Praise for *New York Times* bestselling author Diana Palmer

Dear Reader,

I can't believe that it has been over thirty years since my first Long, Tall Texans book, *Calhoun*, debuted! The series was suggested by my former editor Tara Gavin, who asked if I might like to set stories in a fictional town of my own design. Would I! And the rest is history.

As the years went by, I found more and more sexy ranchers and cowboys to add to the collection. My readers (especially Amy!) found time to gift me with a notebook listing every single one of them, along with their wives and kids and connections to other families in my own Texas town of Jacobsville. Eventually the town got a little too big for me, so I added another smaller town called Comanche Wells and began to fill it up, too.

You can't imagine how much pleasure this series has given me. I continue to add to the population of Jacobs County, Texas, and I have no plans to stop. Ever.

I hope all of you enjoy reading the Long, Tall Texans as much as I enjoy writing them. Thank you all for your kindness and loyalty and friendship. I am your biggest fan!

Love,

Diana Palmer

NEW YORK TIMES BESTSELLING AUTHOR

DIANA PALMER

THE COWBOY CODE

2 Heartfelt Stories
Ethan and *Harley* (Previously published as *The Maverick*)

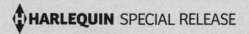

HHARLEQUIN SPECIAL RELEASE

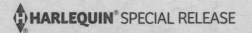

HARLEQUIN® SPECIAL RELEASE

ISBN-13: 978-1-335-14692-2

PLEASE RECYCLE

Recycling programs
for this product may
not exist in your area.

The Cowboy Code

Harlequin Enterprises ULC
22 Adelaide St. West, 41st Floor
Toronto, Ontario M5H 4E3, Canada
www.Harlequin.com

Printed in U.S.A.

CONTENTS

A prolific author of more than one hundred books, **Diana Palmer** got her start as a newspaper reporter. A *New York Times* bestselling author and voted one of the top ten romance writers in America, she has a gift for telling the most sensual tales with charm and humor. Diana lives with her family in Cornelia, Georgia. Visit her website at dianapalmer.com.

Books by Diana Palmer

Long, Tall Texans

Fearless
Heartless
Dangerous
Merciless
Courageous
Protector
Invincible
Untamed
Defender
Undaunted

The Wyoming Men

Wyoming Tough
Wyoming Fierce
Wyoming Bold
Wyoming Strong
Wyoming Rugged
Wyoming Brave

Morcai Battalion

The Morcai Battalion
The Morcai Battalion: The Recruit
The Morcai Battalion: Invictus
The Morcai Battalion: The Rescue

Visit the Author Profile page
at Harlequin.com for more titles.

ETHAN

CHAPTER ONE

ARABELLA WAS DRIFTING. She seemed to be floating along on a particularly fast cloud, high above the world. She murmured contentedly and sank into the fluffy nothingness, aware somewhere of a fleeting pain that began to grow with every passing second until it was a white-hot throb in one of her hands.

"No!" she exclaimed, and her eyes flew open.

She was lying on a cold table. Her dress, her beautiful gray dress, was covered with blood and she felt bruised and cut all over. A man in a white jacket was examining her eyes. She groaned.

"Concussion," the man murmured. "Abrasions, contusions. Compound fracture of the wrist, one ligament almost severed. Type and cross-match her blood, prep her for surgery, and get me an operating room."

"Yes, Doctor."

"Well?" The other voice was harsh, demanding. Very male and familiar, but not her father's.

"She'll be all right," the doctor said with resignation. "Now, will you please go outside and sit down, Mr. Hardeman? While I can appreciate your concern—" and that was an understatement, the physician thought "—you can do her more good by letting us work."

Ethan! The voice was Ethan's! She managed to turn her head, and yes, it was Ethan Hardeman. He looked as if they'd dragged him out of bed. His black hair was rumpled, apparently by his own fingers. His hard, lean face was drawn, his gray eyes so dark with worry that they looked black. His white shirt was half-unbuttoned, as if he'd thrown it on, and his dark jacket was open. He'd all but crushed the brim of the creamy Stetson in his hand.

"Bella," he breathed when he saw her pale, damaged face.

"Ethan," she managed in a hoarse whisper. "Oh, Ethan, my hand!"

His expression tautened as he moved closer to her, despite the doctor's protests. He reached down and touched her poor, bruised cheek. "Baby, what a scare you gave me!" he whispered. His hand actually seemed to be trembling as he brushed back her disheveled long brown hair. Her green eyes were bright with pain and welcome, all mixed up together.

"My father?" she asked with apprehension, because he'd been driving the car.

"They flew him to Dallas. He had an ocular injury, and they've got some of the top men in the field there. He's all right, otherwise. He couldn't take care of you, so he had the hospital call me." Ethan smiled coldly. "God knows, that was a gut-wrenching decision on his part."

She was in too much pain to pick up on the meaning behind the words. "But…my hand?" she asked.

He stood up straight. "They'll talk to you about that later. Mary and the rest will be here in the morning. I'll stay until you're out of surgery."

She caught at his arm with her good hand, feeling the hard muscle tighten. "Make them understand…how important my hand is, please," she pleaded.

"They understand. They'll do what can be done." He touched her cracked lips gently with his forefinger. "I won't leave you," he said quietly. "I'll be here."

She grabbed his hand, holding it, feeling his strength, drawing on his strength for the first time in recent memory. "Ethan," she whispered as the pain built, "remember the swimming hole…?"

His expression closed up. He actually flinched as her face contorted. "My God, can't you give her something?" he asked the doctor, as if the pain were his own.

The doctor seemed to understand at last that it was more than bad temper driving the tall, angry man who'd stormed into the emergency room barely ten minutes ago. The look on those hard features as he'd held the woman's hand had said everything.

"I'll give her something," the doctor promised. "Are you a relative? Her husband, perhaps?"

Ethan's silver eyes cut at him. "No, I'm not a relative. She's a concert pianist, very commercial these days. She lives with her father and she's never been allowed to marry."

The doctor didn't have time for discussion. He settled Ethan with a nurse and vanished gratefully into the emergency room.

HOURS LATER, Arabella drifted in and out of the anesthesia in a private room. Ethan was there again, staring angrily out the window at the pastel colors of the sky at dawn, still in the same clothes he'd been wearing the night before. Arabella was in a floral hospital gown and she felt as she probably looked—weak and wrung out.

"Ethan," she called.

He turned immediately, going to the bedside. He did look terrible, all right. His face was white with strain and bridled anger.

"How are you?" he asked.

"Tired and sore and groggy," she murmured, trying to smile at him. He looked so fierce, just as he had when they were younger. She was almost twenty-three now, and Ethan was thirty, but he'd always been worlds ahead of her in maturity. With Ethan standing over her, it was hard to remember the anguish of the past four years. So many memories, she thought drowsily, watching that dear face. Ethan had been her heart four years ago, but he'd married Miriam. Ethan had forced Miriam into a separation only a little while after they married, but she'd fought Ethan's divorce action tooth and nail for almost four years. Miriam had given up, at last, this year. Their divorce had only become final three months ago.

Ethan was a past master at hiding his feelings, but the deep lines in his face spoke for themselves. Miriam had hurt him dreadfully. Arabella had tried to warn him, in her own shy way. They'd argued over Miriam and because of it, Ethan had shut Arabella out of his life with cold cruelty. She'd seen him in passing since then because she and his sister-in-law were best friends, and visits were inevitable. But Ethan had been remote and unapproachable. Until last night.

"You should have listened to me about Miriam," she said groggily.

"We won't talk about my ex-wife," he said coldly. "You're coming home with me when you're able to get around again. Mother and Mary will look after you and keep you company."

"How's my father?" she asked.

"I haven't found out anything new. I'll check later. Right now, I need breakfast and a change of clothes. I'll come back as soon as I've got my men started at home. We're in the middle of roundup."

"What a time to be landed with me," she said with a deep sigh. "I'm sorry, Ethan. Dad could have spared you this."

He ignored the comment. "Did you have any clothes in the car with you?"

She shook her head. The slight movement hurt, so she stopped. She reached up with her free hand to smooth back the mass of waving dark brown hair from her bruised face. "My clothes are back in the apartment in Houston."

"Where's the key?"

"In my purse. They should have brought it in with me," she murmured drowsily.

He searched in the locker on the other side of the room and found her expensive leather purse. He carried it to the bed with the air of a man holding a poisonous snake. "Where is it?" he muttered.

She stared at him, amused despite the sedatives and the growing pain. "The key is in the zipper compartment," she managed.

He took out a set of keys and she showed him the right one. He put the purse away with obvious relief. "Beats me why women can't use pockets, the way men do."

"The stuff we carry wouldn't fit into pockets," she said reasonably. She lay back on the pillows, her eyes open and curious. "You look terrible."

He didn't smile. He hardly ever had, except for a few magical days when she was eighteen. Before Miriam got her beautiful hands on him. "I haven't had much sleep," he said, his voice sharp and cutting.

She smiled drowsily. "Don't growl at me. Coreen wrote to me last month in Los Angeles. She said you're impossible to live with these days."

"My mother always thought I was impossible to live with," he reminded her.

"She said you'd been that way for three months, since the divorce was final," she replied. "Why did Miriam finally give in? She was the one who insisted on staying married to you, despite the fact that she stopped living with you ages ago."

"How should I know?" he asked abruptly, and turned away.

She saw the way he closed up at the mention of his ex-wife's name, and her heart felt heavy and cold. His marriage had hurt her more than anything in her life. It had been unexpected, and she'd almost gone off the deep end when she'd heard. Somehow she'd always thought that Ethan cared for her. She'd been too young for him at eighteen, but that day by the swimming hole, she'd been sure that he felt more than just a physical attraction for her. Or maybe that had been one more hopeless illusion. Whatever he'd felt, he'd started going around with Miriam immediately after that sweet interlude, and within two months he'd married the woman.

Arabella had mourned him bitterly. He'd been the first man in her life in all the important ways, except for the most intimate one. She was still waiting for that first intimacy, just as she'd waited most of her adult life for Ethan to love her. She almost laughed out loud. Ethan had never loved her. He'd loved Miriam, who'd come to the ranch to film a commercial. She'd watched it happen, watched Ethan falling under the spell of the green-eyed, redheaded model with her sophisticated beauty.

Arabella had never had the measure of self-confidence and teasing sophistication that Miriam had. And Miriam had walked off with Ethan, only to leave him. They said that Ethan had become a woman-hater because of his marriage. Arabella didn't doubt it. He'd never been a playboy in the first place. He was much too serious and stoical. There was nothing happy-go-lucky or carefree about Ethan. He'd had the responsibility for his family for a long time now, and even Arabella's earliest memories of him were of a quiet, hard man who threw out orders like a commanding general, intimidating men twice his age when he was only just out of his teens.

Ethan was watching her, but his scrutiny ceased when she noticed him standing beside the bed. "I'll send someone to your apartment in Houston for your things."

"Thank you." He wouldn't talk to her about Miriam. Somehow, she'd expected that reaction. She took a deep breath and started to lift her hand. It felt heavy. She looked down and realized that it was in a small cast.

Red antiseptic peeked out from under it, stark against her pale skin. She felt the threat of reality and withdrew from it, closing her eyes.

"They had to set the bones," Ethan said. "The cast comes off in six weeks, and you'll have the use of your hand again."

Use of it, yes. But would she be able to play again as she had? How long would it take, and how would she manage to support herself and her father if she couldn't? She felt panic seeping in. Her father had a heart condition. She knew, because he'd used it against her in the early days when she hadn't wanted the years of study, the eternal practice that made it impossible for her to go places with her friends Mary and Jan, Ethan's sister, and Matt, his brother whom Mary had later married.

It was astonishing that her father had called Ethan after the wreck. Ever since Arabella had blossomed into a young woman, her father had made sure that Ethan didn't get too close to her. He'd never liked Ethan. The reverse was also true. Arabella hadn't understood the friction, because Ethan had never made any serious advances toward her, until that day she and Ethan had gone swimming at the creek, and things had almost gone too far. Arabella had told no one, so her father hadn't known about that. It was her own private, special secret. Hers and Ethan's.

She forced her mind back to the present. She couldn't let herself become maudlin now. She had enough complications in her life without asking for more. She vaguely remembered mentioning to Ethan that day she and he had gone swimming together, when she was eighteen. She hoped against hope that he'd been too worried to pay attention to the remark, that she hadn't given away how precious the memory was to her.

"You said I'd stay with you," she began falteringly, trying to make her mind work. "But my father...?"

"Your uncle lives in Dallas, remember?" he asked curtly. "Your father will probably stay there."

"He won't like having me this far away," she said doggedly.

"No, he won't, will he?" He pulled the sheet up to her chin. "Try to sleep. Let the medicine work."

Her wide green eyes opened, holding his. "You don't want me at your house," she said huskily. "You never did. We quarreled over Miriam and you said I was a pain in the neck and you never wanted to have to see me again!"

He actually winced. "Try to sleep," he said tersely.

She was drifting in and out of consciousness, blissfully unaware of the tortured look on the dark face above her. She closed her eyes. "Yes. Sleep..."

The world seemed very far away as the drugs took hold at last and she slept. Her dreams were full of the old days, of growing up with Mary and Matt, of Ethan always nearby, beloved and taciturn and completely unattainable. No matter how hard she tried to act her age, Ethan had never looked at her as a woman in those early days.

Arabella had always loved him. Her music had been her escape. She could play the exquisite classical pieces and put all the love Ethan didn't want into her fingers as she played. It was that fever and need that had given her a start in the musical world. At the age of twenty-one, she'd won an international competition with a huge financial prize, and the recognition had given her a shot at a recording contract.

Classical music was notoriously low-paying for pianists, but Arabella's style had caught on quickly when she tried some pop pieces. The albums had sold well, and she was asked to do more. The royalties began to grow, along with her fame.

Her father had pushed her into personal appearances and tours, and, basically shy in front of people she didn't know, she'd hated the whole idea of it. She'd tried to protest, but her father had dominated her all her life, and she hadn't had the will to fight him. Incredible, that, she told herself, when she could stand up to Ethan and most other people without a qualm. Her father was different. She loved him and he'd been her mainstay when her mother had died so long ago. She couldn't bear to hurt her father by refusing his guidance in her career. Ethan had hated the hold her father had on her, but he'd never asked her to try to break it.

Over the years, while she was growing up in Jacobsville, Ethan had been a kind of protective but distant big brother. Until that day he'd taken her swimming down at the creek and everything had changed. Miriam had been at the ranch even then, starting on a layout with a Western theme for a fashion magazine. Ethan had paid her very little notice until he'd almost lost control with Arabella when they started kissing, but after that day he'd begun pursuing Miriam. It hadn't taken long.

Arabella had heard Miriam bragging to another model that she had the Hardeman fortune in the palm of her hand and that she was going to trade Ethan her body for a life of luxury. It had sickened Arabella to think of the man she loved being treated as a meal ticket and nothing more, so she'd gone to him and tried to tell him what she'd heard.

He hadn't believed her. He'd accused her of being jealous of Miriam. He'd hurt her with his cold remarks about her age and inexperience and naïveté, then he'd ordered her off the ranch. She'd run away, all the way out of the state and back to music school.

How strange that Ethan should be the one to look after her. It was the first time she'd ever been in a hospital, the first time she'd been anything except healthy. She wouldn't have expected Ethan to bother with her, despite her father's request. Ethan had studiously ignored Arabella since his marriage, right down to deliberately disappearing every time she came to visit Mary and Coreen.

Mary and Matt lived with Matt and Ethan's mother, Coreen, at the big rambling Hardeman house. Coreen always welcomed Arabella as if she were family when she came to spend an occasional afternoon with her friend Mary. But Ethan was cold and unapproachable and barely spoke to her.

Arabella hadn't expected more from Ethan, though. He'd made his opinion of her crystal clear when he'd announced his engagement to Miriam shortly after he'd started dating the model. The engagement had shocked everyone, even his mother, and the rushed wedding had been a source of gossip for months. But Miriam wasn't pregnant, so obviously he'd married her for love. If that was the case, it was a brief love. Miriam had gone, bag and baggage, six months later, leaving Ethan alone but not unattached. Arabella had never learned why Miriam had refused the divorce or why Miriam had started running around on a man she'd only just married. It was one of many things about his marriage that Ethan never discussed with anyone.

Arabella felt oblivion stealing her away. She gave in to it at last, sighing as she fell asleep, leaving all her worries and heartaches behind.

CHAPTER TWO

WHEN ARABELLA WOKE up again, it was daylight. Her hand throbbed in its white cast. She ground her teeth together, recalling the accident all too vividly—the impact, the sound of broken glass, her own cry, and then oblivion rushing over her. She couldn't blame the accident on her father; it had been unavoidable. Slick roads, a car that pulled out in front of them, and they'd gone off the pavement and into a telephone pole. She was relieved to be alive, despite the damage to her hand. But she was afraid her father wasn't going to react well to the knowledge that her performing days might be over. She refused to think about that possibility. She had to be optimistic.

Belatedly she wondered what had become of the car they'd been driving. They'd been on their way to Jacobsville from Corpus Christi, where she'd been performing in a charity concert. Her father hadn't told her why they were going to Jacobsville, so she'd assumed that they were taking a brief vacation in their old home town. She'd thought then about seeing Ethan again, and her heart had bounced in her chest. But she hadn't expected to see him under these circumstances.

They'd been very close to Jacobsville, so naturally they'd been taken to the hospital there. Her father had been transferred to Dallas and had called Ethan, but why? She couldn't imagine the reason he should have asked a man he obviously disliked to look after his daughter. She was no closer to solving the mystery when the door opened.

Ethan came in with a cup of black coffee, looking out of sorts, as if he'd never smiled in his life. He had a faint arrogance of carriage that had intrigued her from the first time she'd seen him. He was as individual as his name. She even knew how he'd come by the name. His mother Coreen, a John Wayne fan, had loved the movie *The Searchers*, which came out before Ethan was born. When Coreen became pregnant, she couldn't think of a better name for her firstborn son than the first name John Wayne had been given in the movie. So he became Ethan Hardeman. His middle name was John, but few people outside the family knew it.

Arabella loved looking at him. He had a rodeo rider's physique, powerful shoulders and chest that wedged down to narrow hips, a flat belly and long, muscular legs. His face wasn't bad, either. He was tanned and his eyes were deep-set and very gray, although sometimes they looked silver and other times they had the faintest hint of blue. His hair was dark and conventionally cut. His nose was straight, his mouth sensuous, his cheekbones high and his chin faintly jutting with a slight cleft. He had lean hands with long fingers and neatly trimmed flat nails.

She was staring at him again, helplessly, she supposed. From his blue-checked Western shirt to his gray denims and black boots, he was impeccably dressed, elegant for a cowboy, even if he was the boss.

"You look like hell," he said, and all her romantic dreams were pushed aside at once.

"Thank you," she replied with a little of her old spirit. "That kind of flattery is just what I needed."

"You'll mend." He sounded unruffled; he always did. He sat down in the armchair next to the bed and leaned back with one long leg crossed over the other, sipping his coffee. "Mother and Mary will be in to see you later. How's the hand?"

"It hurts," she said simply. She used the good one to brush back her hair. She could hear Bach preludes and Clementi sonatinas in the back of her mind. Always the music. It gave her life, made her breathe. She couldn't bear to think that she might lose it.

"Have they given you anything?"

"Yes, just a few minutes ago. I'm a little groggy, but I don't hurt as much as I did," she assured him. She'd already seen one orderly run for cover when he walked in. All she needed was to have Ethan bulldoze any more of the staff on her behalf.

He smiled faintly. "I won't cause too much trouble," he assured her. "I just want to make sure you're being treated properly."

"So does the staff," she murmured dryly, "and I hear at least two doctors are thinking of resigning if I'm not released soon."

He looked the least bit uncomfortable. "I wanted to make sure you got the best care possible."

"I did, never fear." She averted her eyes. "From one enemy to another, thanks for the TLC."

He stiffened. "I'm not your enemy."

"No? We didn't part as friends all those years ago." She leaned back, sighing. "I'm sorry things didn't work out for you and Miriam, Ethan," she said quietly. "I hope it wasn't because of anything I said…"

"It's past history," he said curtly. "Let it drop."

"Okay." He intimidated her with those black stares.

He sipped his coffee, allowing his eyes to wander down the length of her slender body. "You've lost weight. You need a rest."

"I haven't been able to afford that luxury," she told him. "We've only begun to break even this year."

"Your father could get a job and help out," he said coldly.

"You don't have the right to interfere in my life, Ethan," she said, staring back at him. "You gave that up years ago."

The muscles in his face contracted, although his gaze didn't waver. "I know better than you do what I gave up." He stared her down and drank some more coffee. "Mother and Mary are fixing up the guest room for you," he told her. "Matt's off at a sale in Montana, so Mary will be glad of the company."

"Doesn't your mother mind having me landed on her?"

"My mother loves you," he said. "She always has, and you've always known it, so there's no need to pretend."

"Your mother is a nice person."

"And I'm not?" He studied her face. "I've never tried to win any popularity contests, if that's what you mean."

She shifted against the pillows. "You're very touchy

these days, Ethan. I wasn't looking for ways to insult you. I'm very grateful for what you've done."

He finished his coffee. His gray eyes met hers and for an instant, they were held against their will. He averted his gaze instantly. "I don't want gratitude from you."

That was the truth; not gratitude or anything else— least of all love.

She let her eyes fall to her hand in its cast. "Did you call the hospital at Dallas to ask about my father?"

"I phoned your uncle early this morning. The eye specialist is supposed to see your father today; they're more optimistic than they were last night."

"Did he ask about me?"

"Of course he asked about you," Ethan replied. "He was told about your hand."

She stiffened. "And?"

"He didn't say another word, according to your uncle." Ethan smiled without humor. "Well, what did you expect? Your hands are his livelihood. He's just seen a future that's going to require him to work for a living again. I expect he's drowning in self-pity."

"Shame on you," she snapped.

He stared at her, unblinking. "I know your father. You do, too, despite the fact that you've spent your life protecting him. You might try living your own way for a change."

"I'm content with my life," she muttered.

His pale eyes caught and held hers, and he was very still. The room was so quiet that they could hear the sound of cars outside the hospital, in the nearby streets of Jacobsville.

"Do you remember what you asked me when they brought you in?"

She shook her head. "No. I was hurting pretty badly just then," she lied, averting her eyes.

"You asked if I remembered the swimming hole."

Her cheeks went hot. She pleated the material of the hospital gown they'd put her in, grimacing. "I can't imagine why I'd ask such a question. That's ancient history."

"Four years isn't ancient history. And to answer the question belatedly, yes, I remember. I wish I could forget."

Well, that was plain enough, wasn't it? she thought, hurt. She couldn't bring herself to meet his gaze. She could imagine the mockery in his eyes. "Why can't you?" she asked, trying to sound as unconcerned as he did. "After all, you told me yourself that I'd asked for it, that you'd been thinking about Miriam."

"Damn Miriam!" He got up, upsetting the coffee cup in the process, splattering a few drops of scalding coffee onto his hand. He ignored the sting, turning away to stare out the window at Jacobsville, his body rigid. He lifted the cup to his lips and sipped the hot liquid again to steady himself. Even the mention of his ex-wife made him tense, wounded him. Arabella had no idea of the hell Miriam had made of his life, or why he'd let her trap him into marriage. It was four years too late for explanations or apologies. His memories of the day he'd made love to Arabella were permanent, unchanged, a part of him, but he couldn't even tell her that. He was so locked up inside that he'd almost forgotten how to feel, until Arabella's father had telephoned him to tell him that Arabella had been injured. Even now, he could taste the sick fear he'd felt, faced all over again the possibility that she might have died. The world had gone black until he'd gotten to the hospital and found her relatively unhurt.

"Do you hear from Miriam anymore?" she asked.

He didn't turn around. "I hadn't since the divorce was final, until last week." He finished the coffee and laughed coldly. "She wants to talk about a reconciliation."

Arabella felt her heart sink. So much for faint hope, she thought. "Do you want her back?"

Ethan came back to the bedside, and his eyes were blazing with anger. "No, I don't want her back," he said. He stared down at her icily. "It took me years to talk her into a divorce. Do you really think I have any plans to put my neck in that noose again?" he asked.

"I don't know you, Ethan," she replied quietly. "I don't think I ever did, really. But you loved Miriam once," she added with downcast eyes. "It's not inconceivable that you could miss her, or want her back."

He didn't answer her. He turned and dropped back down into the armchair by the bed, crossing his legs. Absently, he played with the empty coffee cup. Loved Miriam? He'd wanted her. But love? No. He wished he could tell Arabella that, but he'd become too adept at keeping his deepest feelings hidden.

He put the cup down on the floor beside his chair. "A cracked mirror is better replaced than mended," he said, lifting his eyes back to Arabella's. "I don't want a reconciliation. So, that being the case," he continued, improvising as he began to see a way out of his approaching predicament, "we might be able to help each other."

Arabella's heart jumped. "What?"

He stared at her, his eyes probing, assessing. "Your father raised you in an emotional prison. You never tried to break out. Well, here's your chance."

"I don't understand."

"That's obvious. You used to be better at reading between the lines." He took a cigarette from the pack in his pocket and dangled it from his fingers. "Don't worry, I won't light it," he added when he saw the look she gave him. "I need something to do with my hands. What I meant was that you and I can pretend to be involved."

She couldn't prevent the astonished fear from distorting her features. He'd pushed her out of his life once, and now he had the audacity to want her to pretend to be involved with him? It was cruel.

"I thought you'd be bothered by the suggestion," he said after a minute of watching her expression. "But think about it. Miriam won't be here for another week or two. There's time to map out some strategy."

"Why can't you just tell her not to come?" she faltered.

He studied his boot. "I could, but it wouldn't solve the problem. She'd be dancing in and out of my life from now on. The best way, the only way," he corrected, "is to give her a good reason to stay away. You're the best one I can think of."

"Miriam would laugh herself sick if anyone told her you were involved with me," she said shortly. "I was only eighteen when you married her. She didn't consider me any kind of competition then, and she was right. I wasn't, and I'm not." She lifted her chin with mangled pride. "I'm talented, but I'm not pretty. She'll never believe you see anything interesting about me."

He had to control his expression not to betray the sting of those words. It hurt him to hear Arabella talk so cynically. He didn't like remembering how badly he'd had to hurt her. At the time, it didn't seem that he'd had a choice. But explaining his reasoning to Arabella four years too late would accomplish nothing.

His eyes darkened as he watched Arabella with the old longing. He didn't know how he was going to bear having to let her walk out of his life a second time. But at least he might have a few weeks with her under the pretext of a mutual-aid pact. Better that than nothing. At least he might have one or two sweet memories to last him through the barren years ahead.

"Miriam isn't stupid," he said finally. "You're a young woman now, well-known in your field and no longer a country mouse. She won't know how sheltered you've been, unless you tell her." His eyes slid gently over her face. "Even without your father's interference, I don't imagine you've had much time for men, have you?"

"Men are treacherous," she said without thinking. "I offered you my heart and you threw it in my teeth. I haven't offered it again, to anyone, and I don't intend to. I've got my music, Ethan. That's all I need."

He didn't believe her. Women didn't go that sour over a youthful infatuation, especially when it was mostly physical to begin with. Probably the drugs they'd given her had upset her reasoning, even if he'd give an arm to believe she'd cared that much. "What if you don't have music again?" he asked suddenly.

"Then I'll jump off the roof," she replied with conviction. "I can't live without it. I don't want to try."

"What a cowardly approach." He said the words coldly to disguise a ripple of real fear at the way she'd looked when she said that.

"Not at all," she contradicted him. "At first it was my father's idea to push me into a life of concert tours. But I love what I do. Most of what I do," she corrected. "I don't care for crowds, but I'm very happy with my life."

"How about a husband? Kids?" he probed.

"I don't want or need either," she said, averting her face. "I have my life planned."

"Your damned father has your life planned," he shot back angrily. "He'd tell you when to breathe if you'd let him!"

"What I do is none of your concern," she replied. Her green eyes met his levelly. "You have no right whatsoever to talk about my father trying to dominate me, when you're trying to manipulate me yourself to help you get Miriam out of your hair."

One silvery eye narrowed. "It amazes me."

"What does?" she asked.

"That you hit back at me with such disgusting ease and you won't say boo to your father."

"I'm not afraid of you," she said. She laced her fingers together. "I've always been a little in awe of my father. The only thing he cares about is my talent. I thought if I got famous, he might love me." She laughed bitterly. "But it didn't work, did it? Now he thinks I may not be able to play again and he doesn't want anything to do with me." She looked up with tear-bright eyes. "Neither would you, if it wasn't for Miriam hotfooting it down here. I've never been anything but a pawn where men were concerned, and you think my *father* is trying to run my life?"

He stuck the hand that wasn't holding the cigarette into his pocket. "That's one miserable self-image you've got," he remarked quietly.

She looked away. "I know my failings," she told him. She closed her eyes. "I'll help you keep Miriam at bay, but you won't need to protect me from my father. I very much doubt if I'll ever see him again after what's happened."

"If that hand heals properly, you'll see him again." Ethan tossed the unlit cigarette into an ashtray. "I have to get Mother and Mary and drive them in to see you. The man I sent for your clothes should be back by then. I'll bring your things with us."

"Thank you," she said stiffly.

He paused by the bedside, his eyes attentive. "I don't like having to depend on other people, either," he said. "But you can carry independence too far. Right now, I'm all you've got. I'll take care of you until you're back on your feet. If that includes keeping your father away, I can do that, too."

She looked up. "What do you have in mind to keep Miriam from thinking our relationship is a sham?"

"You look nervous," he remarked. "Do you think I might want to make love to you in front of her?"

Her cheeks went hot. "Of course not!"

"Well, you can relax. I won't ask you for the ultimate sacrifice. A few smiles and some hand-holding ought to get the message across." He laughed bitterly as he looked down at her. "If that doesn't do it, I'll announce our engagement. Don't panic," he added icily when he saw the expression on her face. "We can break it off when she leaves, if we have to go that far."

Her heart was going mad. He didn't know what the thought of being engaged to him did to her. She loved him almost desperately, but it was obvious that he had no such feeling for her.

Why did he need someone to help him get Miriam to leave him alone? she wondered. Maybe he still loved Miriam and was afraid of letting her get to him. Arabella closed her eyes. Whatever his reason, she couldn't let him know how she felt. "I'll go along, then," she said. "I'm so tired, Ethan."

"Get some rest. I'll see you later."

She opened her eyes. "Thank you for coming to see me. I don't imagine it was something you'd have chosen to do, except that Dad asked you."

"And you think I care enough for your father's opinion to make any sacrifices on his behalf?" he asked curiously.

"Well, I don't expect you to make any on mine," she said coolly. "God knows you disliked me enough in the old days. And still do, I imagine. I shouldn't have said anything to you about Miriam—"

She was suddenly talking to thin air. He was gone before the words were out of her mouth.

ETHAN WAS BACK with Coreen and Mary later that day, but he didn't come into the room.

Coreen, small and delicate, was everything Arabella

would have ordered in a custom-made mother. The little woman was spirited and kind, and her battles with Ethan were legendary. But she loved Arabella and Mary, and they were as much her daughters as Jan, her own married daughter who lived out of state.

"It was a blessing that Ethan was home," Coreen told Arabella while Mary, Arabella's best friend in public school, sat nearby and listened to the conversation with twinkling brown eyes. "He's been away from home every few days since his divorce was final, mostly business trips. He's been moody and brooding and restless. I found it amazing that he sent Matt on his last one."

"Maybe he was out making up for lost time after the divorce was final," Arabella said quietly. "After all, he was much too honorable himself to indulge in anything indecent while he was technically married."

"Unlike Miriam, who was sleeping with anything in pants just weeks after they married," Coreen said bluntly. "God knows why she held on to him for so long, when everyone knew she never loved him."

"There's no alimony in Texas." Mary grinned. "Maybe that's why."

"I offered her a settlement," Coreen said, surprising the other two women. "She refused. But I hear that she met someone else down in the Caribbean and there are rumors that she may marry her new man friend. That's more than likely why she agreed to the divorce."

"Then why does she want to come back?" Arabella asked.

"To make as much trouble as she can for Ethan, probably," Coreen said darkly. "She used to say things to him that cut my heart out. He fought back, God knows, but even a strong man can be wounded by ceaseless ridicule and humiliation. My dear, Miriam actually seduced a man at a dinner party we gave for Ethan's business associates. He walked in on them in his own study."

Arabella closed her eyes and groaned. "It must have been terrible for him."

"More terrible than you know," Coreen replied. "He never really loved her and she knew it. She wanted him to worship at her feet, but he wouldn't. Her extramarital activities turned him off completely. He told me that he found her repulsive, and probably he told her, too. That was about the time she started trying to create as many scandals as possible, to embarrass him. And they did. Ethan's a very conventional man. It crushed him that Miriam thought nothing of seducing his business associates." Coreen actually shuddered. "A man's ego is his sensitive spot. She knew it, and used it, with deadly effect. Ethan's changed. He was always quiet and introverted, but I hate what this marriage has done to him."

"He's a hard man to get close to," Arabella said quietly. "Nobody gets near him at all now, I imagine."

"Maybe you can change that," Coreen said, smiling. "You could make him smile when no one else could. You taught him how to play. He was happier that summer four years ago than he ever was before or since."

"Was he?" Arabella smiled painfully. "We had a terrible quarrel over Miriam. I don't think he's ever forgiven me for the things I said."

"Anger can camouflage so many emotions, Bella,"

Coreen said quietly. "It isn't always as cut-and-dried as it seems."

"No, it isn't," Mary agreed. "Matt and I hated each other once, and we wound up married."

"I doubt if Ethan will ever marry anyone again," Arabella said, glancing at Coreen. "A bad burn leaves scars."

"Yes," Coreen said sadly. "By the way, dear," she said then, changing the subject, "we're looking forward to having you with us while you recuperate. Mary and I will enjoy your company so much."

Arabella thought about what Coreen had said long after they left. She couldn't imagine a man as masculine as Ethan being so wounded by any woman, but perhaps Miriam had some kind of hold on him that no one knew about. Probably a sensual one, she thought miserably, because everyone who'd seen them together knew how attracted he'd been to Miriam physically. Miriam had been worldly and sophisticated. It was understandable that he'd fallen so completely under her spell. Arabella had been much too innocent to even begin to compete for him.

A nurse came in, bearing a huge bouquet of flowers, and Arabella's eyes glistened with faint tears at their beauty. There was no card, but she knew by the size and extravagance of the gift that it had to be Coreen. She'd have to remember to thank the older woman the next day.

It was a long night, and she didn't sleep well. Her dreams were troubled, full of Ethan and pain. She lay looking up at the ceiling after one of the more potent

dreams, and her mind drifted back to a late-summer's
day, with the sound of bees buzzing around the wildflowers that circled the spot where the creek widened
into a big hole, deep enough to swim in. She and Ethan
had gone there to swim one lazy afternoon....

She could still see the butterflies and hear the crick-
ets and July flies that populated the deserted area. Ethan
had driven them to the creek in the truck, because it was
a long and tiring walk in the devastating heat of a south
Texas summer. He'd been wearing white trunks that
showed off his powerful body in an all-too-sensuous
way, his broad shoulders and chest tapering to his narrow hips and long legs. He was deeply tanned, and his
chest and flat belly were thick with curling dark hair.
Seeing him in trunks had never bothered Arabella over-
much until that day, and then just looking at him made
her blush and scamper into the water.

She'd been wearing a yellow one-piece bathing suit,
very respectable and equally inexpensive. Her father's
job had supported them frugally, and she was working
part-time to help pay her tuition at the music school in
New York. She was on fire with the promise of being
a superb pianist, and things were going well for her.
She'd come over to spend the afternoon with his sister, Jan, but she and her latest boyfriend had gone to a
barbecue, so Ethan had offered to take her swimming.

The offer had shocked and flattered Arabella, because
Ethan was in his mid-twenties and she was sure his taste
didn't run to schoolgirls. He was remote and unapproachable most of the time, but in the weeks before they went
swimming together, he'd always seemed to be around

when she visited his sister. His eyes had followed Arabella with an intensity that had disturbed and excited her. She'd loved him for so long, ached for him. And then, that day, all her dreams had come true when he'd issued his casual invitation to come swimming with him.

Once he'd rescued her from an overamorous would-be suitor, and another time he'd driven her to a school party along with Jan and Matt and Mary. To everyone's surprise, he'd stayed long enough to dance one slow, lazy dance with Arabella. Jan and Mary had teased her about it mercilessly. That had started the fantasies, that one dance. Afterward, Arabella had watched Ethan and worshipped him from afar.

Once they were at the swimming hole, the atmosphere had suddenly changed. Arabella hadn't understood the way Ethan kept looking at her body, his silver eyes openly covetous, thrilling, seductive. She'd colored delicately every time he glanced her way.

"How do you like music school?" he'd asked while they sat in the grass at the creek's edge, and Ethan quietly smoked a cigarette.

She'd had to drag her eyes away from his broad chest. "I like it," she said. "I miss home, though." She'd played with a blade of grass. "I guess things have been busy for you and Matt."

"Not busy enough," he'd said enigmatically. He'd turned his head and his silver eyes had cut at her. "You didn't even write. Jan worried."

"I haven't had time. I had so much to catch up on."

"Boys?" he questioned, his eyes flickering as he lifted the cigarette to his thin lips.

"No!" She averted her face from that suddenly mocking gaze. "I mean, there hasn't been time."

"That's something." He'd crushed out the cigarette in the grass. "We've had visitors. A film crew, doing a commercial of all things, using the ranch as a backdrop. The models are fascinated by cattle. One of them actually asked me if you really pumped a cow's tail to get milk."

She laughed delightedly. "What did you tell her?"

"That she was welcome to try one, if she wanted to."

"Shame on you, Ethan!" Her face lit up as she stared at him. Then, very suddenly, the smile died and she was looking almost straight into his soul. She shivered with the feverish reaction of her body to that long, intimate look, and Ethan abruptly got to his feet and moved toward her with a stride that was lazy, graceful, almost stalking.

"Trying to seduce me, Bella?" he'd taunted softly, all too aware of how her soft eyes were smoothing over his body as he stopped just above her.

She'd really colored then. "Of course not!" she'd blurted out. "I was…just looking at you."

"You've been doing that all day." He'd moved then, straddling her prone body so that he was kneeling with her hips between his strong thighs. He'd looked at her, his eyes lingering on her breasts for so long that they began to feel tight and swollen. She followed his gaze and found the nipples hard and visible under the silky fabric. She'd caught her breath and lifted her hands to cover them, but his steely fingers had snapped around her wrists and pushed them down beside her head. He'd leaned forward to accomplish that, and now his hips

were squarely over hers and she could feel the contours
of his body beginning to change.

Her shocked eyes met his. "Ethan, what are you…"
she began huskily.

"Don't move your hips," he said, his voice deep and
soft as he eased his chest down over hers and began to
drag it slowly, tenderly, against her taut nipples. "Lock
your fingers into mine," he whispered, and still that
aching, arousing pressure went on and on. He bent, so
that his hard, thin mouth was poised just above hers. He
bit softly at her lower lip, drawing it into his lips, teasing it, while his tongue traced the moist inner softness.

She moaned sharply at the intimacy of his mouth and
his body, her eyes wide-open, astonished.

"Yes," he said, lifting his face enough to see her
eyes, to hold them with his glittering ones. "You and
me. Hadn't you even considered the possibility while
you were being thrown at one eligible man after another
by Jan's ceaseless matchmaking a few months ago?"

"No," she confessed unsteadily. "I thought you
wouldn't be interested in somebody my age."

"A virgin has her own special appeal," he replied.
"And you are still a virgin, aren't you?"

"Yes," she managed, wondering at her inability to
produce anything except monosyllables while Ethan's
body made hers ache all over.

"I'll stop before we do anything risky," he said quietly.
"But we're going to enjoy each other for a long, long time
before it gets to that point. Open your mouth when I kiss
it, little one. Let me feel your tongue touching mine…"

She did moan then, letting his tongue penetrate the

soft recesses of her mouth. The intimacy of it lifted her body against his and he made a deep, rough sound in his throat as he let his hips down over hers completely.

He felt her faint panic and subdued it with soft words and the gentle caress of his lean, strong hands on her back. Under her, the soft grass made a tickly cushion while she looked up into Ethan's quiet eyes.

"Afraid?" he asked gently. "I know you can feel how aroused I am, but I'm not going to hurt you. Just relax. We can lie together like this. I won't lose control, even if you let me do what comes next."

She felt the faint tenderness of her lips as she spoke, tasted him on them with awe. "What…comes next?" she asked.

"This." He lifted up on one elbow and traced his fingers over her shoulder and her collarbone, down onto the faint swell of her breast. He stroked her with the lightest kind of touch, going close to but never actually touching the taut nipple. She couldn't help her own reaction to the intimate feel of his lean fingers on her untouched body. She shuddered with pure pleasure, and the silver eyes above her watched with their own pleasure in her swift response.

"I know what you want," he whispered softly, and holding her gaze, he began to tease the nipple with a light, repetitive stroke that made her arch with each exquisite movement. "Have you ever done this with a man?"

"Never," she confessed jerkily. She shivered all over and her fingers bit into his muscular arms.

His face changed at her admission. It grew harder and his eyes began to glow. He lifted himself away a few inches. "Pull your bathing suit down to your hips," he said with rough tenderness.

"I couldn't!" she gasped, flushing.

"I want to look at you while I touch you," he said. "I want to show you how intimate it is to lie against a man's body with no fabric in the way to blunt the sweetness of touching."

"But I've never..." she protested weakly.

His voice, when he spoke, was slow and soft and solemn. "Bella, is there another man you want this first time to be with?"

That put it all in perspective. "No," she said finally. "I couldn't let anyone else look at me. Only you."

His chest rose and fell heavily. "Only me," he breathed. "Do it."

She did, amazed at her own abandon. She pulled the straps gingerly down her arms and loosened the fabric from her breasts. His eyes slid down with the progress of the bathing suit and when she was nude from the waist up, he hung there above her, just looking at the delicate rise of her hard-tipped breasts, drinking in their beauty.

She gasped and his eyes lifted to hers, as they shared the impact of the first intimate thing they'd ever done together.

"I didn't think it would be you, the first time," she whispered shakily.

"That makes us even," he replied. His hand moved, tracing around her breast. His hips shifted, and she felt his pulsating need with awe as she registered his blatant masculinity.

His hand abruptly covered her breast, his palm taking in the hard nipple, and she moaned as his mouth ground down into hers.

Her body was alive. It wanted him, needed him. She felt her hips twist instinctively upward, seeking an even closer contact. He groaned, and one long, powerful leg insinuated itself between hers, giving her the contact she wanted. But it wasn't enough. It was fever, burning, blistering, and she felt her hands go to his hips, digging in, her voice breaking under the furious crush of his mouth. His hands slid under her, his hair-roughened chest dragged over her soft breasts while his hips thrust down rhythmically against hers and she felt him in a contact that made her cry out.

The cry was what stopped him. He had to drag his mouth away. She saw the effort it took, and he stared down at her with eyes that were frankly frightening. He was barely able to breathe. He groaned out loud. Then he'd arched away from her and gotten jerkily to his feet, to dive headfirst into the swimming hole, leaving a dazed, shocked Arabella on the bank with her bathing suit down around her hips.

She'd only just managed to pull it up when he finally climbed out of the water and stood over her. She was at a definite disadvantage, but she let him pull her to her feet.

He didn't let go of her hand. His fingers lifted it to his mouth, and he put his lips to its soft palm. "I envy the man who gets you, Bella," he said solemnly. "You're very special."

"Why did you do that?" she asked hesitantly.

He averted his eyes. "Maybe I wanted a taste of you,"

he said with a cynical smile before he turned away from her to get his towel. "I've never had a virgin."

"Oh."

He watched her gather up her own things and slip into her shoes as they went back to the pickup truck. "You didn't take that little interlude seriously, I hope?" he asked abruptly as he held the door open for her.

She had, but the look on his face was warning her not to. She cleared her throat. "No, I didn't take it seriously," she said.

"I'm glad. I don't mind furthering your education, but I love my freedom."

That stung. Probably it was meant to. He'd come very close to losing control, and he didn't like it. His anger had been written all over his face.

"I didn't ask you to further my education," she'd snapped.

And he'd smiled, mockingly. "No? It seemed to me that you'd done everything but wear a sign. Or maybe I just read you too well. You wanted me, honey, and I was glad to oblige. But only to a certain point. Virgins are exciting to kiss, but I like an experienced woman under me in bed."

She'd slapped him. It hadn't been something she meant to do, but the remark had stung viciously. He hadn't tried to slap her back. He hadn't said anything. He'd smiled that cold, mocking, arrogant smile that meant he'd scored and nothing else mattered. Then he'd put her in the truck and driven her home.

The next week he'd been seen everywhere with Miriam, and Arabella overheard Miriam telling the other model about her plans for Ethan. Arabella had gone straight to Ethan, despite their strained relationship, to tell him what Miriam had said before it was too late. But he'd laughed at her, accused her of being jealous. And then he'd sent her out of his life with a scorching account of her inadequacies.

Four years ago, and she could still hear every word. She closed her eyes. She wondered if his memories were as bitter and as painful as her own. She doubted it. Surely Miriam had left him with some happy ones.

Finally, worn out and with her wounds reopened, she slept.

CHAPTER THREE

THE HOUSE ETHAN and his family called home was a huge two-story Victorian. Set against the softly rolling land of south Texas, with cattle grazing in pastures that seemed to stretch forever, it was the very picture of an old-time Western movie set. Except that the cattle in their fenced pastures were very real, and the fences were sturdy and purposeful, not picture-perfect and overly neat. Jacobsville was within an easy drive of Houston, and Victoria was even closer. It had a small-town atmosphere that Arabella had always loved, and she'd known the people who lived there most of her life. Like the Ballenger brothers, who ran the biggest feedlot in the territory, and the Jacobs—Tyler and Shelby Jacobs Ballenger—whose ancestor the town was named for.

The elegant old mansion with its bone-white walls and turret and gingerbread latticework was beautiful enough to have been featured in lifestyle magazines from time to time. It contained some priceless antiques both from early Texas and from England, because the first Hardeman had come over from London. The Hardemans were old money. Their fortune dated to an early cattle baron who made his fortune in the latter part of the nineteenth century during a blizzard that wiped out half the cattle ranches in the West. Actually, in the beginning, the family name had been Hartmond, but owing to the lack of formal education of their ancestor, the name was hopelessly misspelled on various documents until it became Hardeman.

Ethan looked like the portrait of that earlier Hardeman that graced the living-room mantel. They were probably much the same personality type, too, Arabella thought as she studied Ethan over the coffee he'd brought to the guest room for her. He was a forbidding-looking man with a cool, very formal manner that kept most people at arm's length.

"Thank you for letting me come here," she said.

He shrugged. "We've got plenty of room." He looked around the high ceiling of the room she'd been given. "This was my grandmother's bedroom," he mused. "Remember hearing Mother talk about her? She lived to be eighty and was something of a hell-raiser. She was a vamp or some such thing back during the twenties, and *her* mother was a dyed-in-the-wool suffragette. One of the bloomer girls, out campaigning for the vote for women."

"Good for her." Arabella laughed.

"She'd have liked you," he said, glancing down at her. "She had spirit, too."

She sipped her coffee. "Do I have spirit?" she mused. "I let my father lead me around by the nose my whole life, and I guess I'd still be doing it if it hadn't been for the accident." She glanced at the cast on her wrist, sighing as she juggled the coffee mug in one hand. "Ethan, what am I going to do? I won't even have a job, and Daddy always took care of the money."

"This is no time to start worrying about the future," he said firmly. "Concentrate on getting well."

"But—"

"I'll take care of everything," he interrupted. "Your father included."

She put the coffee mug down and lay back against the pillows. Her wrist was still uncomfortable and she was taking pain capsules fairly regularly. She felt slightly out of focus, and it was so nice to just lie there and let Ethan make all the decisions.

"Thank you, Ethan," she said and smiled up at him.

He didn't smile back. His eyes slid over her face in an exploration that set all her nerves tingling. "How long has it been since you've had any real rest?" he asked after a minute.

She shifted on the pillows. "I don't know. It seems like forever." She sighed. "There was never any time." Her stomach muscles clenched as she remembered the constant pressure, the practice that never stopped, the planes and motel rooms and concert halls and recording dates and expectant audiences. She felt her body going rigid with remembered stress as she recalled how she'd had to force herself more and more to go out on the stage, to keep her nerve from shattering at the sight of all those people.

"I suppose you'll miss the glamour," Ethan murmured.

"I suppose," she said absently and closed her eyes, missing the odd look that passed over his dark face.

"You'd better get some sleep. I'll check on you later."

The bed rose as he got up and left the room. She didn't even open her eyes. She was safe here. Safe from the specter of failure, safe from her father's long, disapproving face, safe from the cold whip of his eyes. She wondered if he was ever going to forgive her for failing him, and decided that he probably wouldn't. Tears slid down her cheeks. If only he could have loved her, just a bit, for what she was underneath her talent. He'd never seemed to love her.

COREEN SAT WITH her for most of the day. Ethan's little mother was a holy terror when she was upset, but everyone loved her. She was the first person in the door when someone was sick or needed help, and the last to leave. She gave generously of her time and money, and none of her children had a bad word to say about her, even in adulthood. Well, except Ethan, and sometimes Arabella thought he did that just for amusement because he loved to watch his mother throw things in a temper.

Arabella had seen the result of one memorable fight between mother and son, back during her teenage years when she was visiting Ethan's brother and sister with Mary. Arabella, Mary, Jan and Matt had been playing Monopoly on the living-room floor when Ethan and his mother got into it in the kitchen. The voices were loud and angry, and unfortunately for Ethan, his mother had been baking a cake when he provoked her. She threw a whole five-pound bag of flour at him, followed by an open jar of chocolate syrup. Arabella and Mary and Jan and Matt had seen Ethan walk by, covered from Stetson hat to booted feet in white flour and chocolate syrup, leaving a trail of both behind him on the wooden floor as he strode toward the staircase.

Arabella and the others had gaped at him, but one cold-eyed look in their direction dared them to open their mouths. Arabella had hidden behind the sofa and collapsed in silent laughter while the others struggled valiantly to keep straight faces. Ethan hadn't said a word, but Coreen had continued to fling angry insults after him from the kitchen doorway as he stomped upstairs to shower and change. For a long time afterward, Arabella had called him "the chocolate ghost." But not to his face.

Coreen was just a little over five foot three, with the dark hair all her children had inherited, but hers was streaked with silver now. Only Ethan shared her gray eyes. Jan and Matt had dark blue eyes, like their late father.

"Do you remember when you threw the flour at Ethan?" Arabella asked, thinking aloud as she watched Coreen's deft fingers working a crochet hook through a growing black-and-red afghan.

Coreen looked up, her plump face brightening. "Oh, yes, I do," she said with a sigh. "He'd refused to sell that bay gelding you always liked to ride. One of my best friends wanted him, you see, and I knew you'd be away at music school in New York. He wasn't a working horse." She chuckled. "Ethan dug in his heels and then he gave me that smile. You know the one, when he knows he's won and he's daring you to do anything about it. I remember looking at the open flour sack." She cleared her throat and went back to work on the afghan. "The next thing I knew, Ethan was stomping down the hall leaving a trail of flour and chocolate syrup in his wake, and I had to clean it up." She shook her head. "I don't throw things very often these days. Only paper or baskets—and nothing messy."

Arabella smiled at the gentle countenance, wishing deep in her heart that she'd had a mother like Coreen. Her own mother had been a quiet, gentle woman whom she barely remembered. She'd died in a wreck when Arabella was only six. Arabella didn't remember ever hearing her father talk about it, but she recalled that he'd become a different man after the funeral.

She twisted her fingers in the blue quilted coverlet. Her father had discovered by accident that Arabella had a natural talent for the piano, and he'd become obsessed with making her use it. He'd given up his job as a clerk in a law office, and he'd become a one-man public relations firm with his daughter as his only client.

"Don't brood, dear," Coreen said gently when she saw the growing anguish on Arabella's lovely face. "Life is easier when you accept things that happen to you and just deal with them as they crop up. Don't go searching for trouble."

Arabella looked up, shifting the cast with a wince because the break was still tender. They'd taken out the clamps that had held the surgical wound together before they put on the cast, but it still felt as if her arm had been through a meat grinder.

"I'm trying not to," she told Ethan's mother. "I thought my father might have called, at least, since they put me back together. Even if it was just to see if I had a chance of getting my career back."

"Being cynical suits my son. It doesn't suit you," Coreen said, glancing at her over the small reading glasses that she wore for close work. "Betty Ann is making a cherry cobbler for dessert."

"My favorite," Arabella groaned.

"Yes, I know, Ethan told us. He's trying to fatten you up."

She frowned at the older woman. "Is Miriam really trying to come back to him?"

With a long-suffering sigh, Coreen laid the afghan and crochet hook over her knees. "I'm afraid so. It's the last thing in the world he needs, of course, after the way she cut up his pride."

"Maybe she still loves him," Arabella suggested.

Coreen cocked her head. "Do you know what I think? I think she's just lost her latest lover and he's left her pregnant. She'll try to lure Ethan into bed and convince him it's his child, so that he'll take her back."

"You really should write books," Arabella said dryly. "That's a great plot."

Coreen made a face at her. "Don't laugh. I wouldn't put it past her. She isn't as pretty as she used to be. All that hard living and hard drinking have left their mark on her. One of my friends saw her on a cruise recently, and Miriam was pumping her for all sorts of information about Ethan—if he'd remarried or was keeping company with anyone."

"He wants me to keep company with him," Arabella mentioned, "to keep Miriam at bay."

"Is that what he told you?" Coreen smiled gently. "I suppose it's as good an excuse as any."

"What do you mean?" Arabella asked curiously.

Coreen shook her head. "That's for Ethan to tell you. Are you going to keep company with him?"

"It seems little enough to do for him, when he's kind enough to give me a roof over my head and turn the whole household upside down on my account," she said miserably. "I feel like an intruder."

"Nonsense," Coreen said easily. "We all enjoy having you here, and none of us wants Miriam to come back. Do play up to Ethan. It will turn Miriam green with envy and send her running."

"Is she going to stay here?" Arabella asked worriedly.

"Over my dead body," Ethan drawled from the doorway, staring across the room at Arabella.

"Hello, dear. Been rolling in the mud with the horses again?" Coreen asked pleasantly.

He did look that way, Arabella had to admit. He was wearing working gear—chambray shirt, thick denims, weathered old leather chaps, boots that no self-respecting street cowboy would have touched with a stick, and a hat that some horse had stepped on several times. His dark skin had a thin layer of dust on it, and his work gloves were grasped in one lean hand that didn't look much cleaner.

"I've been doctoring calves," he replied. "It's March," he reminded her. "Roundup is in full swing, and we're on the tail end of calving. Guess who's going to be night-hawking the prospective mamas this week?"

"Not Matt," Coreen groaned. "He'll leave home!"

"He needs to," Ethan said imperturbably. "He and Mary can't cuss each other without an audience around here. It's going to affect their marriage sooner or later."

"I know," Coreen said sadly. "I've done my best to persuade Matt that he can make it on his own. God knows, he can afford to build a house and furnish it on his income from those shares Bob left him."

"We're too good to him," Ethan pointed out. "We need to start refusing to speak to him and putting salt in his coffee."

"If you put salt in my coffee, I'd stuff the cup up your…" Coreen began hotly.

"Go ahead," Ethan said when she hesitated, his pale eyes sparkling. "Say it. You won't embarrass me."

"Oh, I'll drink to that," Coreen murmured. "You're too much my son to be embarrassed."

Arabella looked from one to the other. "You do favor each other," she said. "Your eyes are almost exactly the same shade."

"He's taller," Coreen remarked.

"Much taller, shrimp," he agreed, but he smiled when he said it.

Coreen glared at him. "Did you come up here for any particular reason, or do you just enjoy annoying me?"

"I came to ask Arabella if she wanted a cat."

Arabella gaped at him. "A what?"

"A cat," he repeated. "Bill Daniels is out front with a mother cat and four kittens that he's taking to the vet to be put down."

"Yes, I want a cat," Arabella said at once. "Five cats."

She gnawed her lower lip. "God knows what my father will say when he finds out, though. He hates cats."

"Why not think about what *you* want for a change, instead of what your father wants?" Ethan asked curtly. "Or have you ever had your own way?"

"Once, he let me have chocolate ice cream when he told me to get vanilla," she replied.

"That isn't funny," Ethan said darkly.

"Sorry." She leaned back against the pillows. "I guess I've never tried to stand up to him." It was the truth. Even though she'd rebelled from time to time, her father's long-standing domination had made it difficult for her to assert herself. Incredible, when she thought nothing of standing up to Ethan…

"No time like the present. I'll tell Bill we'll keep the cats." He moved away from the doorjamb. "I've got to get back to work."

"Like that?" Coreen asked. "You'll embarrass your men. They won't want to admit they work for someone as filthy as you are."

"My men are even filthier than I am," he replied proudly. "Jealous because you're clean?"

Coreen moved her hand toward the trash basket, but Ethan just smiled and left the room.

"You wouldn't have thrown it at him, would you?" Arabella asked.

"Why not?" Coreen asked. "It doesn't do to let men get the upper hand, Bella. Especially not Ethan," she added, looking at Arabella thoughtfully. "You've learned that much, I see. Ethan is a good man, a strong man. But that's all the more reason to stand up to him. He wants his own way, and he won't give an inch."

"Maybe that was one reason he and Miriam couldn't make a go of it."

"That, and her wild ways. One man just wasn't enough for her," Coreen replied.

"I can't imagine anyone going from Ethan to someone else," Arabella said. "He's unique."

"I think so, even if he is my son." Coreen picked up her afghan and her crochet hook. "How do you feel about him, Bella?"

"I'm very grateful to him for what he's done for me," she said evasively. "He's always been like a big brother...."

"You don't have to pretend," Coreen said gently. "I'm perceptive, even if I don't look it." She lowered her eyes to her crocheting. "He made the mistake of his life by letting you get away. I'm sorry for both of you that it didn't work out."

Arabella studied the coverlet under her nervous hands. "It's just as well that it didn't," she replied. "I have a career that I hope to go back to. Ethan...well, maybe he and Miriam will patch things up."

"God forbid," Coreen muttered. She sighed wearily. "Life goes on. But I'm glad Ethan brought you home with him, Bella." She looked up. "He isn't a carefree man, and he takes on too much responsibility sometimes. He's forgotten how to play. But he changes when he's with you. It makes me happy to see how different he is when you're around. You always could make him smile."

Arabella thought about that long after Coreen had gone downstairs to help Betty Ann in the kitchen. Ethan did smile more with her than he did with other people. He always had. She'd noticed it, but it surprised her that his mother had.

FOR TWO DAYS, Arabella was confined to bed against her will. Doctor's orders, they told her, because she'd been concussed and badly bruised in the wreck. But on the third day, the sun came out and the temperature was unnaturally high that afternoon for early March. She got downstairs by herself, a little wobbly from her enforced leisure, and sat down in the porch swing.

Coreen had gone to a ladies' circle meeting and Mary was shopping, so there was no one to tell her she couldn't go outside. Mary had helped her dress that morning in a snap-front, full denim skirt and a long-sleeved blue sweatshirt. She'd tied her hair back with a blue velvet ribbon. She looked elegant even in such casual attire, and the touch of makeup she'd used made her look more alive. Not that anyone would be around to notice.

And that was where she was mistaken. The pickup truck pulled into the yard and Ethan got out of it, pausing on the steps when he saw her sitting in the swing.

"Who the hell told you to get out of bed?" he demanded.

"I'm tired of staying in bed," she replied. Her heart went wild just at the sight of him. He was wearing faded jeans and a chambray shirt with a beat-up, tan Stetson, and his boots were muddy as he joined her on the porch. "It's a beautiful day," she added hopefully.

"So it is." He lit a cigarette and leaned against the post, his pale eyes lancing over her. "I checked with your uncle this morning."

"Did you?" She watched him curiously.

"Your father left Dallas for New York this morning." His eyes narrowed. "Do you know why?"

She grimaced. "The bank account, I guess. If there's anything in it."

"There's something in it," he said pleasantly enough. "But he won't get to it. I had my attorney slap an injunction on your father, and the bank has orders not to release a penny to him. That's where I've been."

"Ethan!"

"It was that or have him get you by the purse strings," he said quietly. "When you're back on your feet again, you can play twenty questions with him. Right now, you're here to get well, not to have yourself left penniless by your mercenary father."

"Do I have much?" she asked, dreading the answer, because her father had enjoyed a luxurious lifestyle.

"You have twenty-five thousand," he replied. "Not a fortune, but it will keep you if it's invested properly."

She stared at his muscular arms, remembering the strength of them. "I didn't think ahead," she said. "I let him put the money in a joint account because he said it was the best way. I guess I owe you my livelihood, don't I?" she added with a smile.

"You're earning it," he replied quietly.

"By helping you get rid of Miriam," she agreed.

"We'll have to do a little work on you first," he returned. He studied her for a long moment. "You washed your hair."

"Actually, Mary and I washed my hair. I have to get Mary to help me dress with this thing on," she muttered, holding up the arm with the cast and then grimacing at the twinge of pain it caused. "I can't even fasten my bra—" She bit off the rest of the word.

His eyes narrowed. "Embarrassed to talk about undergarments with me?" he asked. "I know what women wear under their clothes." He grew suddenly distant and cold. "I know all too well."

"Miriam hurt you very badly, didn't she, Ethan?" she asked without meeting his eyes. "I suppose having her come back here makes all the scars open up again." She looked up then, catching the bitterness in his expression before he could erase it.

He sighed heavily and lifted the cigarette to his lips with a vicious movement of his fingers. He stared out over the horizon blankly. "Yes, she hurt me. But it was my pride, not my heart, that took a beating. When I threw her out, I vowed that no woman was going to get a second shot at me. So far, no one has."

Was he warning her off? Surely he knew that she'd never have the courage to set her cap for him again. He'd knocked her back hard enough over Miriam.

"Well, don't look at me," she said with a forced smile. "I'm definitely not Mata Hari material."

Some of the tenseness left him. He stubbed out the finished cigarette in an ashtray nearby. "All the same, little one, I can't see you sleeping around. Before or after marriage."

"We go to church," she said simply.

"I go to church myself."

She clasped her hands in her lap. "I read about this poll they took. It said that only four percent of the people in the country didn't believe in God."

"The four percent that produce motion pictures and television programs, no doubt," he muttered dryly.

She burst out laughing. "That was unkind," she said. "They aren't atheists, they're just afraid of offending somebody. Religion and politics are dangerous subjects."

"I've never worried about offending people," Ethan replied. "In fact, I seem to have a knack for it."

She smiled at him. He made her feel alive and free, as if she could do anything. Her green eyes sparkled as they met and held his silver ones, and the same electricity ran between them that had bound them together, years ago, one lazy day in late summer. The look had been translated into physical reality that one time, but now it only made Arabella sad for something she'd never have again. Even so, Ethan didn't look away. Perhaps he couldn't, she thought dazedly, feeling her heart shake her with its beat, her body tingle all over with sweet, remembered pleasure.

He said something rough under his breath and abruptly turned away. "I've got to get down to the holding pens. If you need anything, sing out. Betty Ann's in the kitchen."

He left without a backward glance.

Arabella stared after him with open longing. It seemed that she couldn't breathe without setting him off. And even if he could have felt something for her, he wasn't going to let his guard down again. He'd already said so. Miriam had really done a job on his pride.

She leaned back in the swing and started it swinging. Odd that he hadn't found someone to replace Miriam as soon as his marriage was over. He could have had his pick on looks alone, never mind the fortune behind his name. But he'd been a loner ever since, from what Mary had said. Surely Miriam couldn't have hurt him that much—unless he was still in love with her.

She sighed. She was a little afraid of Ethan. She was much too vulnerable and he was close at hand and alone. Ironically, Miriam's arrival might be her only hope of keeping her heart from being broken by him all over again.

CHAPTER FOUR

ARABELLA HAD SUPPER with the family for the first time that night, and Matt announced that he was taking Mary to the Bahamas for a much-needed vacation.

"Vacation?" Ethan glared at him. "What's that?"

Matt grinned. He looked a lot like his brother, except that he had deep blue eyes and Ethan's were silver. Matt was shorter, less formidable, but a hard worker in spite of his easygoing nature.

"A vacation is a thing I haven't had since I got married. I'm leaving and Mary is going with me."

"It's March," Ethan pointed out. "Calving? Roundup...?"

"I never asked for a honeymoon," Matt replied with an eloquent glance.

Ethan and Coreen exchanged wry looks. "All right. Go ahead," Ethan told him dryly. "I'll just have an extra set of arms put on and manage without you."

"Thanks, Ethan," Mary said gently. Her eyes glanced shyly off his and she smiled at her husband with pure delight.

"Where in the Bahamas did you plan to go?" Ethan asked.

Matt grinned. "That's a secret. If you don't know where I am, you can't look for me."

Ethan glared at him. "I tried that four years ago. You found me."

"That was different," Matt said. "A note came due at the bank and they wouldn't let me arrange the renewal."

"Excuses, excuses," Ethan replied.

"You might look at houses before you come back," Coreen murmured.

Matt shook his finger at her. "Not nice."

"Just a thought," she replied.

"If we leave, who'll save you from Ethan?" Matt asked smugly.

Arabella glanced at Ethan, who looked more approachable tonight than he had since she'd come home from the hospital. She felt suddenly mischievous. She raised her hand. "I volunteer."

Ethan's silvery eyes lanced her way with faint surprise and a little delight in them as he studied her face. "It'll take more than you, cupcake," Ethan said, and he smiled.

The smile reminded her of what Coreen had said, about how easily Ethan had once smiled for Arabella. The knowledge went to her head. She wrinkled her nose at him. "I'll recruit help. At least one of the cowboys was offering to spray you with malathion late this afternoon. I heard him."

"He was offering to spray *me* with insecticide?" Ethan glowered. "Which cowboy?" he demanded, with a look that meant trouble for the man.

"I won't tell. He might come in handy later," Arabella returned.

"Feeling better, are we?" Ethan murmured. He lifted an eyebrow. "Watch out. We'll get in trouble."

Arabella looked around. "I thought there was only one of me."

Ethan felt frankly exhilarated, and that disturbed him. He had to drag his eyes away from Arabella's soft face. He stared at his brother instead. "Why don't you want a house of your own?" Ethan asked him.

"I can't afford one."

"Horsefeathers," Ethan muttered. "You've got a great credit rating."

"I don't like the idea of going that deep in debt."

Ethan sat back in his chair and chuckled. "You don't know what debt is until you spend ninety thousand dollars for a combine."

"If you think that's high for a harvesting machine, just consider the total cost of tractors, hay balers and cattle trailers," Coreen added.

"I know, I know," Matt conceded. "But you're used to it. I'm not. Mary's applied for a job at the new textile plant that just opened. They're looking for secretarial help. If she gets it, we might take the plunge. But first we take a vacation. Right, honey?"

"Right," Mary said eagerly.

"Suit yourself," Ethan said. He finished his coffee and stood up. "I've got to make a couple of phone calls." Involuntarily, his eyes were drawn to Arabella. She looked up in time to meet that searching gaze, and a long, static moment passed during which Ethan's jaw clenched and Arabella flushed.

Arabella managed to look away first, embarrassed even though Coreen and the others were engaged in conversation and hadn't noticed.

Ethan paused by her chair and his lean hand went to her dark hair, lightly brushing it. He was gone before she could question whether it had been accidental or deliberate. Either way, her heart went wild.

She spent the evening listening to Matt and Mary talk about their planned trip, and when bedtime came, she was the first to go up. She was on the bottom step of the staircase when Ethan came out of his study and joined her there.

"Come here, little one, I'll carry you up." He bent, swinging her gently into his arms, careful of the hand that was in the cast.

"It's my arm, not my leg," she stammered.

He started up the stairs, easily taking her weight. He glanced down at her. "I don't want you to overdo it."

She was silent, and he drank in the feel of her in his arms. He'd never managed to forget how she felt close against him, and he'd tried, for years. Of course she didn't need to be carried. But he needed to carry her, to feel her body against him, to bring back the bittersweet memories of the one time he'd made love to her. It had haunted him ever since, especially now that she was here, in his house. He hardly slept at all these days, and when he did, his dreams were full of her. She didn't know that, and he wasn't going to admit it. It was much too soon.

She felt her breath whispering out at the concern in his deep voice. She couldn't think of anything to say. She curled her arms hesitantly around his neck and nuzzled her face into his shoulder. His breath caught and his step faltered for an instant, as if her soft movement had startled and disturbed him.

"Sorry," she whispered.

He didn't answer. He'd felt something when she moved that way. Something that he hadn't felt in a long time. His arms tightened as he savored the warm weight of Arabella's body, the faint scent of flowers that clung to her dark hair.

"You've lost weight," he said as he reached the landing.

"I know." Her breasts rose and fell in a gentle sigh, bringing them into a closer, exciting contact with his chest. "Aren't you glad? I mean, if I weighed twice as much as I do, you might pitch headfirst down the stairs and we'd both wind up with broken necks."

He smiled faintly. "That's one way of looking at it." He shifted her as he reached her bedroom, edging through the doorway. "Hold tight while I close the door."

She did, shivering a little at his closeness. He felt that betraying tremble and stopped dead, lifting his head to look into her wide, bright eyes with a heart-stopping intensity.

"You like being close to me, don't you?" he asked. His senses stirred with a sensuality that he hadn't felt in years.

Arabella went scarlet. She dropped her eyes and went rigid in his arms, struggling for something to say.

Amazingly, her embarrassment intensified the excitement he was feeling. It was like coming to life after being dead. His body rippled with desire and he felt like a man for the first time in four years. He kicked the door shut and carried her to the bed. He tossed her onto it gently and stood over her, his eyes lingering on the soft thrust of her breasts. His eyes darted back up to catch hers, his heart feeding on the helpless desire he found on her face.

So she hadn't forgotten, any more than he had. For one wild minute, he thought about going down beside her, arching his body over her own and kissing her until she gasped. But he moved away from the bed before his body could urge him on. Arabella might want him, but her virginal state was enough of a brake for both of them. She was still bitter about the past, and what he was feeling might not last. He had to be sure....

He lit a cigarette, repocketing his lighter roughly.

"I thought you'd quit, until this afternoon," Arabella said, sitting up. She was uncomfortable with the silence and his sudden withdrawal. Why had he taunted her with that intimate remark and then looked as if she'd asked him to do it? Shades of the past, she thought.

"I had quit until you got yourself banged up in that wreck," he agreed with a cold glance. "That started me back."

"So did having a flat tire in the truck." She began to count off the reasons on one hand. "There was the time the men got drunk the night before roundup started. Then there was the day your horse went lame. And once, a horse bit you...."

"I don't have to have excuses to smoke," he reminded her. "I've always done it and you've always known it." His eyes narrowed as he studied her soft face. "I was smoking that day by the creek. You didn't complain about the taste of it when I kissed you."

She felt the sadness that must have been reflected in her eyes. "I was eighteen," she said. "A couple of boys had kissed me, but you were older and more worldly." She lowered her eyes. "I was trying so hard to behave like a sophisticated woman, but the minute you touched me, I went to pieces." She sighed heavily. "It seems like a hundred years ago. I guess you were right, too; I did throw myself at you. I was besotted with you."

He had to struggle not to go to her, to pull her into his arms and kiss the breath out of her. She felt guilty, when he was the one who'd been wrong. He'd hurt her. He'd wounded her pride, just as Miriam had wounded his, and sent her running. Perhaps her father would never have gotten such a hold on her if he'd told Miriam to go to hell and asked Arabella to marry him.

"What tangled webs we weave," he said quietly. "Even when we aren't trying to deceive people."

"You couldn't help loving Miriam," she replied.

His face froze. Amazing how just the sound of his ex-wife's name could turn him off completely. He lifted the cigarette to his mouth, the hardness in him almost brittle as he stared down at Arabella.

Arabella watched him. "Do you realize how you look when someone mentions her, Ethan?" she asked gently.

"I realize it," he said curtly.

"And you don't want to talk about it. All right, I won't ask," she replied. "I can imagine she dealt your pride a horrible blow. But sometimes all it takes to repair the damage is having your ego built back up again."

His pale eyes pierced hers, and the look they exchanged was even more electric and intimate than the one downstairs.

"Are you offering to give me back my self-esteem?" he asked.

Years seemed to pass while she tried to decide if he meant that question. He couldn't have, she decided finally. He'd made it clear four years ago just how he felt. She shivered. "No, I'm not offering anything, except to give a good performance when Miriam gets here," she told him. "I owe you that much for taking me in while I get well."

His eyes blazed. "You owe me nothing," he said coldly.

"Then I'll do it for old times' sake," she returned with icy pride. "You were like the big brother I never had. I'll do it to pay you back for looking out for me."

He felt as if she'd hit him. The only thing that gave him any confidence was the way she'd reacted to being in his arms. He blew out a cloud of smoke, staring at her with total absorption. "Any reason will do," he said. "I'll see you in the morning."

He turned and started toward the door.

"Well, what do you want me to say?" she burst out. "That I'd do anything you asked me to do short of murder? Are you looking for miracles?"

He stopped with his hand on the doorknob and looked at her. "No, I'm not looking for miracles." He searched her face. Somewhere inside, he felt dead. "I put the cat and kittens in the barn," he said after a minute. "If you'd like to see them, I'll take you down there in the morning."

She hesitated. It was an olive branch of sorts. And if they were going to convince Miriam, they couldn't do it in a state of war. She moved restlessly on the bed. "Yes, I'd like that. Thank you."

"De nada," he said in careless Spanish, a habit because of the Mexican vaqueros who worked for him, who still understood their own language best. Ethan spoke three or four languages fluently, which often surprised visitors who felt his Texas drawl indicated a deprived education.

She watched him leave with pure exasperation. He kept her so confused and upset that she didn't know if she was coming or going.

MARY AND MATT left the next morning. Arabella hugged Mary goodbye, feeling a little lost without her best friend. Ethan's new outlook and the specter of Miriam's approach seemed daunting, to say the least.

"Don't look so worried," Mary said gently. "Ethan and Coreen will take good care of you. And Miriam won't be staying here. Ethan wouldn't have it."

"I hope you're right. I have a feeling Miriam could take skin off with words."

"I wouldn't doubt that," Mary replied, grimacing. "She can be nasty, all right. But I think you might be equal to her, once you got going. You used to be eloquent when you lost your temper. Even Ethan listened." She laughed.

"I haven't had much practice at losing my temper, except with Ethan," Arabella replied. "Wish me luck."

"I will, but you won't need it, I'm sure," Mary said.

Ethan drove them to the airport in Houston so they wouldn't have to take the shuttle flight out of Jacobsville airport. But he was back before Arabella expected him, and he hadn't forgotten about the kittens.

"Come on, if you're still interested." He took her good hand, tugging her along with him, not a trace of emotion showing on his face.

"Shouldn't we tell your mother where we're going?" she protested.

"I haven't told my mother where I was going since I was eight," he said shortly. "I don't need her permission to walk around the ranch."

"I didn't mean it that way," she muttered.

It did no good at all. He ignored her. He was still wearing what he called his city clothes, charcoal slacks with a pale blue shirt and a Western-cut gray-and-black sport jacket.

"You'll get dirty," she said as they entered the wide-aisled barn.

He glanced down at her. "How?"

She could have made a joke about it with a less intimidating man, but not with Ethan. This unapproachable man would have cut her to pieces.

"Never mind." She moved ahead of him, neatly dressed herself in a pair of designer jeans and a pale yellow pullover that would show the least hint of dirt.

She walked down the aisle and went where he gestured, feeling his presence with fear and delight. It was sobering to think that but for the accident that had damaged her hand, she might never have seen Ethan again.

Her hand. She glanced down at it, seeing the help-lessness of it emphasized by the cast. Threads of music drew through her mind. She could hear the keys, feel the chords, the melody, the minors, the subdominants....

She closed her eyes and heard Clementi's *Sonatina*, its three movements one of the first pieces she'd mastered when she began as an intermediary student. She smiled as it was replaced in her thoughts by the exquisite *English Suite* by Bach, and *Finlandia* by Grieg.

"I said, here are the kittens. Where were you?" Ethan asked quietly.

She opened her eyes, and realized as she did that her fingers might never feel those notes again. She might never be able to play a melody in more than a parody of her former ability. Even the pop tunes would be beyond her. She'd have no way to support herself. And she certainly couldn't expect her father to do it, not when he wouldn't even phone or come near her. At least Ethan had managed to save some of her earnings, but they wouldn't last long if her father hadn't paid off the debts.

There was panic in her eyes, in her pale face.

Ethan saw it. He tapped her gently on the nose, the antagonism dying out of him all at once when he saw her tormented expression. He had to stop baiting her. It wasn't her fault that Miriam had crippled him as a man. "Stop trying to live your life all at one time. There's nothing to panic about."

Her eyes met his. "That's what you think."

"Let tomorrow take care of itself." He went down on one knee. "Now, this is worth seeing."

He gestured for her to kneel down beside him, and

all her cares were lost in the magic of four snow-white, newborn kittens. Their mother, too, was a snow-white short hair with deep blue eyes.

"Why, I've never seen a cat like this!" she exclaimed. "A white cat with blue eyes!"

"They're pretty rare, I'm told. Bill found them in his barn, and he's not a cat fancier."

"And they were going to be put to sleep." She groaned. "I'll rent them an apartment if my father gives me any trouble," she said firmly. She smiled at the mother cat and then looked longingly at the kittens. "Will she let me hold one?"

"Of course. Here." He lifted a tiny white kitten and placed it gently in Arabella's hand, which she held close to her body to make sure it didn't fall. She nuzzled its tiny head with her cheek, lost in the magic of the new life.

Ethan watched her, his eyes indulgent and without mockery. "You love little things, don't you?"

"I always have." She handed back the kitten with obvious reluctance, taking the opportunity to stroke it gently. "I always thought that one day I'd get married and have children, but there seemed to be one more concert, one more recording date." She smiled wistfully. "My father was determined to make sure that I never had the chance to get serious about anyone."

"He couldn't risk losing you." Ethan put the kitten back down, stroking the mother's head gently before he rose, bringing Arabella up with him. He brushed back her long, loose dark hair with both hands. Then, in the silence of the barn, which was only broken by an occasional movement or sound from the horses nearby, his hands moved to frame her face. "I used to take you riding. Remember?"

"Yes. I haven't been on a horse since. Ethan, why wouldn't you let your mother sell the horse I used to ride here?" she asked suddenly, remembering what Coreen had said about it.

He shifted restlessly. "I had my reasons."

"And you won't tell me what they were?"

"No." He searched her eyes slowly, hungrily. He felt his heartbeat increasing as the nearness of her began to affect him, just as it had the night before. "It's been a hell of a long time since you and I have been alone together," he said quietly.

She lowered her eyes to his broad chest, watching its heavy rise and fall. "Years," she agreed nervously.

He touched her hair gently, trailing it through his fingers, feeling the silkiness of it. "Your hair was long, then, too," he recalled, catching her soft eyes. "I pillowed you on it in the grass when we made love by the old swimming hole."

Her heart went wild. It was all she could do to hold on to her self-control. "We didn't make love," she said through her teeth. "You kissed me a few times and made sure I didn't take it seriously. It was to 'further my education,' didn't you say?"

"You were grass-green and stupid about men," he said curtly. "You felt my body against yours. You may have been a kid then, but you sure as hell ought to know by now how dangerous the situation was getting when I called a halt."

"It doesn't make any difference now," she said miserably. "As I said, you made sure I didn't take it seriously. I was just being my usual stupid self. Now can we go back to the house?"

He slid his hands roughly into her hair and held her face up to his pale, glittering eyes. "You were eighteen," he said shortly. "A virginal eighteen with a father who hated my guts and had complete control of your life. Only a heartless fool would have seduced you under those circumstances!"

She stared at him, shocked by the fury in his eyes, his voice. "And you were nobody's fool," she agreed, almost shaking with mingled fear and hurt. "But you don't have to pretend that you cared about my feelings, not after the things you said to me…!"

His hands contracted and he drew in a sharp breath. "God in heaven, how can you be so blind?" he groaned. His gaze fell to her mouth and he drew her face up toward his, his lips parting. "I wanted you!"

The words went into her mouth. He was fitting his lips with exquisite slowness to her own in a silence thick with tense emotion. But even as his mouth brushed against hers, even as she felt the sharp intake of his breath and felt the pressure of his hands on her face, a sound broke the spell and froze him in place.

It was the loud roar of a car driving up outside. Ethan's head lifted abruptly and the look in his eyes was almost feverish. His hands had a faint tremor as he drew them away from her face, and he was breathing roughly. So was she. She felt as if her legs wouldn't even support her.

Her eyes asked the question she didn't dare.

"I've been alone a long time," he said curtly, and he gave her a mocking smile. "Isn't that what you'd like to believe?"

Before she could answer, he let go of her and turned toward the front of the barn.

"I'm expecting a buyer this morning," he said gruffly. "That must be him."

He went down the wide aisle ahead of her, almost grateful for the diversion. He'd lost his head just then, gotten drunk on the exquisite promise of Arabella's mouth under his. He hadn't realized how vulnerable he'd become since she'd been here. He was going to have to be more careful. Rushing her would accomplish nothing; he should be thankful that his buyer had interrupted.

But when he reached the yard, the visitor wasn't his buyer at all. It was a taxi, and getting out of the back seat, all leggy glamour and red lipstick, was Miriam Hardeman. If she wasn't going to be a houseguest, obviously nobody had thought to inform her of it, because the cabdriver was slowly getting six expensive suitcases out of the trunk of the car.

Ethan's face went stiff as Arabella joined him and he felt as if he were breaking out in a cold sweat. Miriam. Just the sight of his ex-wife was enough to shake his self-confidence to its foundations. He schooled his face to show nothing as he turned toward Arabella and held out his hand, silently commanding her cooperation, as she'd promised it.

Beside him, Arabella stared at the newcomer as if

she were a particularly vicious disease. Which, in fact, was a fair analogy. She let Ethan's hand envelop hers and she held on for dear life. They were in it together now, for better or worse.

CHAPTER FIVE

MIRIAM RAISED A delicately etched eyebrow as Ethan and Arabella joined her. She stared hard at Arabella, almost incredulously, her eyes sharp and immediately hostile. She noticed that Ethan and the younger woman were holding hands, and for a minute, she seemed to lose a little of her poise. Then she smiled, almost as if by force of will, because there was no joy in her dark green eyes.

"Hello, Ethan." She tossed back her long auburn hair nervously. "I hope you got my telegram?"

He stared back at her, refusing to be taunted. "I got it."

"Pay the cabdriver, would you?" she persisted. "I'm flat broke. I hope you don't mind my staying here, Ethan, because I blew my last dollar on this outfit and I just can't afford a hotel."

Ethan didn't say a word, but his expression grew even more remote.

Arabella watched Ethan pay the driver, then her eyes darted to Miriam. The woman was perfection itself. Flaming red highlights in her long auburn hair, dark green, witchy eyes, an exquisite face and figure. But she was showing her age a bit, and she was heavier than she had been. What Coreen had said about pregnancy came home with full force. Yes, Miriam could be pregnant, all right. That would explain that slight weight gain, mostly in her waist.

"Hello, Arabella," Miriam said as she studied the younger woman coldly. "I've heard enough about you over the years. I remember you, of course. You were only a child when Ethan and I married."

"I've grown up," Arabella said quietly. She stared after Ethan with soft longing. "At least, Ethan thinks so."

Miriam laughed haughtily. "Does he, really?" she asked. "I suppose a very young woman would appeal to him, since she wouldn't know what she was missing."

That was an unexpected taunt. Arabella didn't understand it, or the way Ethan looked when he came back, after gesturing for one of his passing cowboys to carry Miriam's luggage up to the house.

"Tell her why you won't get involved with experienced women, Ethan, dear," Miriam murmured sarcastically.

Ethan stared at her with the intimidating look that Arabella hated. It even seemed to work on Miriam.

"Arabella and I go back a long way. We were involved before you and I were, Miriam," he added, staring levelly at his ex-wife.

Miriam's eyes blazed. "Yes, I remember your mother saying that," she replied.

The expression on Miriam's face did Ethan more good than anything had in years. He drew Arabella close against his side, giving her a quick, pleased glance when she let her body go lax against him. "You weren't expected until next week," he told Miriam.

"I just finished a modeling assignment down in the Caribbean and I thought I'd stop by on my way back to

New York," Miriam replied. She fidgeted with her purse, nervously it seemed.

Arabella stared at Miriam from the shelter of Ethan's hard arm. It was almost rigid around her, which told her plenty about how he was reacting to the woman's presence. She didn't understand the undercurrents. If he still loved Miriam, she didn't see why he couldn't just say it. Why this pretense, when Miriam was obviously still jealous of him?

"How long do you want to stay?" Ethan asked. "We're pretty busy right now and I hope you understand that Arabella and I consider our time together precious."

Miriam lifted an eyebrow. "How convenient that you should turn up just now, Arabella. You've been pursuing your career for several years, I believe?"

"Bella was injured in a wreck. Naturally I want her where I am," Ethan replied with a cool smile. "I hope you'll enjoy spending your evenings talking to Mother."

"I'll manage," Miriam said irritably. "Well, let's go up to the house. I'm tired and I want a drink."

"You won't drink here," Ethan said firmly. "We don't keep liquor in the house."

"Don't keep…!" Miriam gasped. "But we always had a full liquor cabinet!"

"You did," Ethan corrected. "When you left, I had the bottles thrown out. I don't drink."

"You don't do anything," Miriam said with a nasty inflection. "Especially in bed!" she lashed out.

Ethan's arm tightened around her. Arabella was beginning to catch on, or she thought she was. She felt her hair bristling as she stared at the older woman with pure fury. Ethan didn't need defending, and he'd probably be furious that she dared say anything, but this was too much! Miriam had run around on him; what did she expect when he was repulsed by it? Even love would have a hard time excusing that kind of hurt.

Ethan himself was having to bite his tongue. He knew how Miriam would love to provoke him into losing his temper, to give her an excuse to tell Arabella all their dark secrets. He didn't want that, not until he'd had time to tell her himself. His pride demanded that much.

But Arabella got in the first words, her face lifted proudly as she faced the older woman without flinching. "You may have had problems in bed," Arabella said quietly, clinging to Ethan's hand. "Ethan and I don't." Which was the gospel truth, but not the way Miriam took it. Ethan smothered a shocked gasp. He hadn't expected her to sacrifice her reputation for him, certainly not with such surprising courage.

Miriam shuddered with fury. "You little...!"

The word she'd used was dying on the air even as Ethan broke into it, his face fiercely angry at the way Arabella was trembling despite her brave front. "The road is that direction." Ethan indicated. "I'll send a cab after you. No way are you going to exercise your vicious tongue on my future wife!"

Miriam backed down immediately. Arabella didn't do anything; she was too shocked at being referred to as Ethan's future wife.

"I'm sorry," Miriam said on a swallowed breath. "I suppose I did lay it on with a trowel." She glanced at

Ethan, curious and nervous now, unusually so. "I... I guess it shocked me to think you'd gotten over me."

"I meant what I said," he replied, his voice cutting. "If you stay here, it's on my terms. If I hear so much as one sharp word to Bella, off you go. Is that clear?"

"It had better be, isn't that what you mean, Ethan?" Miriam forced a smile. "All right, I'll be the perfect houseguest. I thought we were going to talk about a reconciliation."

"Perhaps you did," Ethan said calmly. "Bella and I are going to be married. There's no room in my life for you now or ever."

Miriam seemed to go pale. She straightened, elegant in her pale gray suit, and smiled again. "That's pretty blunt."

"Blunt is the only way to be with you," Ethan said. "After you," he said, standing aside to let her enter the house.

Arabella was still stunned, although she had the presence of mind to wonder if Miriam's outburst hadn't been prompted by fear rather than anger. Which made her wonder why Miriam was so afraid of having Ethan involved with another woman. Ethan took her hand in his, feeling its soft coldness.

"You're doing fine," he said quietly, so that Miriam couldn't hear. "Don't worry, I won't let her savage you."

"I didn't mean to say that...."

He smiled gently, despite his drawn features. "I'll explain it to you later."

"You don't have to explain anything to me," she said,

her eyes level and unblinking. "I don't care what Miriam says."

He drew in a deep breath. "You're full of surprises."

"So are you. I thought you were going to save the engagement threat as a last resort," she murmured.

"Sorry. This seemed the best time. Come on. Chin up."

She managed a smile and, holding tight to his lean hand, followed him into the house.

Coreen was unwelcoming, but she was too much a lady to show her antagonism for Miriam outright. She camouflaged it behind impeccable manners and cold courtesy. The only time a smile touched her lips was when Ethan sat down close beside Arabella on the sofa and drew her against him with a possessive arm.

It had thrilled Arabella earlier when Ethan had defended her so fiercely. Perhaps it had just been his distaste for Miriam's manners, but it was nice to think that he cared enough to stand up for her. She curled up on the sofa against him, drinking in his nearness, loving the scent and feel of him so close. This was the one nice thing that had come out of Miriam's visit. Arabella could indulge her longing for Ethan without giving herself away. What a pity that he was only pretending, to keep Miriam from seeing how vulnerable he was.

She glanced up at him, watching his lean face as he listened with coolly polite interest to Miriam's monologue about her travels. He was so tense, and she felt that what Miriam had said about him in bed had hurt him. She remembered what Coreen had said about his finding Miriam repulsive and she wondered if that was what Miriam had been referring to. Odd that he'd gone so white at the reference. Well, a woman like that could do plenty of damage even to a strong man's pride. She had a vicious tongue and no tolerance for other people. It wasn't the kind of attitude that kept a marriage together, especially when she'd never given Ethan any kind of fidelity. That must have cut his heart to pieces, loving her as he had.

"What are you doing down here, Arabella?" Miriam asked eventually. "I thought you were in New York."

"I was touring," Arabella replied. "I was on my way back from a charity performance when the car was wrecked."

"She was coming back here," Ethan inserted smoothly with a warning glance at Arabella. "She'd gone with her father. I should have driven her myself."

Arabella let out an inaudible sigh at the way she'd almost slipped up. Miriam would hardly believe that she and Ethan were engaged if Arabella was living in New York and they never saw each other.

"Will you be able to use your hand again, or is your career up the creek?" Miriam asked with a pointed smile. "I guess Ethan wouldn't want you to do anything except have babies anyway."

"As I recall," Ethan said coldly, "you were quite emphatic about not wanting any. That was after I married you, of course," he added meaningfully.

Miriam shifted restlessly. "So I was. Is there anything to do around here? I hate television," she said, quickly changing the subject.

"Ethan and Arabella and I like to watch the nature

specials," Coreen said. "In fact, there's a fascinating program about polar bears on tonight, isn't there, dear?" she asked Ethan.

Ethan exchanged a glance with his mother. "There is, indeed."

Miriam groaned.

It was the longest day Arabella could remember. She managed to dodge Miriam by staying with Ethan, even when he went out to check on the roundup. He usually took a horse, but in deference to Arabella's injured wrist, he was driving the ranch pickup.

He glanced at her. "Doing okay?" he asked.

She smiled. "I'm fine, thanks." He'd changed out of his traveling clothes into his worn jeans and boots and a blue plaid Western-cut shirt. His wide-brimmed hat was tilted at a rakish angle over his forehead. He looked very cowboyish, and Arabella grinned at the thought.

"Something funny?" he asked with a narrow, suspicious gaze.

"I was just thinking how much like a cowboy you look," she replied. "Not bad, for the boss."

"I don't have to wear suits around the men to get their attention."

"I remember." She shuddered.

"Stop that." He took a draw from the smoking cigarette in his hand. "You were a surprise this morning," he said unexpectedly. "You handled Miriam very well."

"Did you expect me to break into tears and run for cover?" she asked. "I've had a lot of practice with bad-tempered people. I lived with my father, remember."

"I remember. Miriam's the one who ran for cover this time."

"You had a few bites of her, yourself. My gosh, what a venomous woman!" she said huskily. "I don't remember her being that bad before."

"You didn't know her before. Or maybe you did," he added quietly. "You saw through her from the beginning."

She studied his averted face for a long moment, wanting to ask him something more, but uncertain of the way to go about it.

He sensed her curiosity and glanced toward her. "Go ahead. Ask me."

She started. "Ask you what?"

He laughed coldly as he drove the truck along the rough track beside the fence, bouncing them both in the seats even with the superior shocks under the truck body. "Don't you want to know why she was surprised when you gave her the impression we were lovers?"

"I thought she was just being sarcastic," she began.

He turned the truck and headed it toward another rutted path. Then abruptly he stopped it and cut off the engine. He had the windows down, and the sounds of birds and the distant bawling of cattle filtered in through it.

He sat with one hand on the steering wheel, the other holding the cigarette. He shifted in the seat and stared at Arabella fully, his silver eyes touching her face while he struggled with an explanation he didn't want to make. But Miriam was bound to say something to Arabella, and he wanted it to come from him, not from his venomous houseguest.

"Miriam took a lover two weeks after we were married," he said quietly. "There was a procession of them until I divorced her. She said that I couldn't satisfy her in bed."

He said it with icy bluntness, his eyes dark with pain, as if it were a reflection on his manhood. Perhaps it was. Arabella had read that a man's ego was the most vulnerable part of him.

She searched his face quietly. "It seems to me that nobody could satisfy her, Ethan. She certainly had a lot of lovers."

He didn't realize that he'd been holding his breath until then. Arabella's attitude took the sting out of the admission. He relaxed a little. "They say everything goes if both partners want it, but I was too old-fashioned to suit Miriam." He smoked his cigarette quietly.

She glanced at him. "Coreen thinks Miriam's pregnant and that's why she came back to try for a reconciliation. She wants to get you into bed and pretend it's yours."

"I told you at the outset, I don't want her," he said bluntly. "In bed or otherwise. She'd have to do a hell of a lot of pretending to get me to go along."

"She could tell people you were the father," she countered.

He sighed. "Yes, she probably could. That may be what she has in mind."

"What are we going to do?" she asked.

"I'll think of something," he said without looking at her. Locking his bedroom door might be the best answer, but wouldn't Miriam enjoy that, he thought bitterly.

"I could help if you'd tell me what to do," she replied. "All I know about sex is what you taught me that day," she added without looking at him.

That got his full attention. His breath was expelled in an audible rush. "My God," he said roughly. "You're kidding."

"I'm afraid not."

"Surely there were other men?"

"Not in the way you mean."

"You had to go out on dates in the past four years," he persisted. "You could be a virgin and still have some experience."

She'd backed herself into a corner now, she thought worriedly. How could she tell him that the thought of any other man's hands and eyes on her body had nauseated her? She looked for a way to change the subject.

"Answer me, Arabella," he said firmly.

She glared at him. "I won't."

He began to smile. "Was it so good with me that you didn't want it with anyone else?" he asked slowly. She blushed and averted her eyes, and he felt as if he were floating.

He reached out unexpectedly and caught a strand of her hair, savoring its silky softness. "I don't know how I managed to stop. You were extraordinarily responsive."

"I was infatuated with you," she replied. "I wanted so desperately to show you that I was grown up." She stared at his broad chest. "I suppose I did, but it didn't help. We'd at least been on relatively friendly terms until then."

He closed the ashtray and sat up straight again to

study her through narrowed eyes. "I suppose you're right. If we're going to pull this off, you and I are going to have to give the appearance of intimacy when we're around Miriam," he said abruptly, changing the subject.

She was glad to return to the present. Discussion about the past was still unpleasant. "You mean, I need to wear low-cut dresses and slink when I walk and sit on your lap and curl your hair around my fingers? Especially in front of Miriam?"

"You're catching on, cupcake," he replied.

"It wouldn't embarrass you?" she asked with a faint grin.

"Well, as long as you don't try to take my clothes off in public," he said. It was the first trace of humor she'd noticed in him since Miriam came. "We wouldn't want to embarrass my mother."

"You'll have to settle for partial seduction right now, I'm afraid," she sighed, indicating her wrist in the cast. "It's hard enough undressing myself without having to undress you, too."

"That reminds me," he murmured with a pointed look at the straps under her blouse, "how do you manage to get undressed?"

She lifted her shoulders. "I can manage most everything. Except what's underneath."

"You might consider going without what's underneath for the duration of Miriam's stay," he suggested somberly. "I'll try not to stare, but it might give her food for thought if you walk around in front of me that way."

"Your mother will have a heart attack," she replied.

"Not my mother. She's been in your corner since

you were eighteen." His eyes darkened as they searched hers. "She never could understand why I preferred Miriam to you."

"I could," she said with a harsh laugh. "Miriam was everything I wasn't. Especially sophisticated and experienced." She stared down at her lap with returning bitterness. "All I had going for me was a little talent. And now I may not even have that."

"None of that," he said curtly. His hand tightened around hers. "We won't think ahead. We won't think about when that cast comes off or your father's reaction. We'll think about Miriam and how to get her out of here. That's our first priority. You give me a hand and I'll do the same for you when your father shows up."

"Will he show up, Ethan?" she asked miserably.

The soft green eyes looking so trustingly into his made his pulse hammer in his throat. She was as pretty as she'd been at eighteen, and just as shyly innocent. He wouldn't have traded her tenderness for all of Miriam's glittery sophistication, but he no longer had that choice. Arabella was only playing a part in this mutual-protection pact. He couldn't lose sight of that fact. Arabella wasn't his. With the bitterness of the past between them, she probably never would be.

"It doesn't matter whether or not he does," he replied. He studied her long, elegant fingers. "I'll take care of you."

She felt little thrills down her spine. If only he meant it! She closed her eyes, drinking in the scent of his cologne, the warmth of his lean, powerful body so close to her.

There had been so little affection in her life. She'd been alone and unloved. Her father had only wanted her talent, not her company. No one had ever loved her, but she wanted Ethan to. She wanted him to care as much as she did. But that would never happen now. Miriam had killed what love there was in him.

"You're so quiet, little one," Ethan said. He tilted her chin up and searched her sad eyes. "What's wrong?"

The softness of his voice brought tears. They stung her eyelids and when she tried to hide them, he held her face firmly in both lean hands and made her look at him.

"Why?" he asked roughly.

Her lower lip trembled and she caught it in her teeth to still it. "It's nothing," she managed. Her eyes closed. She was a hopeless coward, she thought. She wanted to say *why can't you love me*, but she was afraid to.

"Stop trying to live your whole life in one day," he said sharply. "It won't work."

"I guess I worry too much," she confessed, brushing away a shiny tear from her cheek. "But everything's turned upside down. I had a promising career and a nice apartment in New York. I traveled…and now I may be a has-been. My father won't even talk to me," she faltered.

"He'll be in touch," he said. "Your hand will mend. Right now you don't need a job; you've already got one."

"Yes," she said with a weak smile. "Helping you stay single."

He gave her an odd look. "I wouldn't put it that way," he corrected. "The idea is to get Miriam to leave without bloodshed."

She lifted her face. "She's very beautiful," she said, searching his pale silver eyes. "Are you sure you don't want her back, Ethan? You loved her once."

"I loved an illusion," he said. His fingers brushed at a long strand of dark brown hair, moving it behind her ear. "Outward beauty isn't any indication of what's inside, Arabella. Miriam thought that beauty was enough, but a kind spirit and a warm heart mean a lot more to most people than a pretty face."

"She's not quite as cold as she was," she said.

He smiled faintly, searching her eyes. "Are you trying to push me into her arms?"

"No." She lowered her eyes to his hard mouth. "I just wondered if you were sure that getting rid of her is what you really want."

He drew her forehead against his chest, smoothing down her ruffled hair as he stared over her head and out the window. "I'm sure," he replied. "It wasn't much of a marriage to begin with." He drew back and looked at Arabella's soft face, drinking in its delicate beauty, its strength of character. "I wanted her," he said absently. "But wanting isn't enough."

Perhaps wanting was all he was capable of, though, Arabella thought miserably. He'd wanted her years ago, but he hadn't loved her. He said he hadn't loved Miriam, but since he married her, he must have felt something pretty powerful for her.

"What are you thinking about now?" he asked at her forehead.

"Just long thoughts," she confessed. She drew in a

steadying breath and lifted a smile to show him. "I'm all—"

His mouth settled unexpectedly on hers, covering the word even as she spoke it.

She stiffened at the feel of his firm lips on hers. All the years since he'd touched her, and it was as if they'd never been apart. She remembered the scent of him, the way his mouth bit at hers to make it open just as it had the first time he'd ever kissed her. She remembered the sound he made in his throat when he dragged her face under his with rough, warm hands and the feverish intensity of the mouth that grew instantly more demanding and intimate on her lips.

"Kiss me," he whispered, his breath making little chills on her moist lips. "Don't hold back."

"I don't want this—" she protested with her last whisper of will.

"You want me. You always have and I've always known it," he said roughly.

His fingers speared into her long hair, tangling in its dark softness while his mouth crushed down on hers again, pressing her lips firmly apart as he began to build the intensity of the kiss from a slow possession to a devastating intimacy.

She stiffened and he hesitated, his mouth poised just above her own.

"Don't fight me," he said huskily. His hands moved, faintly tremulous where they held her face captive. He was burning. On fire for her. The old need was back, in full force, and she was his, if only for a space of seconds. He wanted her so desperately. She was his heart.

Miriam and all the pain were forgotten in his driving hunger to hold Arabella's soft body in his arms, to feel again the aching sweetness of her mouth under his. "Oh, God, let me love you," he ground out.

"You don't," she said miserably. "You don't, you never did…!"

He took the words into his open mouth. He groaned heavily and his hands slid over her back, bringing her gently against him, so that her breasts flattened against his hard chest while he kissed her. Her hands pressed against his warm shirtfront, but she didn't kiss him back or put her arms around him. She was too afraid that he'd been stirred up by his ex-wife and now he needed an outlet. It was…demeaning.

He felt her lack of response and lifted his head. He could hardly breathe. His chest actually throbbed with the fierce thunder of his heart, and the sight of Arabella's flushed, lovely face under his made it go even faster. She looked frightened, although there was something under the fear, a leashed hunger that she was refusing to satisfy.

And that wasn't the only thing he noticed. Despite the blow Miriam had dealt his pride, he discovered that he was suddenly very much a man. He felt desire as he held Arabella; a raging desire he'd thought for four years he'd never be able to feel again for a woman. The impact of it brought a muffled curse from his lips. Of all the times for it to happen, and with Arabella, of all people!

CHAPTER SIX

ARABELLA COULDN'T MEET Ethan's searching gaze, and the faint tremor in his arms frightened her. He looked and felt out of control, and she knew the strength in that lean body. She tried to pull away, but he drew her even closer, his hard, dark face poised just above her own.

"What's wrong?" he asked roughly.

"You want Miriam," she said through numb lips. "You want her, and I'm substituting, all over again."

He was utterly shocked. His arms loosened and she took advantage of the momentary slackening to pull away from him. She couldn't bear the confinement of the cab a minute longer. She opened the door and climbed down, locking her arms around her breasts as she stared at the flat horizon and listened to the buzzing noise of insects in the heat of the day.

Ethan got out, too, lighting a cigarette. He walked along beside her with apparent carelessness, steering her toward a grove of mesquite trees by the small stream that led eventually to the swimming hole. He leaned against the rough trunk of a huge mesquite tree, smoking quietly while Arabella leaned against a nearby tree and watched butterflies fluttering around a handful of straggly wildflowers on the creek bank.

The silence became unnerving. Ethan's eyes narrowed as he studied Arabella's slender body. "You weren't substituting for Miriam in the truck."

She colored, avoiding his level gaze. "Wasn't I?"

He took a draw from the cigarette and stared at the ripples in the water. "My marriage is over."

"Maybe she's changed," she said, rubbing salt in her own wounds. "It could be a second chance for you."

"Miriam's the one with the second chance," he returned, his cold eyes biting into her face. "To bring me to my knees. The only thing she ever saw in me was the size of my wallet."

And that was the most hurtful part of it, she imagined. He'd loved Miriam and all she'd wanted was his money. She rubbed her cast with a light finger, tracing patterns on it. "I'm sorry. I guess that was rough."

"No man likes being a walking meal ticket," he said shortly. He finished the cigarette and tossed it onto the ground, putting it out with a vicious movement of his boot.

"Then maybe she'll give up and go away," she said.

"Not if you don't help me give her the right impression about our relationship," he said curtly. He pushed away from the tree and walked toward her with somber intent in his pale eyes. "You said you'd need a little cooperation. All right. You'll get it."

"No, Ethan," she choked. Even in her innocence, she recognized the purposeful stride, the glitter in his enveloping gaze. It was the same look he'd had on his face that day at the swimming hole. "Oh, Ethan, don't! It's just a game to you. It's Miriam you want. It's always been Miriam, never me!"

He moved in front of her and his lean hands shot past her to the broad tree trunk, imprisoning her. He held her eyes relentlessly. "No," he said huskily. He searched her face and his heart went wild. Even his body, frozen though it had been for four long years, was alive as never before.

"Don't," she pleaded as her breath caught in her throat. The scent and feel of him was making her weak. She didn't want to be vulnerable again, she didn't want to be hurt. "Please don't."

"Look at me."

She shook her head.

"I said, look at me!"

The sheer force of will in the deep drawl brought her rebellious eyes up, and he trapped them.

Still holding her eyes with his, he lowered his body against hers, letting her feel the raging arousal she'd kindled.

Her eyes dilated. She could barely breathe. After one shocked minute, she tried to struggle, but he groaned and his eyes closed. He shuddered. She stood very still, her lips parted.

He looked down at her for a long time, his eyes dark with desire, his body rigid with it. "My God," he whispered almost reverently. "It's been so long...." His mouth ground into hers with fierce delight. He was a man again, whole again. He could hardly believe what he was feeling.

Arabella was drowning in him. His warm masculine

body was making her ache terribly, but she couldn't afford to give in.

"I won't love you, Ethan," she whispered, her expression tormented as memories of the past wounded her. "I won't, I won't!"

His heart began to swell in his chest. So that was it. The secret fear. He smiled faintly, letting his gaze fall to her soft bow of a mouth as he began to realize how vulnerable she was, and why. "We'll take it one day at a time," he breathed as his head bent. "Do you remember how I taught you to kiss—with your teeth and your tongue as well as your lips?"

She did, but it wouldn't have mattered, because he was teaching her all over again. She felt the brush of his warm, hard lips over her own, felt them tug on her lower lip and then her upper lip, felt the soft tracing of his tongue between them and the gentle bite of his teeth as he coaxed her mouth to open and admit the slow, deliberate penetration of his tongue.

A sound escaped her tight throat. Her body stiffened under his. The fingers of her uninjured hand began to open and close, her nails making tiny scraping sensations even through his shirt to his throbbing chest.

"Open my shirt," he said into her mouth.

She hesitated and he kissed her roughly.

"Do it," he bit off against her lips. "You've never touched me that way. I want you to."

She knew it was emotional suicide to obey him, but her fingers itched to touch his warm, dark skin. She felt his lips playing gently against her mouth while she fumbled the buttons out of the buttonholes until, finally, her fingers could tangle in the thick dark growth of hair over his chest to find the warm, taut skin beneath it.

Unthinking, she drew back to look at where her fingers were touching, fascinated concentration in her soft green eyes as she registered the paleness of her long fingers against the darkness of his hair-matted skin.

"Put your mouth against me," he said unsteadily. "Here. Like this." He caught the back of her head and coaxed her face against him. She breathed in soap and cologne and pure, sweet man as her lips pressed softly where he guided them.

"Ethan?" she whispered uncertainly. This was unfamiliar territory, and she could feel that his body was rigid with desire. He was shuddering with it.

"There's nothing to be afraid of, Arabella," he said at her lips. "Let me lift you… God, baby!" he ground out, shuddering. His hips pinned hers to the tree, but she never felt the rough bark at her spine. Her arms went around him, both of them trembling as the intimate contact locked them together as forcefully as a blazing electric current.

She was crying with the sheer impact of it, her arms holding him even as his full weight came down against her.

"You can't get close enough to me, can you?" he groaned. "I know. I feel the same way! Move your legs, sweet…yes!"

His leg insinuated its powerful length between hers, intensifying the intimacy of the embrace.

"I want you." His hands caught her hips, moving them with slow, deliberate intent into his while his mouth probed hers. "I want you, Arabella. God, I want you so!"

She was incapable of answering him. She felt him pick her up, but her eyes were closed. She was his. Whatever he wanted, whatever he did, she had no desire to stop him.

She felt the wind in her hair and Ethan's mouth on hers. The strength of his arms absorbed the shock of his footsteps as he carried her back to the truck.

He opened the door and put her in the passenger seat, sliding her to the middle of the cab so that he could fit facing her, his eyes intent on her flushed face.

Arabella could hardly breathe for the enormity of what had just happened. She'd never expected Ethan to make such a heavy pass at her with Miriam in residence. But it was because of Miriam, she was sure of it. He just didn't want to admit that his heart was still in bondage to the woman he couldn't satisfy. Her eyes fell to his opened shirt, to the expanse of his muscular chest, and lingered there.

"Nothing to say?" he asked quietly.

She shook her head slowly.

"I won't let you pretend that it didn't happen." He tilted her face up to his. "We made love."

Her cheeks went scarlet. "Not…not quite."

"You wouldn't have stopped me." He traced her lower lip with a long, teasing forefinger. "Four years, and the intensity hasn't lessened. We touch each other and catch fire."

"It's just physical, Ethan," she protested weakly.

He caught her long hair in his hands and drew it around her throat. "No."

"Miriam's here and you're frustrated because she didn't want you...."

He lifted an eyebrow. "Really?"

She folded the arm in the cast and stared at it. "Shouldn't we go back?"

"You were the one asking for cooperation," he reminded her.

"Was that why you kissed me?" she ventured.

"Not really." He brushed his lips over her eyes, closing her eyelids gently. "You make me feel like a man," he whispered huskily. "I'm whole again, with you."

She didn't understand that. He'd said that he couldn't satisfy Miriam, but he was certainly no novice. She was shaking from the intensity of his lovemaking.

"What are you going to do about tonight?" She tried to change the subject. "Miriam will surely make a beeline for your bedroom."

"Let me handle Miriam," he said. "Are you sure you want to go home?"

She wasn't, but she nodded.

He framed her face in his lean hands and made her look at him. "If your body was all I wanted, I could have had it four years ago," he reminded her gently. "You would have given yourself to me that day at the swimming hole."

Her lips parted on a rush of breath. "I don't understand."

"That's obvious." He kissed her roughly and let her go, climbing down out of the cab. He shut the door, went around to get in himself, and started the truck with a jerky motion of his fingers.

"You said it was just to get rid of Miriam, that we'd pretend to be involved," she began dazedly.

He glanced at her, his pale eyes approving the swell of her mouth, the faint flush of her cheeks. "But we weren't pretending just now, were we?" he asked quietly. "I said we'd take it one day at a time, and that's how it's going to be. Just let it happen."

"I don't want to have an affair," she whispered.

"Neither do I." He put the truck in gear and pulled back into the ruts, bouncing them over the pasture. "Light this for me, honey."

He handed her a cigarette and his lighter, but it took her three tries before her trembling fingers would manage the simple action. She handed him the cigarette and then the lighter, her eyes lingering on his hard mouth.

"You've thought about sleeping with me, haven't you?" he asked unexpectedly.

Why lie? she asked herself. She sighed. "Yes."

"There's no reason to be embarrassed. It's a perfectly natural curiosity between two people who've known each other as long as we have." He took a draw from the cigarette. "But you don't want sex outside marriage."

She stared out the windshield. "No," she said honestly.

He glanced at her and then nodded absently. "Okay."

She felt as if she were struggling out of a web of vagueness. Nothing made sense anymore, least of all Ethan's suddenly changed attitude toward her. He wanted her, that was patently obvious. But wasn't it because he couldn't have Miriam? Or was there some reason that she'd missed entirely?

Well, there was going to be plenty of time to figure it out, she supposed. Ethan sat beside her, quietly smoking his cigarette while she shot covert glances his way and tried to understand what he wanted from her. Life was suddenly growing very complicated.

Supper that night was a stilted affair, with Miriam complaining delicately about every dish and eating hardly anything. She glared at Arabella as if she wished her on Mars. Probably, Arabella mused, because she'd seen the two of them when they came in from their ride in the truck. Arabella's hair had been mussed, her makeup missing, her lips obviously swollen. It didn't take a mind reader to know that she and Ethan had been making love.

And in that supposition, Arabella was right. Miriam did recognize the signs and they made her furious. The way Ethan was looking at the younger woman under his thick dark eyelashes was painful to her. Ethan had looked at her that way once, in the early days of their courtship. But now he had eyes only for Arabella, and Miriam's hope for a reconciliation was going up in smoke. Not that she loved Ethan; she didn't. But it hurt her pride that he could love someone else, especially when that someone was Arabella. It had been because of Arabella that Ethan had never fallen completely under Miriam's spell. He'd wanted her, but his heart had always belonged to that young woman sitting beside him. Arabella would have known that, of course, even in the old days. That was why Miriam had fought the divorce.

She'd known that Arabella and Ethan would wind up together, and she hadn't wanted it to happen. But all her efforts hadn't stopped it.

Ethan didn't see Miriam's pointed glare. He was too busy watching the expression on Arabella's face. Her mouth had a soft swell where his had pressed against it, and it made him burn with pride to know how easily she'd given in to him at the last. He was a man again, a whole, capable man again, and for the first time, Miriam's presence didn't unsettle him. She'd wounded his ego to the quick with her taunts and ridicule about his prowess in the bedroom. But now he was beginning to understand that it wasn't strictly a physical problem. Not the way his body had reacted to Arabella earlier.

Miriam saw his smug expression and shifted uncomfortably.

"Thinking long thoughts, darling?" she taunted with a cold smile. "Or are you just reminiscing about the way we used to be together?"

Ethan pursed his thin lips and studied her. The anguish he felt from her taunts was suddenly gone. He knew now that the only failure was hers. She was conceited and cold and cruel, a sexless woman who basically hated men and used her beauty to punish them.

"I was thinking that you must have had a hell of a childhood," he replied.

Miriam went stark white. She dropped her fork and fumbled to pick it up again. "What in the world made you say such a thing?" she faltered.

He went from contempt to pity in seconds. Everything suddenly became crystal clear, and he understood her better now than he ever had before. Not that it changed his feelings. He couldn't want her, or love her. But he hated her less.

"No reason," he replied, but not unkindly. "Eat your beef. To hell with what they say about it, red meat's been sustaining human beings for hundreds of years in this country."

"I do seem to have a rather large appetite these days," Miriam replied. She glanced at Ethan suspiciously and then dropped her eyes.

Arabella had been watching the byplay with cold misery. Ethan was warming to the older woman, she could feel it. So what did she do now? Should she play up to him or not? She only wanted him to be happy. If that meant helping him get Miriam back, then she supposed she could be strong enough to do it.

As if he sensed her regard, he turned his head and smiled at her. He laid his hand on the table, inviting hers. After a second's hesitation, she slid her fingers across the palm and had them warmly, softly enfolded. He brought them to his mouth and kissed them hungrily, oblivious to his mother's shocked delight and Miriam's bridled anger.

Arabella colored and caught her breath. There had been a breathless tenderness in that caress, and the way he was looking at her made her body ripple with the memory of that afternoon.

"Are we really going to sit through a nature special?" Miriam asked, breaking into the tense silence.

Ethan lifted an eyebrow at her. "Why not? I like polar bears."

"Well, I don't," Miriam muttered. "I hate polar bears, in fact. I hate living out in the country, I hate the sound of animals in the distance, I hate this house, and I even hate you!"

"I thought you wanted to talk about a reconciliation," Ethan pointed out.

"How can I, when you've obviously been out in the fields making love with Miss Concert Pianist!"

Arabella flushed, but Ethan just laughed. The sound was unfamiliar, especially to Miriam.

"As it happens, it was in the truck, not in the fields," Ethan said with outrageous honesty. "And engaged people do make love."

"Yes, I remember," Miriam said icily. She threw her napkin down and stood up. "I think I'll lie down. I'll see you all in the morning. Good night."

She left, and Coreen sat back with a loud sigh. "Thank God! Now I can enjoy what's left of my meal." She picked up a homemade roll and buttered it. "What's this about making love in the pickup?" she asked Ethan with a grin.

"We need to keep Miriam guessing," he replied. He leaned back in his chair and watched his mother. "You tell me what we were doing."

"Arabella's a virgin," Coreen pointed out, noting Arabella's discomfort.

"I know that," Ethan said gently and smiled in her direction. "That won't change. Not even to run Miriam off."

"I didn't think it would." Coreen patted Arabella's hand. "Don't look so embarrassed, dear. Sex is part of life. But you aren't the kind of woman Miriam is. Your conscience would beat you to death. And to be perfectly blunt, so would Ethan's. He's a puritan."

"I'm not alone," Ethan said imperturbably. "What would you call a twenty-two-year-old virgin?"

"Sensible," Coreen replied. "It's dangerous to play around these days, and it's stupid to give a man the benefits of marriage without making him assume responsibility for his pleasure. That isn't just old-fashioned morality, it's common sense. I'm a dyed-in-the-wool women's libber, but I'll be damned if I'd give my body to any man without love and commitment."

Ethan stood up calmly, and pushed his chair toward his mother. "Stand on that," he invited. "If you're going to give a sermon, you need to be seen as well as heard, shrimp."

Coreen drew back the hand holding the roll and Ethan chuckled. He bent and picked his little mother up in his arms and kissed her resoundingly on the cheek.

"I love you," he said as he put her down again, flustered and breathless. "Don't ever change."

"Ethan, you just exasperate me," she muttered.

He kissed her forehead. "That's mutual." He glanced at Arabella, whose eyes were adoring him. "I have to make some phone calls. If she comes back downstairs, come into the office and we'll give her something else to fuss about."

Arabella colored again, but she smiled at him. "All right."

He winked and left the two women at the table.

"You still love him, don't you?" Coreen asked as she sipped her coffee.

Arabella shrugged. "It seems to be an illness without a cure," she agreed. "Despite Miriam and the arguments and all the years apart, I've never wanted anyone else."

"It seems to be mutual."

"Seems to be, yes, but that's just the game we're playing to keep Miriam from getting to him again."

"Isn't it odd how he's changed in one day," Coreen said suddenly, watching the younger woman with narrowed eyes. "This morning he was all starch and bristle when Miriam came, and now he's so relaxed and careless of her pointed remarks that he seems like another man." She narrowed one eye. "Just what did you do to him while the two of you were out alone?"

"I just kissed him, honest," Arabella replied "But he is different, isn't he?" She frowned "He said something odd, about being whole again. And he did say that Miriam told him he couldn't satisfy her. Maybe he just needed an ego boost."

His mother smiled secretively and stared down into her coffee. "Maybe he did." She leaned back. "She'll make another play for him, you know. Probably tonight."

"I told him I thought she would, too," Arabella said. "But I couldn't get up enough nerve to offer to sleep with him." She cleared her throat. "He really is a puritan. I thought he'd be outraged if I mentioned it. I could sleep on a chair or something. I didn't mean…" she added, horrified at what his mother might think.

"I know, dear. You don't have to worry about that.

But I do think it might be a good idea if you spend some time in his room tonight. Miriam would think twice before she invaded his bedroom if she thought you were in it with him." She grinned. "It would damage her pride."

"Ethan may damage my ears," Arabella said ruefully. "He won't like it. And what if Miriam tells you about it? You're a puritan, too, about having unmarried people sleeping together under your roof."

"I'll pretend to be horrified and surprised and I'll insist that Ethan set a wedding date," Coreen promised.

"Oh, no, you can't!" Arabella gasped.

Coreen got up and began removing crockery. She darted an amused glance at her houseguest. "Don't worry about a thing. I know something you don't. Help me get these things into the kitchen, would you, dear? Betty Ann went home an hour ago, so you can help me do dishes. Then, you can start making plans for later. Do you have a slinky negligee?"

The whole thing was taking on the dimensions of a dream, Arabella thought as she waited in Ethan's room dressed in the risqué white negligee and peignoir that Coreen had given her. How was she ever going to tell him that this was his mother's idea?

She'd brushed her long hair until it shone. She was still wearing her bra under the low-cut gown because she couldn't unfasten the catch and Coreen had already gone to bed. But it did make her breasts look sexier, and the way the satin clung to her body she felt like a femme fatale.

She draped herself across the foot of Ethan's antique four-poster bed, the white satin contrasting violently with the brown-and-black-and-white plaid of his cover-let. The room was so starkly masculine that she felt a little out of place in it.

There were a couple of heavy leather armchairs by the fireplace, and a few Indian rugs on the floor. The beige draperies at the windows were old and heavy, blocking out the crescent moon and the expanse of open land. The ceiling light fixture was bold and masculine, shaped like a wagon wheel. There was a tallboy against one wall and a dresser and mirror against another, next to the remodeled walk-in closet. It was a big room, but it suited Ethan. He liked a lot of space.

The door began to open and she struck a pose. Perhaps this was Miriam getting a peek in. She tugged the gown off one shoulder, hating the ugly cast that ruined the whole effect. She put it behind her and pushed her breasts forward, staring toward the door with what she hoped was a seductive smile.

But it wasn't Miriam. It was Ethan, and he stopped dead in the doorway, his fingers in the act of unbuttoning his shirt frozen in place.

CHAPTER SEVEN

"OH!" ARABELLA GASPED. She scrambled into a sitting position, painfully aware of how much cleavage she was showing, not to mention the liquid way the satin adhered to her slender curves.

Ethan slammed the door behind him, his face unreadable. He was bareheaded and he looked very tired and worn, but the light in his eyes was fascinating. He stared at her as if he'd never seen a woman's body before, lingering on the thrust of her breasts under the satin with its exquisite, lacy trim.

"My God," he breathed finally. "You could bring a man to his knees."

It wasn't what she'd expected him to say, but it made her efforts with her appearance worthwhile. "I could?" she echoed blankly as delight made her face radiant.

He moved toward her. His shirt was halfway unbuttoned, and he looked rough and dangerous and very sexy with his hair disheveled and that faint growth of beard on his deeply tanned face.

"Is the bra really necessary, or couldn't you get it off?" he asked as he sat down beside her on the coverlet.

She smiled shyly. "I couldn't get it off," she admitted, lifting the cast. "I still can't use these fingers."

He smiled gently. "Come here." He tugged her forward and reached around her, his lean, rough-skinned hands pushing the straps down over her arms to give him access to the fastening. But the bodice was loose and it fell to her waist, giving him a total view of her breasts in their brief, lacy covering.

He caught his breath. His body made a quick, emphatic statement about what her curves did to it and he laughed even through the discomfort. "My God," he said, chuckling deeply.

"What is it?" she asked breathlessly.

"Don't ask." He reached behind her and unfastened the bra, amused at her efforts to catch the front as it fell. She held it against her, but one of his hands went to her smooth, bare back and began to caress it gently.

"Let it fall," he whispered against her lips as he took them.

It was the most erotic experience of her life, even more than the interlude by the swimming hole, because she was a woman now and her love for him had grown. She released the fabric and her good arm went up around his neck, lifting her breasts.

He drew back to look down at them with pure male appreciation. His fingers touched her, and he looked into her eyes, watching the pupils dilate as he teased the soft contour of her breast and brushed his forefinger tenderly over the taut nipple. She bit back a moan and his free hand lanced into the thick hair at her nape and contracted. He held her prisoner with delicious sensuality while his other hand snaked to her waist and around her, lifting her body in a delicate arch.

"I've dreamed of this," he said, lowering his eyes and then his hard, warm mouth to the swollen softness of her breast.

She watched his mouth open as it settled on her, felt the soft, warm suction, felt the rough drag of his tongue, the faint threat of his teeth and a sound she'd never made pushed out of her throat.

He heard it. His arousal grew by the second, until he was shaking with the force of it. She was everything he'd ever wanted. Young, virginal, achingly receptive to his advances, glorying in his need of her, giving of herself without reservation. He could barely believe what was happening.

His dark eyebrows drew together in harsh pleasure as he increased the pressure of his mouth, feeling her shiver as the intensity of the caress grew. He felt her nails digging into his back and he groaned, his lean hand sweeping down her waist to her hip, edging the fabric up until he could touch her soft, bare thigh.

"Ethan, no...!" she whispered frantically, but his head lifted from her breast and he eased her back onto the coverlet, knowing she was helpless now, totally at his mercy in a sensual limbo.

"I'm not going to hurt you," he said gently, bending over her. "Unbutton my shirt." His fingers slid between her legs, tenderly separating them, and he watched her face waver between acceptance and fear of the unknown. He bent to her lips, brushing them with soft reassurance. "I want to make love to you," he whispered. "We don't have to go all the way."

"I don't understand," she choked.

He kissed her accusing eyes shut. "I'll teach you. One way or another, I'm going to be your lover. It might as well begin now. Get my shirt out of the way, sweet," he breathed into her open mouth. "And then lift your body against mine and let me feel your breasts against my skin."

She'd never dreamed that men said things like that to women, but it had an incredible effect on her emotions. She cried out, her hands fumbling buttons out of buttonholes, and then she arched up, pulling him down on her with the one good arm she had. The experience was staggering. She shuddered as his hair-roughened skin dragged against hers in a terribly arousing caress, weeping helplessly in his arms.

He groaned. All his dreams were coming true. This was his Arabella, and she wanted him. She wanted him!

He eased one powerful leg between hers, and he caught her hand without lifting his mouth and pulled it up against his taut stomach.

"I can't!" she protested wildly.

"You can, sweetheart," he said against her mouth. "Touch me like this," he whispered, opening her clenched fingers and splaying them against his body. "Arabella. Arabella, I need you so!" he ground out. His fingers trembled as they guided hers. "Don't stop," he groaned harshly, dragging in an audible breath as his teeth clenched.

She watched his face with astonished awe. He let her watch, glorying in the forbidden pleasure of her touch, aching to tell her how incredible this was for him, but he couldn't get words out.

The sudden opening of the door was a cruel, vicious shock.

"Oh, for God's sake!" Miriam exclaimed, horrified. She went out again, slamming the door, her furious voice echoing down the hall along with her running feet.

Ethan shuddered helplessly above Arabella. He rolled over onto his back, groaning.

She sat up, her breasts still bare, her eyes apprehensive. "Are you all right?" she asked hesitantly.

"Not really," he managed with a rueful smile. He laughed in spite of the throbbing ache in his body. "But, oh, God, what a beautiful ache it is, little one."

She tugged the gown up over her breasts, frowning slightly. "I don't understand, Ethan," she said.

He laughed, keeping his secret to himself. "It's just as well that you don't. Not yet, anyway." He lay breathing deeply until he could control it, until the ache began to subside, and all the while his silver eyes lanced over her face and her body with tender delight.

"Miriam saw us," she said uncomfortably.

"Wasn't that the whole idea?" he asked.

"Well, yes. But…" She colored and averted her eyes.

He sat up, stretching lazily before he brought her face up to his and began to press soft, undemanding kisses over it. "Women have been touching men like that since the beginning of time," he whispered at her closed eyelids. "I'll bet most of your girlfriends at school indulged, including Mary."

"But she wouldn't…!"

"If she was in love, why not?" He lifted his head and searched her worried face. "Arabella, it's not a sin to want someone. Especially not when you care deeply for them. It's a physical expression of something intangible."

"I have a lot of hang-ups…" she began.

He brushed back her damp, disheveled hair. "You have principles. I can understand that. I'm not going to seduce you in my own bed, in case you were wondering." His pale eyes twinkled with humor. He felt alive as never before, masculine, capable of anything. He brushed his mouth lazily over her nose. "We'll save sex for our wedding night."

She stared at him. "I beg your pardon?"

"Marriage is inevitable," he said. "Miriam isn't going to go away, not if you spend every night in here to keep her out. She's the kind of woman who doesn't understand rejection. She's got her mind made up that she's back to stay, and she thinks she can bulldoze me into it."

"She should know better."

"Oh, but she thinks she has an edge," he murmured. He looked down at her hand, clutching the gown to her body. "Let go of that," he murmured. "I love looking at you."

"Ethan!"

He chuckled. "You love letting me, so you can stop pretending. I've spent a lot of years being convinced that I wasn't a man anymore, so you'll have to forgive me for sounding a little arrogant right now. I've just learned something shocking about myself."

"What?" she asked breathlessly.

"That I'm not impotent," he said simply.

She frowned. Didn't that mean that a man couldn't…?

Her eyes widened. "That was what Miriam meant when she taunted you!"

"You've got it," he agreed. "She couldn't arouse me with all her tricks. It was why I was able to get her to leave. But she wouldn't give me a divorce. She was sure she could get me back under her spell. What she didn't realize was that I was never really under it in the first place. I was briefly infatuated in a purely physical sense. But a craving, once indulged, is usually satisfied. Mine was."

"I guessed she'd know what to do in bed," she sighed. "I'm such a coward...."

He drew her face into his warm, damp throat and smoothed her dark hair gently. "Intimacy is hard, even for men, the first time, Arabella," he said at her ear. "You'll get used to it. I'll never hurt you."

"I know that." And she did. But would he ever be able to love her? That was what she wanted most in the world. She clung to him with a long sigh. "You really don't feel that with Miriam?" she asked lazily. "She's so beautiful and experienced."

His hands hardened on her bare back. "She isn't a patch on you," he said huskily. "She never was."

But you married her, she wanted to say. *You loved her, and tonight at supper, you were so gentle with her.* But she never got the words out. His hands had tugged the fabric away from her breasts while she was busy thinking, and he wrapped her up against his bare chest with slow expertise, his fingers warm on her rib cage as he traced it.

She moaned and he smiled against her forehead.

"I'd had women by the time you were eighteen," he

whispered. "But I felt more with you that day by the swimming hole than I'd ever felt with any of the others, and we did less than I'd ever done with a woman. I've dreamed about that day ever since."

"But you married Miriam," she said quietly. She closed her eyes, unaware of Ethan's expression. "And that says it all, doesn't it? You never loved me. You just wanted me. That's all it's ever going to be. Oh, let me go, Ethan!" She wept, pushing at his shoulders.

But he tightened his hold, easing her down on the bed with him. "It isn't just wanting," he said gently. "Don't fight me," he breathed, settling his mouth on hers. "Don't fight me, honey."

Tears rolled down her face into his hard mouth, but he didn't stop until she was pliant and moaning under the crush of his long, powerful body. Only then did he lift his head and look down at her soft, enraptured face.

His silver eyes searched hers. "If desire was all I felt, do you think I'd spare your chastity?"

She swallowed. "I don't guess you would."

"A man in the throes of passion doesn't usually give a damn what he says or does to get a woman's cooperation," he replied. "I could have had you this afternoon. I could have had you just now. But I stopped."

That could also mean that he didn't want her enough to press his advantage, but she didn't say it.

He sat up, his eyes skimming with warm appreciation over her breasts before he covered them himself, pulling the straps of her gown back up her arms. "You don't have much self-confidence, do you?" he asked when she was standing again. He got to his own feet, towering over her, deliciously sensuous with his chest bare and his mouth faintly swollen from her kisses. "I'll have to work on that."

"It's just to keep Miriam at bay, or so you said," she reminded him shakily.

"Yes, I did say that." He ran his forefinger down her nose. "But in order to do this properly, you're going to have to marry me." He grinned. "It won't be that bad. You can sleep with me and we'll make babies. We'll have a good life together, even if that hand won't let you do anything except give piano lessons."

"And you think that would be enough to satisfy me?" she asked sadly.

The smile left his face. He thought she loved him. She'd acted as if she had. Was she telling him that marriage wouldn't be enough, that she wanted her career instead? He scowled.

"Don't you think you could be happy here?" he asked.

She shifted restlessly. "I'm tired, Ethan. I don't want to talk about marriage tonight. All right?"

He drew a cigarette from his pocket and lit it, still frowning down at her. "All right. But sooner or later you and I are going to have a showdown."

"Meanwhile, I'll do everything I can to help you send Miriam off. If you're sure you want to," she added hesitantly.

"You can't think I want her back?" he demanded.

"Can't you?" she asked sadly, her heart in her soft green eyes.

"Didn't you hear what I told you earlier? Do you

know what impotent means?" he added angrily, and gave her the slang for it, watching her face color.

"I—I—know what it means!" she stammered. She moved away from him. "I don't know that I like being a catalyst in that way. Maybe you really want Miriam but you're too afraid of losing her again to...to be capable with her. She betrayed you once...."

"Oh, hell." He took a draw from his cigarette and sighed angrily. He couldn't get through to her what he felt, and he was too tired to try tonight, anyway. There was time. He hoped there was enough. "You'd better get back to your own room before Miriam drags my mother up here and gives her the shock of her life."

"She wouldn't be shocked," she said absently.

"What makes you think so?"

She lifted her eyes. "Because this was her idea. She even gave me the negligee."

"My God! Women!" he burst out.

"We were saving you from Miriam."

"Fair enough. Who's going to save you from me?" he asked, his hands catching her waist and holding fast as he bent toward her mouth. "I want you. Take off your gown and get into bed. I'll love you up to the ceiling."

She tingled all over. "It isn't me you want, it's Miriam!" she sputtered, pulling away from him.

"You blind little bat," he said, shaking his head. "All right, run. But I'll be two steps behind you from now on. I let you get away once. Never again."

She didn't understand that, either. He was saying a lot of strange things. She colored, wondering at his response to her when he said it didn't happen with

Miriam. But she was still certain that it had some psychological basis, that inability, and probably it had been triggered by the fear that Miriam would take his heart and betray him again. She didn't want to think about it. It hurt too much. Ethan's ardor had uplifted and upset her, all at once. She'd have the memory of it, but it would be a bittersweet one. She'd always feel that she was nothing more than a physical substitute for the woman he loved.

"I'll lead my own life, thank you," she said, moving toward the door. "I haven't forgotten what you said to me when you told me not to come back to the ranch all those years ago, Ethan."

"You will," he replied, opening the door for her. "You don't know why I said it."

She looked up at him. "But I do. You wanted me out of the way."

"So that I could marry Miriam," he suggested.

"Yes."

He sighed, letting the cigarette dangle in his hand while he searched Arabella's soft eyes. "There are none so blind as those who will not see," he murmured. "You were eighteen," he said quietly. "You were your father's emotional slave, a talented novice with an incredible career potential and infatuated for the first time in your innocent life. You're almost the age I was then. Think about how it would be for you, if our positions were reversed. Think about what you'd feel, and what you'd think, and what you might do about it."

She stared up at him helplessly. "What did my age have to do with it?" she faltered.

"Everything." His face hardened. "My God, don't you see? Arabella, what if I'd made you pregnant that day by the swimming hole?"

Her face went white. She could imagine the horror her father would have felt. She knew what he'd have done, too. She'd never have been allowed to have a child out of wedlock. Ethan might have insisted on marrying her, if he'd known, but he'd have been forced into it.

"I might not have gotten pregnant," she said hesitantly. "Some women never do."

"A few can't, that's so," he replied. "But the majority of women can and do. I wasn't prepared that day, and I can't for one minute imagine holding back long enough to protect you. There's every chance that we'd have created a child together." His eyes grew darker, warmer. "I'd like that," he said huskily. "Oh, God, I'd like making you pregnant, Arabella."

She felt hot all over. She managed to get her fingers on the doorknob. "I'd better…go to bed, Ethan," she managed unsteadily.

"You'd like it, too, wouldn't you?" he asked knowingly, smiling in a way that made her toes curl.

"We aren't married," she said, trying to hold on to her sanity.

"We will be." He leaned against the door facing her, his eyes possessive on her satin-and-lace-clad body. "I won't mind changing diapers and giving bottles, just for the record. I'm not one of those Neanderthal men who think anything short of football and beer is woman's work."

She stared up at him with a soft glow in her face,

giving in despite her misgivings. "What if I couldn't give you a baby?" she whispered softly.

He smiled tenderly and touched her mouth with his fingertips. "Then you and I would become closer than most couples do, I suppose," he said, his voice deep and gentle. "We'd be inseparable. We could adopt a child, or maybe several of them, or we could do volunteer work that involved children." He bent and kissed her eyes closed. "Don't ever think that you're only of value to me because of your potential as a mother. Children are, and should be, a precious fringe benefit of marriage. They shouldn't be the only reason for it."

She'd never dreamed of hearing Ethan say such a thing to her. Tears ran down her cheeks and she began to sob.

"Oh, for God's sake…!" He bent and picked her up in his arms, shaken by her reaction. "Arabella, don't," he whispered. His mouth covered hers, faintly tremulous as he savored the tear-wet softness of it, the kiss absolutely beyond his experience as he held her, rocking her in his arms. His head began to spin. Her good arm was around his neck, and she was kissing him back, moaning softly under the crush of his lips, trembling in his protective embrace.

"Now, now, I'm all for the spirit of the thing, but let's not carry it to extremes," Coreen Hardeman murmured dryly.

Ethan lifted his head and stared blankly at his mother. She was leaning against the wall, her gray eyes so smugly pleased that Ethan actually flushed.

CHAPTER EIGHT

ARABELLA WAS MUCH more embarrassed than Ethan or his indomitable parent. She colored delicately and stiffened in Ethan's arms.

"Uh, shouldn't you put me down?" Arabella asked.

"Why?" Ethan murmured dryly. "It was just getting to the good part."

"I thought it already had, from what Miriam said," Coreen replied, and then spoiled her disapproving-mother stance by bursting into laughter. "You two are heading straight for a fiery end, or so I'm told. Shameful behavior, and Arabella such an innocent." She raised an eyebrow at Ethan. "How could you, and other platitudes."

Ethan grinned. "I had a lot of cooperation," he returned, with a wicked glance at Arabella.

"Miriam said that, too." Coreen nodded.

"You put me down, you corrupting influence!" Arabella muttered, struggling. "I knew you'd lead me astray if I wasn't careful."

He set her gently on her feet. "Would you like to try again? I seem to remember finding you lying in exquisite repose on my bed…?" He glanced at Coreen. "She said it was your idea, too."

"Actually, it was," Coreen confessed. "I didn't know

what else to do. I was absolutely certain that Miriam would make a play for you, and I had a fairly good idea why. I think she's pregnant."

"So Arabella told me." He rubbed a hand over his broad chest, staring appreciatively at the younger of the two women. "We're getting married. Arabella doesn't know it yet, but you might go ahead and start making the arrangements and we'll get her to the altar before she has time to work it out."

"Good idea." Coreen laughed delightedly. "Oh, Arabella, I couldn't be more pleased. You'll be the most wonderful daughter-in-law."

"But…" Arabella began, looking from mother to son with dazed eyes.

"She will at that," Ethan agreed. "I'll take her downtown tomorrow to buy a ring. What do you think about having the wedding at the Methodist church? Reverend Boland could perform the service."

"Yes, he'll do nicely. And we can have the reception at the Jacobsville Inn. It's big enough. I'll ask Shelby Ballenger if she'll help with the arrangements. She did the most beautiful job with our charity fashion show last month—amazing how well she manages her volunteer work and their two sons at the same time."

"Do that," Ethan replied. "Now, how about the invitations?"

"I don't think—" Arabella tried again.

"That's a good idea. Don't," Ethan said approvingly. He folded his arms across his chest and turned back to his mother. "Can you handle the invitations?"

"It's my wedding!" Arabella burst out. "Surely I can do something to help!"

"Of course you can," Ethan agreed. "You can try on the wedding gown. Take her to the best store in Houston," he told his mother, "and find the most expensive gown they have. Don't let her get away with something ordinary."

"I won't," Coreen promised. "A white wedding," she sighed. "I never thought I'd live to see you happily married, Ethan."

He was watching Arabella with an odd kind of tenderness. "Neither did I. Not like this," he said huskily, and his eyes blazed.

But it's only to get Miriam out of his life for good, Arabella wanted to wail. *He doesn't love me, he wants me. I make him whole again physically. But that's no reason to get married!*

She started to tell him that, but he was already going back into his room.

"I think I'll lock the door, just in case," he chuckled. "Good night, Mother." He stared at Arabella. "Good night, little one."

"Good night, Ethan," Arabella said softly. "But there's just one thing—"

He closed the door before she could tell him what it was.

"I hate to look smug, but I can't help it," Coreen said with a smile as she walked down the hall with Arabella. "Miriam was so certain she could get under Ethan's skin again. I couldn't bear to see her hurt him so badly twice."

"He was different with her at supper," Arabella said, voicing her biggest fear, that Ethan was once again falling under his ex-wife's spell.

Coreen glanced at her. "Ethan is deep. Don't worry. He wouldn't marry you just to chase Miriam away. I can guarantee it," she added, looking as if she wanted to say something more. But she shrugged and smiled faintly. "I'd better get to bed. Sleep tight, darling, and congratulations."

"Nothing happened," Arabella blurted out. "I don't know what Miriam said—"

Coreen patted her cheek gently. "I know you, and I know my son. You don't have to tell me anything. Besides," she added with a grin, "men who aren't frustrated don't look like Ethan looked when he went back into his room. I'm old, but I'm not blind. 'Night!"

Arabella stared after her, nervous and uncertain. She went on down the hall, hoping against hope that she wouldn't encounter Miriam on the way to her room.

She should have known the woman would be lying in wait for her. Miriam opened her door just as Arabella drew even with it. Her face was flushed and her eyes were red. She'd obviously been crying.

"You snake," Miriam accused furiously. She threw back her auburn hair contemptuously. "He's mine! I'm not going to give him up without a fight!"

"Then you can have one," Arabella said quietly. "We're getting married. Ethan told you so."

"He won't marry you," the other woman replied. "He loves me! He always has! He only wants you." She let her eyes punctuate that coldly sarcastic remark. "You're quite a novelty, but you'll wear thin pretty quickly. You'll never get him to the altar."

"He's making the wedding arrangements already."

"He won't marry you, I tell you!" Miriam flashed. "He only divorced me because I ran around on him."

"That seems like a good reason to me," Arabella returned. She was shaking inside, but she wouldn't back down. "You hurt his pride."

"What do you think it did to mine, having you thrown in my face from the day we married?" she burst out. "It was always Arabella this, Arabella that, from the whole damned family! Nobody could have lived up to you, nobody! I hated you from the start, because Ethan wanted you!" Her eyes were wet with tears and she was sobbing as she tried to speak. "Imagine that!" she laughed brokenly. "I had twice your experience and sophistication, I was more beautiful and sought-after than you could ever hope to be. But it was you he wanted, your name he whispered when he made love to me." She leaned against the wall, crying helplessly while Arabella gaped at her.

"Wha…what?" Arabella gasped.

"It was only when I accused him of using me as a substitute for you that he stopped being capable of making love to me," Miriam said, slumping. "He was obsessed with your body. He still is. Probably," she added, rallying a little, "because he's never had it. Now he'll get his fill of you, and then maybe I can have him back. Maybe I can make him want me. He did love me," she whispered achingly. "He loved me, but I couldn't make him want me, too. Damn you, Arabella! He would have wanted me if it hadn't been for you!"

She went back into her room and slammed the door, leaving a shocked, staggered Arabella in the hall.

She managed to get into her room without really seeing where she was going. She fumbled the light switch on and locked the door before she collapsed on the bed.

Was Miriam telling the truth? Had Ethan been so obsessed by her body that it even affected his marriage? Was it possible for a man to love one woman but lust after another? She knew so little, had such a faint experience of men that she didn't know.

The one thing she was certain of was that Ethan still wanted her. It might not be enough to base a marriage on, but she loved him more than her own life. If desire was all he had to give her, perhaps she could build on that and teach him, someday, to love her. She wasn't as beautiful as Miriam, but he'd said once that inner qualities were just as important.

His ardor that afternoon and that night were proof that his so-called impotence with Miriam was just a fluke. Surely if he could want one woman, he could want another? Miriam had hurt his pride and his body had rebelled. But at supper he'd warmed to Miriam, so might that not affect his ability to want the other woman? Miriam had declared war in the hall and Arabella was afraid that she might not be able to compete. Especially when compared to the more beautiful older woman.

Her mind gave her no peace at all. It was much later when she closed her eyes and went to sleep, leaving all the worries behind.

THINGS LOOKED A little brighter when she awoke the next morning. She had to be more confident. She could work at her appearance, at her personality. Perhaps she could become like Miriam, and then Ethan might be able to love her. She might still get Miriam to acknowledge defeat, using her own tactics against her.

She put on her prettiest pale green cotton sundress with its dropped square neck and cinched waist and full skirt. It was a flirty kind of dress and it matched her eyes. She put her hair into a neatly coiled chignon on top of her head and deliberately used more makeup than normal. She had a pair of huge earrings she'd never liked, but she wore those, too. The result was a much more sophisticated version of herself. She smiled seductively and nodded. Yes. If a sophisticated woman was what Ethan wanted, she could be that. Certainly she could!

She went downstairs with a bounce in her stride. If only it wasn't for the stupid cast, she might really look seductive, she thought, glaring at the bulky thing. Well, only a little while longer and it would be off, then she could really do some important shopping for the right clothes.

When she got to the breakfast table, Ethan and Miriam were already there, with Coreen and the housekeeper, Betty Ann, busy alternating between kitchen and dining room with platters of food.

Miriam and Ethan appeared to be in intense conversation, and not a hostile one, because he was smiling gently and Miriam was hanging on his every word. Miriam even looked different this morning. Her long hair was plaited and hanging down her back. She was wearing a T-shirt and jeans and no makeup at all. What a change, Arabella thought almost hysterically. She and the other woman looked their own opposites.

Ethan turned and saw Arabella and his jaw clenched. His eyes narrowed with something she couldn't quite define.

"Well, good morning," she called gaily, bluffing it out. She bent over Ethan's tall figure and brushed her mouth teasingly over his nose. "How are you? And how are you, Miriam? Isn't it a beautiful morning?"

Miriam murmured something appropriate and concentrated on her coffee, giving Arabella a glare before she lifted her cup to her lips.

Arabella sat down, still with a bounce, and poured herself a cup of coffee. "I guess Coreen and I will go to Houston today to find my wedding gown, if you don't mind, Ethan," she said breezily. "I do want something exquisite."

Ethan stared down into his coffee cup. Images of the past were dancing before his eyes. Miriam had said something similar when they became engaged. She'd even looked as Arabella did now, oh, so sophisticated and lighthearted. Had he been completely and totally wrong about Arabella? Did money matter to her now that she was apparently without a career, now that she couldn't earn her own way? Or was she trying to compete with Miriam by becoming the same kind of woman? Mentally he dismissed the latter. Arabella knew he didn't want another Miriam. She wouldn't make the mistake of trying to emulate a woman he despised. He couldn't bear the thought of another mar-

riage like his first one. Why had he committed himself?
He'd wanted to get rid of Miriam, but now it seemed he
might be walking back into the same trap.

Coreen came in with a plate of biscuits, took a look
at Arabella and did a double take. "Arabella? How…
different you look, dear."

"Do you like it?" Arabella asked with a smile. "I
thought I'd try something new. Do you feel like going
to Houston with me today?"

Coreen put the plate of biscuits down. "Certainly. If
you'd like to…."

"By all means, go ahead," Miriam said huskily. "I'll
keep Ethan company," she added with a rather shy smile
at her ex-husband.

Ethan didn't answer. He was still trying to absorb the
change in Arabella.

He didn't say anything to her all through breakfast
and Arabella began to feel nervous. He and Miriam had
been talking earnestly, and now he looked uncomfortable when she'd mentioned the wedding gown. Was he
having second thoughts? Didn't he want to marry her
after all?

Suddenly, he got up from the table and started out of
the room.

"Just a minute, Ethan," Miriam called quickly, seeing
her chance. "I need to ask you something."

She ran to join him, clutching seductively at his arm
as they went outside together.

"WHAT A NICE way to start the morning," Arabella said
over her second cup of coffee about half an hour later.

Coreen patted her hand. "Don't worry so. Let's get going. I'll just run into the kitchen and tell Betty Ann where we'll be."

While Arabella continued to think about the scene at breakfast, the phone rang and she got up to answer it, since Coreen and Betty Ann were occupied.

Considering the sour note the day had started on, she should have expected it to be her father, she thought when his curt voice came over the line.

"How are you?" he asked stiffly.

She curled the cord around her fingers. "I'm much better, thank you," she replied, her tone just as stilted.

"And your hand?"

"I won't know until the cast comes off," she said.

"I hope you had the sense to let an orthopedic surgeon look at it," he said after a minute.

"A specialist was called in, yes," she replied. Her father made her feel ten years old again. "There's a good chance that I may be able to play normally again."

"Your host filed an injunction against me, so that I can't touch the joint account," he told her. "That wasn't kind of you, Arabella. I have to live, too."

She bit her lip. "I… I know, but…"

"You'll have to send me a check," he continued. "I can't live off my brother. I'll need at least five hundred to get me through. Thank God we had good insurance. And I'll want to hear from you as soon as your cast is off and you've seen the specialist."

She hesitated. She wanted to tell him that she was marrying Ethan, but she couldn't get the words out. It was amazing how he intimidated her, and she a grown woman! It was habit, she supposed. He'd always controlled her. He still did. She was just a wimp, she thought angrily.

"I'll…call you," she promised.

"Don't forget the check. You know Frank's address."

That was all. No words of affection, no comfort. He hung up. She stood staring blankly at the receiver. Before she had time to show her concern, Coreen was back and they were off to Houston in Coreen's black Mercedes-Benz.

THEY BROWSED THROUGH the exclusive bridal department at an exclusive store in Houston for an hour before Arabella was able to choose between three exquisite designer gowns. The one she settled on was traditional with Alençon lace over white *peau de soie*, a delicate, modified V neckline that plunged to the waist but in such a way as to be discreet. It was unique and incredibly sensuous all at once. She chose a traditional veil as well, one with yards and yards of fabric which Ethan would be required to lift during the ceremony. Arabella felt the sense of tradition to her toes, because she was going to her wedding bed a virgin.

The pleasure of the day had been faintly spoiled by Ethan's attitude and Miriam's changed image. Arabella still didn't understand what had gone wrong so suddenly, and even as she was choosing the gown she wondered if she'd really get to wear it. Ethan could change his mind. She wouldn't even blame him. Probably he was finding it hard going to give up Miriam, and the divorce had only been final for three months. Coreen had said that he'd been moody during those three months, too. She frowned at the gown as the saleswoman wrapped it with care in its distinctive box.

"What a blessing you're a perfect size," Coreen smiled. "No alterations. That's a good omen."

Arabella managed a wan smile. "I could use one."

The older woman gave her a curious look as she gave the saleswoman her credit card. But it wasn't until they'd completed their shopping, right down to delicate silk-and-lace undergarments and nylon hose, and were on their way back to Jacobsville that she finally asked Arabella what was wrong.

"I wish I knew why Ethan was so distant this morning," she told the other woman.

"Miriam's doing, no doubt," Coreen said curtly. "Don't underestimate her. Ethan's treating her too nicely and she likes it."

"I won't underestimate her." She hesitated. "That phone call I got this morning was from my father. He called and asked me to send him a check…." She cleared her throat. "Well, he's still my father," she said defensively.

"Of course he is."

"I should have paid for the gown," she said suddenly. "Then, if the wedding is called off, it won't put any strain on your budget."

"Listen, dear, our budget doesn't get strained and you know it." She frowned at Arabella. "This was Ethan's idea. He wanted you to have a designer gown."

"I think he's changed his mind. He and Miriam were getting thick before breakfast," Arabella said miserably.

Coreen sighed gently. "Oh, Arabella, I wish I knew what was in my eldest's mind. Surely he isn't letting that woman get under his skin again!"

"Miriam said that he wanted me when he married her," Arabella blurted out. Her lower lip trembled. "She accused me of ruining her marriage."

"Ethan's always wanted you," the older woman said surprisingly. "He should have married you instead of letting your father spirit you away. He was never happy with Miriam. I've always felt that she was just a stop-gap for him, a poor substitute for you. Perhaps Miriam realized it, and that was what went wrong."

"Wanting isn't loving." Arabella twisted her purse in her lap. "I may not be sophisticated, but I know that."

"You look pretty uptown to me today," Coreen comforted with a smile. "That sundress is very attractive, and I like the way you're wearing your hair. Ethan certainly noticed," she added wickedly.

"I thought Miriam was getting his undivided attention this morning and he wasn't snarling at her."

"Men get funny when they start thinking about marriage," Coreen assured her. "Now, stop worrying. Ethan knows what he's doing."

But did he? Arabella wondered. She might be helping him to make an even bigger mistake than he had before.

And when they got back to the ranch, she found more cause than ever to be concerned. Betty Ann was coming down the staircase with a tray when Coreen and Arabella walked in with the huge dress box.

"What are you doing carrying a tray upstairs at this hour?" Coreen asked the housekeeper, and frowned.

Arabella had a faint premonition even as Betty Ann spoke.

"Ethan fell," Betty Ann said tersely. "Had to be took to the hospital and X-rayed, with herself—" she jerked her head toward the staircase "—hanging on him for dear life."

"Is he all right?" Coreen asked the question for both of them.

"Mild concussion, nothing really serious. They wanted to keep him overnight, but he insisted on coming home." The housekeeper sighed. "He's been up in his room ever since, with herself hovering, and when he wasn't demanding things, he was cussing." She glanced warily at Arabella. "I don't know what Miriam told him, but he's been anxious to see Arabella. Too anxious and too angry."

Arabella felt her knees going weak. Could her father have called back and told Ethan about the check he'd demanded? She knew Ethan would be furious. She just hadn't counted on him finding out so quickly. How had he found out?

"I guess I'd better go up and see him," she murmured.

"We both will," Coreen said shortly.

They marched upstairs. Ethan was lying on top of his bed with a faint gash on his forehead that had been stitched, making a red-and-black pattern on the dark skin. He was fully clothed, and Miriam was sitting with an angelic look by his bedside. The ministering angel.

"So you finally came back," Ethan began, glaring at Arabella. "I hope you enjoyed your shopping trip."

"You knew we were going to get my wedding gown," she said, mildly defensive.

"It's lovely, too, one of their most expensive," Coreen seconded. "A designer gown…"

"Yes, I had one of theirs when I was married," Miriam said with a demure flirting glance at Ethan. "Didn't I, darling?"

"What happened to you?" Coreen asked.

"I got tossed," Ethan said shortly. "Every rider comes off now and again. I was helping Randy with that new mustang in the string we bought from Luke Harper. I got pitched into the fence on my way down. It's nothing."

"Except a concussion," Coreen muttered.

"Obviously that didn't bother anybody except Miriam," he said enigmatically, glaring at his mother and Arabella.

Coreen glared back at him. "You're in a sweet mood, I see. Well, I'll help Betty Ann. Are you coming, Miriam?" she added pointedly.

"Oh, no. I'll sit with Ethan. He shouldn't be alone, since he has a concussion," Miriam said, smiling as she laid a protective hand on Ethan's big, lean one.

Coreen went out. Arabella didn't know what to do. Ethan didn't look as if he needed protecting from his ex-wife, and the way he was looking at Arabella made her want to hide.

"Did you hear from my father?" she asked him hesitantly.

"No, I didn't hear from your father," he said coldly. "Get me a beer, will you, Miriam?"

Miriam looked as if leaving was the last thing she wanted to do, but Ethan glared at her and she left, reluctantly, her eyes darting nervously from Ethan to Arabella.

That nervous glance made better sense when she closed the door and Ethan let Arabella have it with both barrels.

"Thank you for your loving concern," he said coldly. "How kind of you to give a damn if I killed myself on a horse!"

She felt her knees going weak. "What do you mean?" she asked.

"You might have told Mother, at least," he persisted. He tried to sit up, grimaced and grabbed his head, but he scowled furiously when she made an automatic move toward him. "Just keep your distance, honey," he said harshly. "I don't want your belated attention. Miriam was here, thank God. She looked after me."

"I don't understand what you're talking about," she said, exasperated.

"You had a phone call before you left the ranch, didn't you?" he demanded.

"Why, yes, of course..." she began.

"Miriam told you I'd been hurt and I needed Mother to drive me in to the hospital, but you didn't say anything," he accused. "Not one word to her. Were you getting even, because I didn't pay you enough attention at breakfast? Or was it a way to get back at me for what happened last night? Did I go too far and scare you out of your virginal wits?"

Her head was swimming. Surely he wasn't quite rational after that knock on the head, with all these wild statements. "Ethan, Miriam didn't call me," she protested. "I didn't know you were hurt!"

"You just admitted that you got the phone call, so don't bother denying it," he added furiously when she started to do just that, to explain that it was her father who called, not Miriam. "I should never have divorced Miriam. When the chips were down, she cared and you didn't. I hope that damned dress you bought is returnable, honey, because I wouldn't marry you on a bet! Now get out of my room!"

"Ethan!" she burst out, horrified that he could actually believe her capable of such hard-boiled behavior.

"I only took you in because I felt sorry for you," he said, giving her a cold appraisal with silver eyes. "I wanted you like hell, but marriage is too high a price to pay for a mercenary virgin with eyes like cash registers. It's all too plain now that I was right, that all you were interested in was financial security for you, and probably for your damned father!" Before she could answer that unfounded charge, he sat straight up in bed, glaring. "I said get out! I don't want to see you again!"

"If you believe I'm that mercenary, then I'll go," she replied, shaking with mingled hurt and fury. "I'm glad to know how you really feel about me, that it was only desire and pity all along."

His eyes flashed silver fire. "The same goes for me.

You're no different than Miriam was—out for all you can get. You even look like she used to!"

So that was it. Too late, she realized how her sudden change of appearance and her interest in an expensive wedding gown must have seemed to a man who'd already been used for his wealth once.

"You don't understand," she began.

"Oh, yes, I do," he returned hotly. His head was throbbing. Somewhere inside, he knew he was being unreasonable, but he could hardly think at all for pain and outrage. "Will you get out!"

She went. She could barely see through her tears, almost bumping into a satisfied-looking Miriam as she went down the hall toward her own room. Her temper flared at the smug expression on the older woman's face.

"Congratulations," she flashed at Miriam. "You've got what you wanted. I hope your conscience lets you enjoy it—if you have one."

Miriam shifted uncomfortably. "I told you he's mine," she said defensively.

"He was never yours," Arabella said, brushing angrily at her tears. "He was never mine, either, but at least I loved him! You only wanted what he had, I heard you say so before you married him. It isn't your heart that he broke, it was your ego. He was the one who got away, and you couldn't take it! So now you're going to get him back, but you'll be cheating him. You don't love him, even now. And if you're not pregnant, I'm a brain surgeon!"

Miriam went white. "What did you say?" she gasped.

"You heard me," Arabella said. "What are you going

to do, get Ethan to the altar and pretend it's his? That's just what he needs now, to have you come back and finish what you started. You almost destroyed him once. Are you going to finish the job?"

"I need someone!" Miriam protested.

"Try the father of the child you're carrying," Arabella replied.

Miriam wrapped her arms around her chest. "My child is none of your business. And neither is Ethan. If he loved you, he'd never have believed you could ignore him when he was hurt."

Arabella nodded quietly. "Yes, I know that," she said, pain deepening her tone. "And that's the only reason I'm leaving. If I thought he cared, even a little, I'd stay and fight you to the death. But if it's you he wants, then I can bow out gracefully." She laughed bitterly. "I should be used to it. I did it four years ago, and look how happy you made him."

Miriam grimaced. "It could be different this time."

"It could. But it won't. You don't love him," Arabella said. "That's what makes it so terrible, even if he loves you." She turned away and went into her room sickened by the thought. It was like history repeating itself.

The wedding gown, in its box, was lying on her bed. She tossed it into a chair and threw herself across the bed, crying her heart out. It didn't matter that Miriam was the snake who'd betrayed her, it was the fact that Ethan didn't believe she was innocent. That was what hurt the most. If he didn't trust her, he certainly didn't love her. She'd been living in a fool's paradise, thinking his ardor might lead to love. Now she knew that it wouldn't. Desire was never enough to compensate for a lack of real feeling.

She pleaded a headache and spent the rest of the night in her room, even refusing supper. Having to watch Miriam gloat would be the last straw, and she had no stomach for any more arguments with Ethan. She knew from painful experience that once his mind was made up, nothing was going to change it. She'd have to leave in the morning. At least she did still have a little money and her credit cards. She could manage on that. She could go to a hotel.

Her eyes were red with tears. Damn Miriam! The other woman had found the perfect way to foul up everything. Now she'd have Ethan again, just as she'd planned. Well, Arabella thought viciously, they deserved each other. So much for all the pretense. Ethan had admitted that it had only been desire that he felt, that he'd pitied her and that's why he'd invited her here. Probably the excuse of keeping Miriam at bay had been fictitious—like his so-called impotence. She'd never believe another word he said, she told herself firmly. If they were quits, it was just fine with her. If Miriam was what he wanted, he could have her. She put on her gown, turned out the light, and lay down. Amazingly, she slept.

COREEN FINALLY FOUND five minutes alone with her son, Miriam having given in to drowsiness and gone to bed.

"Can I bring you anything?" Coreen asked him. "We didn't have a proper supper. Arabella went to bed hours ago with a headache."

"Too bad," Ethan said coldly.

Coreen scowled at him. "What's eating you? Come on, out with it!"

"Miriam phoned the house before you and Arabella left for Houston to tell you I needed a ride to the hospital," he said curtly. "Arabella didn't even bother to tell you. Apparently the shopping trip meant more than any little injury of mine."

Coreen gaped at him. "What are you talking about? There was only one phone call and it was from Arabella's father!"

"Is that what she told you?" he asked with a hard laugh. "Did you talk to him, or hear him? Did Betty Ann?"

Coreen moved close to the bed, her eyes full of disapproval and concern. "I had hoped that you cared about Arabella," she said. "I hoped that you'd be able to see through Miriam's glitter this time to the cold, selfish woman underneath. Perhaps that kind of woman really appeals to you because you're as incapable of real love as she is."

Ethan's eyebrows went straight up. "I beg your pardon?"

"You heard me. I don't need proof that Arabella didn't lie. She wouldn't walk away and leave an injured animal, much less an injured person. I believe that because I know her, because I care about her." She stared down at him. "Love and trust are two sides of one coin, Ethan. If you can believe Arabella capable of such a cold-blooded act, then I'd suggest that you forget marriage and put Miriam's ring back through your nose. God knows, right now I think the two of you deserve each other."

She turned and left him there. He picked up a cup

from the table and slammed it furiously at the closed door. He knew he was fuddled, but his mother had no right to say things like that to him. Why would Miriam lie about a phone call that he could certainly check? All he had to do was get the record of where the call originated from the phone company to prove a lie. Anyway, Miriam had been different lately, very caring and warm, and he'd actually enjoyed her company. He knew all about the man she was in love with, and he'd done his best to encourage her to go back to the Caribbean and try again. So that meant she wasn't interested in him as a man anymore, and it gave her no reason to try and break up his apparent romance with Arabella.

Or was it all a ruse on Miriam's part to get him back? Could Arabella be innocent of what he'd accused her of? He didn't want to think about that, because if she was, he'd just ruined everything. Again. He groaned. It was the way Arabella had dressed, the things she'd said about getting an expensive wedding gown, and then the way it had hurt when Miriam said Arabella was going to Houston anyway, despite his condition.

He was concussed and his mind wasn't working properly. He'd been sure that Arabella loved him, but when Miriam said she wouldn't come to see about him, he thought he'd been mistaken. Then he'd worked himself into a lather thinking that she'd only wanted to use him, as Miriam once had. Miriam had been so different lately that he'd been sure she'd changed, that she wasn't the same self-seeking woman she had been. But was she different? Or was he just susceptible because his head was throbbing and Arabella had hurt him?

He lay down and closed his eyes. He wouldn't—he couldn't—think about that right now. He'd think about it in the morning, instead, when his throbbing head was a little clearer. Then he'd face the future, if he still had one with Arabella.

CHAPTER NINE

ARABELLA WOKE TO the sound of voices the next morning. She sat up in bed, her pale blue gown twisted around her slender body, her long brown hair a tangle around her shoulders, just as Mary knocked briefly then opened the door, rushing inside.

"Hello!" she said, laughing, as she hugged Arabella and placed a bag of souvenir items on the bed. Mary was tan and relaxed and looked lovely. "These are all for you," she said. "T-shirts, shell things, necklaces, skirts, and even a few postcards. Did you miss me?"

"Oh, Mary, yes, I did," Arabella said with a long sigh, hugging her back. Mary was the best, and the only, real friend she'd ever had. "Things are getting so complicated."

"I heard you and Ethan are going to be married," Mary continued, all eyes.

Arabella's face fell. "Yes. Well, that was just what we told Miriam. The wedding is off."

"But your gown!" Mary protested, nodding toward the box in the armchair. "Coreen told us all about it."

"It's going back today," Arabella said firmly. "Ethan broke off the engagement last night. He wants Miriam back."

Mary sat very still. "He what?"

"Wants Miriam back," Arabella said quietly. "She's changed, or so he says. They've gotten real thick in the past couple of days." Which was odd, she told herself, because she herself had gotten real thick with Ethan in the past couple of days. She felt sick all over. "And I'm leaving," she added, giving in to a decision she'd made the night before. "I hate to ask when you're just off the plane, but could you drive me into Jacobsville later?"

Mary almost refused, but the look in her friend's eyes killed all her hopeful words. Whatever had happened, Arabella had been terribly hurt by it. "All right," she said with a forced smile. "I'll be glad to. Does Ethan know you're going?"

"Not yet," Arabella said. "He doesn't need to. He fell yesterday and got concussed." She had to bite back all her concern for him. She couldn't afford to let it show. "He's all right. Miriam's taking care of him, and that's the way he wants it. He said so."

Mary knew there had to be more to it than that, but she kept her silence. "I'll let you dress and pack. I gather that I'm not to tell anyone you're going?"

"Please."

"All right. Come downstairs when you're ready."

"I'll do that. Could you…take that with you?" she asked, nodding toward the box.

Mary picked it up, thinking privately that it was a pity Ethan had waited until she bought the dress to call off the wedding. He didn't seem to care very much for Arabella's feelings, either, because she was obviously crushed.

"I'll see you directly," Arabella said as Mary went out and closed the door.

She got dressed, minus the bra that she still couldn't fasten, in a suit with a thick jacket that she buttoned up. She packed her few things with her good hand and tied a scarf around her neck to hold the cast at her waist. It got heavy when she moved around very much. She picked up her suitcase, then, after a final glance in the mirror at her pale face without makeup, left the room where she'd been so happy and so sad.

There was one last thing she wanted to do. She had to say goodbye to Ethan. She wouldn't admit, even to herself, how much she hoped he'd changed his mind.

Actually, at that moment, Ethan was having a long talk with a quiet and dejected Miriam. He'd asked for the truth, and she'd reluctantly given it to him, her conscience pricked by the conversation that Ethan didn't know she'd had with Arabella the night before.

"I shouldn't have done it," she told him, smiling mistily. "You've been so different, and I saw the way things could have been if you'd loved me when we first married. I knew I didn't stand a chance against Arabella, so I had other men to get even," she confessed for the first time. She met his eyes apologetically. "You should have married her. I'm sorry I made things difficult for you. And I'm very sorry about the lie I told yesterday."

Ethan was having trouble breathing properly. All he could think of was what he'd said to Arabella the night before. He'd been out of his muddled head with anger.

"I called off the wedding," he said absently, and winced.

"She'll forgive you," Miriam said sadly. "I'm sure she feels the same way about you." She reached out and touched his face. "I do love my Jared, you know." She sighed. "I ran because of the baby. I thought he wouldn't want it, but now I'm not so sure. I could at least give him the benefit of the doubt, I suppose. I didn't sleep last night thinking about it. I'll phone him this morning and see what develops."

"You may find he wants the baby as much as you do," he replied. He smiled at her. "I'm glad we can part as friends."

"So am I," she said fervently. "Not that I deserve it. I know I've been a royal pain in the neck."

"Not so much anymore," he assured her.

"I'll go and make that call. Thank you, Ethan, for everything. I'm so sorry about what I did. You deserve more than I ever gave you." She bent and kissed him with warm tenderness.

He reached up, giving her back the kiss, for old times' sake. A kiss of parting, between friends, with no sexual overtones.

That was what Arabella saw when she stopped in the open door. A kiss that wasn't sexual and held such exquisite tenderness that it made her feel like a voyeur. She knew she'd gone white. So it was that way. They'd reconciled. Miriam loved him and now they were going to remarry and live happily ever after. Miriam had won.

She smiled bitterly and retraced her steps so that they didn't even know she'd been in the room.

She ran into Coreen going down the staircase.

"I'm just on my way to see Ethan…." She stopped dead, staring at Arabella's suitcase.

"Mary's driving me to town," Arabella said, her voice a little wobbly. "And I wouldn't disturb Ethan just now, if I were you. He's rather involved with Miriam."

"Oh, this is getting completely out of hand!" Coreen said harshly. "Why won't he listen?"

"He's in love with her, Coreen," the younger woman said. "He can't help that, you know. He said last night that it was really only out of pity that he asked me here. He wanted me, but he loves Miriam. It would never have worked. It's best that I leave now, so that I won't be an embarrassment to him."

"My dear," Coreen said miserably. She hugged Arabella warmly. "You know the door is always open. I'll miss you."

"I'll miss you, too. Mary was going to take the dress back to the store for me, but…but Miriam might like it," she said bravely. "All it would need is a little alteration."

"I'll take care of the dress," Coreen said. "Will you be all right? Where will you go?"

"I'll go to a motel for the time being. I'll phone my father when I've settled in. Don't worry, I've got money, thanks to Ethan's intervention. I won't go hungry, and I can take care of myself. But thank you for all you've done for me. I'll never forget you."

"I'll never forget you either, darling," Coreen said quietly. "Keep in touch, won't you?"

"Of course," Arabella lied with a smile. That was the very last thing she intended doing now, for Ethan's sake.

She followed Mary out to the car after exchanging

farewells with Betty Ann and a puzzled Matt. She didn't even look back as the car wound down the driveway to the road.

Just as Arabella was going out to the car, Miriam was lifting her head and smiling at Ethan. "Not bad. I'm sorry we didn't make it. Shall I go downstairs and explain it all to Arabella and your mother?" she asked with a grimace. "I guess they'll pitch me out the back door on my head when I get through."

"It's my head that's going to be in danger, I'm afraid," he said ruefully. "No, I'll handle it. You'd better go and call your Caribbean connection."

"I'll do that. Thanks."

He watched her go, and lay back against the pillows. He'd heard Matt and Mary come in and he was waiting for them to come and say hello. Maybe he could get Arabella up here and try to sort things out before it was too late. He heard a car door slam twice and an engine rev up, and he frowned. Surely Mary and Matt weren't leaving already.

Minutes later, a coldly furious Coreen walked into his room and glared at him.

"Well, I hope you're happy," she told him. "You've got what you wanted. She just left."

He sat up, scowling at her. "Who just left?" he asked with a chilling sense of loss.

"Arabella," Coreen informed him. "She said you'd called off the wedding. She left her dress for Miriam and said to congratulate you on your forthcoming remarriage."

"Oh, for God's sake!" he burst out. He threw his legs off the bed and tried to get up, but his head was still spinning with the aftereffects of the day before. He sat down again and rubbed his forehead. "I'm not marrying Miriam! Where in hell did she get that idea?"

"From you, I suppose, after the bite you apparently took out of her last night. And something must have been going on in here when she left, because she said you and Miriam were involved when she came downstairs."

She'd seen Miriam kiss him. He remembered the kiss, realized how it would look to an outsider, and he groaned out loud. "My God, I've got a knack for ruining my life," he said with a rough sigh. "I must have a deep-buried death wish. Where did she go?"

"To a motel," she said. "Mary will know which one."

He lifted his head, and his eyes were anguished. "She'll call her father," he said. "He'll be here like a shot to take her over again."

"Do remember who pushed her out of the door, won't you, dear boy?" his mother asked with smiling venom.

"I thought she'd deserted me!" he burst out.

"As if Arabella would do any such thing," she scoffed. "How could you have believed it?"

"Because I had a concussion and I was half out of my head," he returned angrily.

"And what did she see on her way out that convinced her Miriam needed the wedding gown?" Coreen added.

"I kissed her. She kissed me," he corrected. He threw up his hands. "Miriam's going back to the Caribbean to marry the father of her child, if everything works out all right," he said. "It was a goodbye kiss."

"You fool," Coreen said evenly. "Four years ago, you put Arabella's welfare above your own. You married the wrong woman and cheated her as well as yourself, and now you've thrown away the second chance you might have had. Why didn't you tell Arabella how you feel about her!"

He lowered his eyes. Some things he couldn't share, even with his mother. "She's career-minded. She always was. She came here because she was hurt and needed some security. She was reluctant from the first when I tried to get her to marry me. I think she was afraid that she'd be able to play again and be stuck here with me."

"More likely she was afraid you were just using her as a blind for the feelings you had for Miriam," Coreen replied. "She said you only wanted her, but you loved Miriam. She believed it."

Ethan sighed heavily and lay back down. "I'll go after her, when I get my head together."

"Never mind," Coreen said. "She won't come back. She's let you cut up her heart twice already. She won't risk it again."

His eyes opened. "What do you mean, cut up her heart?"

"Ethan," she said patiently, "she was in love with you four years ago. Desperately in love. She thought Miriam just wanted what you had, not you. She was trying to protect you, but you accused her of interfering and God knows what else. She ran then, too, and kept running. Didn't you ever wonder why she arranged to come here to see Jan, and later Mary, only when she knew you wouldn't be here?"

"No, because I was too busy making sure I didn't have to see her," he said doggedly. He averted his eyes. "It hurt too much. I was married, Miriam wouldn't divorce me...." His broad shoulders rose and fell. "I couldn't bear the torment of seeing her and not being able to touch her honorably." He looked up at his mother. "How do you know how she felt about me?" he asked.

"It's obvious," she said simply. "She chose music as a substitute, just as you chose Miriam. You're both fools. What a horrible waste of time."

Ethan was inclined to agree. So Arabella had loved him. He lay back down and closed his eyes, trying to imagine how it would have been if he'd given up his plans to save her from what he thought would have been a mistake, if he'd married her instead. They'd have children by now, they'd be a family. Arabella would sleep in his arms every night and love him. He couldn't bear the images that haunted him. He'd driven her away a second time with his idiotic accusations, and now he'd probably never be able to get her back. He heard his mother leave, but he didn't bother to open his eyes.

ARABELLA GOT A room in a downtown Jacobsville motel. There were several to choose from, but her favorite was an adobe-style one with a Spanish flavor. She settled into her room, trying not to think how bare and austere and impersonal it was compared to the one she'd had at the Hardeman ranch.

Mary hadn't wanted to leave her there, but she'd insisted. She couldn't stay in the house now that she knew how it was between Ethan and Miriam. It was too painful. A clean break was best. She picked up the phone when she'd unpacked and phoned her father in Dallas. The cast came off in nine days. Her father would meet her here then and they'd go back to Houston. He'd sublet their apartment there while he was in Dallas, but they could get another temporarily. Odd that it didn't even bother her to think about being back with her parent again. She didn't feel intimidated anymore.

Time went by slowly. Mary came to visit, but Arabella was reluctant to listen to any news from the ranch, especially about Ethan. She didn't want to hear what was going on at the house, it would be too painful. The only reality was that Ethan hadn't bothered to call or come by or even drop her a postcard, even though he knew by now—or so Mary had said before Arabella protested listening to news of Ethan—that Miriam had lied about the phone call. He knew, but he wouldn't apologize for the things he'd said. He never apologized, she reflected. Since Miriam was still with him, why should he bother? He and Arabella were now past history.

Meanwhile, Ethan was trying to come to grips with his own idiocy. He was certain that Arabella wouldn't listen to him. He couldn't blame her; he'd certainly been eloquent in his condemnation. He thought it would be better if he let things cool down for a few days before they had a showdown. In the meantime, Miriam's man was on his way up to Texas. They'd reconciled and Miriam had been on a cloud ever since, barely coherent except when she was talking about the planter she was going to marry. Ethan enjoyed her company, especially now that he was well and truly off the hook, now that he was able to understand the past and why things had happened the way they had. Miriam had suffered an unfortunate experience with a family friend as a child.

As a result, she'd become brittle in her dealings with men, and very hostile toward them. Only now, secure in her pregnancy and the love of her planter, was she able to come to grips with the past that had made her what she was when she'd married Ethan.

Ethan's only regret was that he'd married her in the first place. It had been unfair to her, to Arabella and even to himself. He should have followed his instincts, which were to marry Arabella and let the chips fall where they may. He'd never been able to give Miriam anything except the dregs of his desires for another woman and, eventually, not even that. He hadn't understood that Miriam's childhood had made it impossible for her to give herself wholly to any man. She'd been looking for love in a series of impossible physical liaisons that were only briefly satisfying. She'd wanted Ethan's love, but he'd withheld it, and she'd tried to punish him. Arabella, though, had suffered as well, trapped in a career that her father controlled, with no hope of escape.

It had thrilled him when Coreen had told him Arabella had once loved him. But he didn't know what she felt now. She probably hated him. He'd started for town three times in the past several days, but he'd stopped. She needed time. So did he.

Mary came up the steps as he was going down them, and he stopped her, trying not to look as unhappy as he felt.

"How is she?" he asked bluntly, because he was certain she'd been to see her friend.

"Lonely," Mary said, her voice gentle. "The cast comes off Tuesday."

"Yes." He stared off over the tree-lined horizon. "Is her father here yet?"

"He'll be here Tuesday." Mary was nervous of Ethan, but she hesitated. "She won't talk about you," she said. "She doesn't look well."

He glanced down at her with flashing silver eyes. "Nobody told her to leave," he said cuttingly, stung by the remark.

"How could she stay, knowing that you're going to marry Miriam all over again?" she asked. "I guess you two do deserve each other," she added with the first show of spirit Ethan had ever seen in her, and she was gone before he could correct her impression of the situation.

What made everyone think Miriam was marrying him? He sighed angrily as he went down the steps. Probably because neither of them had told the rest of the family what was going on. Well, when her planter arrived they'd get the picture. For now, he couldn't let himself dwell on how bad Arabella looked. If he thought about it long enough, he was sure he'd go stark, raving mad.

Mary and Matt had studiously ignored Miriam since Arabella's departure, and Coreen had been so coldly polite to the woman that she might as well have had icicles dripping off her. Ethan tried to make up for his family, which only reinforced their speculation about Miriam's status in his life.

Miriam's intended and Arabella's father arrived in town at the same time. While Jared was being introduced to the Hardemans, Arabella was having the cast off and being told that her hand and wrist had healed almost to perfection. Her father had beamed at the specialist. But only at first.

"Almost to perfection," Dr. Wagner repeated, frowning at Arabella's father. "Translated, that means that Miss Craig will play the piano again. Unfortunately it also means that she will never regain her former mastery. Severed tendons are never the same when they heal, for the primary reason that they're shortened by the process of reattaching them. I'm sorry."

Arabella didn't realize how much she'd been counting on a favorable prognosis. She collapsed into tears.

Her father forgot his own disappointment when he saw hers. Clumsily, he took her in his arms and held her, patting her ineffectually on the back while he murmured words of comfort.

He took her out to dinner that night. She dressed in her one good cocktail dress, black with a scattering of sequins, and knotted her long hair at her nape. She looked elegant, but even with the unwieldy cast off, she felt dowdy. The skin that had been under the cast was unnaturally pale and there were scars. But she kept her hand in her lap and in the dark atmosphere of the restaurant and lounge, she was certain that nobody noticed.

"What will we do?" Arabella asked quietly.

Her father sighed. "Well, for now, I'll see about releasing some of the new recordings and re-releasing the older ones." He looked across the table at her. "I haven't been much of a father, have I? Deserting you after the wreck… I guess you thought I didn't want you without a career to keep us up."

"Yes, I did," she confessed.

"The wreck brought back your mother's accident," he said. It was a subject he'd never discussed before, but she sensed that he was getting something off his chest. "Arabella, she died because I had one drink too many at a party. I was driving, and my reaction time was down. Oh, there were no charges," he said with a cold laugh when he saw her expression. "I wasn't even legally drunk. But the police knew, and I knew, that I could have reacted quicker and avoided the other car. She died instantly. I've lived with that guilt for so long." He leaned back in his chair, making patterns in the condensation on his water glass. "I couldn't admit my mistake. I buried the past in my mind and concentrated on you. I was going to be noble, I was going to dedicate my life to your talent, to your glorious career." He studied her wan face. "But you didn't want a career, did you? You wanted Ethan Hardeman."

"And he wanted Miriam, so what difference does it make now? In fact," she added without looking at him, "Miriam is back and they're reconciling."

"I'm sorry," he said. He studied her. "You know, the wreck brought it all back," he continued. "Your mother's death, trying to cope without her, trying to live with my guilt." He studied his locked-together fingers on the table. "You needed me and I couldn't bear to face you. I came so close to losing you the way I lost her…."

His voice broke and Arabella suddenly saw her father as a man. Just a man, with all the fears and failings of any other human. It shocked her to realize that he wasn't omnipotent. Parents always seemed to be, somehow.

"I didn't remember how Mama died," she said, searching for words. "And I certainly didn't blame you for our wreck. There was nothing you could have done. Really," she emphasized when he lifted tormented eyes to hers. "Dad, I don't blame you."

He bit his lower lip hard and looked away. "Well, I blamed me," he said. "I called Ethan because there was no one else, but I thought in a way, it might make up to you what I'd cheated you out of. I figured with your hand in that shape, Ethan might decide to stop being noble and give you a chance."

"Thank you," she said gently. "But all Ethan wants is his ex-wife. Maybe that's just as well. Four years ago, I worshipped the ground he walked on, but I'm older now...."

"And still in love with him," he finished for her. He shook his head. "All my efforts backfired, didn't they? All right, Arabella. What do you want to do now?"

She was amazed that he was asking her opinion. It was a first—like realizing that he was human and fallible. She liked him much better this way. It was a whole new relationship, because he was treating her like an adult for the first time. "Well, I don't want to stay in Jacobsville," she said firmly. "The sooner we can leave here, the better."

"I guess I'll have to go to Houston and find a place, first," he said. "Then I'll see what I can do about finding myself a job." He waved aside her objections. "I've spent altogether too much time in the past. You have a right to your own life. I'm only sorry that it took another near-fatal wreck to bring me to my senses."

Arabella slid her hand into his and clasped it warmly. "You've been very good to me, Dad," she said gently. "I don't have any complaints."

"Are you sure about Miriam?" he asked with a frown. "Because I don't believe Ethan really wanted to marry her in the first place. And I know he was damned near crazy when I phoned him about you being hurt in the wreck."

"I'm sure," she said, closing the book on that subject forever.

He relented. "All right. We'll start again. And don't worry about that hand," he added. "You can always teach, if everything else fails." He smiled at her gently. "There's a great deal of satisfaction in seeing someone you've coached become famous. Take my word for it."

She smiled at him. "I can live with that," she said. Inwardly, she was almost relieved. She loved to play the piano, but she'd never wanted the tours, the endless road trips, the concerts. Now they were gone forever, and she wasn't really sorry.

Her father left the next morning for Houston in the car he'd rented for the trip to Jacobsville. Arabella was lazy, not rising until late morning. She decided to have lunch in the restaurant and went early.

Their seafood was delicious, so she ordered that and settled back to wait for it.

Incredible how her life had changed, she thought as she came to grips finally with what the surgeon had told her about her hand. What could have been traumatic wasn't that at all. She accepted it with relative ease. Of course, her father's new attitude had helped.

She felt a shadow fall over her and turned with an automatic smile to face the waiter. But it wasn't a waiter. It was Ethan Hardeman.

CHAPTER TEN

ARABELLA SCHOOLED HER features not to show any of the emotions she was feeling. She stared up at him with a blank expression, while her poor heart ran wild and fed on the sight of him.

"Hello, Ethan," she said. "Nice to see you. Is Miriam with you?" she added with a pointed glance behind him.

He put his hat on an empty seat and lowered himself into the chair beside hers. "Miriam is getting married."

"Yes, I know," she began.

So Mary had already told her, he thought. That wasn't surprising, Mary came to see her almost every day. He caught her eyes, but she quickly lowered her gaze to the beige sport coat he was wearing with dark slacks, a white silk shirt and striped tie.

He toyed with the utensils at his place. "I wanted to come sooner, but I thought you needed a little time to yourself. What did the doctor say about your hand?" he added.

She managed to disguise her broken heart very well. To save her pride, she was going to have to lay it on thick. She couldn't let him know her predicament. Besides, he was getting married, and she wished the best for him. He didn't need her problems to mar his happiness. "It's fine," she said. "I have to have a little physical therapy and then I'm back to New York, by way of Houston, to take up where I left off."

His face hardened. He couldn't help it. He'd thought for certain that she'd never use that hand again, knowing how much damage had been done to it. Of course, these days they had all sorts of methods of repairing damaged tendons, so maybe there was a new technique. But it didn't help his pride. He'd left things too late. If he'd told her how he felt at the beginning, if he'd revealed his feelings, things might have been different. His whole life seemed to be falling apart, and all because of his lousy timing.

He stared at her across the table. "Then you've got what you want," he said.

"Yes. But so have you," she reminded him with a forced smile. "I hope you and Miriam will be very happy. I really do, Ethan."

He gaped at her. Meanwhile, the waiter appeared with her salad and paused to ask Ethan if he was ready to order. Absently, he ordered a steak and salad and coffee and sat back heavily in the chair when the man left.

"Arabella, I'm not getting married."

She blinked. "You said you were."

"I said Miriam was."

"What's the difference?" she asked.

He sighed heavily. "She's marrying a man she met down in the Caribbean," he said. "He's the father of her child."

"Oh." She watched the way he twirled his water glass, his eyes downcast, his face heavily lined. "Ethan, I'm so sorry," she said gently. She reached out hesitantly and touched one of his hands.

Electric current shot through him. He lifted his eyes to catch hers while his fingers linked around and through her own. He'd missed her more than he even wanted to admit. The house, and his life, had been empty without her. "Care to console me?" he asked half seriously. "She and her fiancé are staying for a few days." He lowered his eyes to their linked hands so that she wouldn't see the hunger in them. "You could come back with me and help me bluff it out until they leave."

She closed her eyes briefly. "I can't."

"Why not? It's only for a couple of days. You could have your old room. Coreen and Mary would enjoy your company."

She weakened, but her pride was still smarting from the beating it had taken. "I shouldn't, Ethan."

His fingers tightened. "Will it help if I apologize?" he asked quietly. "I never meant to be so rough on you. I should have known better, but I was half out of my mind and I swallowed everything Miriam said."

"I thought you knew me better than that," she said sadly. "I suppose you have to love people to trust them, though."

He flinched. He felt as if he'd had a stake put through his heart. Yes, he should have trusted her. He hadn't, and now she was running away because he'd hurt her. He couldn't let her get away from him now. No matter what it took.

"Listen, honey," he said softly, coaxing her eyes up to

his, "it's been hard on all of us, having Miriam around. But she'll be gone soon."

Taking his heart with her, Arabella thought. She wished, oh, how she wished, that he could love her. "My father and I are going to Houston as soon as he finds a place for us," she said.

His jaw clenched. He hadn't counted on that complication, although he should have expected it. She had her career to think of, and that was her father's grubstake. "You could stay with us until he finds one," he said curtly.

"I'm happy here in the motel," she protested.

"Well, I'm not happy with you here," he said, his own voice arctic. His eyes began to kindle with feeling. "It's my fault you left. We were off to a good start, until I started jumping to conclusions."

"That's just as well." She searched his face. "I guess it's pretty painful for you. Losing her again."

"If you only knew," he replied, his voice deep and slow, but he wasn't thinking of Miriam. He brought her fingers to his lips and nibbled at them, watching the reaction color her face and bring a soft, helpless light to her green eyes. "Come home with me," he said. "You can sprawl across my bed in that satin gown and we'll make love again."

"Hush!" she exclaimed, looking around to make sure they weren't overheard.

"You're blushing."

"Of course I'm blushing. I want to forget that it ever happened!" she muttered. She tried to draw her fingers away, but he held them tightly.

"We could give Miriam and her intended a grand send-off," he coaxed. "By the time she left, she'd be convinced that I didn't have a broken heart."

"And why should I want to do you another favor?" she demanded.

He looked her right in the eye. "I can't think of a single reason," he confessed with a warm, quiet smile. "But I hope you'll come, all the same. Maybe I can make up for the way I treated you."

Her fingers jerked in his and she went scarlet. "By making love to me again? Do you think I care so much that I'll be grateful for any crumbs left over from your relationship with Miriam?" she asked bluntly.

"No. I don't think that at all." He held her gaze, trying to find any sign that she still cared, that he hadn't quite ruined everything. That he might have one last chance before she resumed her career to make her understand how deeply involved his feelings were, how much he cared.

"I've heard you play." He lowered his eyes to her hands, caressing them gently. "You have genius in your hands. I'm glad you haven't lost that talent, Arabella, even if it means that I have to let you go again." And he might, but now he had the hope that it might not be a permanent loss this time. If he could convince her that he cared, she might yet come back to him one day.

She wanted to tell him. She started to tell him, to draw him out, to try to make him tell her if wanting was all he felt. But the waiter arrived with their order, and the moment was lost. She couldn't find the nerve to reopen the subject, especially when he started talking about Miriam's husband-to-be and the way he'd come dashing across the sea to get her.

After lunch, Ethan waited while she packed and left a message at the desk for her father to call her at the Hardeman ranch. Going back was against her better judgment, but she couldn't resist the temptation. In the long years ahead, at least she'd have a few bittersweet memories.

He drove her out to the ranch, his eyes thoughtful, his face quiet and brooding.

"Roundup's over," he announced as they sped down the road out of Jacobsville. "It feels good to have a little free time."

"I imagine so." She glanced off the highway at the massive feedlot that seemed to stretch forever toward the horizon. "Do the Ballenger brothers still own that feedlot?"

"They certainly do," he mused, following her glance. "Calhoun and Justin are making a mint on it. Good thing, too, the way they're procreating. Calhoun and Abby have a son and a daughter and Justin and Shelby have two sons."

"Whatever happened to Shelby's brother, Tyler?" she asked absently.

"Tyler married an Arizona girl. They don't have any kids yet, but their dude ranch just made headlines— Tyler and his wife have expanded it to include a whole authentic Old-West adobe village as a tourist attraction, and they've enlarged their tourist facilities. It looks as if they're going to make a mint, too."

"Good for them," Arabella said. She stared down at

the floorboard of the car. "It's nice to hear about local people making good."

"That's what we thought about you," he said, "when you started making headlines. We all knew you had the talent."

"But not the ambition," she confessed. "My father had that, for both of us. I only loved music. I still do."

"Well, you'll be on your way again when you get the physical therapy out of the way, I guess," he said, his voice hardening.

"Of course," she mumbled numbly and moved her damaged hand to stare down at its whiteness. She flexed the muscles, knowing she'd never be the same again.

Ethan caught a glimpse of the expression on her face. It kept him puzzled and quiet all the way home.

Miriam and her fiancé were beaming like newlyweds. Even Coreen seemed to have warmed toward her, and Miriam went out of her way to make Arabella feel comfortable.

"I'm really sorry for messing things up between you and Ethan," the older woman said when she and Arabella were briefly alone during the long afternoon. In her newfound happiness, she could afford to be generous, and she'd seen the misery she'd caused Ethan already. "I was evening up old scores, but it wasn't Ethan's fault, or yours, that he couldn't love me." She glanced toward Jared, a tall, pleasant man with elegance and obvious breeding, and her face softened with emotion. "Jared is everything I dreamed of in a husband. I ran because I didn't think he'd want our child, as I did. My emotions were all over the place. I guess I had some wild idea of

getting Ethan to marry me again to get even with Jared."
She looked at Arabella with quiet apology. "I'm sorry.
I hope this time you and Ethan will make a go of it."

That wasn't possible now, but it was kind of Miriam
to think, even belatedly, of Ethan's happiness. She managed a smile. "Thank you. I hope you'll be happy, too."

"I don't deserve it, but so do I," Miriam murmured.
She smiled self-consciously and went back to her fiancé.

Mary was giving Arabella curious looks. Later on,
she dragged her friend to one side.

"What's going on? You could have knocked me over
with a feather when I saw Ethan walk in with you," she
whispered. "Have you made up?"

"Not really. He wants me to help him put on a good
front so Miriam won't think she's broken his heart,"
Arabella said, her eyes going to Ethan like homing pi-
geons.

Mary watched the look and smiled secretly. "I don't
think she could get that impression, not considering
the way he's been sneaking looks at you ever since he
brought you in."

Arabella laughed halfheartedly. "He's just putting
on an act," she said.

"Is that what it's called?" Mary murmured dryly.
"Well, ignore it while you can."

"I thought I was...." Her voice trailed off as she en-
countered a long, simmering gaze from Ethan's silver
eyes and got lost in the fierce hunger in them. The rest
of the people seemed to vanish. She didn't look away
and neither did he, and electricity sizzled between them
for one long, achingly sweet minute. Then Coreen di-

verted his attention and Arabella was able to breathe again.

For the remainder of the day, he didn't leave the house. After supper, while the rest of the family watched a movie in the living room on the VCR, Arabella excused herself and changed into comfortable jeans and a white tank top before she sneaked back downstairs and went into the library to try the piano for the first time since the wreck.

She closed the door quietly, so that no one would hear her. She positioned the piano bench carefully and sat down, easing up the cover over the keyboard. It was a grand piano, because Coreen played herself, and it was in perfect tune. She touched middle C and ran a scale one octave lower with her left hand.

Very nice, she thought, smiling. Then she put her right hand on the keyboard. It trembled and the thumb protested when she tried to turn it under on F. She grimaced. All right, she thought after a minute. Perhaps scales would be just too difficult right now. Perhaps a simple piece would be easier.

She chose a Chopin nocturne, a beginner's piece she'd played in her early days at the piano. She began very slowly, but it made no difference. Her hand was lax and trembly and totally uncooperative. She groaned and her hands crashed down despairingly on the keyboard, seeing months of work ahead before she could even do a scale, perhaps years before she could play again normally, if at all.

She didn't hear Ethan come in. She didn't hear him close the door behind him and stand staring at her down-bent head for a long time. He'd heard the crash of her hands on the piano and it had made him curious. He knew she was probably feeling frustrated, that it would take a long time for her hand to be able to stand the torment of long practice.

It was only when he came up to her and straddled the piano bench facing her that she looked up.

"You can't play," he said. He'd heard her from outside the door. He knew the truth now. She gritted her teeth, waiting for the blow to fall. "It will take time," he said. "Don't be impatient."

She let out a slow breath. So he didn't know. At least her pride was safe.

"That's right." She met his eyes and felt her heart drop. "So you don't have to feel sorry for me. I can still play, Ethan. I'll just need a little more time to heal, and then a lot of practice."

"Of course." He looked down at the keyboard. "Hurt, didn't it? What I said about feeling sorry for you."

"The truth is always the best way," she said numbly.

He shifted, his eyes pinning hers. "What are you and your father going to do until you're proficient again?"

"He's going to see about releasing some of my new recordings and re-releasing some of the older ones," she replied. Her left hand touched the keyboard reverently and she mourned fiercely the loss of her abilities. She couldn't even show it, couldn't cry her eyes out on Ethan's broad chest, because she didn't dare admit it to him. "So, you see, I won't have any financial worries right away. Dad and I will look after each other."

He drew in a short, angry breath. "Is he going to win again?" he asked coldly.

She drew away, puzzled by the fury in his tone. "Again?"

"I let him take you away from here once," he said, his jaw taut, his silver eyes flashing. "I let you walk away, because he convinced me that you needed him and music more than you needed me. But I can't do that again, Arabella."

She hesitated. "You…you loved Miriam."

His face hardened. "No."

"You only want me," she began again, searching his eyes while her heart threatened to run away with her. "And not enough to marry me."

"No."

He was confusing her. She pushed back her long, dark hair nervously. "Can't you say something besides just 'no'?" she asked slowly.

"Put your leg over here." He readjusted her so that she was facing him on the long, narrow piano bench. Then he pulled her jean-clad legs gently over his so that they were in the most intimate position they'd ever shared. His lean hands held her hips, pulling them hard into his, and then he looked down into her eyes and deliberately moved her so that she felt, with shocking emphasis, the slow arousal of his body.

Her nails dug into his shoulders. "Ethan, for heaven's sake!" she protested in shocked outrage.

But he held her there despite her struggles. His jaw was taut and his breathing unsteady. "I'll be damned if I'll let you go," he said huskily. "You're going to marry me."

She couldn't believe what she was hearing. The feel of him against her was making reason almost impossible, anyway.

"Say yes," he said, bending to her mouth. "Say it now, or so help me God, I'll have you where you sit!" His hands pulled her closer and she felt the physical reality of the threat.

"Yes, Ethan," she could manage that, barely. Not because she was afraid of him, but because she loved him too much to refuse him a second time. Then his lips were against hers and she was clinging to him like ivy, only living through his mouth and his hands and his body.

Somehow he managed to get his shirt and hers out of the way, and she felt him from the waist up, bare and hair-roughened muscles warm and hard against her sensitive breasts while he kissed her until her mouth ached. His strong hands slid up and down her back, moving her in a new and shameless rhythm against his thighs, making her moan with the intimacy of their position.

"It will be like this in bed," he whispered, his deep voice shaken as it made tiny chills against her moist, swollen lips. "Except that we'll join in the most intimate way of all first. Then I'll rock you against me… like this…and we'll have each other on crisp, white sheets in my bed…!"

His tongue penetrated her mouth. She arched against him, moaning, her hands trembling as they caught in his hair and held his mouth against her own. She could see them—Ethan's lean, dark-skinned body over hers, the light glistening on his damp skin, the movement of it against her own pale flesh in a rhythm as deep, as slow, as waves against the beach. His strained face above hers, his breath shaking, as hers would be, his mouth moving to her breasts…

She caught her breath. Sensations of pleasure made her shudder as his hands clenched on her hips and forced her even closer.

"I want you," he groaned against her mouth. His fingers trembled as they slid under the waistband of her jeans.

"I know," she whispered feverishly. Her hands slid to his thighs, trembling too. "I want…you, too."

He shuddered with the fierce need to give in to what he was feeling, what she was feeling. But it couldn't happen like this. No, he told himself. No! He eased back a breath and looked down into her soft, misty eyes. "Not like this," he bit off. "Our first time shouldn't be on a piano bench in an unlocked room. Should it?"

She stared up at him, shivering. It had only then occurred to her where they were. "I saw us," she whispered unsteadily. "In bed."

His face clenched. "My God, so did I, twisting against each other in a fever so hot it burned." He buried his face in her throat, and it was burning hot. His arms contracted.

His hands smoothed against her bare back and he touched her soft breasts. He lifted his head, looking down at the rose-tipped softness in his hands. "Did you ever dream that we'd be like this together one day?" he asked, almost in awe, and lifted his eyes to hold hers. "Sitting alone in a quiet room with your body open to my eyes and my hands, and so natural that we both accepted it without embarrassment?"

"I dreamed of it," she confessed in a soft whisper. She looked down at the darkness of his hands against the creamy beauty of her breasts. She trembled, and didn't mind letting him see. She belonged to him now. If wanting was all he felt, she could live with it. She'd have to.

"So did I," he whispered huskily. "Every long, lonely night." And he bent to take one small, perfect breast into his mouth.

She arched to him, clinging to his hair, gasping at the delicious sensations that washed over her, loving the warm moist suction of his mouth on her.

"It will be like this in bed, too," he whispered against her flushed skin. "Except that I'll kiss more than your breasts this way, and I won't stop until you're as satisfied as I am."

She drew her mouth over his eyes, his cheekbones, his nose, his mouth. "I hope you won't be sorry," she said quietly.

He lifted his head and looked down at her. If she'd ever loved him, he'd killed it. He was bulldozing her into this wedding, but it seemed the only way out. Perhaps love could be taught. "We'll have a white wedding, with all the trimmings," he added. "Complete with a wedding night. There won't be any anticipating our vows, and to hell with modern attitudes." He kissed her gently. "This is what marriage should be. A good marriage, with respect on both sides and honor to make it all perfect."

Respect. Honor. No mention of love, but perhaps she was being greedy. "Your mother was right. You are a puritan," she teased.

"So are you." He lifted her away from him with rueful reluctance and fastened her clothes again, then his. "I like the idea of a blushing, shy bride," he murmured, watching her face color. "Do you mind?"

"No," she assured him. "Not at all. I've waited so long to be one."

"As long as I've waited for you," he replied, his face almost a stranger's with its hard restraint. He moved away from her. "We'll make it together this time," he said. "Despite your father and Miriam and all the other obstacles, this time we'll make it."

She looked up at him with hope and quiet adoration. "Yes. This time we'll make it," she whispered.

They had to. She knew that she'd never survive having to leave him again. Later, she'd explain about her father and the peace they'd made. For now, it was enough that they were facing a future with each other. Love might come later, if she could be the kind of wife he wanted, and needed. In the meantime, she'd live one day at a time.

Her only worry was what he was going to think if he found out that her career was over. He might think again that she was marrying him for security.

SHE PHONED HER father that night and explained the situation to him. Oddly enough, he wasn't disappointed, and he even congratulated her. He'd make do, he promised, and she'd get the lion's share of the deals he was working on her behalf.

That reassured her. She'd have her little nest egg. Then, in the future, when Ethan finally tired of her body, she'd have something to fall back on. She could have a kind of life, even though it wouldn't include him.

She slept fitfully, wondering if she'd made the right decision. Was it right for Ethan, who was losing the woman he really loved? Or should she have let him go for good? By morning, she was no closer to a decision.

CHAPTER ELEVEN

"SO IT'S BACK on again," Coreen said with a nod, eyeing her son warily as he and a somber Arabella broke the news to her. "Uh-huh. For how long this time?"

"For good." He lifted his chin. "You took the gown back, I suppose," he added.

"No, I didn't take the gown back," Coreen replied. "I stuck it in the closet because I was reasonably sure that you inherited enough of my common sense not to duplicate the worst mistake of your life."

He stared at her. "You kept it?"

"Yes." She smiled at Arabella. "I hoped he'd come to his senses. I just wasn't sure that he could get past his old doubts. Especially," she added, with a grim glance in Miriam's direction, "when the past started to interfere with the present."

"I'll tell you all about that, someday," Ethan promised his mother. "In the meantime, how about those plans for the wedding?"

"I'll call Shelby tonight. Is that all right with you, Arabella?"

"I'd like that," Arabella said with downcast eyes. "Are you sure Shelby will have time to help us?"

"She'll make it. Her mother and I were best friends,

many years ago. This time, don't let Arabella get away," Coreen cautioned her son.

He looked down at Arabella with open hunger. "Not on your life. Not this time."

Arabella was trying not to look as nervous as she felt. That hunger in Ethan's eyes was real, even if he didn't love her, and she was suddenly uncertain about being able to satisfy it. If it hadn't dimmed in four years, how was she, a virgin, going to be woman enough to quench it?

He saw that fear in her eyes and misinterpreted it. He drew her to one side, scowling. "You aren't getting cold feet?"

"It's a big step, marriage," she said, hedging. "I'll get my nerve back."

"I'll give you anything you want," he said curtly. "You can have the moon, if you like."

She averted her gaze to Miriam and her fiance. They looked the picture of coming nuptial bliss. Nothing like Arabella and Ethan, so tense and nervous with each other, stepping gingerly around the big issues they still had to face.

"I don't want the moon," she said. "I'll settle for a good marriage."

"We come from similar backgrounds and we have a lot in common," he said stubbornly. "We'll make it."

SHELBY JACOBS BALLENGER came by the next morning to talk to Arabella while Coreen and Mary listened in. She was a beautiful woman, much prettier than Miriam, and there had been a lot of gossip about the rocky romance she and her husband, Justin, had weathered. If it was true, none of it showed on her supremely happy face, and even the birth of two sons hadn't ruined her slender figure.

"I can't tell you how much we appreciate your help," Arabella said, smiling at Shelby. "I've never had to worry about arrangements of this sort before."

"It's my pleasure," Shelby replied, beaming. "I have a special place in my heart for weddings. My own was something to remember—unfortunately, for all the wrong reasons. But even with a bad start, it's been a miracle of togetherness. Justin is all I ever wanted, he and my boys."

"How do you manage any free time?" Arabella asked.

"It's not easy, with preschoolers," Shelby laughed, "but my sister-in-law is a jewel. Abby's keeping them while she's confined to the house. It's their third child on the way, you know. Justin said he was going to have a long talk with Calhoun and see if he knew what was causing them!"

Everyone laughed. It was well-known around Jacobsville that Calhoun and Abby would have loved an even dozen.

"Now." Shelby got out a notebook. "Let me run you through the possibilities and then we'll sort out the particulars."

It took the better part of the morning. Shelby left just before lunch and Arabella's head was swimming with it all.

"I don't want a wedding," she moaned to Coreen. "It's too complicated."

"We could elope," Ethan suggested.

Coreen glared at him. "Mary and Matt already did

that. I won't let you. It's a church wedding or you'll live in sin!"

"Mother!" Ethan gave a theatrical expression of shock.

"It won't be that difficult. We already have the bride and the dress; all we have to worry about are invitations and food."

"Well, we could phone the guests and have a barbecue," he replied.

"Go away, Ethan," Coreen invited.

"Only if Arabella comes with me. I thought she might like to see the kittens. They've grown since she's been away," he added offhandedly.

She was tempted, but she wasn't sure she wanted to be alone with him. She'd successfully avoided him the night before, because of that look in his eyes that made her skin tingle.

"Come on, chicken," he taunted, so handsome in his jeans and chambray shirt that he looked the epitome of the movie cowboy.

"All right." She capitulated, following him out the door, to Coreen and Mary's amusement.

He caught her hand in his as they walked, linking her fingers sensuously through his own. He glanced down, his silver eyes approving of her gray slacks and gray-and-yellow patterned sweater. "You look good with your hair down like that."

She smiled. "It gets in my eyes."

He tilted his hat low over his eyes as they went out into the sunlight. "It's going to get hot today. We might go swimming."

"No, thanks," she said. Too quickly. She felt his eyes probing.

"Afraid history might repeat itself?" he asked softly. He stopped at the barn door and turned her, his hands gentle, his eyes questioning. "We're engaged. I might not draw back this time. I might take you."

She dropped her eyes to his chest. "I want a white wedding."

His own eyes were looking for telltale signs, for anything that would give him a hint of what she really was feeling. "So do I. Will it be any less white if we express what we feel for each other with our bodies?"

Her gaze shot up, her face flaming with bad temper. "That's all you feel for me, though. You said so. Wanting. You want me. I'm something you'd like to use…!"

He let her go abruptly, literally pushing her away from him. "My God, I can't get through to you, can I?" he asked bitterly.

She wrapped her arms across her breasts. "I wouldn't put it like that," she replied. "You wanted me four years ago, but you married Miriam. You loved her, not me."

"Four years ago, Miriam told me she was pregnant," he said, his face hardening at the memory. "By the time I realized she wasn't, we were married."

Her face tightened. She knew what he was saying. He and Miriam had anticipated their wedding vows. Probably by the time he'd made love to her at the swimming hole, he'd already been intimate with Miriam. She felt sick.

She started past him, but he caught her arms and held her. "No!" he said roughly. "It wasn't like that! It was you from the very beginning. Miriam was the substitute, Arabella, not you." He pulled her back against him, his teeth grinding together in anguish. "I knew that afternoon that if I didn't do something, I'd have you in spite of all my noble intentions. Miriam was handy and willing." He bent his head over hers. "I used her, and she knew it, and hated me for it. I cheated all three of us. She came to me and told me she thought she was pregnant, so I married her. You had your career and I didn't think you were old enough to cope with marriage, so I let you go. My God, don't you think I paid for that decision? I paid for it for four long years. I'm still paying!"

Time slowed to a standstill as what he was saying penetrated her mind. "You made love to Miriam because you wanted me?" she asked wanly. That was just what Miriam had said. That it had been a physical obsession on his part.

"Yes," he said with a heavy sigh. His fingers smoothed over the fabric of her sweater, caressing her shoulders. "And couldn't have you." His mouth pressed her hair away from her neck and sought it, warm and hard and fiercely passionate. "I wouldn't have been able to stop, Arabella," he whispered huskily. "Once I had you, I couldn't have stopped." His mouth opened, warm and moist against the tender flesh, arousing and slow. "You'd never have been able to leave, don't you see, baby? You'd have been mine. Totally mine."

Her eyes closed as the arousing movement of his lips made her knees go weak. He was seducing her with words. She shouldn't let him do this to her. She was weak.

He edged her into the deserted barn, against the inside of the closed door, so that the weight of his lean body pinned her there from breast to thighs. He shuddered with his need.

"I'm going to make you marry me," he said into her mouth. "If it takes seduction, that's all right, too. I'll get you to the altar any way I have to."

"Blackmailer," she protested shakenly.

"Kiss me back." He moved against her and felt her begin to tremble. Her mouth lifted and he took it with slow, aching movements that made her moan under the crush of the kiss, that made her give it back in a feverish surge of passion.

A long time later, he dragged her arms from around his neck and stepped away from her, a reddish burn along his cheeks, a tremor in the lean, sure hands that held her wrists.

"You can have a month," he said with savage hunger just barely held in check. "If the ring isn't on your finger by then, look out. I won't wait a night longer."

He turned and left her there, still shaking, with her back to the wall.

EXACTLY ONE MONTH LATER, she spoke her vows in the small Jacobsville Methodist church with her father there to give her away and half of Jacobsville in attendance. Ethan hadn't touched her since that day in the barn, but his eyes threatened her every time he looked at her. He might not love her, but his passion for her was as alive and hot as the weather.

Miriam had long since gone back to the Caribbean with Jared, and she'd sent them a wedding invitation.

She'd beaten Ethan to the altar by two weeks, but Ethan hadn't seemed to mind. He'd been busy, and away a good bit recently on ranch business. Coreen remarked dryly that it was probably just as well, because his moods were making everyone nervous.

Only Arabella understood exactly what those moods were about, and tonight she was going to have to cope with the cause of them. He'd reserved a hotel room for them at a resort on the Gulf of Mexico, and she was more nervous than she'd ever been in her life. All the walls were going to come down and she'd be alone with Ethan and his fierce desire for her. She didn't know how she was going to survive a possession that was purely physical.

"You made a beautiful bride," Coreen said, kissing her just before she went upstairs to change. She wiped away tears. "I just know you and Ethan are going to make it this time."

"I hope so," Arabella confessed, radiant despite her fears as she paused to kiss Mary and Matt and to thank Shelby.

"It was my pleasure," Shelby assured her, and tightened her grip on her tall husband's hand. Justin Ballenger was altogether too much man for the average woman, but Shelby had moved in under his heart, and he looked as if he didn't mind one bit. He smiled down at her, his lean face briefly radiant as his dark eyes swept over her with possession and pride.

"I won't forget all you've done for me," Arabella murmured, a little shy of Justin. She leaned forward and kissed Shelby's cheek. "Thank you."

"I hope you'll be very happy," Shelby said gently.

"You get out of marriage what you put into it," Justin added and smiled at her. "Give a little and take a little. You'll do fine."

"Thanks," Arabella replied.

He and Shelby moved off, hand in hand, and Arabella watched them with pure envy.

Ethan caught her hand, pulling her around. He searched her eyes with a light in his that puzzled her. It was the first time he'd come near her since he'd said, "I do," and he hadn't kissed her at the altar, to everyone's surprise and puzzlement.

"The luggage is in the car. Let's go," he said quietly, his eyes narrowing as they smoothed over her body. "I want you to myself."

"But…aren't we going to change?" She faltered.

"No." He framed her face in his lean hands and pulled it up to the descent of his. "I want to take that dress off you myself," he whispered, and his lips touched hers in a promise of a kiss that made her knees go weak. "Come along, Mrs. Hardeman."

He made the name sound new and sweet. She took his hand and let him lead her out, coping somehow with the shock and amusement of all the people who'd gathered around them here. The reception was supposed to be held in the fellowship hall, but Ethan had apparently decided that they were going to forego the traditional celebration. He grinned, whispered something to his delighted mother, and they left in a hail of rice and confetti and good wishes.

They drove to Galveston in his mother's Mercedes-

Benz, since his own car had been left as a decoy for well-wishers with their soap and tin cans. His mother's car was untouched, and he grinned at Arabella's expression when she saw it.

"We're too old for all that," he chided as he put her in the car. "Tin cans and soaped windows—my God."

She made a face at him. "Some of us sure grow up too fast," she muttered.

"Not quite fast enough, in your case." He started the car and took off around the back of the church, glancing with amusement at the rearview mirror where he could see a few friends were just staring after them with astonished faces. "I could very happily have married you at the age of sixteen, but I had a guilty conscience about robbing the cradle."

She was faintly shocked at the admission, not sure if she should even take the remark seriously. But he wasn't smiling.

"Don't believe me?" he asked with a quick glance. "Wait until we get to Galveston. You've got a lot of surprises coming."

"Have I?" She wondered what they were. She had a feeling the biggest one was going to be the wedding night she'd secretly dreaded. Love on one side wasn't going to be enough to get her through that, and she knew it.

He kept music playing until they reached the lovely brick hotel on the beach and checked in. Their room overlooked the beach and Galveston Bay, and it was a remote spot, for all its closeness to town. Sea gulls dipped down on the beach and she watched them wistfully.

"Change into some jeans and a top and we'll walk

down the beach," he suggested, sensing her discomfort. "It's a bit cool today for swimming."

"Okay." She hesitated, wondering if he was going to expect her to undress in front of him.

"You can have the bathroom. I'll change in here," he said easily.

She gave him a grateful smile and got her things out of her suitcase. By the time she'd changed into her jeans and a gray pullover shirt, he was wearing jeans and a blue-and-white-striped shirt.

"Let's go." He didn't give her time to be self-conscious about sharing the big room with its two double beds. He led her out onto the beach and they spent the afternoon looking for shells and talking. Later they had a seafood supper in a restaurant located in an old lighthouse, and sat on the big deck after dark and watched the ships pass.

By the time they went back into their room, Arabella was relaxed and so much in love that she didn't even protest when Ethan took her in his arms in the doorway and began to kiss her with fervent hunger.

He didn't turn on the light. He closed and locked the door in the dark and picked Arabella up, carrying her to the first of the two beds.

She was lost in his hard, deep kisses, in the caressing movements of his lean hands as he undressed her with slow delight, discovering her body with his lips first, then his hands. She stretched like a cat while he undressed and when she felt the first touch of his naked skin against her own, she gasped with shocked pleasure.

His mouth covered hers then, gentling her. As the minutes began to move faster, as the heat began to burn inside her, as the kisses grew endless and his hands made her shiver and cry out, she forgot her fear and gave him what he wanted. When he moved over her, she welcomed the hard thrust of his body with trusting abandon.

He pushed down and she clung to him. There was a flash of pain, and then it was feverish movement and growing pleasure that finally exploded into an ecstasy that bordered on pain in its sweeping fulfillment.

"No," he groaned when she made a hesitant movement, aeons later. His hands swept her back, hard against him, and he shuddered as he held her there, against his sweat-dampened body. "Stay here."

"Are you all right?" she whispered into his throat.

"Now, I am," he replied. His lips brushed tenderly over her face. "You love me. We couldn't have made love like this out of desire alone," he whispered huskily. "Not with this kind of tenderness."

She closed her eyes. So he knew. It wasn't surprising. That had probably been her biggest fear, that when he made love to her, he was going to realize how much she cared.

Her fingers moved gently in his thick, damp hair. "Yes," she confessed then. "I love you. I always have. I don't think they've invented a cure for it."

"God forbid that they ever should," he whispered back. He cradled her intimately in the curve of his legs with a long sigh. His hand smoothed over her waist, her breast, with slow possession and he laughed. "You're mine," he said with gruff amusement. "I'm never going to let you go now. You're going to live with me and bear my children and we're going to be everything to each other for the rest of our lives."

"Even though you only want me?" she asked sadly.

"I want you, yes," he replied. His hands smoothed her back against him, so that her body could feel the urgent press of his. "I want you to the point of madness and beyond. If it were only desire that I felt, any woman's body would do. But that isn't the case." He held her hips to his. "Not only was there no Miriam, there was no other woman for four years. Is that enough proof of love?"

Her breath caught. She turned in his grasp, her eyes trying to see his through the moonlit darkness. "You love me?"

"My God, with all my heart," he said huskily. "You little blind fool, didn't you know? My mother did. Mary and Matt did. Everyone knew what I felt, including Miriam, so why didn't you?"

She laughed, on fire with the first daring certainty of shared love, belonging. "Because I was a blind little fool! Oh, Ethan, I love you, I love you, I love…!"

That was as far as she got. He rolled her into him and his hands grew quickly urgent, like the hard mouth that had cut off her hasty admission. He moved against her and she moved to accommodate him, and for a long time, they said nothing while their bodies spoke in a new and intimate language of love.

"God knows how I'll share you with the stage," he groaned much later when they were propped up together sharing a soft drink he'd retrieved from the refrigerator in the room. "But I'll manage."

"Oh. That." She grimaced and laid her face against his warm, bare shoulder. "Well, I sort of lied."

"What?"

"I sort of lied," she repeated. "I will be able to use my hand again, and play again, but not like I did before." She sighed, nuzzling her cheek against him with a loving sigh. "I can teach, but I can't perform. And before you say it, I'm not sorry. I'd rather have you than be as great as Van Cliburn."

He couldn't speak. If he needed proof of her love, that gave it to him. He bent and kissed her eyes with breathless tenderness. "Truly, Arabella?" he asked softly.

"Truly, Ethan." She nibbled at his lips and simultaneously set the ice-cold bottom of the soft drink on his warm, flat belly.

His voice exploded in the darkness and he jumped. Arabella laughed with endless delight, anticipating a delicious reprisal.

"Why, you little…" he began, and she could see the smile, hear the loving threat, see the quick movement in her direction.

She put the drink on the bedside table and reached out to him, drawing him to her, accepting her fate with arms that would accept everything life had to offer for the rest of her life. Ethan in her arms. Heaven.

* * * * *

HARLEY

To Julie Benefiel, who designed my cowboy quilt
(hand pieced by Nancy Caudill),

To Nancy Mason, who quilted it,

And to Janet Borchert, who put together
a 2007 hardcover book of all my covers,
including foreign ones, along with Jade, Tracy,
Nancy, Carey, Amy, Renata, Maria, LeeAnn, Efy,
Kay, Peggy, Hang, Ronnie, Mona and Debbie
of the Diana Palmer Bulletin Board.

Also to everyone who participated in
the compendium summaries of all my books,
and to Nancy for the quilted covers
for the loose-leaf notebooks.

With many thanks and much love.

CHAPTER ONE

HARLEY FOWLER WAS staring so hard at his list of chores that he walked right into a young brunette as he headed into the hardware store in Jacobsville, Texas. He looked up, shocked, when she fell back against the open door, glaring at him.

"I've heard of men getting buried in their work, but this is too much," she told him with a speaking look. She smoothed over her short black hair, feeling for a bump where she'd collided with the door. Deep blue eyes glared up into his pale blue ones. She noticed that he had light brown hair and was wearing a baseball cap that seemed to suit him. He was sexy-looking.

"I'm not buried in my work," he said curtly. "I'm trying to get back to work, and shopping chores are keeping me from it."

"Which doesn't explain why you're assaulting women with doors. Does it?" she mused.

His eyes flared. "I didn't assault you with a door. You walked into me."

"I did not. You were staring at that piece of paper so hard that you wouldn't have seen a freight train coming." She peered over his arm at the list. "Pruning shears? Two new rakes?" She pursed her lips, but smiling blue eyes stared at him. "You're obviously somebody's gardener," she said, noting his muddy shoes and baseball cap.

His eyebrows met. "I am not a gardener," he said indignantly. "I'm a cowboy."

"You are not!"

"Excuse me?"

"You don't have a horse, you're not wearing a cowboy hat, and you don't have on any chaps." She glanced at his feet. "You aren't even wearing cowboy boots!"

He gaped at her. "Did you just escape from intense therapy?"

"I have not been in any therapy," she said haughtily. "My idiosyncrasies are so unique that they couldn't classify me even with the latest edition of the DSM-IV, much less attempt to psychoanalyze me!"

She was referring to a classic volume of psychology that was used to diagnose those with mental challenges. He obviously had no idea what she was talking about.

"So, can you sing, then?"

He looked hunted. "Why would I want to sing?"

"Cowboys sing. I read it in a book."

"You can read?" he asked in mock surprise.

"Why would you think I couldn't?" she asked.

He nodded toward the sign on the hardware store's door that clearly said, in large letters, PULL. She was trying to push it.

She let go of the door and shifted her feet. "I saw that," she said defensively. "I just wanted to know if you were paying attention." She cocked her head at him. "Do you have a rope?"

"Why?" he asked. "You planning to hang yourself?"

She sighed with exaggerated patience. "Cowboys carry ropes."

"What for?"

"So they can rope cattle!"

"Don't find many head of cattle wandering around in hardware stores," he murmured, looking more confident now.

"What if you did?" she persisted. "How would you get a cow out of the store?"

"Bull. We run purebred Santa Gertrudis bulls on Mr. Parks's ranch," he corrected.

"And you don't have any cows?" She made a face. "You don't raise calves, then." She nodded.

His face flamed. "We do so raise calves. We do have cows. We just don't carry them into hardware stores and turn them loose!"

"Well, excuse me!" she said in mock apology. "I never said you did."

"Cowboy hats and ropes and cows," he muttered. He opened the door. "You going in or standing out here? I have work to do."

"Doing what? Knocking unsuspecting women in the head with doors?" she asked pleasantly.

His impatient eyes went over her neat slacks and wool jacket, to the bag she was holding. "I said, are you going into the store?" he asked with forced patience, holding the door open.

"Yes, as a matter of fact, I am," she replied, moving closer. "I need some tape measures and Super Glue and matches and chalk and push pins and colored string and sticky tape."

"Don't tell me," he drawled. "You're a contractor."

"Oh, she's something a little less conventional than that, Harley," Police Chief Cash Grier said as he came up the steps to the store. "How's it going, Jones?" he asked.

"I'm overflowing in DBs, Grier," she replied with a grin. "Want some?"

He held up his hands. "We don't do a big business in homicides here. I'd like to keep it that way." He scowled. "You're out of your territory a bit, aren't you?"

"I am. I was asked down here by your sheriff, Hayes Carson. He actually does have a DB. I'm working the crime scene for him per his request through the Bexar County medical examiner's office, but I didn't bring enough supplies. I hope the hardware store can accommodate me. It's a long drive back to San Antonio when you're on a case."

"On a case?" Harley asked, confused.

"Yes, on a case," she said. "Unlike you, some of us are professionals who have real jobs."

"Do you know him?" Cash asked her.

She gave Harley a studied appraisal. "Not really. He came barreling up the steps and hit me with a door. He says he's a cowboy," she added in a confidential tone. "But just between us, I'm sure he's lying. He doesn't have a horse or a rope, he isn't wearing a cowboy hat or boots, he says he can't sing, and he thinks bulls roam around loose in hardware stores."

Harley stared at her with more mixed emotions than he'd felt in years.

Cash choked back a laugh. "Well, he actually is a

cowboy," Cash defended him. "He's Harley Fowler, Cy Parks's foreman on his cattle ranch."

"Imagine that!" she exclaimed. "What a blow to the image of Texas if some tourist walks in and sees him dressed like that!" She indicated Harley's attire with one slender hand. "They can't call us the cowboy capital of the world if we have people working cattle in baseball caps! We'll be disgraced!"

Cash was trying not to laugh. Harley looked as if he might explode.

"Better a horseless cowboy than a contractor with an attitude like yours!" Harley shot back, with glittery eyes. "I'm amazed that anybody around here would hire you to build something for them."

She gave him a superior look. "I don't build things. But I could if I wanted to."

"She really doesn't build things," Cash said. "Harley, this is Alice Mayfield Jones," he introduced. "She's a forensic investigator for the Bexar County medical examiner's office."

"She works with dead people?" Harley exclaimed, and moved back a step.

"Dead bodies," Alice returned, glaring at his obvious distaste. "DBs. And I'm damned good at my job. Ask him," she added, nodding toward Cash.

"She does have a reputation," Cash admitted. His dark eyes twinkled. "And a nickname. Old Jab-'Em-in-the-Liver Alice."

"You've been talking to Marc Brannon," she accused.

"You did help him solve a case, back when he was still a Texas Ranger," he pointed out.

"Now they've got this new guy, transferred up from Houston," she said on a sigh. "He's real hard going. No sense of humor." She gave him a wry look. "Kind of like you used to be, in the old days when you worked out of the San Antonio district attorney's office, Grier," she recalled. "A professional loner with a bad attitude."

"Oh, I've changed." He grinned. "A wife and child can turn the worst of us inside out."

She smiled. "No kidding? If I have time, I'd love to see that little girl everybody's talking about. Is she as pretty as her mama?"

He nodded. "Oh, yes. Every bit."

Harley pulled at his collar. "Could you stop talking about children, please?" he muttered. "I'll break out in hives."

"Allergic to small things, are you?" Alice chided.

"Allergic to the whole subject of marriage," he emphasized with a meaningful stare.

Her eyebrows arched. "I'm sorry, were you hoping I was going to ask you to marry me?" she replied pleasantly. "You're not bad-looking, I guess, but I have a very high standard for prospective bridegrooms. Frankly," she added with a quick appraisal, "if you were on sale in a groom shop, I can assure you that I wouldn't purchase you."

He stared at her as if he doubted his hearing. Cash Grier had to turn away. His face was going purple.

The hardware-store door opened and a tall, black-haired, taciturn man came out it. He frowned. "Jones? What the hell are you doing down here? They asked for Longfellow!"

She glared back. "Longfellow hid in the women's restroom and refused to come out," she said haughtily. "So they sent me. And why are you interested in Sheriff Carson's case? You're a fed."

Kilraven put his finger to his lips and looked around hastily to make sure nobody was listening. "I'm a policeman, working on the city force," he said curtly.

Alice held up both hands defensively. "Sorry! It's so hard to keep up with all these secrets!"

Kilraven glanced at his boss and back at Alice. "What secrets?"

"Well, there's the horseless cowboy there—" she pointed at Harley "—and the DB over on the Little Carmichael River..."

Kilraven's silver eyes widened. "On the river? I thought it was in town. Nobody told me!"

"I just did," Alice said. "But it's really a secret. I'm not supposed to tell anybody."

"I'm local law enforcement," Kilraven insisted. "You can tell me. Who is he?"

Alice gave him a bland look and propped a hand on her hip. "I only looked at him for two minutes before I realized I needed to get more investigative supplies. He's male and dead. He's got no ID, he's naked, and even his mother wouldn't recognize his face."

"Dental records..." Kilraven began.

"For those, you need identifiable teeth," Alice replied sweetly.

Harley was turning white.

She glanced at him. "Are you squeamish?" she asked hopefully. "Listen, I once examined this dead guy whose girlfriend caught him with a hooker. After she offed him, she cut off his… Where are you going?"

Harley was making a beeline for the interior of the hardware store.

"Bathroom, I imagine." Grier grinned at Kilraven, who chuckled.

"He works around cattle and he's squeamish?" Alice asked, delighted. "I'll bet he's a lot of fun when they round up the calves!"

"Not nice," Kilraven chided. "Everybody's got a weak spot, Jones. Even you."

"I have no weak spots," she assured him.

"No social life, either," Grier murmured. "I heard you tried to conduct a postmortem on a turkey in North Carolina during a murder investigation there."

"It met with fowl play," she said, straight-faced.

Both men chuckled.

"I have to get to work," she said, becoming serious. "This is a strange case. Nobody knows who this guy is or where he came from, and there was a serious attempt to make him unidentifiable. Even with DNA, when I can get a profile back from state—and don't hold your breath on the timetable—I don't know if we can identify him. If he has no criminal record, he won't be on file anywhere."

"At least we don't get many of these," Kilraven said quietly.

Jones smiled at him. "When are you coming back up to San Antonio?" she asked. "You solved the Pendleton kidnapping and helped wrap up the perps."

"Just a few loose ends to tie up," he said. He nodded at her and his boss. "I'll get back on patrol."

"Brady's wife made potato soup and real corn bread for lunch. Don't miss it."

"Not me, boss."

Alice stared after the handsome officer. "He's a dish. But isn't he overstaying his purpose down here?" she asked Cash.

He leaned down. "Winnie Sinclair works for the 911 center. Local gossip has it that he's sweet on her. That's why he's finding excuses not to leave."

Alice looked worried. "And he's dragging around a whole past that hardly anybody knows about. He's pretending it never happened."

"Maybe he has to."

She nodded. "It was bad. One of the worst cases I ever worked. Poor guy." She frowned. "They never solved it, you know. The perp is still out there, running around loose. It must have driven Kilraven and his brother, Jon Blackhawk, nuts, wondering if it was somebody they arrested, somebody with a grudge."

"Their father was an FBI agent in San Antonio, before he drank himself to death after the murders. Blackhawk still is," Cash replied thoughtfully. "Could have been a case any one of the three men worked, a perp getting even."

"It could," she agreed. "It must haunt the brothers. The guilt would be bad enough, but they wouldn't want to risk it happening again, to someone else they got involved with. They avoid women. Especially Kilraven."

"He wouldn't want to go through it again," Cash said.

"This Sinclair woman, how does she feel about Kilraven?"

Cash gave her a friendly smile. "I am not a gossip."

"Bull."

He laughed. "She's crazy about him. But she's very young."

"Age doesn't matter, in the long run," Alice said with a faraway look in her eyes. "At least, sometimes." She opened the door. "See you around, Grier."

"You, too, Jones."

She walked into the hardware store. There at the counter was Harley, pale and out of sorts. He glared at her.

She held up both hands. "I wasn't even graphic," she said defensively. "And God only knows how you manage to help with branding, with that stomach."

"I ate something that didn't agree with me," he said icily.

"In that case, you must not have a lot of friends…."

The clerk doubled over laughing.

"I do not eat people!" Harley muttered.

"I should hope not," she replied. "I mean, being a cannibal is much worse than being a gardener."

"I am not a gardener!"

Alice gave the clerk a sweet smile. "Do you have chalk and colored string?" she asked. "I also need double-A batteries for my digital camera and some antibacterial hand cleaner."

The clerk looked blank.

Harley grinned. He knew this clerk very well. Sadly, Alice didn't. "Hey, John, this is a real, honest-to-goodness crime scene investigator," he told the young man. "She works out of the medical examiner's office in San Antonio!"

Alice felt her stomach drop as she noted the bright fascination in the clerk's eyes. The clerk's whole face became animated. "You do, really? Hey, I watch all those CSI shows," he exclaimed. "I know about DNA profiles. I even know how to tell how long a body's been dead just by identifying the insects on it…!"

"You have a great day, Ms. Jones," Harley told Alice, over the clerk's exuberant monologue.

She glared at him. "Oh, thanks very much."

He tipped his bibbed cap at her. "See you, John," he told the clerk. Harley picked up his purchases, smiling with pure delight, and headed right out the front door.

The clerk waved an absent hand in his general direction, never taking his eyes off Alice. "Anyway, about those insects," he began enthusiastically.

Alice followed him around the store for her supplies, groaning inwardly as he kept talking. She never ran out of people who could tell her how to do her job these days, thanks to the proliferation of television shows on forensics. She tried to explain that most labs were understaffed, under-budgeted, and that lab results didn't come back in an hour, even for a department like hers, on the University of Texas campus, which had a national reputation for excellence. But the bug expert here was on a roll and he wasn't listening. She resigned herself to the lecture and forced a smile. Wouldn't do to make enemies here, not when she might be doing more business with him later. She was going to get even with that smug cowboy the next time she saw him, though.

THE RIVERBANK WAS spitting out law enforcement people. Alice groaned as she bent to the poor body and began to take measurements. She'd already had an accommodating young officer from the Jacobsville Police Department run yellow police tape all around the crime scene. That didn't stop people from stepping over it, however.

"You stop that," Alice muttered at two men wearing deputy sheriff uniforms. They both stopped with one foot in the air at the tone of her voice. "No tramping around on my crime scene! That yellow tape is to keep people *out*."

"Sorry," one murmured sheepishly, and they both went back on their side of the line. Alice pushed away a strand of sweaty hair with the back of a latex-gloved hand and muttered to herself. It was almost Christmas, but the weather had gone nuts and it was hot. She'd already taken off her wool jacket and replaced it with a lab coat, but her slacks were wool and she was burning up. Not to mention that this guy had been lying on the riverbank for at least a day and he was ripe. She had Vicks Salve under her nose, but it wasn't helping a lot.

For the hundredth time, she wondered why she'd ever chosen such a messy profession. But it was very satisfying when she could help catch a murderer, which she had many times over the years. Not that it substituted for a family. But most men she met were repelled by her profession. Sometimes she tried to keep it to herself. But inevitably there would be a movie or a TV show that would mention some forensic detail and Alice would hold forth on the misinformation she noted. Sometimes it was rather graphic, like with the vengeful cowboy in the hardware store.

Then there would be the forced smiles. The excuses. And so it went. Usually that happened before the end of the first date. Or at least the second.

"I'll bet I'm the only twenty-six-year-old virgin in the whole damned state of Texas," she muttered to herself.

"Excuse me?" one of the deputies, a woman, exclaimed with wide, shocked eyes.

"That's right, you just look at me as if I sprouted horns and a tail," she murmured as she worked. "I know I'm an anachronism."

"That's not what I meant," the deputy said, chuckling. "Listen, there are a lot of women our ages with that attitude. I don't want some unspeakable condition that I catch from a man who passes himself around like a dish of peanuts at a bar. And do you think they're going to tell you they've got something?"

Alice beamed. "I like you."

She chuckled. "Thanks. I think of it as being sensible." She lowered her voice. "See Kilraven over there?" she asked, drawing Alice's eyes to the arrival of another local cop—even if he really was a fed pretending to be one. "They say his brother, Jon Blackhawk, has never had a woman in his life. And we think we're prudes!"

Alice chuckled. "That's what I heard, too. Sensible man!"

"Very." The deputy was picking up every piece of paper, every cigarette butt she could find with latex gloves on, bagging them for Alice for evidence. "What about that old rag, Jones, think I should put it in a bag, too? Look at this little rusty spot."

Alice glanced at it, frowning. It was old, but there was a trace of something on it, something newer than the rag. "Yes," she said. "I think it's been here for a while, but that's new trace evidence on it. Careful not to touch the rusty-looking spot."

"Blood, isn't it?" She nodded.

"You're good," Alice said.

"I came down from Dallas P.D.," she said. "I got tired of big-city crime. Things are a little less hectic here. In fact, this is my first DB since I joined Sheriff Carson's department."

"That's a real change, I know," Alice said. "I work out of San Antonio. Not the quietest place in the world, especially on weekends."

Kilraven had walked right over the police tape and came up near the body.

"What do you think you're doing?" Alice exclaimed. "Kilraven…!"

"Look," he said, his keen silver eyes on the grass just under the dead man's right hand, which was clenched and depressed into the mud. "There's something white."

Alice followed his gaze. She didn't even see it at first. She'd moved so that it was in shadow. But when she shifted, the sunlight caught it. Paper. A tiny sliver of paper, just peeping out from under the dead man's thumb. She reached down with her gloved hand and brushed away the grass. There was a deep indentation in the soft, mushy soil, next to his hand; maybe a footprint.

"I need my camera before I move it," she said, holding out her hand. The deputy retrieved the big digital camera from its bag and handed it to Alice, who documented the find and recorded it on a graph of the crime scene. Then, returning the camera, she slid a pencil gently under the hand, moving it until she was able to see the paper. She reached into her kit for a pair of tweezers and tugged it carefully from his grasp.

"It's a tiny, folded piece of paper," she said, frowning. "And thank God it hasn't rained."

"Amen," Kilraven agreed, peering at the paper in her hand.

"Good eyes," she added with a grin.

He grinned back. "Lakota blood." He chuckled. "Tracking is in my genes. My great-great-grandfather was at Little Big Horn."

"I won't ask on which side," she said in a loud whisper.

"No need to be coy. He rode with Crazy Horse's band."

"Hey, I read about that," the deputy said. "Custer's guys were routed, they say."

"One of the Cheyenne people said later that a white officer was killed down at the river in the first charge," he said. "He said the officer was carried up to the last stand by his men, and after that the soldiers seemed to lose heart and didn't fight so hard. They found Custer's brother, Tom, and a couple of ranking officers from other units, including Custer's brother-in-law, with Custer. It could indicate that the chain of command changed several times. Makes sense, if you think about it. If there was a charge, Custer would have led it. Several historians think that Custer's unit made it into the river before the Cheyenne came flying into it after them. If Custer was killed early, he'd have been carried up to the last stand ridge—an enlisted guy, they'd have left there in the river."

"I never read that Custer got killed early in the fight," the deputy exclaimed.

"I've only ever seen the theory in one book—a warrior was interviewed who was on the Indian side of the fight, and he said he thought Custer was killed in the first charge," he mused. "The Indians' side of the story didn't get much attention until recent years. They said there were no surviving eyewitnesses. Bull! There were several tribes of eyewitnesses. It was just that nobody thought their stories were worth hearing just after the battle. Not the massacre," he added before the deputy could speak. "Massacres are when you kill unarmed people. Custer's men all had guns."

The deputy grinned. "Ever think of teaching history?"

"Teaching's too dangerous a profession. That's why I joined the police force instead." Kilraven chuckled.

"Great news for law enforcement," Alice said. "You have good eyes."

"You'd have seen it for yourself, Jones, eventually," he replied. "You're the best."

"Wow! Did you hear that? Take notes," Alice told the deputy. "The next time I get yelled at for not doing my job right, I'm quoting Kilraven."

"Would it help?" he asked.

She laughed. "They're still scared of you up in San Antonio," she said. "One of the old patrolmen, Jacobs, turns white when they mention your name. I understand the two of you had a little dustup?"

"I threw him into a fruit display at the local supermarket. Messy business. Did you know that blackberries leave purple stains on skin?" he added conversationally.

"I'm a forensic specialist," Alice reminded him. "Can I ask why you threw him into a fruit display?"

"We were working a robbery and he started making these remarks about fruit with one of the gay officers standing right beside me. The officer in question couldn't do anything without getting in trouble." He grinned. "Amazing, how attitudes change with a little gentle adjustment."

"Hey, Kilraven, what are you doing walking around on the crime scene?" Cash Grier called from the sidelines.

"Don't fuss at him," Alice called back. "He just spotted a crucial piece of evidence. You should give him an award!"

There were catcalls from all the officers present.

"I should get an award!" he muttered as he went to join his boss. "I never take days off or vacations!"

"That's because you don't have a social life, Kilraven," one of the officers joked.

Alice stood up, staring at the local law enforcement uniforms surrounding the crime scene tape. She recognized at least two cars from other jurisdictions. There was even a federal car out there! It wasn't unusual in a sleepy county like Jacobs for all officers who weren't busy to congregate around an event like this. It wasn't every day that you found a murder victim in your area. But a federal car for a local murder?

As she watched, Garon Grier and Jon Blackhawk of the San Antonio district FBI office climbed out of the BuCar—the FBI's term for a bureau car—and walked over the tape to join Alice.

"What have you found?" Grier asked.

She pursed her lips, glancing from the assistant director of the regional FBI office, Grier, to Special Agent Jon Blackhawk. What a contrast! Grier was blond and Blackhawk had long, jet-black hair tied in a ponytail. They were both tall and well-built without being flashy about it. Garon Grier, like his brother Cash, was married. Jon Blackhawk was unattached and available. Alice wished she was his type. He was every bit as good-looking as his half brother Kilraven.

"I found some bits and pieces of evidence, with the deputy's help. Your brother," she told Jon, "found this." She held up the piece of paper in an evidence bag. "Don't touch," she cautioned as both men peered in. "I'm not unfolding it until I can get it into my lab. I won't risk losing any trace evidence out here."

Blackhawk pulled out a pad and started taking notes. "Where was it?" he asked.

"Gripped in the dead man's fingers, out of sight. Why are you here?" she asked. "This is a local matter."

Blackhawk was cautious. "Not entirely," he said.

Kilraven joined them. He and Blackhawk exchanged uneasy glances.

"Okay. Something's going on that I can't be told about. It's okay." She held up a hand. "I'm used to being a mushroom. Kept in the dark and fed with…"

"Never mind," Garon told her. He softened it with a

smile. "We've had a tip. Nothing substantial. Just something that interests us about this case."

"And you can't tell me what the tip was?"

"We found a car in the river, farther down," Cash said quietly. "San Antonio plates."

"Maybe his?" Alice indicated the body.

"Maybe. We're running the plates now," Cash said.

"So, do you think he came down here on his own, or did somebody bring him in a trunk?" Alice mused.

The men chuckled. "You're good, Alice," Garon murmured.

"Of course I am!" she agreed. "Could you," she called to the female deputy, "get me some plaster of Paris out of my van, in the back? This may be a footprint where we found the piece of paper! Thanks."

She went back to work with a vengeance while two sets of brothers looked on with intent interest.

CHAPTER TWO

ALICE FELL INTO her bed at the local Jacobsville motel after a satisfying soak in the luxurious whirlpool bathtub. Amazing, she thought, to find such a high-ticket item in a motel in a small Texas town. She was told that film crews from Hollywood frequently chose Jacobs County as a location and that the owner of the motel wanted to keep them happy. It was certainly great news for Alice.

She'd never been so tired. The crime scene, they found, extended for a quarter of a mile down the river. The victim had fought for his life. There were scuff marks and blood trails all over the place. So much for her theory that he'd traveled to Jacobsville in the trunk of the car they'd found.

The question was, why had somebody brought a man down to Jacobsville to kill him? It made no sense.

She closed her eyes, trying to put herself in the shoes of the murderer. People usually killed for a handful of reasons. They killed deliberately out of jealousy, anger or greed. Sometimes they killed accidentally. Often, it was an impulse that led to a death, or a series of acts that pushed a person over the edge. All too often, it was drugs or alcohol that robbed someone of impulse control, and that led inexorably to murder.

Few people went into an argument or a fight intending to kill someone. But it wasn't as if you could take it back even seconds after a human life expired. There were thousands of young people in prison who would have given anything to relive a single incident where they'd made a bad choice. Families suffered for those choices, along with their children. So often, it was easy to overlook the fact that even murderers had families, often decent, law-abiding families that agonized over what their loved one had done and paid the price along with them.

Alice rolled over, restlessly. Her job haunted her from time to time. Along with the coroner, and the investigating officers, she was the last voice of the deceased. She spoke for them, by gathering enough evidence to bring the killer to trial. It was a holy grail. She took her duties seriously. But she also had to live with the results of the murderer's lack of control. It was never pleasant to see a dead body. Some were in far worse conditions than others. She carried those memories as certainly as the family of the deceased carried them.

Early on, she'd learned that she couldn't let herself become emotionally involved with the victims. If she started crying, she'd never stop, and she wouldn't be effective in her line of work.

She found a happy medium in being the life of the party at crime scenes. It diverted her from the misery of her surroundings and, on occasion, helped the crime scene detectives cope as well. One reporter, a rookie, had given her a hard time because of her attitude. She'd invited him to her office for a close-up look at the world of a real forensic investigator.

The reporter had arrived expecting the corpse, always tastefully displayed, to be situated in the tidy, high-tech surroundings that television crime shows had accustomed him to seeing.

Instead, Alice pulled the sheet from a drowning victim who'd been in the water three days.

She never saw the reporter again. Local cops who recounted the story, always with choked-back laughter, told her that he'd turned in his camera the same day and voiced an ambition to go into real estate.

Just as well, she thought. The real thing was pretty unpleasant. Television didn't give you the true picture, because there was no such thing as Smell-O-Vision. She could recall times when she'd gone through a whole jar of Vicks Salve trying to work on a drowning victim like the one she'd shown the critical member of the Fourth Estate.

She rolled over again. She couldn't get her mind to shut down long enough to allow for sleep. She was reviewing the meager facts she'd uncovered at the crime scene, trying to make some sort of sense out of it. Why would somebody drive a murder victim out of the city to kill him? Maybe because he didn't know he was going to become a murder victim. Maybe he got in the car voluntarily.

Good point, she thought. But it didn't explain the crime. Heat of passion wouldn't cover this one. It was too deliberate. The perp meant to hide evidence. And he had.

She sighed. She wished she'd become a detective instead of a forensic specialist. It must be more fun solving crimes than being knee-deep in bodies. And prospective dates wouldn't look at you from a safe distance with that expression of utter distaste, like that gardener in the hardware store this afternoon.

What had Grier called him, Fowler? Harley Fowler, that was it. Not a bad-looking man. He had a familiar face. Alice wondered why. She was sure she'd never seen him before today. She was sure she'd remember somebody that disagreeable.

Maybe he resembled somebody she knew. That was possible. Fowler. Fowler. No. It didn't ring any bells. She'd have to let her mind brood on it for a couple of days. Sometimes that's all it took to solve such puzzles— background working of the subconscious. She chuckled to herself. *Background workings*, she thought, *will save me yet.*

AFTER HOURS OF almost-sleep, she got up, dressed and went back to the crime scene. It was quiet, now, without the presence of almost every uniformed officer in the county. The body was lying in the local funeral home, waiting for transport to the medical examiner's office in San Antonio. Alice had driven her evidence up to San Antonio, to the crime lab, and turned it over to the trace evidence people, specifically Longfellow.

She'd entrusted Longfellow with the precious piece of paper, which might yield dramatic evidence, once unfolded. There had clearly been writing on it. The dead man had grasped it tight in his hand while he was being killed, and had managed to conceal it from his killer. It must have something on it that he was desperate to preserve. Amazing. She wanted to know what it was. Tomorrow, she promised herself, their best trace evidence specialist, Longfellow, would have that paper turned every which way but loose in her lab, and she'd find answers for Alice. She was one of the best CSI people Alice had ever worked with. When Alice drove right back down to Jacobsville, she knew she'd have answers from the lab soon.

Restless, she looked around at the lonely landscape, bare in winter. The local police were canvassing the surrounding area for anyone who'd seen something unusual in the past few days, or who'd noticed an out-of-town car around the river.

Alice paced the riverbank, a lonely figure in a neat white sweatshirt with blue jeans, staring out across the ripples of the water while her sneakers tried to sink into the damp sand. It was cooler today, in the fifties, about normal for a December day in south Texas.

Sometimes she could think better when she was alone at the crime scene. Today wasn't one of those days. She was acutely aware of her aloneness. It was worse now, after the death of her father a month ago. He was her last living relative. He'd been a banker back in Tennessee, where she'd taken courses in forensics. The family was from Floresville, just down the road from San Antonio. But her parents had moved away to Tennessee when she was in her last year of high school, and that had been a wrench. Alice had a crush on a boy in her class, but the move killed any hope of a relationship. She really had been a late bloomer, preferring to hang out in the biology lab rather than think about dating. Amoeba under the microscope were so much more interesting.

Alice had left home soon after her mother's death, the year she started college. Her mother had been a live wire, a happy and well-adjusted woman who could do almost anything around the house, especially cook. She despaired of Alice, her only child, who watched endless reruns of the old TV show *Quincy*, about a medical examiner, along with archaic *Perry Mason* episodes. Long before it was popular, Alice had dreamed of being a crime scene technician.

She'd been an ace at biology in high school. Her science teachers had encouraged her, delighting in her bright enthusiasm. One of them had recommended her to a colleague at the University of Texas campus in San Antonio, who'd steered her into a science major and helped her find local scholarships to supplement the small amount her father could afford for her. It had been an uphill climb to get that degree, and to add to it with courses from far-flung universities when time and money permitted; one being courses in forensic anthropology at the University of Tennessee in Knoxville. In between, she'd slogged away with other techs at one crime scene after another, gaining experience.

Once, in her haste to finish gathering evidence, due to a rare prospective date, she'd slipped up and mislabeled blood evidence. That had cost the prosecution staff a conviction. It had been a sobering experience for Alice, especially when the suspect went out and killed a young boy before being rearrested. Alice felt responsible for that boy's death. She never forgot how haste had put the nails in his coffin, and she never slipped up again. She gained a reputation for being precise and meticulous in evidence-gathering. And she never went home early again. Alice was almost always the last person to leave the lab, or the crime scene, at the end of the day.

A revved-up engine caught her attention. She turned as a carload of young boys pulled up beside her white van at the river's edge.

"Lookie there, a lonely lady!" one of them called. "Ain't she purty?"

"Shore is! Hey, pretty thing, you like younger men? We can make you happy!"

"You bet!" Another one laughed.

"Hey, lady, you feel like a party?!" another one cat-called.

Alice glared. "No, I don't feel like a party. Take a hike!" She turned back to her contemplation of the river, hoping they'd give up and leave.

"Aww, that ain't no way to treat prospective boy-friends!" one yelled back. "Come on up here and lie down, lady. We want to talk to you!"

More raucous laughter echoed out of the car.

So much for patience. She was in no mood for teenagers acting out. She pulled out the pad and pen she always carried in her back pocket and walked up the bank and around to the back of their car. She wrote down the license plate number without being obvious about it. She'd call in a harassment call and let local law enforcement help her out. But even as she thought about it, she hesitated. There had to be a better way to handle this bunch of loonies without involving the law. She was overreacting. They were just teenagers, after all. Inspiration struck as she reemerged at the driver's side of the car.

She ruffled her hair and moved closer to the tow-headed young driver. She leaned down. "I like your tires," she drawled with a wide grin. "They're real nice. And wide. And they have treads. I *like* treads." She wiggled her eyebrows at him. "You like treads?"

He stared at her. The silly expression went into eclipse. "Treads?" His voice sounded squeaky. He tried again. "Tire…treads?"

"Yeah. Tire treads." She stuck her tongue in and out and grinned again. "I *reeaaally* like tire treads."

He was trying to pretend that he wasn't talking to a lunatic. "Uh. You do. Really."

She was enjoying herself now. The other boys seemed even more confused than the driver did. They were all staring at her. Nobody was laughing.

She frowned. "No, you don't like treads. You're just humoring me. Okay. If you don't like treads, you might like what I got in the truck," she said, lowering her voice. She jerked her head toward the van.

He cleared his throat. "I might like what you got in the truck," he parroted.

She nodded, grinning, widening her eyes until the whites almost gleamed. She leaned forward. "I got bodies in there!" she said in a stage whisper and levered her eyes wide-open. "Real dead bodies! Want to see?"

The driver gaped at her. Then he exclaimed, "Dead… bod…. Oh, Good Lord, no!"

He jerked back from her, slammed his foot down on the accelerator, and spun sand like dust as he roared back out onto the asphalt and left a rubber trail behind him.

She shook her head. "Was it something I said?" she asked a nearby bush.

She burst out laughing. She really did need a vacation, she told herself.

HARLEY FOWLER SAW the van sitting on the side of the road as he moved a handful of steers from one pasture to another. With the help of Bob, Cy Parks's veteran cattle dog, he put the little steers into their new area and closed the gate behind him. A carload of boys roared up beside the van and got noisy. They were obviously hassling the crime scene woman. Harley recognized her van.

His pale blue eyes narrowed and began to glitter. He didn't like a gang of boys trying to intimidate a lone woman. He reached into his saddlebag and pulled out his gunbelt, stepping down out of the saddle to strap it on. He tied the horse to a bar of the gate and motioned Bob to stay. Harley strolled off toward the van.

He didn't think he'd have to use the pistol, of course. The threat of it would be more than enough. But if any of the boys decided to have a go at him, he could put them down with his fists. He'd learned a lot from Eb Scott and the local mercs. He didn't need a gun to enforce his authority. But if the sight of it made the gang of boys a little more likely to leave without trouble, that was all right, too.

He moved into sight just at the back of Alice's van. She was leaning over the driver's side of the car. He couldn't hear what she said, but he could certainly hear what the boy exclaimed as he roared out onto the highway and took off.

Alice was talking to a bush.

Harley stared at her with confusion.

Alice sensed that she was no longer alone, and she turned. She blinked. "Have you been there long?" she asked hesitantly.

"Just long enough to see the Happy Teenager Gang take a powder," he replied. "Oh, and to hear you asking a bush about why they left." His eyes twinkled. "Talk to bushes a lot in your line of work, do you?"

She was studying him curiously, especially the low-slung pistol in its holster. "You on your way to a gunfight and just stopped by to say hello?"

"I was moving steers," he replied. "I heard the teenagers giving you a hard time and came to see if you needed any help. Obviously not."

"Were you going to offer to shoot them for me?" she asked.

He chuckled. "Never had to shoot any kids," he said with emphasis.

"You've shot other sorts of people?"

"One or two," he said pleasantly, but this time he didn't smile.

She felt chills go down her spine. If her livelihood made him queasy, the way he looked wearing that side-arm made her feel the same way. He wasn't the easy-going cowboy she'd met in town the day before. He reminded her oddly of Cash Grier, for reasons she couldn't put into words. There was cold steel in this man. He had the self-confidence of a man who'd been tested under fire. It was unusual, in a modern man. Unless, she considered, he'd been in the military, or some paramilitary unit.

"I don't shoot women," he said when she hesitated.

"Good thing," she replied absently. "I don't have any bandages."

He moved closer. She seemed shaken. He scowled. "You okay?"

She shifted uneasily. "I guess so."

"Mind telling me how you got them to leave so quickly?"

"Oh. That. I just asked if they'd like to see the dead bodies in my van."

He blinked. He was sure he hadn't heard her right. "You asked if…?" he prompted.

She sighed. "I guess it was a little over the top. I was going to call Hayes Carson and have him come out and save me, but it seemed a bit much for a little catcalling."

He didn't smile. "Let me tell you something. A little catcalling, if they get away with it, can lead to a little harassment, and if they get away with that, it can lead to a little assault, even if drugs or alcohol aren't involved. Boys need limits, especially at that age. You should have called it in and let Hayes Carson come out here and scare the hell out of them."

"Well, aren't you the voice of experience!"

"I should be," he replied. "When I was sixteen, an older boy hassled a girl in our class repeatedly on campus after school and made fun of me when I objected to it. A few weeks later, after she'd tried and failed to get somebody to do something about him, he assaulted her."

She let out a whistle. "Heavy stuff."

"Yes, and the teacher who thought I was overreacting when I told him was later disciplined for his lack of response," he added coldly.

"We live in difficult times," she said.

"Count on it."

She glanced in the direction the car had gone. "I still have the license plate number," she murmured.

"Give it to Hayes and tell him what happened," he encouraged her. "Even if you don't press charges, he'll keep an eye on them. Just in case."

She studied his face. "You liked that girl."

"Yes. She was sweet and kind-natured. She…"

She moved a little closer. "She…?"

"She killed herself," he said tightly. "She was very religious. She couldn't live with what happened, especially after she had to testify to it in court and everyone knew."

"They seal those files…" she began.

"Get real," he shot back. "It happened in a small town just outside San Antonio, not much bigger than Jacobsville. I was living there temporarily with a nice older couple and going to school with her when it happened. The people who sat on the jury and in the courtroom were all local. They knew her."

"Oh," she said softly. "I'm sorry."

He nodded.

"How long did the boy get?"

"He was a juvenile," he said heavily. "He was under eighteen when it happened. He stayed in detention until he was twenty-one and they turned him loose."

"Pity."

"Yes." He shook himself as if the memory had taken him over and he wanted to be free of it. "I never heard anything about him after that. I hope he didn't prosper."

"Was he sorry, do you think?"

He laughed coldly. "Sorry he got caught, yes."

"I've seen that sort in court," she replied, her eyes darkening with the memory. "Cocky and self-centered, contemptuous of everybody around them. Especially people in power."

"Power corrupts," he began.

"And absolute power corrupts absolutely," she finished for him. "Lord Acton," she cited belatedly.

"Smart gent." He nodded toward the river. "Any new thoughts on the crime scene?"

She shook her head. "I like to go there alone and think. Sometimes I get ideas. I still can't figure how he died here, when he was from San Antonio, unless he came voluntarily with someone and didn't know they were going to kill him when they arrived."

"Or he came down here to see somebody," he returned, "and was ambushed."

"Wow," she said softly, turning to face him. "You're good."

There was a faint, ruddy color on his high cheekbones. "Thanks."

"No, I mean it," she said when she saw his expression. "That wasn't sarcasm."

He relaxed a little.

"We got off to a bad start, and it's my fault," Alice admitted. "Dead bodies make me nervous. I'm okay once I get started documenting things. It's the first sight of it that upsets me. You caught me at a bad time, at the hardware store. I didn't mean to embarrass you."

"Nothing embarrasses me," he said easily.

"I'm sorry, just the same."

He relaxed a little more.

She frowned as she studied his handsome face. He really was good-looking. "You look so familiar to me," she said. "I can't understand why. I've never met you before."

"They say we all have a doppelgänger," he mused. "Someone who looks just like us."

"Maybe that's it," she agreed. "San Antonio is a big city, for all its small-town atmosphere. We've got a lot of people. You must resemble someone I've seen."

"Probably."

She looked again at the crime scene. "I hope I can get enough evidence to help convict somebody of this. It was a really brutal murder. I don't like to think of people who can do things like that being loose in society."

He was watching her, adding up her nice figure and her odd personality. She was unique. He liked her. He wasn't admitting it, of course.

"How did you get into forensic work?" he asked. "Was it all those crime shows on TV?"

"It was the *Quincy* series," she confessed. "I watched reruns of it on TV when I was a kid. It fascinated me.

I liked him, too, but it was the work that caught my attention. He was such an advocate for the victims." Her eyes became soft with reminiscence. "I remember when evidence I collected solved a crime. It was my first real case. The parents of the victim came over and hugged me after the prosecutor pointed me out to them. I always went to the sentencing if I could get away, in cases I worked. That was the first time I realized how important my work was." She grinned wickedly. "The convicted gave me the finger on his way out of the courtroom with a sheriff's deputy. I grinned at him. Felt good. Really good."

He laughed. It was a new sound, and she liked it.

"Does that make me less spooky?" she asked, moving a step closer.

"Yes, it does."

"You think I'm, you know, normal?"

"Nobody's really normal. But I know what you mean," he said, and he smiled at her, a genuine smile. "Yes, I think you're okay."

She cocked her head up at him and her blue eyes twinkled. "Would you believe that extraordinarily handsome Hollywood movie stars actually call me up for dates?"

"Do they, really?" he drawled.

"No, but doesn't it sound exciting?"

He laughed again.

She moved another step closer. "What I said, about not purchasing you if you were on sale in a groom shop... I didn't really mean it. There's a nice ring in that jewelry shop in Jacobsville," she said dreamily. "A man's wedding ring." She peered up through her lashes. "I could buy it for you."

He pursed his lips. "You could?"

"Yes. And I noticed that there's a minister at that Methodist Church. Are you Methodist?"

"Not really."

"Neither am I. Well, there's a justice of the peace in the courthouse. She marries people."

He was just listening now. His eyes were wide.

"If you liked the ring, and if it fit, we could talk to the justice of the peace. They also have licenses."

He pursed his lips again. "Whoa," he said after a minute. "I only met you yesterday."

"I know." She blinked. "What does that have to do with getting married?"

"I don't know you."

"Oh. Okay. I'm twenty-six. I still have most of my own teeth." She displayed them. "I'm healthy and athletic, I like to knit but I can hunt, too, and I have guns. I don't like spinach, but I love liver and onions. Oh, and I'm a virgin." She smiled broadly.

He was breathless by this time. He stared at her intently.

"It's true," she added when he didn't comment. She scowled. "Well, I don't like diseases and you can't look at a man and tell if he has one." She hesitated. Frowned worriedly. "You don't have any...?"

"No, I don't have any diseases," he said shortly. "I'm fastidious about women."

"What a relief!" she said with a huge sigh. "Well, that covers all the basics." Her blue eyes smiled up at him and she batted her long black eyelashes. "So when do we see the justice of the peace?"

"Not today," he replied. "I'm washing Bob."

"Bob?"

He pointed toward the cattle dog, who was still sitting at the pasture gate. He whistled. Bob came running up to him, wagging her long, silky tail and hassling. She looked as if she was always smiling.

"Hi, Bob," Alice said softly, and bent to offer a hand, which Bob smelled. Then Alice stroked the silky head. "Nice boy."

"Girl," he corrected. "Bob's a girl."

She blinked at him.

"Mr. Parks said if Johnny Cash could have a boy named Sue, he could have a girl dog named Bob."

"He's got a point," she agreed. She ruffled Bob's fur affectionately. "You're a beaut, Bob," she told the dog.

"She really is. Best cattle dog in the business, and she can get into places in the brush that we can't, on horseback, to flush out strays."

"Do you come from a ranching family?" she asked absently as she stroked the dog.

"Actually I didn't know much about cattle when I went to work for Mr. Parks. He had one of his men train me."

"Wow. Nice guy."

"He is. Dangerous, but nice."

She lifted her head at the use of the word and frowned slightly. "Dangerous?"

"Do you know anything about Eb Scott and his outfit?"

"The mercenary." She nodded. "We all know about his training camp down here. A couple of our officers use his firing range. He made it available to everyone in law enforcement. He's got friends in our department."

"Well, he and Mr. Parks and Dr. Micah Steele were part of a group who used to make their living as mercenaries."

"I remember now," she exclaimed. "There was a shoot-out with some of that drug lord Lopez's men a few years ago!"

"Yes. I was in it."

She let out a breath. "Brave man, to go up against those bozos. They carry automatic weapons."

"I noticed." That was said with a droll expression worth a hundred words.

She searched his eyes with quiet respect. "Now, I really want to see the justice of the peace. I'd be safe anywhere."

He laughed. "I'm not that easy. You haven't even brought me flowers, or asked me out to a nice restaurant."

"Oh, dear."

"What?"

"I don't get paid until Friday, and I'm broke," she said sorrowfully. She made a face. "Well, maybe next week? Or we could go Dutch…"

He chuckled with pure delight. "I'm broke, too."

"So, next week?"

"We'll talk about it."

She grinned. "Okay."

"Better get your van going," he said, holding out a palm-up hand and looking up. "We're going to get a rain shower. You could be stuck in that soft sand when it gets wet."

"I could. See you."

"See you."

She took off running for the van. Life was looking up, she thought happily.

CHAPTER THREE

HARLEY WENT BACK to the ranch house with Bob racing beside his horse. He felt exhilarated for the first time in years. Usually he got emotionally involved with girls who were already crazy about some other man. He was the comforting shoulder, the listening ear. But Alice Jones seemed to really like him.

Of course, there was her profession. He felt cold when he thought about her hands working on dead tissue. That was a barrier he'd have to find some way to get past. Maybe by concentrating on what a cute woman she was.

Cy Parks was outside, looking over a bunch of young bulls in the corral. He looked up when Harley dismounted.

"What do you think, Harley?" he asked, nodding toward several very trim young Santa Gertrudis bulls.

"Nice," he said. "These the ones you bought at the auction we went to back in October? Gosh, they've grown!"

He nodded. "They are. I brought them in to show to J. D. Langley. He's looking for some young bulls for his own herd. I thought I'd sell him a couple of these. Good thing I didn't have to send them back."

Harley chuckled. "Good thing, for the seller. I remember the lot we sent back last year. I had to help you deliver them."

"Yes, I remember," Cy replied. "He slugged you and I slugged him."

Harley resisted a flush. It made him feel good, that Mr. Parks liked him enough to defend him. He could hardly recall his father. It had been years since they'd had any contact at all. He felt a little funny recalling how he'd lied to his boss about his family, claiming that his mother could help brand cattle and his father was a mechanic. He'd gone to live with an older couple he knew after a fight with his real folks. It was a small ranch they owned, but only the wife lived on it. Harley had stayed in town with the husband at his mechanic's shop most of the time. He hadn't been interested in cattle at the time. Now, they were his life and Mr. Parks had taken the place of his father, although Harley had never put it into words. Someday, he guessed, he was going to have to tell his boss the truth about himself. But not today.

"Have any trouble settling the steers in their new pasture?" Cy asked.

"None at all. The forensic lady was out at the river."

"Alice Jones?"

"Yes. She said sometimes she likes to look around crime scenes alone. She gets impressions." He smiled. "I helped her with an idea about how the murder was committed."

Parks looked at him and smiled. "You've got a good brain, Harley."

He grinned. "Thanks."

"So what was your idea?"

"Maybe the victim was here to see somebody and got ambushed."

Parks's expression became solemn. "That's an interesting theory. If she doesn't share it with Hayes Carson, you should. There may be somebody local involved in all this."

"That's not a comforting thought."

"I know." He frowned as he noted the gun and holster Harley was wearing. "Did we have a gunfight and I wasn't invited?"

"This?" Harley fingered the butt of the gun. "Oh. No! There were some local boys trying to harass Alice. I strapped it on for effect and went to help her, but she'd already sent them running."

"Threatened to call the cops, huh?" he asked pleasantly.

"She invited them to her van to look at bodies," he said, chuckling. "They left tread marks on the highway."

He grinned back. "Well! Sounds like she has a handle on taking care of herself."

"Yes. But we all need a little backup, from time to time," Harley said.

Cy put a hand on Harley's shoulder. "You were mine, that night we had the shoot-out with the drug dealers. You're a good man under fire."

"Thanks," Harley said, flushing a little with the praise. "You'll never know how I felt, when you said that, after we got home."

"Maybe I do. See about that cattle truck, will you? I think it's misfiring again, and you're the best mechanic we've got."

"I'll do it. Just don't tell Buddy you meant it," he pleaded. "He's supposed to be the mechanic."

"Supposed to be is right," Cy huffed. "But I guess you've got a point. Try to tell him, in a nice way, that he needs to check the spark plugs."

"You could tell him," Harley began.

"Not the way you can. If I tell him, he'll quit." He grimaced. "Already lost one mechanic that way this year. Can't afford to lose another. You do it."

Harley laughed. "Okay. I'll find a way."

"You always do. Don't know what I'd do without you, Harley. You're an asset as a foreman." He studied the younger man quietly. "I never asked where you came from. You said you knew cattle, but you really didn't. You learned by watching, until I hooked you up with old Cal and let him tutor you. I always respected the effort you put in, to learn the cattle business. But you're still as mysterious as you were the day you turned up."

"Sometimes it's better to look ahead, and not backward," Harley replied.

Parks smiled. "Enough said. See you later."

"Sure."

He walked off toward the house where his young wife, Lisa, was waiting with one preschool-aged boy and one infant boy in her arms. Of all the people Harley would never have expected to marry, Mr. Parks was first on his list. The rancher had been reclusive, hard to get along with and, frankly, bad company. Lisa had changed him. Now, it was impossible to think of him as anything except a family man. Marriage had mellowed him.

Harley thought about what Parks had said, about how mysterious he was. Maybe Mr. Parks thought he was running from the law. That was a real joke. Harley was running from his family. He'd had it up to his neck with monied circles and important people and parents who thought position was everything. They'd argued heatedly one summer several years ago, when Harley was sixteen, about Harley's place in the family and his lack of interest in their social life. He'd walked out.

He had a friend whose aunt and uncle owned a small ranch and had a mechanic's shop in Floresville. He'd taken Harley down there and they'd invited him to move in. He'd had his school files transferred to the nearest high school and he'd started his life over. His parents had objected, but they hadn't tried to force him to come back home. He graduated and went into the Army. But, just after he returned to Texas following his release from the Army, he went to see his parents and saw that nothing had changed at all. He was expected to do his part for the family by helping win friends and influencing the right people. Harley had left that very night, paid cash for a very old beat-up pickup truck and turned himself into a vagabond cowhand looking for work.

He'd gone by to see the elderly couple he'd lived with during his last year of high school, but the woman had died, the ranch had been sold and the mechanic had moved to Dallas. Discouraged, Harley had been driving through Jacobsville looking for a likely place to hire on when he'd seen cowboys working cattle beside the road. He'd talked to them and heard that Cy Parks was hiring. The rest was history.

He knew that people wondered about him. He kept his silence. It was new and pleasant to be accepted at face value, to have people look at him for who he was and what he knew how to do rather than at his background. He was happy in Jacobsville.

He did wonder sometimes if his people missed him. He read about them in the society columns. There had been a big political dustup just recently and a landslide victory for a friend of his father's. That had caught his attention. But it hadn't prompted him to try to mend fences. Years had passed since his sudden exodus from San Antonio, but it was still too soon for that. No, he liked being just plain Harley Fowler, cowboy. He wasn't risking his hard-won place in Jacobsville for anything.

ALICE WAITED FOR Hayes Carson in his office, frowning as she looked around. Wanted posters. Reams of paperwork. A computer that was obsolete, paired with a printer that was even more obsolete. An old IBM Selectric typewriter. A battered metal wastebasket that looked as if it got kicked fairly often. A CB unit. She shook her head. There wasn't one photograph anywhere in the room, except for a framed one of Hayes's father, Dallas, who'd been sheriff before him. Nothing personal.

Hayes walked in, reading a sheet of paper.

"You really travel light, don't you?" Alice mused.

He looked up, surprised. "Why do you say that?"

"This is the most impersonal office I've ever walked into. Wait." She held up a hand. "I take that back. Jon Blackhawk's office is worse. He doesn't even have a photograph in his."

"My dad would haunt me if I removed his." He chuckled, sitting down behind the desk.

"Heard anything from the feds?"

"Yes. They got a report back on the car. It was reported missing by a woman who works for a San Antonio politician yesterday. She has no idea who took it."

"Damn." She sighed and leaned back. "Well, Longfellow's working on that piece of paper I found at the crime scene and we may get something from the cast I made of the footprint. We did find faint sole markings, from a sneaker. FBI lab has the cast. They'll track down which company made the shoe and try to trace where it was sold."

"That's a damned long shot."

"Hey, they've solved crimes from chips of paint."

"I guess so."

She was deep in thought. "Odd, how that paper was pushed into the dirt under his hand."

"Somebody stepped on it," Hayes reminded her.

"No." Her eyes narrowed. "It was clenched in the victim's hand and hidden under it."

Hayes frowned. "Maybe the victim was keeping it hidden deliberately?"

She nodded. "Like, maybe he knew he was going to die and wanted to leave a clue that might bring his killer to justice."

Hayes chuckled. "Jones, you watch too many crime dramas on TV."

"Actually, to hear the clerk at the hardware tell it I don't watch enough," she sighed. "I got a ten-minute lecture on forensic entomology while he hunted up some supplies I needed."

"Bug forensics?" he asked.

She nodded. "You can tell time of death by insect activity. I've actually taken courses on it. And I've solved at least one murder with the help of a bug expert." She pushed back a stray wisp of dark hair. "But what's really interesting, Carson, is teeth."

He frowned. "Teeth?"

She nodded. "Dentition. You can tell so much about a DB from its teeth, especially if there are dental records available. For example, there's Carabelli's cusp, which is most frequently found in people of European ancestry. Then there's the Uto-Aztecan upper premolar with a bulging buccal cusp, which is found only in Native Americans. You can identify Asian ancestry in shovel-shaped incisors... Well, anyway, your ancestry, even the story of your life, is in your teeth. Your diet, your age..."

"Whether you got in bar fights," he interrupted.

She laughed. "Missing some teeth, are we?"

"Only a couple," he said easily. "I've calmed right down in my old age."

"You and Kilraven," she agreed dubiously.

He laughed. "Not that yahoo," he corrected. "Kilraven will never calm down, and you can quote me."

"He might, if he can ever slay his demons." She frowned thoughtfully and narrowed her eyes. "We have a lot of law enforcement down here that works in San Antonio." She was thinking out loud. "There's Garon Grier, the assistant SAC in the San Antonio field office. There's Rick Marquez, who works as a detective for San Antonio P.D. And then there's Kilraven."

"You trying to say something?" he asked.

She shook her head. "I'm linking unconnected facts.

Sometimes it helps. Okay, here goes. A guy comes down here from San Antonio and gets whacked. He's driving somebody else's stolen car. He's messed up so badly that his own mother couldn't identify him. Whoever killed him didn't want him ID'd."

"Lots of reasons for that, maybe."

"Maybe. Hear me out. I'm doing pattern associations." She got up, locked her hands behind her waist, and started pacing, tossing out thoughts as they presented themselves. "Of all those law enforcement people, Kilraven's been the most conspicuous in San Antonio lately. He was with his brother, Jon, when they tried to solve the kidnapping of Gracie Marsh, Jason Pendleton's stepsister..."

"Pendleton's wife, now," he interrupted with a grin.

She returned it. "He was also connected with the rescue of Rodrigo Ramirez, the DEA agent kidnapping victim whose wife, Glory, was an assistant D.A. in San Antonio."

Hayes leaned back in his chair. "That wasn't made public, any of it."

She nodded absently.

"Rick Marquez has been pretty visible, too," he pointed out. He frowned. "Wasn't Rick trying to convince Kilraven to let him reopen that murder case that involved his family?"

"Come to think of it, yes," she replied, stopping in front of the desk. "Kilraven refused. He said it would only resurrect all the pain, and the media would dine out on it. He and Jon both refused. They figured it was a random crime and the perp was long gone."

"But that wasn't the end of it."

"No," she said. "Marquez refused to quit. He promised to do his work on the QT and not reveal a word of it to anybody except the detective he brought in to help him sort through the old files." She grimaced. "But the investigation went nowhere. Less than a week into their project, Marquez and his fellow detective were told to drop the investigation."

Hayes pursed his lips. "Now isn't that interesting?"

"There's more," she said. "Marquez and the detective went to the D.A. and promised to get enough evidence to reopen the case if they were allowed to continue. The D.A. said to let him talk to a few people. The very next week, the detective who was working with Marquez on the case was suddenly pulled off Homicide and sent back to the uniformed division as a patrol sergeant. And Marquez was told politely to keep his nose out of the matter and not to pursue it any further."

Hayes was frowning now. "You know, it sounds very much as if somebody high up doesn't want that case reopened. And I have to ask why?"

She nodded. "Somebody is afraid the case may be solved. If I'm guessing right, somebody with an enormous amount of power in government."

"And we both know what happens when power is abused," Hayes said with a scowl. "Years ago, when I was still a deputy sheriff, one of my fellow deputies— a new recruit—decided on his own to investigate rumors of a house of prostitution being run out of a local motel. Like a lamb, he went to the county council and brought it up in an open meeting."

Alice grimaced, because she knew from long experience what most likely happened after that. "Poor guy!"

"Well, after he was fired and run out of town," Hayes said, "I was called in and told that I was not to involve myself in that case, if I wanted to continue as a deputy sheriff in this county. I'd made the comment that no law officer should be fired for doing his job, you see."

"What did you do?" she asked, because she knew Hayes. He wasn't the sort of person to take a threat like that lying down.

"Ran for sheriff and won," he said simply. He grinned. "Turns out the head of the county council was getting kickbacks from the pimp. I found out, got the evidence and called a reporter I knew in San Antonio."

"That reporter?" she exclaimed. "He got a Pulitzer Prize for the story! My gosh, Hayes, the head of the county council went to prison! But it was for more than corruption…"

"He and the pimp also ran a modest drug distribution ring," he interrupted. "He'll be going up before the parole board in a few months. I plan to attend the hearing." He smiled. "I do so enjoy these little informal board meetings."

"Ouch."

"People who go through life making their money primarily through dishonest dealings don't usually reform," he said quietly. "It's a basic character trait that no amount of well-meaning rehabilitation can reverse."

"We live among some very unsavory people."

"Yes. That's why we have law enforcement. I might

add, that the law enforcement on the county level here is exceptional."

She snarled at him. He just grinned.

"What's your next move?" she asked.

"I'm not making one until I know what's in that note. Shouldn't your assistant have something by now, even if it's only the text of the message?"

"She should." Alice pulled out her cell phone and called her office. "But I'm probably way off base about Kilraven's involvement in this. Maybe the victim just ticked off the wrong people and paid for it. Maybe he had unpaid drug bills or something."

"That's always a possibility," Hayes had to agree.

The phone rang and rang. Finally it was answered. "Crime lab, Longfellow speaking."

"Did you know that you have the surname of a famous poet?" Alice teased.

The other woman was all business, all the time, and she didn't get jokes. "Yes. I'm a far-removed distant cousin of the poet, in fact. You want to know about your scrap of paper, I suppose? It's much too early for any analysis of the paper or ink…"

"The writing, Longfellow, the writing," Alice interrupted.

"As I said, it's too early in the analysis. We'd need a sample to compare, first, and then we'd need a handwriting expert…"

"But what does the message *say*?" Alice blurted out impatiently. Honest to God, the other woman was so ponderously slow sometimes!

"Oh, that. Just a minute." There was a pause, some

paper ruffling, a cough. Longfellow came back on the line. "It doesn't say anything."

"You can't make out the letters? Is it waterlogged, or something?"

"It doesn't have letters."

"Then what does it have?" Alice said with the last of her patience straining at the leash. She was picturing Longfellow on the floor with herself standing over the lab tech with a large studded bat...

"It has numbers, Jones," came the droll reply. "Just a few numbers. Nothing else."

"An address?"

"Not likely."

"Give me the numbers."

"Only the last six are visible. The others apparently were obliterated by the man's sweaty palms when he clenched it so tightly. Here goes."

She read the series of numbers.

"Which ones were obliterated?" Alice asked.

"Looks like the ones at the beginning. If it's a telephone number, the area code and the first of the exchange numbers is missing. We'll probably be able to reconstruct those at the FBI lab, but not immediately. Sorry."

"No, listen, you've been a world of help. If I controlled salaries, you'd get a raise."

"Why, thank you, Jones," came the astonished reply. "That's very kind of you to say."

"You're very welcome. Let me know if you come up with anything else."

"Of course I will."

Alice hung up. She looked at the numbers and frowned.

"What have you got?" Hayes asked.

"I'm not sure. A telephone number, perhaps."

He moved closer and peered at the paper where she'd written those numbers down. "Could that be the exchange?" he asked, noting some of the numbers.

"I don't know. If it is, it could be a San Antonio number, but we'd need to have the area code to determine that, and it's missing."

"Get that lab busy."

She glowered at him. "Like we sleep late, take two-hour coffee breaks, and wander into the crime lab about noon daily!"

"Sorry," he said, and grinned.

She pursed her full lips and gave him a roguish look. "Hey, you law enforcement guys live at doughnut shops and lounge around in the office reading sports magazines and playing games on the computer, right?"

He glowered back.

She held out one hand, palm up. "Welcome to the stereotype club."

"When will she have some more of those numbers?"

"Your guess is as good as mine. Has anybody spoken to the woman whose car was stolen to ask if someone she knew might have taken it? Or to pump her for information and find out if she really loaned it to him?" she added shrewdly.

"No, nobody's talked to her. The feds in charge of the investigation wanted to wait until they had enough information to coax her into giving them something they needed," he said.

"As we speak, they're roping Jon Blackhawk to his

desk chair and gagging him," she pronounced with a grin. "His first reaction would be to drag her downtown and grill her."

"He's young and hotheaded. At least to hear his brother tell it."

"Kilraven loves his brother," Alice replied. "But he does know his failings."

"I wouldn't call rushing in headfirst a failing," Hayes pointed out.

"That's why you've been shot, Hayes," she said.

"Anybody can get shot," he said.

"Yes, but you've been shot twice," she reminded him. "The word locally is that you'd have a better chance of being named king of some small country than you'd have getting a wife. Nobody around here is rushing to line up and become a widow."

"I've calmed down," he muttered defensively. "And who's been saying that, anyway?"

"I heard that Minette Raynor was," she replied without quite meeting his eyes.

His jaw tautened. "I have no desire to marry Miss Raynor, now or ever," he returned coldly. "She helped kill my brother."

"She didn't, and you have proof, but suit yourself," she said when he looked angry enough to say something unforgivable. "Now, do you have any idea how we can talk to that woman before somebody shuts her up? It looks like whoever killed that poor man on the river wouldn't hesitate to give him company. I'd bet my reputation that he knew something that could bring down someone powerful, and he was stopped dead first. If the woman has any info at all, she's on the endangered list."

"Good point," Hayes had to admit. "Do you have a plan?"

She shook her head. "I wish."

"About that number, you might run it by the 911 operators," he said. "They deal with a lot of telephone traffic. They might recognize it."

"Now that's constructive thinking," she said with a grin. "But this isn't my jurisdiction, you know."

"The crime was committed in the county. That's my jurisdiction. I'm giving you the authority to investigate."

"Won't your own investigator feel slighted?"

"He would if he was here," he sighed. "He took his remaining days off and went to Wyoming for Christmas. He said he'd lose them if he didn't use them by the end of the year. I couldn't disagree and we didn't have much going on when I let him go." He shook his head. "He'll punch me when he gets back and discovers that we had a real DB right here and he didn't get to investigate it."

"The way things look," she said slowly, "he may still get to help. I don't think we're going to solve this one in a couple of days."

"Hey, I saw a murder like this one on one of those CSI shows," he said with pretended excitement. "They sent trace evidence out, got results in two hours and had the guy arrested and convicted and sent to jail just before the last commercial!"

She gave him a smile and a gesture that was universal before she picked up her purse, and the slip of paper, and left his office.

SHE WAS EATING lunch at Barbara's Café in town when the object of her most recent daydreams walked in, tall and handsome in real cowboy duds, complete with a shepherd's coat, polished black boots and a real black Stetson cowboy hat with a brim that looked just like the one worn by Richard Boone in the television series *Have Gun Will Travel* that she used to watch videos of. It was cocked over his eyes and he looked as much like a desperado as he did a working cowboy.

He spotted Alice as he was paying for his meal at the counter and grinned at her. She turned over a cup of coffee and it spilled all over the table, which made his grin much bigger.

Barbara came running with a towel. "Don't worry, it happens all the time," she reassured Alice. She glanced at Harley, put some figures together and chuckled. "Ah, romance is in the air."

"It is not," Alice said firmly. "I offered to take him to a movie, but I'm broke, and he won't go Dutch treat," she added in a soft wail.

"Aww," Barbara sympathized.

"I don't get paid until next Friday," Alice said, dabbing at wet spots on her once-immaculate oyster-white wool slacks. "I'll be miles away by then."

"I get paid this Friday," Harley said, straddling a chair opposite Alice with a huge steak and fries on a platter. "Are you having a salad for lunch?" he asked, aghast at the small bowl at her elbow. "You'll never be able to do any real investigating on a diet like that. You need protein." He indicated the juicy, rare steak on his own plate.

Alice groaned. He didn't understand. She'd spent so

many hours working in her lab that she couldn't really eat a steak anymore. It was heresy here in Texas, so she tended to keep her opinions to herself. If she said anything like that, there would be a riot in Barbara's Café.

So she just smiled. "Fancy seeing you here," she teased.

He grinned. "I'll bet it wasn't a surprise," he said as he began to carve his steak.

"Whatever do you mean?" she asked with pretended innocence.

"I was just talking to Hayes Carson out on the street and he happened to mention that you asked him where I ate lunch," he replied.

She huffed. "Well, that's the last personal question I'll ever ask him, and you can take that to the bank!"

"Should I mention that I asked him where *you* ate lunch?" he added with a twinkle in his pale eyes.

Alice's irritated expression vanished. She sighed. "Did you, really?" she asked.

"I did, really. But don't take that as a marriage proposal," he said. "I almost never propose to crime scene investigators over lunch."

"Crime scene investigators?" a cowboy from one of the nearby ranches exclaimed, leaning toward them. "Listen, I watch those shows all the time. Did you know that they can tell time of death by…!"

"Oh, dear, I'm so sorry!" Alice exclaimed as the cowboy gaped at her. She'd "accidentally" poured a glass of iced tea all over him. "It's a reflex," she tried to explain as Barbara came running, again. "You see, every time somebody talks about the work I do, I just get all excited and start throwing things!" She picked up her salad bowl. "It's a helpless reflex, I just can't stop…"

"No problem!" the cowboy said at once, scrambling to his feet. "I had to get back to work anyway! Don't think a thing about it!"

He rushed out the door, trailing tea and ice chips, leaving behind half a cup of coffee and a couple of bites of pie and an empty plate.

Harley was trying not to laugh, but he lost it completely. Barbara was chuckling as she motioned to one of her girls to get a broom and pail.

"I'm sorry," Alice told her. "Really."

Barbara gave her an amused glance. "You don't like to talk shop at the table, do you?"

"No. I don't," she confessed.

"Don't worry," Barbara said as the broom and pail and a couple of paper towels were handed to her. "I'll make sure word gets around. Before lunch tomorrow," she added, still laughing.

CHAPTER FOUR

AFTER THAT, nobody tried to engage Alice in conversation about her job. The meal was pleasant and friendly. Alice liked Harley. He had a good personality, and he actually improved on closer acquaintance, as so many people didn't. He was modest and unassuming, and he didn't try to monopolize the conversation.

"How's your investigation coming?" he asked when they were on second cups of black coffee.

She shrugged. "Slowly," she replied. "We've got a partial number, possibly a telephone number, a stolen car whose owner didn't know it was stolen and a partial sneaker track that we're hoping someone can identify."

"I saw a program on the FBI lab that showed how they do that," Harley replied. He stopped immediately as soon as he realized what he'd said. He sat with his fork poised in midair, eyeing Alice's refilled coffee mug.

She laughed. "Not to worry. I'll control my reflexes. Actually the lab does a very good job running down sneaker treads," she added. "The problem is that most treads are pretty common. You get the name of a company that produces them and then start wearing out shoe leather going to stores and asking for information about people who bought them."

"What about people who paid cash and there's no record of their buying them?"

"I never said investigation techniques were perfect," she returned, smiling. "We use what we can get."

He frowned. "Those numbers, it shouldn't be that hard to isolate a telephone number, should it? You could narrow it down with a computer program."

"Yes, but there are so many possible combinations, considering that we don't even have the area code." She groaned. "And we'll have to try every single one."

He pursed his lips. "The car, then. Are you sure the person who owned it didn't have a connection to the murder victim?"

She raised her eyebrows. "Ever considered a career in law enforcement?"

He laughed. "I did, once. A long time ago." He grimaced, as if the memory wasn't a particularly pleasant one.

"We're curious about the car," she said, "but they don't want to spook the car's owner. It turns out that she works for a particularly unpleasant member of the political community."

His eyebrows lifted. "Who?"

She hesitated.

"Come on. I'm a clam. Ask my boss."

"Okay. It's the senior U.S. senator from Texas who lives in San Antonio," she confessed.

Harley made an ungraceful movement and sat back in his chair. He stared toward the window without really seeing anything. "You think the politician may be connected in some way?"

"There's no way of knowing right now," she sighed.

"Everybody big in political circles has people who work for them. Anybody can get involved with a bad person and not know it."

"Are they going to question the car owner?"

"I'm sure they will, eventually. They just want to pick the right time to do it."

He toyed with his coffee cup. "So, are you staying here for a while?"

She grimaced. "A few more days, just to see if I can develop any more leads. Hayes Carson wants me to look at the car while the lab's processing it, so I guess I'll go up to San Antonio for that and come back here when I'm done."

He just nodded, seemingly distracted.

She studied him with a whimsical expression. "So, when are we getting married?" she asked.

He gave her an amused look. "Not today. I have to move cattle."

"My schedule is very flexible," she assured him.

He smiled. "Mine isn't."

"Rats."

"Now, that's interesting, I was just thinking about rats. I have to get cat food while I'm in town."

She blinked. "Cat food. For rats?"

"We keep barn cats to deal with the rat problem," he explained. "But there aren't quite enough mice and rats to keep the cats healthy, so we supplement."

"I like cats," she said with a sigh and a smile. "Maybe we could adopt some stray ones when we get married." She frowned. "Now that's going to be a problem."

"Cats are?"

"No. Where are we going to live?" she persisted. "My job is in San Antonio and yours is here. I know," she said, brightening. "I'll commute!"

He laughed. She made him feel light inside. He finished his coffee. "Better work on getting the bridegroom first," he pointed out.

"Okay. What sort of flowers do you like, and when are we going on our first date?"

He pursed his lips. She was outrageously forward, but behind that bluff personality, he saw something deeper and far more fragile. She was shy. She was like a storefront with piñatas and confetti that sold elegant silverware. She was disguising her real persona with an exaggerated one.

He leaned back in his chair, feeling oddly arrogant at her interest in him. His eyes narrowed and he smiled. "I was thinking we might take in a movie at one of those big movie complexes in San Antonio. Friday night."

"Ooooooh," she exclaimed, bright-eyed. "I like science fiction."

"So do I, and there's a remake of a 1950's film playing. I wouldn't mind seeing it."

"Neither would I."

"I'll pick you up at your motel about five. We'll have dinner and take in the movie afterward. That suit you?"

She was nodding furiously. "Should I go ahead and buy the rings?" she asked with an innocent expression.

He chuckled. "I told you, I'm too tied up right now for weddings."

She snapped her fingers. "Darn!"

"But we can see a movie."

"I like movies."

"Me, too."

They paid for their respective meals and walked out together, drawing interest from several of the café patrons. Harley hadn't been taking any girls around with him lately, and here was this cute CSI lady from San Antonio having lunch with him. Speculation ran riot.

"They'll have us married by late afternoon," he remarked, nodding toward the windows, where curious eyes were following their every move.

"I'll go back in and invite them all to the wedding, shall I?" she asked at once.

"Kill the engine, dude," he drawled in a perfect imitation of the sea turtle in his favorite cartoon movie.

"You so totally rock, Squirt!" she drawled back.

He laughed. "Sweet. You like cartoon movies, too?"

"Crazy about them," she replied. "My favorite right now is *WALL-E*, but it changes from season to season. They just get better all the time."

"I liked *WALL-E*, too," he agreed. "Poignant story. Beautiful soundtrack."

"My sentiments, exactly. That's nice. When we have kids, we'll enjoy taking them to the theater to see the new cartoon movies."

He took off his hat and started fanning himself. "Don't mention kids or I'll faint!" he exclaimed. "I'm already having hot flashes, just considering the thought of marriage!"

She glared at him. "Women have hot flashes when they enter menopause," she said, emphasizing the first word.

He lifted his eyebrows and grinned. "Maybe I'm a woman in disguise," he whispered wickedly.

She wrinkled her nose up and gave him a slow, interested scrutiny from his cowboy boots to his brown hair. "It's a really good disguise," she had to agree. She growled, low in her throat, and smiled. "Tell you what, after the movie, we can undress you and see how good a disguise it really is."

"Well, I never!" he exclaimed, gasping. "I'm not that kind of man, I'll have you know! And if you keep talking like that, I'll never marry you. A man has his principles. You're just after my body!"

Alice was bursting at the seams with laughter. Harley followed her eyes, turned around, and there was Kilraven, in uniform, staring at him.

"I read this book," Kilraven said after a minute, "about a Scot who disguised himself as a woman for three days after he stole an English payroll destined for the turncoat Scottish Lords of the Congregation who were going to try to depose Mary, Queen of Scots. The family that sheltered him was rewarded with compensation that was paid for centuries, even after his death, they say. He knew how to repay a debt." He frowned. "But that was in the sixteenth century, and you don't look a thing like Lord Bothwell."

"I should hope not," Harley said. "He's been dead for over four hundred years!"

Alice moved close to him and bumped him with her hip. "Don't talk like that. Some of my best friends are dead people."

Harley and Kilraven both groaned.

"It was a joke," Alice burst out, exasperated. "My goodness, don't you people have a sense of humor?"

"He doesn't," Harley said, indicating Kilraven.

"I do so," Kilraven shot back, glaring. "I have a good sense of humor." He stepped closer. "And you'd better say that I do, because I'm armed."

"You have a great sense of humor," Harley replied at once, and grinned.

"What are you doing here?" Alice asked suddenly. "I thought you were supposed to be off today."

Kilraven shrugged. "One of our boys came down with flu and they needed somebody to fill in. Not much to do around here on a day off, so I volunteered," he added.

"There's TV," Alice said.

He scoffed. "I don't own a TV," he said huffily. "I read books."

"European history?" Harley asked, recalling the mention of Bothwell.

"Military history, mostly, but history is history. For instance," he began, "did you know that Hannibal sealed poisonous snakes in clay urns and had his men throw them onto the decks of enemy ships as an offensive measure?"

Harley was trying to keep a straight face.

Alice didn't even try. "You're kidding!"

"I am not. Look it up."

"I'd have gone right over the side into the ocean!" Alice exclaimed, shivering.

"So did a lot of the enemy combatants." Kilraven chuckled. "See what you learn when you read, instead of staying glued to a television set?"

"How can you not have a television set?" Harley exclaimed. "You can't watch the news…"

"Don't get me started," Kilraven muttered. "Corporate news, exploiting private individuals with personal problems for the entertainment of the masses! Look at that murder victim who was killed back in the summer, and the family of the accused is still getting crucified nightly in case they had anything to do with it. You call that news? I call it bread and circuses, just like the arena in ancient Rome!"

"Then how do you know what's going on in the world?" Alice had to know.

"I have a laptop computer with Internet access," he said. "That's where the real news is."

"A revolutionary," Harley said.

"An anarchist," Alice corrected.

"I am an upstanding member of law enforcement," Kilraven retorted. He glanced at the big watch on his wrist. "And I'm going to be late getting back on duty if I don't get lunch pretty soon."

Harley was looking at the watch and frowning. He knew the model. It was one frequently worn by mercs. "Blade or garrote?" he asked Kilraven, nodding at the watch.

Kilraven was surprised, but he recovered quickly. "Blade," he said. "How did you know?"

"Micah Steele used to wear one just like it."

Kilraven leaned down. "Guess who I bought it from?" he asked. He grinned. With a wave, he sauntered into the café.

"What were you talking about?" Alice asked curiously.

"Trade secret," Harley returned. "I have to get going. I'll see you Friday."

He turned away and then, just as suddenly turned back. "Wait a minute." He pulled a small pad and pencil out of his shirt pocket and jotted down a number. He tore off the paper and handed it to her. "That's my cell phone number. If anything comes up, and you can't make it Friday, you can call me."

"Can I call you anyway?" she asked.

He blinked. "What for?"

"To talk. You know, if I have any deeply personal problems that just can't wait until Friday?"

He laughed. "Alice, it's only two days away," he said.

"I could be traumatized by a snake or something."

He sighed. "Okay. But only then. It's hard to pull a cell phone out of its holder when you're knee-deep in mud trying to extract mired cattle."

She beamed. "I'll keep that in mind." She tucked the number in the pocket of her slacks. "I enjoyed lunch."

"Yeah," he said, smiling. "Me, too."

She watched him walk away with covetous eyes. He really did have a sensuous body, very masculine. She stood sighing over him until she realized that several pair of eyes were still watching her from inside the café. With a self-conscious grin in their direction, she went quickly to her van.

THE PATTERN IN the tennis shoes was so common that Alice had serious doubts that they'd ever locate the seller, much less the owner. The car was going to be a much better lead. She went up to the crime lab while they were processing it. There was some trace evidence that was promising. She also had Sergeant Rick Marquez, who worked out of San Antonio P.D., get as much information as he could about the woman the murdered man had stolen the car from.

The next morning in Jacobsville, on his way to work in San Antonio, Rick stopped by Alice's motel room to give her the information he'd managed to obtain. "She's been an employee of Senator Fowler for about two years," Rick said, perching on the edge of the dresser in front of the bed while she paced. "She's deeply religious. She goes to church on Sundays and Wednesdays. She's involved in an outreach program for the homeless, and she gives away a good deal of her salary to people she considers more needy." He shook his head. "You read about these people, but you rarely encounter them in real life. She hasn't got a black mark on her record anywhere, unless you consider a detention in high school for being late three days in a row when her mother was in the hospital."

"Wow," Alice exclaimed softly.

"There's more. She almost lost the job by lecturing the senator for hiring illegal workers and threatening them with deportation if they asked for higher wages."

"What a sweetheart," Alice muttered.

"From what we hear, the senator is the very devil to work for. They say his wife is almost as hard-nosed. She was a state supreme court judge before she went into the import/export business. She made millions at it. Finances a good part of the senator's reelection campaigns."

"Is he honest?"

"Is any politician?" Marquez asked cynically. "He sits on several powerful committees in Congress, and was once accused of taking kickbacks from a Mexican official."

"For what?"

"He was asked to oppose any shoring up of border security. Word is that the senator and his contact have their fingers in some illegal pies, most notably drug trafficking. But there's no proof. The last detective who tried to investigate the senator is now working traffic detail."

"A vengeful man."

"Very."

"I don't suppose that detective would talk to me?" she wondered aloud.

"She might," he replied surprisingly. "She and I were trying to get the Kilraven family murder case reopened, if you recall, when pressure was put on us to stop. She turned her attention to the senator and got kicked out of the detective squad." He grimaced. "She's a good woman. Got an invalid kid to look after and an ex-husband who's a pain in the butt, to put it nicely."

"We heard about the cold case being closed. You think the senator might have been responsible for it?" she wondered aloud.

"We don't know. He has a protégé who's just been elected junior senator from Texas, and the protégé has some odd ties to people who aren't exactly the crème of society. But we don't dare mention that in public." He smiled. "I don't fancy being put on a motorcycle at my age and launched into traffic duty."

"Your friend isn't having to do that, surely?" she asked.

"No, she's working two-car patrols on the night shift, but she's a sergeant, so she gets a good bit of desk work." He studied her. "What's this I hear about you trying to marry Harley?"

She grinned. "It's early days. He's shy, but I'm going to drown him in flowers and chocolate until he says yes."

"Good luck," he said with a chuckle.

"I won't even need it. We're going to a movie together Friday."

"Are you? What are you going to see?"

"The remake of that fifties movie. We're going to dinner first."

"You are a fast worker, Alice," he said with respect. He checked his watch. "I've got to get back to the precinct."

She glanced at his watch curiously. "You don't have a blade or a wire in that thing, do you?"

"Not likely," he assured her. "Those watches cost more than I make, and they're used almost exclusively by mercs."

"Mercs?" She frowned.

"Soldiers of fortune. They work for the highest bidder, although our local crowd had more honor than that."

Mercs. Now she understood Harley's odd phrasing about "trade secrets."

"Where did you see a watch like that?" he asked.

She looked innocent. "I heard about one from Harley. I just wondered what they were used for."

"Oh. Well, I guess if you were in a tight spot, it might save your life to have one of those," he agreed, distracted.

"Before you go, can you give me the name and address of that detective in San Antonio?" she asked.

He hesitated. "Better let me funnel the questions to her, Alice," he said with a smile. "She doesn't want anything to slip out about her follow-ups on that case. She's still working it, without permission."

She raised an eyebrow. "So are you, unless I miss my guess. Does Kilraven know?"

He shook his head. Then he hesitated. "Well, I don't think he does. He and Jon Blackhawk still don't want us nosing around. They're afraid the media will pick up the story and it will become the nightly news for a year or so." He shook his head. "Pitiful, how the networks don't go out and get any real news anymore. They just create it by harping on private families mixed up in tragedies, like living soap operas."

"That's how corporate media works," she told him. "If you want real news, buy a local weekly newspaper."

He laughed. "You're absolutely right. Take care, Alice."

"You, too. Thanks for the help."

"Anytime." He paused at the door and grinned at her. "If Harley doesn't work out, you could always pursue me," he invited. "I'm young and dashing and I even have long hair." He indicated his ponytail. "I played semi-professional soccer when I was in college, and I have a lovely singing voice."

She chuckled. "I've heard about your singing voice, Marquez. Weren't you asked, very politely, to stay out of the church choir?"

"I wanted to meet women," he said. "The choir was

full of unattached ones. But I can sing," he added bel-ligerently. "Some people don't appreciate real talent."

She wasn't touching that line with a pole. "I'll keep you in mind."

"You do that." He laughed as he closed the door.

Alice turned back to her notes, spread out on the desk in the motel room. There was something nagging at her about the piece of paper they'd recovered from the mur-der victim. She wondered why it bothered her.

HARLEY PICKED HER up punctually at five on Friday night for their date. He wasn't overdressed, but he had on slacks and a spotless sports shirt with a dark blue jacket. He wasn't wearing his cowboy hat, either.

"You look nice," she said, smiling.

His eyes went to her neat blue sweater with embroi-dery around the rounded neckline and the black slacks she was wearing with slingbacks. She draped a black coat with fur collar over one arm and picked up her purse.

"Thanks," he said. "You look pretty good yourself, Alice."

She joined him at the door. "Ooops. Just a minute. I forgot my cell phone. I was charging it."

She unplugged it and tucked it into her pocket. It rang immediately. She grimaced. "Just a minute, okay?" she asked Harley.

She answered the phone. She listened. She grimaced. "Not tonight," she groaned. "Listen, I have plans. I never do, but I really have plans tonight. Can't Clancy cover for me, just this once? Please? Pretty please? I'll do the same for her. I'll even work Christmas Eve…okay? Thanks!" She beamed. "Thanks a million!"

She hung up.

"A case?" he asked curiously.

"Yes, but I traded out with another investigator." She shook her head as she joined him again at the door. "It's been so slow lately that I forgot how hectic my life usually is."

"You have to work Christmas Eve?" he asked, surprised.

"Well, I usually volunteer," she confessed. "I don't have much of a social life. Besides, I think parents should be with children on holidays. I don't have any, but all my coworkers do."

He paused at the door of his pickup truck and looked down at her. "I like kids," he said.

"So do I," she replied seriously, and without joking. "I've just never had the opportunity to become a parent."

"You don't have to be married to have kids," he pointed out.

She gave him a harsh glare. "I am the product of generations of Baptist ministers," she told him. "My father was the only one of five brothers who went into business instead. You try having a modern attitude with a mother who taught Sunday School and uncles who spent their lives counseling young women whose lives were destroyed by unexpected pregnancies."

"I guess it would be rough," he said.

She smiled. "You grew up with parents who were free thinkers, didn't you?" she asked, curious.

He grimaced. He put her into the truck and got in

beside her before he answered. "My father is an agnostic. He doesn't believe in anything except the power of the almighty dollar. My mother is just like him. They wanted me to associate with the right people and help them do it. I stayed with a friend's aunt and uncle for a while and all but got adopted by them—he was a mechanic and they had a small ranch. I helped in the mechanic's shop. Then I went into the service, came back and tried to work things out with my real parents, but it wasn't possible. I ran away from home, fresh out of the Army Rangers."

"You were overseas during the Bosnia conflict, weren't you?" she asked.

He snapped his seat belt a little violently. "I was a desk clerk," he said with disgust. "I washed out of combat training. I couldn't make the grade. I ended up back in the regular Army doing clerical jobs. I never even saw combat. Not in the Army," he added.

"Oh."

"I left home, came down here to become a cowboy barely knowing a cow from a bull. The friends that I lived with had a small ranch, but I mostly stayed in town, working at the shop. We went out to the ranch on weekends, and I wasn't keen on livestock back then. Mr. Parks took me on anyway. He knew all along that I had no experience, but he put me to work with an old veteran cowhand named Cal Lucas who taught me everything I know about cattle."

She grinned. "It took guts to do that."

He laughed. "I guess so. I bluffed a lot, although I am a good mechanic. Then I got in with this Sunday

merc crew and went down to Africa with them one week
on a so-called training mission. All we did was talk to
some guys in a village about their problems with foreign relief shipments. But before we could do anything,
we ran afoul of government troops and got sent home."
He sighed. "I bragged about how much I'd learned, what
a great merc I was." He glanced at her as they drove
toward San Antonio, but she wasn't reacting critically.
Much the reverse. He relaxed a little. "Then one of the
drug lords came storming up to Mr. Parks's house with
his men and I got a dose of reality—an automatic in
my face. Mr. Parks jerked two combat knives out of his
sleeves and threw them at the two men who were holding me. Put them both down in a heartbeat." He shook
his head, still breathless at the memory. "I never saw
anything like it, before or since. I thought he was just
a rancher. Turns out he went with Micah Steele and Eb
Scott on real merc missions overseas. He listened to me
brag and watched me strut, and never said a word. I'd
never have known, if the drug dealers hadn't attacked.
We got in a firefight with them later."

"We heard about that, even up in San Antonio," she
said.

He nodded. "It got around. Mr. Parks and Eb Scott
and Micah Steele got together to take out a drug distribution center near Mr. Parks's property. I swallowed my
pride and asked to go along. They let me." He sighed.
"I grew up in the space of an hour. I saw men shot and
killed, I had my life saved by Mr. Parks again in the
process. Afterward, I never bragged or strutted again.
Mr. Parks said he was proud of me." He flushed a lit-

tle. "If my father had been like him, I guess I'd still be at home. He's a real man, Mr. Parks. I've never known a better one."

"He likes you, too."

He laughed self-consciously. "He does. He's offered me a few acres of land and some cattle, if I'd like to start my own herd. I'm thinking about it. I love ranching. I think I'm getting good at it."

"So we'd live on a cattle ranch." She pursed her lips mischievously. "I guess I could learn to help with branding. I mean, we wouldn't want our kids to think their mother was a sissy, would we?" she asked, laughing.

Harley gave her a sideways glance and grinned. She really was fun to be with. He thought he might take her by the ranch one day while she was still in Jacobsville and introduce her to Mr. Parks. He was sure Mr. Parks would like her

CHAPTER FIVE

THE RESTAURANT HARLEY took Alice to was a very nice one, with uniformed waiters and chandeliers.

"Oh, Harley, this wasn't necessary," she said quickly, flushing. "A hamburger would have been fine!"

He smiled. "We all got a Christmas bonus from Mr. Parks," he explained. "I don't drink or smoke or gamble, so I can afford a few luxuries from time to time."

"You don't have any vices? Wow. Now I really think we should set the date." She glanced at him under her lashes. "I don't drink, smoke or gamble, either," she added hopefully.

He nodded. "We'll be known as the most prudish couple in Jacobsville."

"Kilraven's prudish, too," she pointed out.

"Yes, but he won't be living in Jacobsville much longer. He's been reassigned, we're hearing. After all, he's really a fed."

She studied the menu. "I'll bet he could be a heartbreaker with a little practice."

"He's breaking Winnie Sinclair's heart, anyway, by leaving," Harley said, repeating the latest gossip. "She's really got a case on him. But he thinks she's too young."

"He's only in his thirties," she pointed out.

"Yes, but Winnie's the same age as her brother's new wife," he replied. "Boone Sinclair thought Keely Welsh was too young for him, too."

"But he gave in, in the end. You know, the Ballenger brothers in Jacobsville both married younger women. They've been happy together, all these years."

"Yes, they have."

The waiter came and took their orders. Alice had a shrimp cocktail and a large salad with coffee. Harley gave her a curious look.

"Aren't you hungry?" he asked.

She laughed. "I told you in Jacobsville, I love salads," she confessed. "I mostly eat them at every meal." She indicated her slender body. "I guess that's how I keep the weight off."

"I can eat as much as I like. I run it all off," he replied. "Working cattle is not for the faint of heart or the out-of-condition rancher."

She grinned. "I believe it." She smiled at the waiter as he deposited coffee in their china cups and left. "Why did you want to be a cowboy?" she asked him.

"I loved old Western movies on satellite," he said simply. "Gary Cooper and John Wayne and Randolph Scott. I dreamed of living on a cattle ranch and having animals around. I don't even mind washing Bob when she gets dirty, or Puppy Dog."

"What's Puppy Dog's name?" she asked.

"Puppy Dog."

She gave him an odd look. "Who's on first, what's on second, I don't know's on third?"

"I don't give a damn's our shortstop?" he finished the

old Abbott and Costello comedy routine. He laughed. "No, it's not like that. His name really is Puppy Dog. We have a guy in town, Tom Walker. He had an outlandish dog named Moose that saved his daughter from a rattlesnake. Moose sired a litter of puppies. Moose is dead now, but Puppy Dog, who was one of his offspring, went to live with Lisa Monroe, before she married my boss. She called him Puppy Dog and figured it was as good a name as any. With a girl dog named Bob, my boss could hardly disagree," he added on a chuckle.

"I see."

"Do you like animals?"

"I love them," she said. "But I can't have animals in the apartment building where I live. I had cats and dogs and even a parrot when I lived at home."

"Do you have family?"

She shook her head. "My dad was the only one left. He died a month ago. I have uncles, but we're not close."

"Did you love your parents?"

She smiled warmly. "Very much. My dad was a banker. We went fishing together on weekends. My mother was a housewife who never wanted to run a corporation or be a professional. She just wanted a houseful of kids, but I was the only child she was able to have. She spoiled me rotten. Dad tried to counterbalance her." She sipped coffee. "I miss them both. I wish I'd had brothers or sisters." She looked at him. "Do you have siblings?"

"I had a sister," he said quietly.

"Had?"

He nodded. He fingered his coffee cup. "She died when she was seven years old."

She hesitated. He looked as if this was a really bad memory. "How?"

He smiled sadly. "My father backed over her on his way down the driveway, in a hurry to get to a meeting."

She grimaced. "Poor man."

He cocked his head and studied her. "Why do you say that?"

"We had a little girl in for autopsy, about two years ago," she began. "Her dad was hysterical. Said the television fell over on her." She lifted her eyes. "You know, we don't just take someone's word for how an accident happens, even if we believe it. We run tests to check out the explanation and make sure it's feasible. Well, we pushed over a television of the same size as the one in the dad's apartment. Sure enough, it did catastrophic damage to a dummy." She shook her head. "Poor man went crazy. I mean, he really lost the will to live. His wife had died. The child was all he had left. He locked himself in the bathroom with a shotgun one night and pulled the trigger with his toe." She made a harsh sound. "Not the sort of autopsy you want to try to sleep after."

He was frowning.

"Sorry," she said, wincing. "I tend to talk shop. I know it's sickening, and here we are in a nice restaurant and all, and I did pour a glass of tea on a guy this week for doing the same thing to me…"

"I was thinking about the father," he said, smiling to relieve her tension. "I was sixteen when it happened. I grieved for her, of course, but my life was baseball and girls and video games and hamburgers. I never considered how my father might have felt. He seemed to just get on with his life afterward. So did my mother."

"Lots of people may seem to get over their grief. They don't."

He was more thoughtful than ever. "My mother had been a…lawyer," he said after a slight hesitation that Alice didn't notice. "She was very correct and proper. After my sister died, she changed. Cocktail parties, the right friends, the best house, the fanciest furniture…she went right off the deep end."

"You didn't connect it?"

He grimaced. "That was when I ran away from home and went to live with the mechanic and his wife," he confessed. "It was my senior year of high school. I graduated soon after, went into the Army and served for two years. When I got out, I went home. But I only stayed for a couple of weeks. My parents were total strangers. I didn't even know them anymore."

"That's sad. Do you have any contact with them?"

He shook his head. "I just left. They never even looked for me."

She slid her hand impulsively over his. His fingers turned and enveloped hers. His light blue eyes searched her darker ones curiously. "I never thought of crime scene investigators as having feelings," he said. "I thought you had to be pretty cold-blooded to do that sort of thing."

She smiled. "I'm the last hope of the doomed," she said. "The conscience of the murdered. The flickering candle of the soul of the deceased. I do my job so that murderers don't flourish, so that killers don't escape justice. I think of my job as a holy grail," she said solemnly. "I hide my feelings. But I still have them. It hurts to see a life extinguished. Any life. But especially a child's."

His eyes began to twinkle with affection. "Alice, you're one of a kind."

"Oh, I do hope so," she said after a minute. "Because if there was another one of me, I might lose my job. Not many people would give twenty-four hours a day to the work." She hesitated and grinned. "Well, not all the time, obviously. Just occasionally, I get taken out by handsome, dashing men."

He laughed. "Thanks."

"Actually I mean it. I'm not shrewd enough to lie well."

The waiter came and poured more coffee and took their orders for dessert. When they were eating it, Alice frowned thoughtfully.

"It bothers me."

"What does?" he asked.

"The car. Why would a man steal a car from an upstanding, religious woman and then get killed?"

"He didn't know he was going to get killed."

She forked a piece of cheesecake and looked at it. "What if he had a criminal record? What if he got involved with her and wanted to change, to start over? What if he had something on his conscience and he wanted to spill the beans?" She looked up. "And somebody involved knew it and had to stop him?"

"That's a lot of ifs," he pointed out.

She nodded. "Yes, it is. We still don't know who the car was driven by, and the woman's story that it was stolen is just a little thin." She put the fork down. "I want to talk to her. But I don't know how to go about it. She works for a dangerous politician, I'm told. The feds have backed off. I won't do myself any favors if I charge in and start interrogating the senator's employee."

He studied her. "Let me see if I can find a way. I used to know my way around political circles. Maybe I can help."

She laughed. "You know a U.S. senator?" she teased.

He pursed his lips. "Maybe I know somebody who's related to one," he corrected.

"It would really help me a lot, if I could get to her before the feds do. I think she might tell me more than she'd tell a no-nonsense man."

"Give me until tomorrow. I'll think of something."

She smiled. "You're a doll."

He chuckled. "So are you."

She flushed. "Thanks."

They exchanged a long, soulful glance, only interrupted by the arrival of the waiter to ask if they wanted anything else and present the check. Alice's heart was doing double-time on the way out of the restaurant.

HARLEY WALKED HER to the door of the motel. "I had a good time," he told her. "The best I've had in years."

She looked up, smiling. "Me, too. I turn off most men. The job, you know. I do work with people who aren't breathing."

"It doesn't matter," he said.

She felt the same tension that was visible in his tall, muscular body. He moved a step closer. She met him halfway.

He bent and drew his mouth softly over hers. When she didn't object, his arms went around her and pulled her close. He smiled as he increased the gentle pressure of his lips and felt hers tremble just a little before they relaxed and answered the pressure.

His body was already taut with desire, but it was too soon for a heated interlude. He didn't want to rush her. She was the most fascinating woman he'd ever known. He had to go slow.

He drew back after a minute and his hands tightened on her arms. "Suppose we take in another movie next week?" he asked.

She brightened. "A whole movie?"

He laughed softly. "At least."

"I'd like that."

"We'll try another restaurant. Just to sample the ones that are available until we find one we approve of," he teased.

"What a lovely idea! We can write reviews and put them online, too."

He pursed his lips. "What an entertaining thought."

"Nice reviews," she said, divining his mischievous thoughts.

"Spoilsport."

He winked at her, and she blushed.

"Don't forget," she said. "About finding me a way to interview that woman, okay?"

"Okay," he said. "Good night."

"Good night."

She stood, sighing, as he walked back to his truck. But when he got inside and started it, he didn't drive away. She realized belatedly that he was waiting until she went inside and locked the door. She laughed and waved. She liked that streak of protectiveness in him. It might not be modern, but it certainly made her feel cherished. She slept like a charm.

THE NEXT MORNING, he called her on his cell phone before she left the motel. "I've got us invited to a cocktail party tonight," he told her. "A fundraiser for the senator."

"Us? But we can't contribute to that sort of thing! Can we?" she added.

"We don't have to. We're representing a contributor who's out of the country," he added with a chuckle. "Do you have a nice cocktail dress?"

"I do, but it's in San Antonio, in my apartment."

"No worries. You can go up and get it and I'll pick you up there at six."

"Fantastic! I'll wear something nice and I won't burp the theme songs to any television shows," she promised.

"Oh, that's good to know," he teased. "Got to get back to work. I told Mr. Parks I had to go to San Antonio this afternoon, so he's giving me a half day off. I didn't tell him why I needed the vacation time, but I think he suspects something."

"Don't mention this to anybody else, okay?" she asked. "If Jon Blackhawk or Kilraven find out, my goose will be cooked."

"I won't tell a soul."

"See you later. I owe you one, Harley."

"Yes," he drawled softly. "You do, don't you? I'll phone you later and get directions to your apartment."

"Okay."

She laughed and hung up.

THE SENATOR LIVED in a mansion. It was two stories high, with columns, and it had a front porch bigger than Alice's whole apartment. Lights burned in every room, and in the gloomy, rainy night, it looked welcoming and beautiful.

Luxury sedans were parked up and down the driveway. Harley's pickup truck wasn't in the same class, but he didn't seem to feel intimidated. He parked on the street and helped Alice out of the truck. He was wearing evening clothes, with a black bow tie and highly polished black wingtip shoes. He looked elegant. Alice was wearing a simple black cocktail dress with her best winter coat, the one she wore to work, a black one with a fur collar. She carried her best black evening bag and she wore black pumps that she'd polished, hoping to cover the scuff marks. On her salary, although it was a good one, she could hardly afford haute couture.

They were met at the door by a butler in uniform. Harley handed him an invitation and the man hesitated and did a double take, but he didn't say anything.

Once they were inside, Alice looked worriedly at Harley.

"It's okay," he assured her, smiling as he cradled her hand in his protectively. "No problem."

"Gosh," she said, awestruck as she looked around her

at the company she was in. "There's a movie star over there," she said under her breath. "I recognize at least two models and a Country-Western singing star, and there's the guy who won the golf tournament...!"

"They're just people, Alice," he said gently.

She gaped at him. "Just people? You're joking, right?" She turned too fast and bumped into somebody. She looked up to apologize and her eyes almost popped. "S-sorry," she stammered.

A movie star with a martial arts background grinned at her. "No problem. It's easy to get knocked down in here. What a crowd, huh?"

"Y-yes," she agreed, nodding.

He laughed, smiled at Harley, and drew his date, a gorgeous blonde, along with him toward the buffet table.

Harley curled his fingers into Alice's. "Rube," he teased softly. "You're starstruck."

"I am, I am," she agreed at once. "I've never been in such a place in my life. I don't hang out with the upper echelons of society in my job. You seem very much at home," she added, "for a man who spends his time with horses and cattle."

"Not a bad analogy, actually," he said under his breath. "Wouldn't a cattle prod come in handy around here, though?"

"Harley!" She laughed.

"Just kidding." He was looking around the room. After a minute, he spotted someone. "Let's go ask that woman if they know your employee."

"Okay."

"What's her name?" he whispered.

DIANA PALMER   281

She dug for it. "Dolores."

He slid his arm around her shoulders and led her forward. She felt the warmth of his jacketed arm around her with real pleasure. She felt chilled at this party, with all this elegance. Her father had been a banker, and he hadn't been poor, but this was beyond the dreams of most people. Crystal chandeliers, Persian carpets, original oil paintings—was that a Renoir?!

"Hi," Harley said to one of the women pouring more punch into the Waterford crystal bowl. "Does Dolores still work here?"

The woman stared at him for a minute, but without recognition. "Dolores? Yes. She's in the kitchen, washing dishes. You look familiar. Do I know you?"

"I've got that kind of face," he said easily, smiling. "My wife and I know Dolores, we belong to her church. I promised the minister we'd give her a message from him if we came tonight," he added.

"One of that church crowd," the woman groaned, rolling her eyes. "Honestly, it's all she talks about, like there's nothing else in the world but church."

"Religion dies, so does civilization," Alice said quietly. She remembered that from her Western Civilization course in college.

"Whatever," the woman replied, bored.

"In the kitchen, huh? Thanks," Harley told the woman.

"Don't get her fired," came the quick reply. "She's a pain, sometimes, but she works hard enough doing dishes. If the senator or his wife see you keeping her from her job, he'll fire her."

"We won't do that," Harley promised. His lips made a thin line as he led Alice away.

"Surely the senator wouldn't fire her just for talking to us?" Alice wondered aloud.

"It wouldn't surprise me," Harley said. "We'll have to be circumspect."

Alice followed his lead. She wondered why he was so irritated. Perhaps the woman's remark offended his sense of justice.

The kitchen was crowded. It didn't occur to Alice to ask how Harley knew his way there. Women were bent over tables, preparing platters, sorting food, making canapés. Two women were at the huge double sink, washing dishes.

"Don't they have a dishwasher?" Alice wondered as they entered the room.

"You don't put Waterford crystal and Lenox china in a dishwasher," he commented easily.

She looked up at him with pure fascination. He didn't seem aware that he'd given away knowledge no working cowboy should even possess.

"How do we know which one's her?" he asked Alice.

Alice stared at the two women. One was barely out of her teens, wearing a nose ring and spiky hair. The other was conservatively dressed with her hair in a neat bun. She smiled, nodding toward the older one. She had a white apron wrapped around her. "The other woman said she was washing dishes," she whispered. "And she's a churchgoer."

He grinned, following her lead.

They eased around the curious workers, smiling.

"Hello, Dolores," Alice called to the woman.

The older woman turned, her red hands dripping water and soap, and started at the two visitors with wide brown eyes. "I'm sorry, do I know you?" she asked.

"I guess you've never seen us dressed up, huh? We're from your church," he told her, lying through his teeth. "Your minister gave us a message for you."

She blinked. "My minister…?"

"Could we talk, just for a minute?" Alice asked urgently.

The woman was suspicious. Her eyes narrowed. She hesitated, and Alice thought, *we've blown it*. But just then, Dolores nodded. "Sure. We can talk for a minute. Liz, I'm taking my break, now, okay? I'll only be ten minutes."

"Okay," Liz returned, with only a glance at the elegantly dressed people walking out with Dolores. "Don't be long. You know how he is," she added quickly.

Once they were outside, Dolores gave them a long look. "I know everyone in my church. You two don't go there," Dolores said with a gleam in her eyes. "Who are you and what do you want?"

Alice studied her. "I work for…out-of-town law enforcement," she improvised. "We found your car. And the man who was driving it."

The older woman hesitated. "I told the police yesterday, the car was stolen," she began weakly.

Alice stepped close, so that they couldn't be overheard. "He was beaten to death, so badly that his mother wouldn't know him," she said in a steely tone. "Your car was pushed into the river. Somebody didn't want him to be found. Nobody," she added softly, "should ever have to die like that. And his murderer shouldn't get away with it."

Dolores looked even sicker. She leaned back against the wall. Her eyes closed. "It's my fault. He said he wanted to start over. He wanted to marry me. He said he just had to do something first, to get something off his conscience. He asked to borrow the car, but he said if something happened, if he didn't call me back by the next morning, to say it was stolen so I wouldn't get in trouble. He said he knew about a crime and if he talked they might kill him."

"Do you know what crime?" Alice asked her.

She shook her head. "He wouldn't tell me anything. Nothing. He said it was the only way he could protect me."

"His name," Alice persisted. "Can you at least tell me his name?"

Dolores glanced toward the door, grimacing. "I don't know it," she whispered. "He said it was an alias."

"Then tell me the alias. Help me find his killer."

She drew in a breath. "Jack. Jack Bailey," she said. "He said he'd been in jail once. He said he was sorry. I got him going to church, trying to live a decent life. He was going to start over…" Her voice broke. "It's my fault."

"You were helping him," Alice corrected. "You gave him hope."

"He's dead."

"Yes. But there are worse things than dying. How long did you know him?" Alice asked.

"A few months. We went out together. He didn't own a car. I had to drive…"

"Where did he live?"

Dolores glanced at the door again. "I don't know. He always met me at a little strip mall near the tracks, the Weston Street Mall."

"Is there anything you can tell me that might help identify him?" Alice asked.

She blinked, deep in thought. "He said something happened, that it was an accident, but people died because of it. He was sorry. He said it was time to tell the truth, no matter how dangerous it was to him…"

"Dolores!"

She jumped. A tall, imposing figure stood in the light from the open door. "Get back in here! You aren't paid to socialize."

Harley stiffened, because he knew that voice.

"Yes, sir!" Dolores cried, rushing back inside. "Sorry. I was on my break…!"

She ran past the elegant older man. He closed the door and came storming toward Alice and Harley, looking as if he meant to start trouble.

"What do you mean, interrupting my workers when I have important guests? Who the hell are you people and how did you get in here?" he demanded.

Harley moved into the light, his pale eyes glittering at the older man. "I had an invitation," he said softly.

The older man stopped abruptly. He cocked his head, as if the voice meant more to him than the face did. "Who…are you?" he asked huskily.

"Just a ghost, visiting old haunts," he said, and there was ice in his tone.

The older man moved a step closer. As he came into the light, Alice noticed that he, too, had pale eyes, and gray-streaked brown hair.

"H-Harley?" he asked in a hesitant tone.

Harley caught Alice's hand in his. She noticed that his fingers were like ice.

"Sorry to have bothered you, Senator," Harley said formally. "Alice and I know a pastor who's a mutual friend of Dolores. He asked us to tell her about a family that needed a ride to church Sunday. Please excuse us."

He drew Alice around the older man, who stood frozen watching them as they went back into the kitchen.

Harley paused by Dolores and whispered something in her ear quickly before he rejoined Alice and they sauntered toward the living room. The senator moved toward them before they reached the living room, stared after them with a pained expression and tried to speak.

It was too late. Harley walked Alice right out the front door. On the way, a dark-eyed, dark-haired man in an expensive suit scowled as they passed him. Harley noticed that the senator stopped next to the other man and started talking to him.

THEY MADE IT back to the truck without being challenged, and without a word being spoken.

Harley put Alice inside the truck, got in and started it.

"He knew you," she stammered.

"Apparently." He nodded at her. "Fasten your seat belt."

"Sure." She snapped it in place, hoping that he might add something, explain what had happened. He didn't.

"You've got something to go on now, at least," he said.

"Yes," she agreed. "I have. Thanks, Harley. Thanks very much."

"My pleasure." He glanced at her. "I told Dolores what we said to the senator, so that our stories would match. It might save her job."

"I hope so," she said. "She seemed like a really nice person."

"Yeah."

He hardly said two words the whole rest of the way to her apartment. He parked in front of the building.

"You coming back down to Jacobsville?" he asked.

"In the morning," she said. "I still have some investigating to do there."

"Lunch, Monday, at Barbara's?" he invited.

She smiled. "I'd like that."

He smiled back. "Yeah. Me, too. Sorry we didn't get to stay. The buffet looked pretty good."

"I wasn't really hungry," she lied.

"You're a sweetheart. I'd take you out for a late supper, but my heart's not in it." He pulled her close and bent to kiss her. His mouth was hard and a little rough. "Thanks for not asking questions."

"No problem," she managed, because the kiss had been something, even if he hadn't quite realized what he was doing.

"See you Monday."

He went back to the truck and drove away. This time, he didn't wait for her to go in and close the door, an indication of how upset he really was.

CHAPTER SIX

HARLEY DROVE BACK to the ranch and cut off the engine outside the bunkhouse. It had been almost eight years since he'd seen the senator. He hadn't realized what a shock it was going to be, to come face-to-face with him. It brought back all the old wounds.

"Hey!"

He glanced at the porch of the modern bunkhouse. Charlie Dawes was staring at him from a crack in the door. "You coming in or sleeping out there?" the other cowboy called with a laugh.

"Coming in, I guess," he replied.

"Well!" Charlie exclaimed when he saw how the other man was dressed. "I thought you said you were just going out for a drive."

"I took Alice to a party, but we left early. Neither of us was in the mood," he said.

"Alice. That your girl?"

Harley smiled. "You know," he told the other man, "I think she is."

ALICE DROVE BACK down to Jacobsville late Sunday afternoon. She'd contacted Rick Marquez and asked if he'd do some investigating for her in San Antonio, to look for any rap sheet on a man who used a Jack Bailey alias and to see if they could find a man who'd been staying at a motel near the Weston Street Mall. He might have been seen in the company of a dark-haired woman driving a 1992 blue Ford sedan. It wasn't much to go on, but he might turn up something.

Meanwhile, Alice was going to go back to the crime scene and wander over it one more time, in hopes that the army of CSI detectives might have missed something, some tiny scrap of information that would help break the case.

SHE WAS DRESSED in jeans and sneakers and a green sweatshirt with CSI on it, sweeping the bank of the river, when her cell phone rang. She muttered as she pulled it out and checked the number. She frowned. Odd, she didn't recognize that number in any conscious way, but it struck something in the back of her mind.

"Jones," she said.

"Hi, Jones. It's Kilraven. I wondered if you dug up anything on the murder victim over the weekend?"

She sighed, her mind still on the ground she was searching. "Only that he had an alias, that he was trying to get something off his conscience, that he didn't own a car and he'd been in trouble with the law. Oh, and that he lived somewhere near the Weston Street Mall in San Antonio."

"Good God!" he exclaimed. "You got all that in one weekend?"

She laughed self-consciously. "Well, Harley helped. We crashed a senator's fundraiser and cornered an employee of his who'd been dating the… Oh, damn!" she exclaimed. "Listen, your brother will fry me up toasty and feed me to sharks if you tell him I said that. The feds didn't want anybody going near that woman!"

"Relax. Jon was keen to go out and talk to her himself, but his office nixed it. They were just afraid that some heavy-handed lawman would go over there and spook her. You share what you just told me with him, and I guarantee nobody will say a word about it. Great work, Alice."

"Thanks," she said. "The woman's name is Dolores. She's a nice lady. She feels guilty that he got killed. She never even fussed about her car and now it's totaled. She said she loaned him the car, but he told her to say it was stolen if he didn't call her in a day, in case somebody went after him. He knew he could get killed."

"He said he wanted to get something off his conscience," he reminded her.

"Yes. He said something happened that was an accident but that people died because of it. Does that help?"

"Only if I had ESP," he sighed. "Any more luck on that piece of paper you found in the victim's hand?"

"None. I hope to hear something in a few days from the lab. They're working their fingers to the bone. Why are holidays such a great time for murders and suicides?" she wondered aloud. "It's the holidays. You'd think it would make people happy."

"Sadly, as we both know, it doesn't. It just emphasizes what they've lost, since holidays are prime time for families to get together."

"I suppose so."

"We heard that you were going out with Harley Fowler," he said after a minute, with laughter in his deep voice. "Is it serious?"

"Not really," she replied pertly. "I mean, I ask him to marry me twice a day, but that's not what you'd call serious, is it?"

"Only if he says yes," he returned.

"He hasn't yet, but it's still early. I'm very persistent."

"Well, good luck."

"I don't need luck. I'm unspeakably beautiful, have great language skills, I can boil eggs and wash cars and... Hello? Hello!"

He'd hung up on her, laughing. She closed the flip phone. "I didn't want to talk to you, anyway," she told the phone. "I'm trying to work here."

She walked along the riverbank again, her sharp eyes on the rocks and weeds that grew along the water's edge. She was letting her mind wander, not trying to think in any conscious way. Sometimes, she got ideas that way.

The dead man had a past. He was mixed up in some sort of accident in which a death occurred that caused more deaths. He wanted to get something off his conscience. So he'd borrowed a car from his girlfriend and driven to Jacobsville. To see whom? The town wasn't that big, but it was pretty large if you were trying to figure out who someone a man with a criminal past was trying to find. Who could it be? Someone in law enforcement? Or was he just driving through Jacobsville on his way to talk to someone?

No, she discarded that possibility immediately. He'd

been killed here, so someone had either intercepted him or met him here, to talk about the past.

The problem was, she didn't have a clue who the man was or what he'd been involved in. She hoped that Rick Marquez came up with some answers.

But she knew more than she'd known a few days earlier, at least, and so did law enforcement. She still wondered at the interest of Jon Blackhawk of the San Antonio FBI office. Why were the feds involved? Were they working on some case secretly and didn't want to spill the beans to any outsiders?

Maybe they were working a similar case, she reasoned, and were trying to find a connection. They'd never tell her, of course, but she was a trained professional and this wasn't her first murder investigation.

What if the dead man had confessed, first, to the minister of Dolores's church?

She gasped out loud. It was like lightning striking. Of course! The minister might know something that he could tell her, unless he'd taken a vow of silence, like Catholic priests. They couldn't divulge anything learned in the confessional. But it was certainly worth a try!

She dug Harley's cell phone number out of her pocket and called him. The phone rang three times while she kicked at a dirt clod impatiently. Maybe he was knee-deep in mired cattle or something…

"Hello?"

"Harley!" she exclaimed.

"Now, just who else would it be, talking on Harley's phone?" came the amused, drawling reply.

"You, I hope," she said at once. "Listen, I need to talk to you…"

"You are," he reminded her.

"No, in person, right now," she emphasized. "It's about a minister…"

"Darlin', we can't get married today," he drawled. "I have to brush Bob the dog's teeth," he added lightly.

"Not that minister," she burst out. "Dolores's minister!"

He paused. "Why?"

"What if the murdered man confessed to him before he drove down to Jacobsville and got killed?" she exclaimed.

Harley whistled. "What if, indeed?"

"We need to go talk to her again and ask his name."

"Oh, now that may prove difficult. There's no party."

She realized that he was right. They had no excuse to show up at the senator's home, which was probably surrounded by security devices and armed guards. "Damn!"

"You can just call the house and ask for Dolores," he said reasonably. "You don't have to give your name or a reason."

She laughed softly. "Yes, I could do that. I don't know why I bothered you."

"Because you want to marry me," he said reasonably. "But I'm brushing the dog's teeth today. Sorry."

She glared at the phone. "Excuses, excuses," she muttered. "I'm growing older by the minute!"

"Why don't I bring you over here to go riding?" he

wondered aloud. "You could meet my boss and his wife and the boys, and meet Puppy Dog."

She brightened. "What a nice idea!"

"I thought so myself. I'll ask the boss. Next weekend, maybe? I'll beg for another half day on Saturday and take you riding around the ranch. We've got plenty of spare horses." When she hesitated, he sighed. "Don't tell me. You can't ride."

"I can so ride horses," she said indignantly. "I ride horses at amusement parks all the time. They go up and down and round and round, and music plays."

"That isn't the same sort of riding. Well, I'll teach you," he said. "After all, if we get married, you'll have to live on a ranch. I'm not stuffing myself into some tiny apartment in San Antonio."

"Now that's the sort of talk I love to hear," she sighed.

He laughed. "Wear jeans and boots," he instructed. "And thick socks."

"No blouse or bra?" she exclaimed in mock outrage.

He whistled. "Well, you don't have to wear them on my account," he said softly. "But we wouldn't want to shock my boss, you know."

She laughed at that. "Okay. I'll come decently dressed. Saturday it is." She hesitated. "Where's the ranch?"

"I'll come and get you." He hesitated. "You'll still be here next Saturday, won't you?"

She was wondering how to stretch her investigation here by another week. Then she remembered that Christmas was Thursday and she relaxed. "I get Christmas off," she said. Then she remembered that she'd promised to work Christmas Eve already. "Well, I get

Christmas Day. I'll ask for the rest of the week. I'll tell them that the case is heating up and I have two or three more people to interview."

"Great! Can I help?"

"Yes, you can find me two or three more people to interview," she said. "Meanwhile, I'll call Dolores and ask her to give me her minister's name." She grimaced. "I'll have to be sure I don't say that to whoever answers the phone. We told everybody we were giving her a message from her minister!"

"Good idea. Let me know what you find out, okay?"

"You bet. See you." She hung up.

She had to dial information to get the senator's number and, thank God, it wasn't unlisted. She punched the numbers into her cell phone and waited. A young woman answered.

"May I please speak to Dolores?" Alice asked politely.

"Dolores?"

"Yes."

There was a long pause. Alice gritted her teeth. They were going to tell her that employees weren't allowed personal phone calls during the day, she just knew it.

But the voice came back on the line with a long sigh. "I'm so sorry," the woman said. "Dolores isn't here anymore."

That wasn't altogether surprising, but it wasn't a serious setback. "Can you tell me how to get in touch with her? I'm an old friend," she added, improvising.

The sigh was longer. "Well, you can't. I mean, she's dead."

Alice was staggered. "Dead?!" she exclaimed.

"Yes. Suicide. She shot herself through the heart," the woman said sadly. "It was such a shock. The senator's wife found her... Oh, dear, I can't talk anymore, I'm sorry."

"Just a minute, just one minute, can you tell me where the funeral is being held?" she asked quickly.

"At the Weston Street Baptist Church," came the reply, almost in a whisper, "at two tomorrow afternoon. I have to go. I'm very sorry about Dolores. We all liked her."

The phone went dead.

Alice felt sick. Suicide! Had she driven the poor woman to it, with her questions? Or had she been depressed because of her boyfriend's murder?

Strange, that she'd shot herself through the heart. Most women chose some less violent way to die. Most used drugs. Suicides by gun were usually men.

She called Harley back.

"Hello?" he said.

"Harley, she killed herself," she blurted out.

"Who? Dolores? She's dead?" he exclaimed.

"Yes. Shot through the heart, I was told. Suicide."

He paused. "Isn't that unusual for a woman? To use a gun to kill herself, I mean?"

"It is. But I found out where her pastor is," she added. "I'm going to the funeral tomorrow. Right now, I'm going up to San Antonio to my office."

"Why?" he asked.

"Because in all violent deaths, even those ascribed to suicide, an autopsy is required. I wouldn't miss this one for the world."

"Keep in touch."

"You bet."

Alice hung up and went back to her van. She had a hunch that a woman as religious as Dolores wouldn't kill herself. Most religions had edicts against it. That didn't stop people from doing it, of course, but Dolores didn't strike Alice as the suicidal sort. She was going to see if the autopsy revealed anything.

THE OFFICE WAS, as usual on holidays, overworked. She found one of the assistant medical examiners poring over reports in his office.

He looked up as she entered. "Jones! Could I get you to come back and work for us in autopsy again if I bribed you? It's getting harder and harder to find people who don't mind hanging around with the dead."

She smiled. "Sorry, Murphy," she said. "I'm happier with investigative work these days. Listen, do you have a suicide back there? First name Dolores, worked for a senator…?"

"Yep. I did her myself, earlier this evening." He shook his head. "She had small hands and the gun was a .45 Colt ACP," he replied. "How she ever cocked the damned thing, much less killed herself with it, is going to be one of the great unsolved mysteries of life. Added to that, she had carpal tunnel in her right hand. She'd had surgery at least once. Weakens the muscle, you know. We'd already ascertained that she was right-handed because there was more muscle attachment there—usual on the dominant side."

"You're sure it was suicide?" she pressed.

He leaned back in his chair, eyeing her through thick

corrective lenses. "There was a rim burn around the entrance wound," he said, referring to the heat and flare of the shot in close-contact wounds. "But the angle of entry was odd."

She jumped on that. "Odd, how?"

"Diagonal," he replied. He pulled out his digital camera, ran through the files and punched up one. He handed her the camera. "That's the wound, anterior view. Pull up the next shot and you'll see where it exited, posterior."

She inhaled. "Wow!"

"Interesting, isn't it? Most people who shoot themselves with an automatic handgun do it holding the barrel to the head or under the chin. This was angled downward. And as I said before, her hand was too weak to manage this sort of weapon. There's something else."

"What?" she asked, entranced.

"The gun was found still clenched in her left hand."

"So?"

"Remember what I said about the carpal tunnel? She was right-handed."

She cocked her head. "Going to write it up as suspected homicide?"

"You're joking, right? Know who she worked for?"

She sighed. "Yes. Senator Fowler."

"Would you write it up as a suspected homicide or would you try to keep your job?"

That was a sticky question. "But if she was murdered…"

"The 'if' is subjective. I'm not one of those TV forensic people," he reminded her. "I'm two years from retirement, and I'm not risking my pension on a possibility. She goes out as a suicide until I get absolute proof that it wasn't."

Alice knew when that would be. "Could you at least put 'probable suicide,' Murphy?" she persisted. "Just for me?"

He frowned. "Why? Alice, do you know something that I need to know?"

She didn't dare voice her suspicions. She had no proof. She managed a smile. "Humor me. It won't rattle any cages, and if something comes up down the line, you'll have covered your butt. Right?"

He searched her eyes for a moment and then smiled warmly. "Okay. I'll put probable. But if you dig up something, you tell me first, right?"

She grinned. "Right."

HER NEXT MOVE was to go to the Weston Street Baptist Church and speak to the minister, but she had to wait until the funeral to do it. If she saw the man alone, someone might see her and his life could be in danger. It might be already. She wasn't sure what to do.

She went to police headquarters and found Detective Rick Marquez sitting at his desk. The office was almost empty, but there he was, knee-deep in file folders.

She tapped on the door and walked in at the same time.

"Alice!" He got to his feet. "Nice to see you."

"Is it? Why?" she asked suspiciously.

He glanced at the file folders and winced. "Any reason to take a break is a good one. Not that I'm sorry to see you," he added.

"What are you doing?" she asked as she took a seat in front of the desk.

"Poring over cold cases," he said heavily. "My lieutenant said I could do it on my own time, as long as I didn't advertise why I was doing it."

"Why are you doing it?" she asked curiously.

"Your murder down in Jacobsville nudged a memory or two," he said. "There was a case similar to it, also unsolved. It involved a fourteen-year-old girl who was driving a car reported stolen. She was also unrecognizable, but several of her teeth were still in place. They identified her by dental records. No witnesses, no clues."

"How long ago was this?" she asked.

He shrugged. "About seven years," he said. "In fact, it happened some time before Kilraven's family was killed."

"Could there be a connection?" she wondered aloud.

"I don't know. I don't see how the death of a teenage girl ties in to the murder of a cop's family." He smiled. "Maybe it's just a coincidence." He put the files aside. "Why are you up here?"

"I came to check the results of an autopsy," she said. "The woman who worked for Senator Fowler supposedly killed herself, but the bullet was angled downward, her hand was too weak to have pulled the trigger and the weapon was found clutched in the wrong hand."

He blew out his breath in a rush. "Some suicide."

"My thoughts, exactly."

"Talk to me, Jones."

"She was involved with the murder victim in Jacobsville, remember?" she asked him. "She wouldn't tell me his name, she swore she didn't know it. But she gave me the alias he used—the one I called and gave you— and she said he'd spoken to the minister of her church. He told her there was an accident that caused a lot of other people to die. He had a guilty conscience and he wanted to tell what he knew."

Marquez's dark eyes pinned hers. "Isn't that interesting."

"Isn't it?"

"You going to talk to the minister?"

"I want to, but I'm afraid to be seen doing it," she told him. "His life may be in danger if he knows something. Whatever is going on, it's big, and it has ties to powerful people."

"The senator, maybe?" he wondered aloud.

"Maybe."

"When did you talk to her?"

"There was a fundraiser at the senator's house. Harley Fowler took me…" She hadn't connected the names before. Now she did. The senator's name was Fowler. Harley's name was Fowler. The senator had recognized Harley, had approached him, had talked to him in a soft tone…

"Harley *Fowler*?" Marquez emphasized, making the same connection she did. "Harley's family?"

"I don't know," she said. "He didn't say anything to me. But the senator acted really strangely. He seemed to recognize Harley. And when Harley took me to my apartment, he didn't wait until I got inside the door. That's not like him. He was distracted."

"He comes from wealth and power, and he's working cattle for Cy Parks," Marquez mused. "Now isn't that a curious thing?"

"It is, and if it's true, you mustn't tell anybody," Alice replied. "It's his business."

"I agree. I'll keep it to myself. Who saw you talk to the woman at the senator's house?"

"Everybody, but we told them we knew her minister and came to tell her something for him."

"If she went to church every week, wouldn't that seem suspicious that you were seeing her to give her a message from her minister?"

Alice smiled. "Harley told them he'd asked us to give her a message about offering a ride to a fellow worshipper on Sunday."

"Uh, Alice, her car was pulled out of the Little Carmichael River in Jacobsville…?"

"Oh, good grief," she groaned. "Well, nobody knew that when we were at the party."

"Yes. But maybe somebody recognized you and figured you were investigating the murder," he returned.

She grimaced. "And I got her killed," she said miserably.

"No."

"If I hadn't gone there and talked to her…!" she protested.

"When your time's up, it's up, Jones," he replied philosophically. "It wouldn't have made any difference. A car crash, a heart attack, a fall from a high place…it could have been anything. Intentions are what matter. You didn't go there to cause her any trouble."

She managed a wan smile. "Thanks, Marquez."

"But if she was killed," he continued, "that fits into your case somehow. It means that the murderer isn't taking any chance that somebody might talk."

"The murderer…?"

"Your dead woman said the victim knew something damaging about several deaths. Who else but the murderer would be so hell-bent on eliminating evidence?"

"We still don't know who the victim is."

Marquez's sensuous lips flattened as he considered the possibilities. "If the minister knows anything, he's already in trouble. He may be in trouble if he doesn't know anything. The perp isn't taking any chances."

"What can we do to protect him?"

Marquez picked up the phone. "I'm going to risk my professional career and see if I can help him."

Alice sat and listened while he talked. Five minutes later, he hung up the phone.

"Are you sure that's the only way to protect him?" she asked worriedly.

"It's the best one I can think of, short of putting him in protective custody," he said solemnly. "I can't do that without probable cause, not to mention that our budget is in the red and we can't afford protective custody."

"Your boss isn't going to like it. And I expect Jon Blackhawk will be over here with a shotgun tomorrow morning, first thing."

"More than likely."

She smiled. "You're a prince!"

His eyebrows arched. "You could marry me," he suggested.

She shook her head. "No chance. If you really are

a prince, if I kissed you, by the way the laws of probability work in my life, you'd turn right into a frog."

He hesitated and then burst out laughing.

She grinned. "Thanks, Marquez. If I can help you, anytime, I will."

"You can. Call my boss tomorrow and tell him that you think I'm suffering from a high fever and hallucinations and I'm not responsible for my own actions."

"I'll do that very thing. Honest."

THE NEXT MORNING, the local media reported that the pastor of a young woman who'd committed suicide was being questioned by police about some information that might tie her to a cold case. Alice thought it was a stroke of pure genius. Only a total fool would risk killing the pastor now that he was in the media spotlight. It was the best protection he could have.

Marquez's boss was, predictably, enraged. But Alice went to see him and, behind closed doors, told him what she knew about the murder in Jacobsville. He calmed down and agreed that it was a good call on his detective's part.

Then Alice went to see Reverend Mike Colman, early in the morning, before the funeral.

He wasn't what she expected. He was sitting in his office wearing sneakers, a pair of old jeans and a black sweatshirt. He had prematurely thinning dark hair, wore glasses, and had a smile as warm as a summer day.

He got up and shook hands with Alice after she introduced herself.

"I understand that I might be a candidate for admittance to your facility," he deadpanned. "Detective Marquez decided that making a media pastry out of me could save my life."

"I hope he's right," she said solemnly. "Two people have died in the past two weeks who had ties to this case. We've got a victim in Jacobsville that we can't even identify."

He grimaced. "I was sorry to hear about Dolores. I never thought she'd kill herself, and I still don't."

"It's sad that she did so much to help a man tortured by his past, and paid for it with her life. Isn't there a saying, that no good deed goes unpunished?" she added with wan humor.

"It seems that way sometimes, doesn't it?" he asked with a smile. "But God's ways are mysterious. We aren't meant to know why things happen the way they do at all times. So what can I do to help you?"

"Do you think you could describe the man Dolores sent to talk to you? If I get a police artist over here with his software and his laptop, can you tell him what the man looked like?"

"Oh, I think I can do better than that."

He pulled a pencil out of his desk drawer, drew a thick pad of paper toward him, peeled back the top and proceeded with deft strokes to draw an unbelievably lifelike pencil portrait of a man.

"That's incredible!" Alice exclaimed, fascinated by the expert rendering.

He chuckled as he handed it over to her. "Thanks. I wasn't always a minister," he explained. "I was on my way to Paris to further my studies in art when God

tapped me on the shoulder and told me He needed me."
He shrugged. "You don't say no to Him," he added with
a kind smile.

"If there isn't some sort of pastor/confessor bond
you'd be breaking, could you tell me what you talked
about with him?"

"There's no confidentiality," he replied. "But he
didn't really tell me anything. He asked me if God could
forgive any sin, and I told him yes. He said he'd been a
bad man, but he was in love, and he wanted to change.
He said he was going to talk to somebody who was involved in an old case, and he'd tell me everything when
he got back." He grimaced. "Except he didn't get back,
did he?"

"No," Alice agreed sadly. "He didn't."

CHAPTER SEVEN

ALICE TOOK THE drawing with her. She phoned Marquez's office, planning to stop by to show the drawing to him, but he'd already gone home. She tucked it into her purse and went to her own office. It was now Christmas Eve, and she'd promised to work tonight as a favor to the woman who'd saved her date with Harley.

She walked into the medical examiner's office, waving to the security guard on her way inside. The building, located on the University of Texas campus, was almost deserted. Only a skeleton crew worked on holidays. Most of the staff had families. Only Alice and one other employee were still single. But the medical examiner's office was accessible 24/7, so someone was always on call.

She went by her colleague's desk and grimaced as she saw the caseload sitting in the basket, waiting for her. It was going to be a long night.

She sat down at her own desk and started poring over the first case file. There were always deaths to investigate, even when foul play wasn't involved. In each one, if there was an question as to how the deceased had departed, it was up to her to work with the detectives to determine a cause of death. Her only consolation was that the police detectives were every bit as overloaded as she, a medical examiner investigator, was. Nobody did investigative work to get rich. But the job did have other rewards, she reminded herself. Solving a crime and bringing a murderer to justice was one of the perks. And no amount of money would make up for the pleasure it gave her to see that a death was avenged. Legally, of course.

She opened the first file and started working up the notes on the computer into a document easily read by the lead police detective on the case, as well as the assistant district attorney prosecuting it. She waded through crime scene photographs, measurements, witness statements and other interviews, but as she did, she was still wondering about the coincidence of Harley's last name and the senator's. The older man had recognized him, had called him Harley. They obviously knew each other, and there was some animosity there. But if the senator was a relation, why hadn't Harley mentioned it when he and Alice stopped by the house for the fundraiser?

Maybe he hadn't wanted Alice to know. Maybe he didn't want anyone to know, especially anyone in Jacobsville. Perhaps he wanted to make it on his own, without the wealth and power of his family behind him. He'd said that he no longer felt comfortable with the things his parents wanted him to do. If they were in politics and expected him to help host fundraisers and hang out with the cream of high society, he might have felt uncomfortable. She recalled her own parents and how much she'd loved them, and how close they'd been.

They'd never asked her to do anything she didn't feel comfortable with. Harley obviously hadn't had that sort of home life. She was sad for him. But if things worked out, she promised herself that she'd do what she could to make up for what he missed. First step in that direction, she decided, was a special Christmas present.

SHE SLEPT LATE on Christmas morning. But when she woke up, she got out her cell phone and made a virtual shopping trip around town, to discover which businesses were open on a holiday. She found one, and it carried just the item she wanted. She drove by there on her way down to Jacobsville.

Good thing she'd called ahead about keeping her motel room, she thought when she drove into the parking lot. The place was full. Obviously some locals had out-of-town family who didn't want to impose when they came visiting on the holidays. She stashed her suitcase and called Harley's number.

"Hello," came a disgruntled voice over the line.

"Harley?" she asked hesitantly.

There was a shocked pause. "Alice? Is that you?"

She laughed. "Well, you sound out of sorts."

"I am." There was a splash. "Get out of there, you walking steak platter!" he yelled. "Hold the line a minute, Alice, I have to put down the damn…phone!"

There was a string of very unpleasant language, most of which was mercifully muffled. Finally Harley came back on the line.

"I hate the cattle business," he said.

She grimaced. Perhaps she shouldn't have made that shopping trip after all. "Do you?" she asked. "Why?"

"Truck broke down in the middle of the pasture while I was tossing out hay," he muttered. "I got out of the truck and under the hood to see what was wrong. I left the door open. Boss's wife had sent me by the store on the way to pick up some turnip greens for her. Damned cow stuck her head into the truck and ate every damned one of them! So now, I'm mired up to my knees in mud and the truck's sinking, and once I get the truck out, I've got to go all the way back to town for a bunch of turnips on account of the stupid cow… Why are you laughing?"

"I thought you ran purebred bulls," she said.

"You can't get a purebred bull without a purebred cow to drop it," he said with exaggerated patience.

"Sorry. I wasn't thinking. Say, I'm just across the street from a market. Want me to go over and get you some more turnips and bring them to you?"

There was an intake of breath. "You'd do that? On Christmas Day?"

"I sort of got you something," she said. "Just a little something. I wanted an excuse to bring it to you, anyway."

"Doggone it, Alice, I didn't get you anything," he said shamefully.

"I didn't expect you to," she said at once. "But you took me to a nice party and I thought… Well, it's just a little something."

"I took you to a social shooting gallery and didn't even buy you supper," he said, feeling ashamed.

"It was a nice party," she said. "Do you want turnips or not?"

He laughed. "I do. Think you can find Cy Parks's ranch?"

"Give me directions."

He did, routing her the quickest way.

"I'll be there in thirty minutes," she said. "Or I'll call for more directions."

"Okay. Thanks a million, Alice."

"No problem."

SHE DRESSED IN her working clothes, jeans and boots and a coat, but she added a pretty white sweater with a pink poinsettia embroidered on it, for Christmas. She didn't bother with makeup. It wouldn't help much anyway, she decided with a rueful smile. She bought the turnips and drove the few miles to the turnoff that led to Cy Parks's purebred Santa Gertrudis stud ranch.

Harley was waiting for her less than half a mile down the road, at the fork that turned into the ranch house. He was covered in mud, even his once-brown cowboy hat. He had a smear of mud on one cheek, but he looked very sexy, Alice thought. She couldn't think of one man out of thirty she knew who could be covered in mud and still look so good. Harley did.

He pushed back his hat as he walked up to the van, opening the door for her.

She grabbed the turnips in their brown bag and handed them to him. She jumped down with a small box in her hand. "Here," she said, shoving it at him.

"Wait a sec." He put the turnips in his truck and

handed her a five-dollar bill. "Don't argue," he said at once, when she tried to. "I had money to get them with, even allowing for cow sabotage." He grinned.

She grinned back. "Okay." She put the bill in her jeans pocket and handed him the box.

He gave her an odd look. "What's it for?"

"Christmas," she said.

He laughed. "Boss gives me a bonus every Christmas. I can't remember the last time I got an actual present."

She flushed.

"Don't get self-conscious about it," he said, when he noticed her sudden color. "I just felt bad that I didn't get you something."

"I told you, the party…"

"Some party," he muttered. He turned the small box in his hands, curious. He pulled the tape that held the sides together and opened it. His pale eyes lit up as he pulled the little silver longhorn tie tack out of the box. "Hey, this is sweet! I've been looking for one of these, but I could never find one small enough to be in good taste!"

She flushed again. "You really like it?"

"I do! I'll wear it to the next Cattlemen's Association meeting," he promised. "Thanks, Alice."

"Merry Christmas."

"It is, now," he agreed. He slid an arm around her waist and pulled her against him. "Merry Christmas, Alice." He bent and kissed her with rough affection.

She sighed and melted into him. The kiss was warm, and hard and intoxicating. She was a normal adult woman with all the usual longings, but it had been a long time since a kiss had made her want to rip a man's clothes off and push him down on the ground.

She laughed.

He drew back at once, angry. "What the hell…!"

"No, it's not… I'm not laughing at you! I was wondering what you'd think if I started ripping your clothes off…!"

He'd gone from surprise to anger to indignation, and now he doubled over laughing.

"Was it something I said?" she wondered aloud.

He grabbed her up in his arms and spun her around, catching her close to kiss her hungrily again and again. He was covered in mud, and now she was covered in it, too. She didn't care.

Her arms caught around his neck. She held on, loving the warm crush of his mouth in the cold rain that was just starting to fall. Her eyes closed. She breathed, and breathed him, cologne and soap and coffee…

After a few seconds, the kiss stopped being fun and became serious. His hard mouth opened. His arm dragged her breasts against his broad chest. He nudged her lips apart and invaded her mouth with deliberate sensuality.

He nibbled her lower lip as he carried her to the pickup truck. He nudged the turnips into the passenger seat while he edged under the wheel, still carrying Alice. He settled her in his lap and kissed her harder while his hands slid under the warm sweater and onto her bare back, working their way under the wispy little bra she was wearing.

His hands were cold and she jumped when they found her pert little breasts, and she laughed nervously.

"They'll warm up," he whispered against her mouth.

She was going under in waves of pleasure. It had been such a long time since she'd been held and kissed, and even the best she'd had was nothing compared to this. She moaned softly as his palms settled over her breasts and began to caress them, ever so gently.

She held on for dear life. She hoped he wasn't going to suggest that they try to manage an intimate session on the seat, because there really wasn't that much room. On the other hand, she wasn't protesting...

When he drew back, she barely realized it. She was hanging in space, so flushed with delight that she was feeling oblivious to everything else.

He was looking at her with open curiosity, his hands still under her top, but resting on her rib cage now, not intimately on her breasts.

She blinked, staring up at him helplessly. "Is something wrong?" she asked in a voice that sounded drowsy with passion.

"Alice, you haven't done much of this, have you?" he asked very seriously.

She bit her lip self-consciously. "Am I doing it wrong?"

"There's no right or wrong way," he corrected gently. "You don't know how to give it back."

She just stared at him.

"It's not a complaint," he said when he realized he was hurting her feelings. He bent and brushed his warm mouth over her eyelids. "For a brash woman, you're amazingly innocent. I thought you were kidding, about being a virgin."

She went scarlet. "Well, no, I wasn't."

He laughed softly. "I noticed. Here. Sit up."

She did, but she popped back up and grabbed the turnips before she sat on them. "Whew," she whistled. "They're okay."

He took them from her and put them up on the dash.

She gave him a mock hurt look. "Don't you want to ravish me on the truck seat?" she asked hopefully.

He lifted both eyebrows. "Alice, you hussy!" He laughed.

She grimaced. "Sorry."

"I was teasing!"

"Oh."

He drew her close and hugged her with rough affection. "Yes, I'd love to ravish you on the seat, but not on Christmas Day in plain view of the boss and any cowhand who wandered by."

"Are they likely to wander by?" she wondered out loud.

He let her go and nodded in the direction of the house. There were two cowboys coming their way on horseback. They weren't looking at them. They seemed to be talking.

"It's Christmas," she said.

"Yes, and cattle have to be worked on holidays as well as workdays," he reminded her.

"Sorry. I forgot."

"I really like my tie tack," he said. "And thanks a million for bringing me the turnips." He hesitated. "But I have to get back to work. I gave up my day off so that John could go and see his kids," he added with a smile.

She beamed. "I gave up my Christmas Eve for the same reason. But that's how I got to go to the movie with you. I promised to work for him last night."

"We're both nice people," he said, smiling.

She sighed. "I could call a minister right now."

"He's busy," he said with a grin. "It's Christmas."

"Oh. Right."

He got out of the truck and helped her down. "Thanks for my present. Sorry I didn't get you one."

"Yes, you did," she said at once, and then laughed and flushed.

He bent and kissed her softly. "I got an extra one myself," he whispered. "Are we still going riding Saturday?"

"Oh, yes," she said. "At least, I think so. I've got to run up to San Antonio in the morning to talk to Rick Marquez. The minister of the murdered woman was able to draw the man she sent to him."

"Really?" he asked, impressed.

"Yes, and so now we have a real lead." She frowned thoughtfully. "You know, I wonder if Kilraven might recognize the guy. He works out of San Antonio. He might make a copy and show it to his brother, too."

"Good idea." He drew in a long breath. "Alice, you be careful," he added. "If the woman was killed because she talked to us, the minister might be next, and then you." He didn't add, but they both knew, that he could be on the firing line, too.

"The minister's okay. Marquez called a reporter he

knew and got him on the evening news." She chuckled. "They'd be nuts to hurt him now, with all the media attention."

"Probably true, and good call by Marquez. But you're not on the news."

"Point taken. I'll watch my back. You watch yours, too," she added with a little concern.

"I work for a former mercenary," he reminded her drolly. "It would take somebody really off balance to come gunning for me."

"Okay. That makes me feel better." She smiled. "But if this case heats up in San Antonio, I may have to go back sooner than Saturday…"

"So? If you can't come riding, I can drive up there and we can catch a movie or go out to eat."

"You would?" she exclaimed, surprised.

He glowered at her. "We're going steady. Didn't you notice?"

"No! Why didn't you tell me?" she demanded.

"You didn't ask. Go back to the motel and maybe we can have lunch tomorrow at Barbara's. I'll phone you."

She grinned. "That would be lovely."

"Meanwhile, I've got more cattle to feed," he said on a weary sigh. "It was a nice break, though."

"Yes, it was."

He looked at the smears of mud on her once-pristine shirt and winced. "Sorry," he said.

She looked down at the smears and just laughed. "It'll wash," she said with a shy smile.

He beamed. He loved a woman who didn't mind a

little dirt. He opened her van door and she climbed up into it. "Drive carefully," he told her.

She smiled. "I always do."

"See you."

"See you."

She was halfway back to the motel before she realized that she hadn't mentioned his connection to Senator Fowler. Of course, that might be just as well, considering that the newest murder victim had ties to the senator, and the original murder victim did, too, in a roundabout way.

ON HER WAY to see Hayes Carson at the sheriff's office, Alice phoned Marquez at home—well, it was a holiday, so she thought he might be at home with his foster mother, Barbara. She found out that Marquez had been called back to San Antonio on a case. She grimaced. She was never going to get in touch with him, she supposed.

She walked into Carson's office. He was sitting at his desk. He lifted both eyebrows. "It's December twenty-fifth," he pointed out.

She lifted both eyebrows. "Ho, ho, ho?" she said.

He chuckled. "So I'm not the only person who works holidays. I had started to wonder." He indicated the empty desks around his office in the county detention center.

"My office looked that way last night, too," she confessed. She sat down by his desk. "I questioned a woman who worked for Senator Fowler about the man who drove her car down here and got killed next to the river."

"Find out much?" he asked, suddenly serious.

"That I shouldn't have been so obvious about questioning her. She died of an apparent suicide, but I pestered the attending pathologist to put 'probable' before 'suicide' on the death certificate. She shot herself through the heart with the wrong hand and the bullet was angled down." She waited for a reaction.

He leaned back in his chair. "Wonders will never cease."

"I went to see her minister, who spoke to the man we found dead by the river. The minister was an art student. He drew me this." She pulled out a folded sheet of paper from her purse and handed it to him.

"Hallelujah!" he burst out. "Alice, you're a wonder! You should be promoted!"

"No, thanks, I like fieldwork too much," she told him, grinning. "It's good, isn't it? That's what your murder victim looks like." Her smile faded. "I'm just sorry I got the woman killed who was trying to help him restart his life."

He looked up with piercing eyes. "You didn't. Life happens. We don't control how it happens."

"You're good for my self-esteem. I was going to show that to Rick Marquez, but he's become rather elusive."

"Something happened in San Antonio. I don't know what. They called in a lot of off-duty people."

"Was Kilraven one of them, or do you know?" she asked.

"I don't, but I can find out." He called the dispatch

center and gave Kilraven's badge number and asked if Kilraven was on duty.

"Yes, he is. Do you want me to ask him to place you a twenty-one?" she asked, referring to a phone call.

"Yes, thanks, Winnie," he said, a smile in his voice as he recognized dispatcher Winnie Sinclair.

"No problem. Dispatch out at thirteen hundred hours."

He hung up. "She'll have him call me," he told Alice. "What did the minister tell you about the murdered man?" he asked while they waited.

"Not much. He said the guy told him he'd been a bad man, but he wanted to change, that he was going to speak to somebody about an old case and that he'd talk to the minister again after he did it. It's a real shame. Apparently he'd just discovered that there was more to life than dodging the law. He had a good woman friend, he was starting to go to church—now he's lying in the morgue, unidentifiable."

"Not anymore," Hayes told her, waving the drawing.

"Yes, but he could be anybody," she replied.

"If he has a criminal background, he's got fingerprints on file and a mug shot. I have access to face recognition software."

"You do? How?" she asked, fascinated.

"Tell you what," he said, leaning forward. "I'll give you my source if you'll tell me how you got hold of that computer chip emplacement tech for tagging bodies."

She caught her breath. "Well! You do get around, don't you? That's cutting-edge and we don't advertise it."

"My source doesn't advertise, either."

"We'll trade," she promised. "Now, tell me…"

The phone rang. Hayes picked it up. He gave Alice a sardonic look. "Yes, the sheriff's office is open on Christmas. I just put away my reindeer and took off my red suit… Yes, Alice Jones is here with an artist's sketch of the murdered man… Hello? Hello?" He hung up with a sigh. "Kilraven," he said, answering the unasked question.

Alice sighed. "I get that a lot, too. People hanging up on me, I mean. I'll bet he's burning rubber, trying to get here at light speed."

"I wouldn't doubt it." He chuckled.

Sure enough, just a minute or two later, they heard squealing tires turning into the parking lot outside the window. A squad car with flashing blue lights slammed to a stop just at the front door and the engine went dead. Seconds later, Kilraven stormed into the office.

"Let's see it," he said without preamble.

Hayes handed him the drawing.

Kilraven looked at it for a long time, frowning.

"Recognize him?" Alice asked.

He grimaced. "No," he said gruffly. "Damn! I thought it might be somebody I knew."

"Why?" Hayes asked.

"I work out of San Antonio as a rule," he said. "And I was a patrol officer, and then a detective, on the police force there for some years. If the guy had a record in San Antonio, I might have had dealings with him. But I don't recognize this guy."

Hayes took the sketch back. "If I make a copy, could you show it to Jon and see if he looks familiar to him?"

"Sure." He glanced at Alice. "How'd you get a sketch of the dead man? Reconstructive artist?"

"No. That woman I talked to about him killed herself…"

"Like hell she did," Kilraven exclaimed. "That's too pat!"

"Just what I thought. I talked to the forensic pathologist who did the autopsy," she added. "He said she was right-handed, but shot herself through the heart with her left hand. Good trick, too, because she had carpal tunnel syndrome, plus surgery, and the gun was a big, heavy .45 Colt ACP. He said she'd have had hell just cocking it."

"He labeled it a suicide?"

She shook her head. "He's trying not to get caught up in political fallout. She worked for the senator, you know, and he's not going to want to be a media snack over a possible homicide that happened on his own property."

"The pathologist didn't label it a suicide?" he persisted.

"I got him to add 'probable' to the report."

"Well, that's something, I guess. Damned shame, about the woman. She might have been able to tell us more, in time." He smiled at Alice. "I'm glad you went to see her, anyway. What we have is thanks to you." He frowned. "But how did you get the sketch?"

"The woman's minister," she said simply. "He'd talked to the man who was killed and before he became a minister, he was an artist. He didn't add much to what the woman had already told me. He did say that the guy had a guilty conscience and he was going to talk to somebody about an old case."

Kilraven was frowning again. "An old case. Who was he going to talk to? People in law enforcement, maybe?"

"Very possibly," Alice agreed. "I'm not through digging. But I need to identify this man. I thought I might go to the motel where he was staying and start interviewing residents. It's a start."

"Not for you," Kilraven said sternly. "You've put yourself in enough danger already. You leave this to me and Jon. We get paid for people to shoot at us. You don't."

"My hero," Alice sighed, batting her eyelashes at him and smiling. "If I wasn't so keen to marry Harley Fowler, I swear I'd be sending you candy and flowers."

"I hate sweets and I'm allergic to flowers," he pointed out.

She wrinkled her nose. "Just as well, then, isn't it?"

"I'll copy this for you," Hayes said, moving to the copy machine in the corner. "We're low on toner, though, so don't expect anything as good as the original drawing."

"Why don't you get more toner?" Alice asked.

Hayes glowered. "I have to have a purchase order from the county commission, and they're still yelling at me about the last several I asked for."

"Which was for...?" Kilraven prompted.

Hayes made the copy, examined it and handed it to

Kilraven. "A cat, and an electrician, and an exterminator."

Alice and Kilraven stared at him.

He moved self-consciously back to his desk and sat
down. "I bought this cheap cat," he emphasized. "It only
cost fifteen bucks at the pet store. It wasn't purebred or
anything."

"Why did you buy a cat?" Alice asked.

He sighed. "Do you remember the mouse that lived
in Tira Hart's house before she became Simon Hart's
wife?"

"Well, I heard about it," Kilraven admitted.

"One of my deputies caught two field mice and was
going to take them home to his kids for a science project. He put them in a wood box and when he went to
get them out, they weren't there." Hayes sighed. "They
chewed their way out of the box, they chewed up the
baseboards and two electrical wires, and did about three
hundred dollars worth of damage to county property.
I called an electrician for that. Then I tried traps and
they wouldn't work, so I bought a cat."

"Did the cat get the mice?" Alice asked.

Hayes shook his head. "Actually," he replied, "the
mice lay in wait for the cat, chomped down on both his
paws at the same time, and darted back into the hole in
the wall they came out of. Last time I saw the cat, he
was headed out of town by way of the city park. The
mice are still here, though," he added philosophically.
"Which is why I had to have authorization to pay for
an exterminator. The chairman of our county commis-

sion found one of the mice sitting in his coffee cup." He sighed. "Would you believe, I got blamed for that, too?"

"Well, that explains why the commission got mad at you," Alice said. "I mean, for the cat and the electrician."

"No, that's not why they got mad."

"It wasn't?"

He looked sheepish. "It was the engine for a 1996 Ford pickup truck."

Alice stared at him. "Okay, now I'm confused."

"I had to call an exterminator. While he was looking for the mice, they got under the hood of his truck and did something—God knows what, but it was catastrophic. When he started the truck, the engine caught fire. It was a total loss."

"How do you know the mice did it?" Kilraven wanted to know.

"One of my deputies—the same one who brought the damned rodents in here in the first place—saw them coming down the wheel well of the truck just before the exterminator got in and started it."

Alice laughed. She got to her feet. "Hayes, if I were you, I'd find whoever bought Cag Hart's big albino python and borrow him."

"If these mice are anything like Tira's mouse, fat chance a snake will do what a cat can't."

As he spoke, the lights started dimming. He shook his head. "They're back," he said with sad resignation.

"Better hide your firearms," Kilraven advised as he and Alice started for the door.

"With my luck, they're better shots than I am." Hayes

laughed. "I'm going to show this drawing around town and see if anybody recognizes the subject. If either of you find out anything else about the murdered man, let me know."

"Will do," Alice promised.

CHAPTER EIGHT

ALICE FOLLOWED KILRAVEN out the door. He stood on the steps of the detention center, deep in thought.

"Why did you think you might know the murder victim?" Alice asked him.

"I told you…"

"You lied."

He looked down at her with arched eyebrows.

"Oh, I'm psychic," she said easily. "You know all those shows about people with ESP who solve murders, well, I get mistaken for that dishy one all the time…"

"You're not psychic, Alice," he said impatiently.

"No sense of humor," she scoffed. "I wonder how you stay sane on the job! Okay, okay—" she held up both hands when he glowered "—I'll talk. It was the way you rushed over here to look at the drawing. Come on, give me a break. Nobody gets in that sort of hurry without a pretty sturdy reason."

He rested his hand on the holstered butt of his pistol. His eyes held that "thousand-yard stare" that was so remarked on in combat stories. "I've encouraged a former San Antonio detective to do some digging into the files on my cold case," he said quietly. "And you aren't to mention that to Marquez. He's in enough trouble. We're not going to tell him."

She wouldn't have dared mention that she already knew about the detective working on the case, and so did Marquez. "Have you got a lead?" she asked.

"I thought this case might be one," he said quietly. "A guy comes down here from San Antonio, and gets killed. It's eerie, but I had a feeling that he might have been looking for me. Stupid, I know…"

"There are dozens of reasons he might have driven down here," she replied. "And he might have been passing through. The perp might have followed him and ambushed him."

"You're right, of course." He managed a smile. "I keep hoping I'll get lucky one day." The smile faded into cold steel. "I want to know who it was. I want to make him pay for the past seven miserable years of my life."

She cocked her head, frowning. "Nothing will make up for that," she said quietly. "You can't take two lives out of someone. There's no punishment on earth that will take away the pain, or the loss. You know that."

"Consciously, I do," he said. He drew in a sharp breath. "I worked somebody else's shift as a favor that night. If I hadn't, I'd have been with them…"

"Stop that!" she said in a tone short enough to shock him. "Lives have been destroyed with that one, stupid word. *If!* Listen to me, Kilraven, you can't appropriate the power of life and death. You can't control the world. Sometimes people die in horrible ways. It's not right, but it's just the way things are. You have to go forward. Living in regret is only another way the perp scores off you."

He didn't seem to take offense. He was actually listening.

"I hear it from victims' families all the time," she continued. "They grieve, they hate, they live for vengeance. They can't wait for the case to go to trial so they can watch the guilty person burn. But, guess what, juries don't convict, or perps make deals, or sometimes the case even gets thrown out of court because of a break in the chain of evidence. And all that anger has no place to go, except in sound bites for the six-o'clock news. Then the families go home and the hatred grows, and they end up with empty lives full of nothing. Nothing at all. Hate takes the place that healing should occupy."

He stared down at her for a long moment. "I guess I've been there."

"For about seven years," she guessed. "Are you going to devote your life to all that hatred? You'll grow old with nothing to show for those wasted years except bitter memories."

"If my daughter had lived," he said in a harsh tone, "she'd be ten years old next week."

She didn't know how to answer him. The anguish he felt was in every word.

"He got away with it, Jones," he said harshly.

"No, he didn't," she replied. "Someone knows what happened, and who did it. One day, a telephone will ring in a detective's office, and a jilted girlfriend or boyfriend will give up the perp out of hurt or revenge or greed."

He relaxed a little. "You really think so?"

"I've seen it happen. So have you."

"I guess I have."

"Try to stop living in the past," she counseled gently. "It's a waste of a good man."

He lifted an eyebrow, and the black mood seemed to drop away. His silver eyes twinkled. "Flirting with me?"

"Don't go there," she warned. "I've seen too many wives sitting up watching the late show, hoping their husbands would come home. That's not going to be me. I'm going to marry a cattle rancher and sleep nights."

He grinned. "That's no guarantee of sleep. Baby bulls and cows almost always get born in the wee hours of the morning."

"You'd know," she agreed, smiling. "You and Jon have that huge black Angus ranch in Oklahoma, don't you?"

He nodded. "Pity neither of us wants to sit around and babysit cattle. We're too career conscious."

"When you get older, it might appeal."

"It might," he said, but not with any enthusiasm. "We hold on to it because Jon's mother likes to have company there." He grimaced. "She's got a new prospect for Jon."

"I heard." Alice chuckled. "He had her arrested in his own office for sexual harassment. I understand Joceline Perry is still making him suffer for it."

"It really was sexual harassment," Kilraven corrected. "The woman is a call girl. We both tried to tell my stepmom, but her best friend is the woman's mother. She won't believe us. Mom keeps trying to get her to the ranch, with the idea that Jon will like her better if he sees her in blue jeans."

"Fat chance," Alice said. "Jon should tell Joceline the truth."

"He won't lower his dignity that far. He said if she wants to think he's that much of a scoundrel, let her. They don't get along, anyway."

"No offense, but most women don't get along with your brother," she replied. "He doesn't really like women very much."

He sighed. "If you had my stepmother as a mom, you wouldn't, either." He held up a hand. "She has her good qualities. But she has blind spots and prejudices that would choke a mule. God help the woman who really falls in love with Jon. She'll have to get past Jon's mother, and it will take a tank."

She pursed her lips. "I hear Joceline has the personality of a tank."

He chuckled. "She does. But she hates Jon." He hesitated. "If you get any new leads, you'll tell me, right?"

"Right."

"Thanks for the lecture," he added with twinkling eyes. "You're not bad."

"I'm terrific," she corrected. "Just you wait. Harley Fowler will be rushing me to the nearest minister any day now."

"Poor guy."

"Hey, you stop that. I'm a catch, I am. I've got movie stars standing in line trying to marry me… Where are you going?"

"Back to work while there's still time," he called over his shoulder.

Before she could add to her bragging, he hopped into his squad car and peeled out of the parking lot.

Alice stared after him. "You'd be lucky if I set my sights on you," she said to nobody in particular. "It's your loss!" she called after the retreating squad car.

A deputy she hadn't heard came up behind her. "Talking to yourself again, Jones?" he mused.

She gave him a pained glance. "It's just as well that I do. I'm not having much luck getting people to listen to me."

"I know just how that feels," he said with a chuckle.

He probably did, she thought as she went back to her van. People in law enforcement were as much social workers as law enforcers. They had to be diplomatic, keep their tempers under extraordinary provocation, hand out helpful advice and firm warnings, sort out domestic problems, handle unruly suspects and even dodge bullets.

Alice knew she was not cut out for that sort of life, but she enjoyed her job. At least, she chuckled, she didn't have to dodge bullets.

SATURDAY, SHE WAS still in Jacobsville, waiting for one last piece of evidence that came from the site of the car that was submerged in the river. A fisherman had found a strange object near the site and called police. Hayes Carson had driven out himself to have a look. It was a metal thermos jug that the fisherman had found in some weeds. It looked new and still had liquid in it. Could have been that some other pedestrian lost it, Hayes confided, but it paid to keep your options open.

Hayes had promised that Alice could have it, but she'd promised to go riding with Harley. So she'd told Hayes she'd pick it up at his office late that afternoon.

"And you think the sheriff himself sits at his desk waiting for people on a Saturday?" Hayes queried on the phone in mock horror.

"Listen, Hayes, I have it on good authority that you practically sleep at the office most nights and even keep a razor and toothbrush there," she said with droll humor. "So I'll see you about seven."

He sighed. "I'll be here, working up another budget proposal."

"See?" She hung up.

CY PARKS WASN'T what she'd expected. He was tall and lean, with black hair showing just threads of gray, and green eyes. His wife, Lisa, was shorter and blonde with light eyes and glasses. They had two sons, one who was a toddler and the other newborn. Lisa was holding one, Cy had the oldest.

"We've heard a lot about you," Cy mused as Alice stood next to Harley. They were all wearing jeans and long-sleeved shirts and coats. It was a cold day.

"Most of it is probably true," Alice sighed. "But I have great teeth—" she displayed them "—and a good attitude."

They laughed.

"We haven't heard bad things," Lisa assured her, adjusting her glasses on her pert nose.

"Yes, we have." Cy chuckled. "Not really bad ones. Harley says you keep proposing to him, is all."

"Oh, that's true," Alice said, grinning. "I'm wearing him down, day by day. I just can't get him to let me buy him a ring."

Cy pursed his lips and glanced at Harley. "Hey, if you can get him in a suit, I'll give him away," he promised.

Harley grinned at him. "I'll remind you that you said that," he told his boss.

Cy's eyes were more kind than humorous. "I mean it."

Harley flushed a little with pleasure. "Thanks."

"Does that mean yes?" Alice asked Harley, wide-eyed.

He gave her a mock glare. "It means I'm thinking about it."

"Darn," she muttered.

"How's your murder investigation coming?" Cy asked suddenly.

"You mean the DB on the river?" she asked. "Slowly. We've got evidence. We just can't puzzle out what it means."

"There are some messed-up people involved, is my guess," Cy said, somber. "I've seen people handled the way your victim was. It usually meant a very personal grudge."

Alice nodded. "We've found that most close-up attacks, when they aren't random, are done by people with a grudge. I never cease to be amazed at what human beings are capable of."

"Amen." Cy slid an arm around Lisa. "We'd better get these boys back into a warm house. We've been through the mill with colds already." He chuckled. "Nice to meet you, Alice. If you can get him—" he pointed at Harley "—to marry you, I've already promised him some land and a seed herd of my best cattle."

"That's really nice of you," Alice said, and meant it.

Cy glanced at Harley warmly. "I'd kind of like to keep him close by," he said with a smile. "I'd miss him."

Harley seemed to grow two feet. "I'm not going anywhere," he drawled, but he couldn't hide that he was flattered.

"Come back again," Lisa told Alice. "It's hard to find two minutes to talk with little guys like these around—" she indicated her babies "—but we'll manage."

"I'd love to," Alice told her.

The Parks family waved and went into the house.

"They're nice," Alice said to Harley.

He nodded. "Mr. Parks has been more of a father to me than my own ever was."

Alice wanted to comment, to ask about the senator. But the look on Harley's face stopped her. It was traumatic. "I haven't been on a horse in about two years," she told him. "I had to go out with the Texas Rangers to look at some remains in the brush country, and it was the only way to get to the crime scene." She groaned. "Six hours on horseback, through prickly pear cactus and thorny bushes! My legs were scratched even through thick jeans and they felt like they were permanently bowed when I finally got back home."

"I've been there, too." He laughed. "But we won't go six hours, I promise."

He led her into the barn, where he already had two horses saddled. Hers was a pinto, a female, just the right size.

"That's Bean," he said. "Colby Lane's daughter rides her when she comes over here."

"Bean?" she asked as she mounted.

"She's a pinto," he said dryly.

She laughed. "Oh!"

He climbed into the saddle of a black Arabian gelding and led off down the trail that ran to the back of the property.

IT WAS A nice day to go riding, she thought. It had rained the night before, but it was sunny today, if cold. There were small mud patches on the trail, and despite the dead grass and bare trees, it felt good to be out-of-doors on a horse.

She closed her eyes and smelled the clean scent of country air. "If you could bottle this air," she commented, "you could outsell perfume companies."

He chuckled. "You sure could. It's great, isn't it? People in cities don't even know what they're missing."

"You lived in a city once, didn't you?" she asked in a conversational tone.

He turned his head sideways. Pale blue eyes narrowed under the wide brim of his hat as he pondered the question. "You've been making connections, Alice."

She flushed a little. "No, I really haven't. I've just noticed similarities."

"In names," he replied.

"Yes," she confessed.

He drew in a breath and drew in the reins. So did she. He sat beside her quietly, his eyes resting on the horizon.

"The senator is your father," she guessed.

He grimaced. "Yes."

She averted her gaze to the ground. It was just faintly muddy and the vegetation was brown. The trees in the distance were bare. It was a cold landscape. Cold, like Harley's expression.

"My parents were always in the middle of a cocktail party or a meeting. All my life. I grew up hearing the sound of ice clinking in glasses. We had politicians and other rich and famous people wandering in and out. I was marched out before bedtime to show everybody what a family man the politician was." He laughed coldly. "My mother was a superior court judge," he added surprisingly. "Very solemn on the bench, very strict at home. My sister died, and suddenly she was drinking more heavily than my father at those cocktail parties. She gave up her job on the bench to become an importer." He shook his head. "He changed, too. When he was younger, he'd play ball with me, or take me to the movies. After my sister died, everything was devoted to his career, to campaigning, even when he wasn't up for reelection. I can't tell you how sick I got of it."

"I can almost imagine," she said gently. "I'm sorry."

He turned back to her, frowning. "I never connected those two facts. You know, my sister's death with the changes in my parents. I was just a kid myself, not really old enough to think deeply." He glanced back at the horizon. "Maybe I was wrong."

"Maybe you were both wrong," she corrected. "Your father seemed very sad when he saw you."

"It's been almost eight years," he replied. "In all that

time, not one card or phone call. It's hard to square that with any real regret."

"Sometimes people don't know how to reach out," she said. "I've seen families alienated for years, all because they didn't know how to make the first contact, take the first step back to a relationship that had gone wrong."

He sighed, fingering the bridle. "I guess that describes me pretty well."

"It's pride, isn't it?" she asked.

He laughed faintly. "Isn't it always?" he wondered aloud. "I felt that I was the wronged party. I didn't think it was up to me to make the first move. So I waited."

"Maybe your father felt the same way," she suggested.

"My father isn't the easiest man to approach, even on his good days," he said. "He has a temper."

"You weren't singing happy songs the day I called you, when the cow ate your turnips," she replied, tongue-in-cheek.

He laughed. "I guess I've got a temper, too."

"So do I. It isn't exactly a bad trait. Only if you carry it to extremes."

He looked down at his gloved hands. "I guess."

"They're not young people anymore, Harley," she said quietly. "If you wait too much longer, you may not get the chance to patch things up."

He nodded. "I've been thinking about that."

She hesitated. She didn't want to push too hard. She nudged her horse forward a little, so that she was even with him. "Have you thought about what sort of ring you'd like?"

He pursed his lips and glanced over at her. "One to go on my finger, or one to go through my nose?"

She laughed. "Stop that."

"Just kidding." He looked up. "It's getting cloudy. We'd better get a move on, or we may get caught in a rain shower."

She knew the warning was his way of ending the conversation. But she'd got him thinking. That was enough, for now. "Suits me."

HE WALKED HER back to the van, his hands in his pockets, his thoughts far away.

"I enjoyed today," she told him. "Thanks for the riding lesson."

He stopped at the driver's door of the van and looked down at her, a little oddly. "You don't push, do you?" he asked solemnly. "It's one of the things I like best about you."

"I don't like being pushed, myself," she confided. She searched his eyes. "You're a good man."

He drew his hand out of his pocket and smoothed back her windblown dark hair, where it blew onto her cheek. The soft leather of the glove tickled. "You're a good woman," he replied. "And I really mean that."

She started to speak.

He bent and covered her mouth with his before she could say anything. His lips parted, cold and hungry on her soft, pliable lips. She opened them with a sigh and reached around him with both arms, and held on tight. She loved kissing him. But it was more than affection. It was a white-hot fire of passion that made her ache from head to toe. She felt swollen, hot, burning, as his arms contracted.

"Oh, God," he groaned, shivering as he buried his mouth in her neck. "Alice, we're getting in too deep, too quick."

"Complaints, complaints," she grumbled into his coat.

He laughed despite the ache that was almost doubling him over. "It's not a complaint. Well, not exactly." He drew in a calming breath and slowly let her go. His eyes burned down into hers. "We can't rush this," he said. "It's too good. We have to go slow."

Her wide, dark blue eyes searched his languidly. She was still humming all over with pleasure. "Go slow." She nodded. Her eyes fell to his mouth.

"Are you hearing me?"

She nodded. Her gaze was riveted to the sensuous lines of his lips. "Hearing."

"Woman...!"

He caught her close again, ramming his mouth down onto hers. He backed her into the door of the van and ground his body against hers in a fever of need that echoed in her harsh moan.

For a long time, they strained together in the misting rain, neither capable of pulling back. Just when it seemed that the only way to go was into the back of the van, he managed to jerk his mouth back from hers and step away. His jaw was so taut, it felt as if his mouth might break. His pale blue eyes were blazing with frustrated need.

Her mouth was swollen and red. She leaned back against the door, struggling to breathe normally as she stared up at him with helpless adoration. He wasn't obviously muscular, but that close, she felt every taut line of his body. He was delicious, she thought. Like candy. Hard candy.

"You have to leave. Now." He said it in a very strained tone.

"Leave." She nodded again.

"Leave. Now."

She nodded. "Now."

"Alice," he groaned. "Honey, there are four pairs of eyes watching us out the window right now, and two pairs of them are getting a hell of a sex education!"

"Eyes." She blinked. "Eyes?"

She turned. There, in the living-room window, were four faces. The adult ones were obviously amused. The little ones were wide-eyed with curiosity.

Alice blushed. "Oh, dear."

"You have to go. Right now." He moved her gently aside and opened the door. He helped her up onto the seat. He groaned. "I'm not having supper in the big house tonight, I can promise you that," he added.

She began to recover her senses and her sense of humor. Her eyes twinkled. "Oh, I see," she mused. "I've compromised you. Well, don't you worry, sweetheart," she drawled. "I'll save your reputation. You can marry me tomorrow."

He laughed. "No. I'm trimming horses' hooves."

She glowered at him. "They have farriers to do that."

"Our farrier is on Christmas vacation," he assured her.

"One day," she told him, "you'll run out of excuses."

He searched her eyes and smiled softly. "Of course I

will." He stepped back. "But not today. I'll phone you." He closed the door.

She started the engine and powered down the window. "Thanks for the ride."

He was still smiling. "Thanks for the advice. I'll take it."

"Merry Christmas."

He cocked his head. "Christmas is over."

"New Year's is coming."

"That reminds me, we have a New Year's celebration here," he said. "I can bring you to it."

"I'll be back in San Antonio then," she said miserably.

"I'll drive you down here and then drive you home."

"No. I'll stay in the motel," she said. "I don't want you on the roads after midnight. There are drunk drivers."

His heart lifted. His eyes warmed. "You really are a honey."

She smiled. "Hold that thought. See you."

He winked at her and chuckled when she blushed again. "See you, pretty girl."

She fumbled the van into gear and drove off jerkily. It had been a landmark day.

CHAPTER NINE

ALICE WAS BACK in her office the following week. She'd turned the thermos from the river in Jacobsville over to Longfellow first thing in the morning. She was waiting for results, going over a case file, when the door opened and a tall, distinguished-looking gentleman in an expensive dark blue suit walked in, unannounced. He had brown hair with silver at the temples, and light blue eyes. She recognized him at once.

"Senator Fowler," she said quietly.

"Ms. Jones," he replied. He stood over the desk with his hands in his pockets. "I wonder if you could spare me a few minutes?"

"Of course." She indicated the chair in front of her desk.

He took his hands out of his pockets and sat down, crossing one long leg over the other. "I believe you know my son."

She smiled. "Yes. I know Harley."

"I… My wife and I haven't seen him for many years," he began. "We made terrible mistakes. Now, it seems that we'll never be able to find our way back to him. He's grown into a fine-looking young man. He…has a job?"

She nodded. "A very good one. And friends."

"I'm glad. I'm very glad." He hesitated. "We didn't know how to cope with him. He was such a cocky youngster, so sure that he had all the answers." He looked down at his shoes. "We should have been kinder."

"You lost your daughter," Alice said very gently.

He lifted his eyes and they shimmered with pain and grief. "I killed…my daughter," he gritted. "Backed over her with my car rushing to get to a campaign rally." He closed his eyes. "Afterward, I went mad."

"So did your wife, I think," Alice said quietly.

He nodded. He brushed at his eyes and averted them. "She was a superior court judge. She started drinking and quit the bench. She said she couldn't sit in judgment on other people when her own mistakes were so terrible. She was on the phone when it happened. She'd just told our daughter, Cecily, to stop interrupting her and go away. You know, the sort of offhand remark parents make. It doesn't mean they don't love the child. Anyway, Cecily sneaked out the door and went behind the car, unbeknownst to me, apparently to get a toy she'd tossed under it. I jumped in without looking to see if there was anybody behind me. I was late getting to a meeting… Anyway, my wife never knew Cecily was outside until I started screaming, when I knew what I'd done." He leaned forward. "We blamed each other. We had fights. Harley grieved. He blamed me, most of all. But he seemed to just get right on with his life afterward."

"I don't think any of you did that," Alice replied. "I don't think you dealt with it."

He looked up. His blue eyes were damp. "How do you know so much?"

"I deal with death every day," she said simply. "I've seen families torn apart by tragedies. Very few people admit that they need help, or get counseling. It is horrible to lose a child. It's traumatic to lose one the way you did. You should have been in therapy, all of you."

"I wasn't the sort of person who could have admitted that," he said simply. "I was more concerned with my image. It was an election year, you see. I threw myself into the campaign and thought that would accomplish the same thing. So did my wife." He shook his head. "She decided to start a business, to keep busy." He managed a smile. "Now we never see each other. After Harley left, we blamed each other for that, too."

She studied the older man curiously. "You're a politician. You must have access to investigators. You could have found Harley any time you wanted to."

He hesitated. Then he nodded. "But that works both ways, Ms. Jones. He could have found us, too. We didn't move around."

"Harley said you wanted him to be part of a social set that he didn't like."

"Do you think I like it?" he asked suddenly and gave a bitter laugh. "I love my job. I have power. I can do a lot of good, and I do. But socializing is part of that job. I do more business at cocktail parties than I've ever done in my office in Washington. I make contacts, I get networks going, I research. I never stop." He sighed. "I tried to explain that to Harley, but he thought I meant that I wanted to use him to reel in campaign workers." He laughed. "It's funny now. He was so green, so naive. He thought he knew all there was to know about politics and life." He looked up. "I hope he's learned that nothing is black or white."

"He's learned a lot," she replied. "But he's been running away from his past for years."

"Too many years. I can't approach him directly. He'd take off." He clasped his hands together. "I was hoping you might find it in your heart to pave the way for me. Just a little. I only want to talk to him."

She narrowed her eyes. "This wouldn't have anything to do with the woman we talked to at your fundraising party…?"

He stared at her with piercing blue eyes just a shade lighter than Harley's. "You're very quick."

"I didn't start this job yesterday," she replied, and smiled faintly.

He drew in a long breath. "I gave Dolores a hard time. She was deeply religious, but she got on my nerves. A man who's forsaken religion doesn't like sermons," he added, laughing bitterly. "But she was a good person. My wife had a heart attack earlier this year. I hired a nurse to sit with her, when she got home from the hospital. Unknown to me, the nurse drugged my wife and left the house to party with her boyfriend. Dolores made sure I found out. Then she sat with my wife. They found a lot to talk about. After my wife got back on her feet, she began to change for the better. I think it was Dolores's influence." He hung his head. "I was harsh to

Dolores the night of the fundraiser. That's haunted me, too. I have a young protégé, our newest senator. He's got a brother who makes me very nervous…" He lifted his eyes. "Sorry. I keep getting off the track. I do want you to help me reconnect with my son, if you can. But that's not why I'm here."

"Then why are you here, Senator?" she asked.

He looked her in the eye. "Dolores didn't commit suicide."

Her heart jumped, but she kept a straight face. She linked her hands in front of her on the desk and leaned forward. "Why do you think that?"

"Because once, when I was despondent, I made a joke about running my car into a tree. She was eloquent on the subject of suicide. She thought it was the greatest sin of all. She said that it was an insult to God and it caused so much grief for people who loved you." He looked up. "I'm not an investigator, but I know she was right-handed. She was shot in the right side of her body." He shook his head. "She wasn't the sort of person to do that. She hated guns. I'm sure she never owned one. It doesn't feel right."

"I couldn't force the assistant medical examiner to write it up as a homicide. He's near retirement, and it was your employee who died. He's afraid of you, of your influence. He knows that you stopped the investigation on the Kilraven case stone-cold."

"I didn't," he said unexpectedly, and his mouth tightened. "Will Sanders is the new junior senator from Texas," he continued. "He's a nice guy, but his brother is a small-time hoodlum with some nasty contacts, who mixes with dangerous people. He's involved in illegal enterprises. Will can't stop him, but he does try to protect him. Obviously he thinks Hank knows something about the Kilraven case, and he doesn't want it discovered."

Alice's blue eyes began to glitter. "Murder is a nasty business," she pointed out. "Would you like to know what was done to Kilraven's wife and three-year-old daughter?" she added. "He saw it up close, by accident. But I have autopsy photos that I've never shown anyone, if you'd like to see what happened to them."

The senator paled. "I would not," he replied. He stared into space. "I'm willing for Kilraven to look into the case. Rick Marquez's colleague was sent to work in traffic control. I'm sorry for that. Will persuaded me to get her off the case. She's a bulldog when it comes to homicide investigation, and she stops at nothing to solve a crime." He looked up. "Will's rather forceful in his way. I let him lead me sometimes. But I don't want either of us being shown as obstructing a murder investigation, even one that's seven years old. He's probably afraid that his brother, Hank, may have knowledge of the perpetrator and Will's trying to shield him. He's done that all his life. But he has no idea what the media would do to him if it ever came out that he'd hindered the discovery of a murderer, especially in a case as horrific as this."

"I've seen what happens when people conceal evidence. It's not pretty," Alice said. "How can you help Kilraven?"

"For one thing, I can smooth the way for Marquez's

colleague. I'll go have a talk with the police commissioner when I leave here. He'll get her reassigned to Homicide. Here." He scribbled a number on a piece of paper and handed it to her. "That's my private cell number. I keep two phones on me, but only a few people have access to this number. Tell Kilraven to call me. Or do you have his number?"

"Sure." She pulled out her own cell phone, pushed a few buttons and wrote down Kilraven's cell phone number on a scrap of paper. Odd, how familiar that number looked on paper. She handed it to the senator. "There."

"Thanks. Uh, if you like," he added with a smile as he stood up, "you could share my private number with Harley. He can call me anytime. Even if I'm standing at a podium making a speech somewhere. I won't mind being interrupted."

She stood up, too, smiling. "I'm going down there Wednesday for the New Year's Eve celebration in town, as it happens, with Harley. I'll pass it along. Thanks, Senator Fowler."

He shook hands with her. "If I can pave the way for you in the investigation into Dolores's death, I'll be glad to," he added.

"I'll keep you in mind. Kilraven will be grateful for your help, I'm sure."

He smiled, waved and left.

Alice sat down. Something wasn't right. She pulled up her notes on the Jacobsville murder investigation and scrolled down to the series of numbers that Longfellow had transcribed from the piece of paper in the victim's hand. Gasping, she pulled up Kilraven's cell phone number on her own cell phone and compared them. The digits that were decipherable were a match for everything except the area code, which was missing. It wasn't conclusive, but it was pretty certain that the murder victim had come to contact Kilraven. Which begged the question, did the victim know something about the old murder case?

Her first instinct was to pick up the phone and call Kilraven. But her second was caution. Without the missing numbers, it could be a coincidence. Better to let the senator call Kilraven and get him some help— Marquez's detective friend—and go from there. Meanwhile, Alice would press Longfellow about the faded, wet portion of the paper where the first few numbers were, so far, unreadable. The FBI lab had the technology enabling them to pull up the faintest traces of ink. They might work a miracle for the investigation.

THE THERMOS CONTAINED a tiny residue of coffee laced with a narcotic drug, Longfellow told Alice. "If it's connected to your case," the assistant investigator told Alice, "it could explain a lot. It would make the victim less able to defend himself from an attacker."

"Fingerprints?"

Longfellow shook her head. "It was clean. Wiped, apparently, and just tossed away. It's as if," she added, frowning, "the killer was so confident that he left the thermos deliberately, to show his superiority."

Alice smiled faintly. "I love it when perps do that," she said. "When we catch them, and get them into court, that cockiness usually takes a nosedive. It's a kick to see it."

"Indeed," Longfellow added. "I'll keep digging, though," she assured Alice.

"You do that. We'll need every scrap of evidence we have to pin this murder on somebody. The killer's good. Very good." She frowned. "He's probably done this before and never got caught."

"That might explain his efficiency," the other woman agreed. "But he missed that scrap of paper in the victim's hand."

"Every criminal slips up eventually. Let's hope this is his swan song."

"Oh, yes."

ALICE DROVE DOWN to Jacobsville in her personal car, a little Honda with terrific gas mileage, and checked in at the motel. She'd reserved a room, to make sure she got one, because out-of-town people came for the New Year's Eve celebration. Once she was checked in, she phoned Harley.

"I was going to come up and get you," he protested.

"I don't want you on the roads at night, either, Harley," she replied softly.

He sighed. "What am I going to do with you, Alice?"

"I have several suggestions," she began brightly.

He laughed. "You can tell me tonight. Barbara's Café is staying open for the festivities. Suppose I come and get you about six, and we'll have supper. Then we'll go to the Cattlemen's Association building where the party's being held."

"That sounds great."

"It's formal," he added hesitantly.

"No worries. I brought my skimpy little black cocktail dress and my sassy boa."

He chuckled. "Not a live one, I hope."

"Nope."

"I'll see you later, then," he said in a low, sexy tone.

"I'll look forward to it."

He hung up. So did she. Then she checked her watch. It was going to be a long afternoon.

HARLEY CAUGHT HIS breath when she opened the door. She was dressed in a little black silk dress with spaghetti straps and a brief, low-cut bodice that made the most of her pert breasts. The dress clung to her hips and fell to her knees in silky profusion. She wore dark hose and black slingback pumps. She'd used enough makeup to give her an odd, foreign appearance. Her lips, plumped with glossy red stay-on lipstick, were tempting. She wore a knitted black boa with blue feathery wisps and carried a small black evening bag with a long strap.

"Will I do?" Alice asked innocently.

Harley couldn't even speak. He nudged her back into the room, closed and locked the door, took off his hat and his jacket and pushed her gently onto the bed.

"Sorry," he murmured as his mouth took hers like a whirlwind.

She moaned as he slid onto her, teasing her legs apart so that he could ease up her skirt and touch the soft flesh there with a lean, exploring hand.

His mouth became demanding. His hands moved up and down her yielding body, discovering soft curves and softer flesh beneath. With his mouth still insistent on her parting lips, he brushed away the spaghetti straps and bared her to the waist. He lifted his head to look at her taut, mauve-tipped breasts. "Beautiful," he whispered, and his mouth diverted to the hardness, covered it delicately, and with a subtle suction that arched her off the bed in a stab of pleasure so deep that it seemed to make her swell all over.

She forced his head closer, writhing under him as the hunger built and built in the secret silence of the room. All she wanted was for him never to stop. She whispered it, moaning, coaxing, as the flames grew higher and higher, and his hands reached under her, searching for a waistband...

Her cell phone blared out the theme from the original *Indiana Jones* movie. They both jumped at the sound. Harley, his mind returning to normal, quickly drew his hands out from under Alice's skirt with a grimace, and rolled away. He lay struggling to get his breath while she eased off the bed and retrieved her purse from the floor, where she'd dropped it.

"Jones," she managed in a hoarse tone.

"Alice?" Hayes Carson asked, because she didn't sound like herself.

"Yes," she said, forcing herself to breathe normally. "Hayes?"

"Yes. I wanted to know if you found out anything about that thermos." He hesitated. "Did I call at a bad time?"

She managed a laugh. "We could debate that," she said. "Actually the thermos was clean. No fingerprints, but the liquid in it had traces of a narcotic laced in it," she replied. "But Longfellow's still looking. We've got the note at the FBI lab. Hopefully they'll be able to get the missing numbers for us. But they've got a backlog and it's the holidays. Not much hope for anything this week."

"I was afraid of that."

"Well, we live in hope," she said, and glanced at Harley, who was now sitting up and looking pained.

"We do. Coming to the celebration tonight?"

"Sure am. You coming?"

"I never miss it. Uh, is Harley bringing you?"

She laughed. "He is. We'll see you there."

"Sure thing." He hung up.

She glanced at Harley with a wicked smile. "Well, we can think of Hayes as portable birth control tonight, can't we?"

He burst out laughing despite his discomfort. He managed to get to his feet, still struggling to breathe normally. "I can think of a few other pertinent adjectives that would fit him."

"Unprintable ones, I'll bet." She went up to him and put her hands on his broad chest. She reached up to kiss him softly. "It was good timing. I couldn't have stopped."

"Yeah. Me, neither," he confessed, flushing a little. "It's been a long dry spell." He bent and brushed his mouth over hers. "But we've proven that we're physically compatible," he mused.

"Definitely." She pursed her lips. "So how about we get married tomorrow morning?"

He chuckled. "Can't. I'm brushing bulls for a regional show."

"Brushing bulls?" she wondered aloud.

"Purebred herd sires. They have to be brushed and combed and dolled up. The more ribbons we win, the higher we can charge for their, uh, well, for straws."

Of semen, he meant, but he was too nice to say it bluntly. "I know what straws are, Harley." She grinned. "I get the idea."

"So not tomorrow."

"I live in hope," she returned. She went to the mirror in the bathroom to repair her makeup, which was royally smeared. "Better check your face, too," she called. "This never-smear lipstick has dishonest publicity. It does smear."

He walked up behind her. His shirt was undone. She remembered doing that, her hands buried in the thick hair that covered his chest, tugging it while he kissed her. She flushed at the memory.

He checked his face, decided it would pass, and lowered his eyes to Alice's flushed cheeks in the mirror. He put his hands on her shoulders and tightened them. "We can't get married tomorrow. But I thought, maybe next week. Friday, maybe," he said softly. "I can take a few days off. We could drive down to Galveston. To the beach. Even in winter, it's beautiful there."

She'd turned and was staring up at him wide-eyed. "You mean that? It isn't you're just saying it so I'll stop harassing you?"

He bent and kissed her forehead with breathless tenderness. "I don't know how it happened, exactly," he said in a husky, soft tone. "But I'm in love with you."

She slid her arms around his neck. "I'm in love with you, too, Harley," she said in a wondering tone, searching his eyes.

He lifted her up to him and kissed her in a new way, a different way. With reverence, and respect, and aching tenderness.

"I'll marry you whenever you like," she said against his mouth.

He kissed her harder. The passion returned, riveting them together, locking them in a heat of desire that was ever more formidable to resist.

He drew back, grinding his teeth in frustration, and moved her away from him. "We have to stop this," he said. "At least until after the wedding. I'm really old-fashioned about these things."

"Tell me about it," she said huskily. "I come from a whole family of Baptist ministers. Need I say more?"

He managed a smile. "No. I know what you mean." He drew a steadying breath and looked in the mirror. He grimaced. "Okay, now I believe that publicity was a load of bull," he told her. "I'm smeared, too, and it's not my color."

"It definitely isn't," she agreed. She wet a washcloth and proceeded to clean up both of them. Then, while he got his suit coat back on, and his hair combed, she finished her own makeup. By the time she was done, he was waiting for her at the door. He smiled as she approached him.

"You look sharp," he said gently.

She whirled the boa around her neck and smiled from ear to ear. "You look devastating," she replied.

He stuck out an arm. She linked her hand into it. He opened the door and followed her out.

THERE WAS A BAND. They played regional favorites, and Harley danced with Alice. Practically the whole town had gathered in the building that housed the local Cattlemen's Association, to celebrate the coming of the new year. A pair of steer horns, the idea of Calhoun Ballenger, their new state senator, waited to fall when midnight came.

Hayes Carson was wearing his uniform, and Alice teased him about it.

"Hey, I'm on duty," he replied with a grin. "And I'm only here between calls."

"I'm not arguing. It's a big turnout. Is it always like this?"

"Always," Hayes replied. He started to add to that when a call came over his radio. He pressed the button on his portable and told the dispatcher he was en route to the call. "See what I mean?" he added with a sigh. "Have fun."

"We will," Harley replied, sliding an arm around her.

Hayes waved as he went out the door.

"Is he sweet on you?" Harley asked with just a hint of jealousy in his tone.

She pressed close to him. "Everybody but Hayes knows that he's sweet on Minette Raynor, but he's never going to admit it. He's spent years blaming her for his younger brother's drug-related death. She wasn't responsible, and he even knows who was because there was a confession."

"That's sad," Harley replied.

"It is." She looked up at him and smiled. "But it's not our problem. You said we'd get married next Friday. I'll have to ask for time off."

He pursed his lips. "So will I. Do you want to get married in church?"

She hesitated. "Could we?"

"Yes. I'll make the arrangements. What sort of flowers do you want, for your bouquet?"

"Yellow and white roses," she said at once. "But, Harley, I don't have a wedding gown. You don't want a big reception?"

"Not very big, no, but you should have a wedding gown," he replied solemnly. "If we have a daughter, she could have it for her own wedding one day. Or it could be an heirloom, at least, to hand down."

"A daughter. Children…" She caught her breath. "I hadn't thought about… Oh, yes, I want children! I want them so much!"

His body corded. "So do I."

"I'll buy a wedding gown, first thing when I get home," she said. "I'll need a maid of honor. You'll need a best man," she added quickly.

"I'll ask Mr. Parks," he said.

She smiled. "I don't really have many women friends. Do you suppose Mrs. Parks would be my matron of honor?"

"I think she'd be honored," Harley replied. "I'll ask them."

"Wow," she said softly. "It's all happening so fast." She frowned. "Not too fast, is it?" she worried aloud.

"Not too fast," he assured her. "We're the same sort of people, Alice. We'll fit together like a puzzle. I promise you we will. I'll take care of you all my life."

"I'll take care of you," she replied solemnly. "I want to keep my job."

He smiled. "Of course you do. You can commute, can't you?"

She smiled. "Of course. I have a Honda."

"I've seen it. Nice little car. I've got a truck, so we can haul stuff. Mr. Parks is giving me some land and some cattle from his purebred herd. There's an old house on the land. It's not the best place to set up housekeeping, but Mr. Parks said the minute I proposed, to let him know and he'd get a construction crew out there to remodel it." He hesitated. "I told him Saturday that I was going to propose to you."

Her lips parted. "Saturday?"

He nodded. "That's when I knew I couldn't live without you, Alice."

She pressed close into his arms, not caring what anybody thought. "I felt that way, too. Like I've always known you."

He kissed her forehead and held her tight. "Yes. So we have a place to live. The boss will have it in great shape when we get back from our honeymoon." He lifted his head. "Will you mind living on a ranch?"

"Are you kidding? I want to keep chickens and learn to can and make my own butter."

He laughed. "Really?"

"Really! I hate living in the city. I can't even keep a cat in my apartment, much less grow things there." She beamed. "I'll love it!"

He grinned back. "I'll bring you one of my chicken catalogs. I like the fancy ones, but you can get regular hens as well."

"Chicken catalogs? You like chickens?"

"Boss keeps them," he said. "I used to gather eggs for Mrs. Parks, years ago. I like hens. I had my mind on a small ranch and I thought chickens would go nicely with cattle."

She sighed. "We're going to be very happy, I think."

"I think so, too."

THE PARKSES SHOWED UP, along with the Steeles and the Scotts. Harley and Alice announced their plans, and the Parkses agreed with delightful speed to take part in the wedding. Other local citizens gathered around to congratulate them.

Midnight came all too soon. The steer horns lowered to the loud count by the crowd, out under the bright Texas stars to celebrate the new year. The horns made it to the ground, the band struck up "Auld Lang Syne" and everybody kissed and cried and threw confetti.

"Happy New Year, Alice," Harley whispered as he bent to kiss her.

"Happy New Year." She threw her arms around him and kissed him back.

HE LEFT HER at her motel with real reluctance. "I won't come in," he said at once, grinning wickedly. "We've already discovered that I have no willpower."

"Neither do I," she sighed. "I guess we're very strange. Most people who get married have been living together for years. We're the odd couple, waiting until after the ceremony."

He became serious. "It all goes back to those old ideals, to the nobility of the human spirit," he said softly. "Tradition is important. And I love the idea of chastity. I'm only sorry that I didn't wait for you, Alice. But, then, I didn't know you were going to come along. I'd decided that I'd never find someone I wanted to spend my life with." He smiled. "What a surprise you were."

She went close and hugged him. "You're the nicest man I've ever known. No qualms about what I do for a living?" she added.

He shrugged. "It's a job. I work with cattle and get sunk up to my knees in cow manure. It's not so different from what you do. We both get covered up in disgusting substances to do our jobs."

"I never thought of it like that."

He hugged her close. "We'll get along fine. And we'll wait, even if half the world thinks we're nuts."

"Speaking for myself, I've always been goofy."

"So have I."

"Besides," she said, pulling back, "I was never one to go with the crowd. You'll call me?"

"Every day," he said huskily. "A week from Friday."

She smiled warmly. "A week from Friday. Happy New Year."

He kissed her. "Happy New Year."

He got back into his truck. He didn't drive away until she was safely inside her room.

CHAPTER TEN

ALICE HAD FORGOTTEN, in the excitement, to tell Harley about the senator's message. But the following day, when he called, he didn't have time to talk. So she waited until Friday, when he phoned and was in a chatty mood.

"I have a message for you," she said hesitantly. "From your father."

"My father?" he said after a minute, and he was solemn.

"He said that he'd made some dreadful mistakes. He wants the opportunity to apologize for them. Your sister's death caused problems for both your parents that they never faced."

"Yes, and I never realized it. When did you talk to him?"

"He came to see me Monday, at my office. I like him," she added quietly. "I think he was sincere, about wanting to reconnect with you. He gave me his private cell phone number." She hesitated. "Do you want it?"

He hesitated, too, but only for a moment. "Yes."

She called out the numbers to him.

"I'm not saying I'll call him," he said after a minute. "But I'll think about it."

"That's my guy," she replied, and felt warm all over at the thought. She'd had some worries, though. "Harley?"

"Hmm?"

"You know that we've only known each other for a few weeks…" she began.

"And you're afraid we're rushing into marriage?"

She shrugged. "Aren't we?"

He laughed softly. "Alice, we can wait for several months or several years, but in the end, we'll get married. We have so much in common that no sane gambler would bet against us. But if you want to wait, honey, we'll wait." He cleared his throat. "It's just that my willpower may not be up to it. Just don't expect to get married in a white gown, okay?"

She remembered their close calls and laughed. "Okay, I'm convinced. We'll get married a week from Friday."

"Wear a veil, will you," he added seriously. "It's old-fashioned, but it's so beautiful."

"Say no more. I'll shop veils-are-us this very day."

"There's such a place?" he asked.

"I'll let you know."

"Deal. I'll call you tonight."

She felt a flush of warmth. "Okay."

"Bye, darlin'," he drawled, and hung up.

Alice held the phone close, sighing, until Longfellow walked by and gave her a strange look.

Alice removed the phone from her chest and put it carefully on the desk. "Magnetism, Longfellow," she said facetiously. "You see, a burst of magnetism caught my cell phone and riveted it to my chest. I have only just managed to extricate it." She waited hopefully for the reply.

Longfellow pursed her lips. "You just stick to that

story, but I have reason to know that you have recently become engaged. So I'll bet your boyfriend just hung up."

"Who told you I was engaged?" Alice demanded.

Longfellow started counting them off on her fingers. "Rick Marquez, Jon Blackhawk, Kilraven, Hayes Carson…"

"How do you know Kilraven?" Alice wanted to know.

"He keeps bugging me about that telephone number," she sighed. "As if the FBI lab doesn't have any other evidence to process. Give me a break!" She rolled her eyes.

"If they call you, get in touch with me before you tell Kilraven anything, okay?" she asked. "I want to make sure he's not running off into dead ends on my account."

"I'll do that," Longfellow promised. She stared at Alice. "If you want to shop for a wedding gown, I know just the place. And I'll be your fashion consultant."

Alice looked dubious.

"Wait a sec," Longfellow said. "I have photos of my own wedding, three years ago." She pulled them up on her phone and showed them to Alice. "That's my gown."

Alice caught her breath. "Where in the world did you find such a gown?"

"At a little boutique downtown, would you believe it? They do hand embroidery—although in your case, it will probably have to be machined—and they have a pretty good selection for a small shop."

"Can we go after work?" Alice asked enthusiastically.

Longfellow laughed. "You bet."

"Thanks."

"Not a problem."

ALICE PICKED OUT a dream of a gown, white satin with delicate pastel silk embroidery on the hem in yellow and pink and blue. There was a long illusion veil that matched it, with just the ends embroidered delicately in silk in the same pastel colors. It wasn't even that expensive.

"Why aren't you on the news?" Alice asked the owner, a petite little brunette. "I've never seen such beautiful wedding gowns!"

"We don't appeal to everybody," came the reply. "But for the few, we're here."

"I'll spread the word around," Alice promised.

"I already have." Longfellow chuckled.

Outside the shop, with her purchase safely placed in the backseat of her car, Alice impulsively hugged Longfellow. "Thanks so much."

"It was my pleasure," Longfellow replied. "Where will you live?"

"He's got a small ranch," she said proudly. "We're going to raise purebred Santa Gertrudis cattle. But until we make our first million at it, he's going to go on working as a ranch foreman, and I'll keep my job here. I'll commute."

"You always wanted to live in the country," Longfellow recalled.

Alice smiled. "Yes. And with the right man. I have definitely found him." She sighed. "I know it sounds like a rushed thing. We've known each other just a short time…"

"My sister met her husband and got married in five days," Longfellow said smugly. "They just celebrated their thirty-seventh wedding anniversary."

"Thirty-seven years?" Alice exclaimed.

"Well, he liked *Star Trek*, she said," Longfellow explained. "She said that told her everything she needed to know about him—that he was intelligent, tolerant, inquisitive, optimistic about the future, unprejudiced and a little quirky." She shrugged and laughed. "Not bad for a quick character reading, was it?"

"Not at all. Good for her!"

"You do the same," Longfellow lectured. "I don't want to see you in divorce court a month after you say your vows."

"I believe we can safely say that won't happen," Alice replied, and she felt and sounded confident. She frowned. "I wonder if he likes *Star Trek*," she wondered aloud.

In fact, she asked him when he called that night. "I do," he replied. "All the series, all the movies, and especially the new one, about Kirk, Spock and McCoy as cadets." He paused. "How about you?"

"I love it, too." She laughed, and then explained why she'd asked the question.

He was serious then. "That's a long time," he said of Longfellow's sister's marriage. "We'll give her a run for her money, won't we, Alice?"

She smiled. "Yes, we will."

There was a long pause. "You're wondering if I called that number you gave me," Harley said.

She laughed in surprise. "You read minds! That's great! If we ever have an argument, you'll know why I was mad and just what to do about it!"

"I only read minds occasionally," he told her, "so

let's not have arguments. But I did call my father. We had a long talk. I think we may get together one day, with my mother, and try to iron things out."

"That's wonderful," she said softly.

"It won't be easy to get over the past, but at least we're all willing to try. I did mention the wedding to him."

"And?"

"He said that if he showed up, we'd be a media lunch. I have to agree," he added. "I don't want that. Neither do you. But we're invited to their house for a potluck dinner the day we get back from our honeymoon."

"I'd enjoy that."

"Me, too."

"I bought a wedding gown. With a veil. It's beautiful."

"On you, any gown would be. You're delicious, Alice."

She laughed softly. "That's just the right thing to say."

"I mean it, too."

"I know."

"Game for a movie tomorrow night?" he asked. "There's a Christmas-themed one we could go see."

"That would be fun. Yes."

"I'll pick you up at six and we'll have supper first."

"That's a date."

"Uh, and no stopping by your apartment after. I go home."

"Yes, Harley. You go home."

There was a brief pause and they both burst out laughing.

HE DID GO HOME, but only after a heated session on her sofa that ended with him actually pulling away and running for the door. He waved as he slammed it behind him, leaving a disheveled Alice laughing her head off.

IT WAS RAINING on their wedding day. Alice carried an umbrella over her gown and Lisa Parks held up the train as they rushed into the church just ahead of a thunderbolt. Cy Parks was waiting at the altar with Harley, who looked devastating in a tuxedo, a conventional black one with a white shirt and black bow tie. Harley couldn't take his eyes off Alice.

Lisa went to her seat. The full church quieted. Alice smiled as the "Wedding March" struck up on the organ and she adjusted her train before she picked up the pretty bouquet he'd ordered for her. The fingertip veil just hid the wetness in her eyes as she wished with all her heart that her parents had been here to see her marry.

She walked slowly down the aisle, aware of friendly, curious eyes admiring her dress. Leo Hart and his wife, Janie, were sitting on the aisle. Alice didn't know, but Janie had dated Harley while she was trying to get over Leo. It hadn't been serious. In fact, Harley had dated several local women, including one who'd cast him off like a wet shoe and hurt his pride. It had seemed to many people as if Harley would always be the stand-in for some other man. But here he was with a really pretty, professional woman, and she had a reputation as a keen investigator. Many people in Jacobsville watched the crime scene investigation shows. They grinned as they considered how nice it was going to be, having somebody local who could answer all those questions they wanted to ask about homicide investigation.

Alice paused at the altar, looked up at Harley and felt a moment of panic. They hardly knew each other. They were almost strangers. This was insane…!

Just then, as if he knew what she was feeling, Harley's big hand reached over and linked itself unobtrusively into her cold fingers and pressed them, very gently. She looked into his eyes. He was smiling, with love and pride and confidence. All at once, she relaxed and smiled back.

The minister cleared his throat.

"Sorry," Alice mouthed, and turned her attention to him instead of Harley.

The minister, who had a daughter just Alice's age, grinned at her and began the service.

It was brief, but poignant. At the end of it, Harley lifted the exquisite veil and kissed his bride. Alice fought back tears as she returned the tender kiss.

They ran out of the church amid a shower of confetti and well wishes.

"Good thing you aren't having a reception," Cash Grier remarked as they waited for the limousine Cy Parks had ordered to take them to the airport, one of several wedding presents.

"A reception?" Alice asked, curious. "Why?"

"Our local district attorney, Blake Kemp, had one," Cash explained. "He and his wife went home instead to dress for their honeymoon. While they were gone, there was an altercation. One of my officers was wearing the punch, another salvaged just the top layer of the wedding cake and most of the guests went to jail." He grinned. "Jacobsville weddings are interesting."

They both laughed, and agreed that it was probably a good thing after all.

Cy Parks paused with Lisa when the limo drove up and the driver came around to open the rear door.

Cy shook hands with Harley. "Your house will be ready when you get back," he told Harley. "You did good."

Harley beamed. "You'll never know how much it meant to me, that you and Lisa stood up with us. Thanks."

Cy was somber. "You're a good man, Harley. I hope my sons will be like you."

Harley had to bite down hard. "Thanks," he managed.

"Go have a nice honeymoon," Cy told the couple. He grinned. "I won't let the Hart boys near your house, either."

"The Hart boys?" Alice parroted.

Leo Hart leaned over her shoulder. "We have a reputation for making weddings interesting," he told her, and grinned.

"Not so much these days." Janie grinned from beside him.

A tall, silver-eyed man in a police uniform walked up beside them. Kilraven. Grinning. "I'm giving the limo a police escort to the airport," he told them.

"That's very nice of you," Alice told him.

He sighed. "Might as well, since there's no reception. Weddings are getting really somber around here."

"Why don't you get married and have a reception?" Cash Grier suggested.

Kilraven gave him a look. "And have women throwing themselves over cliffs because I went out of circulation? In your dreams, Grier!"

Everybody laughed.

CORPUS CHRISTI WAS a beautiful little city on the Gulf of Mexico. It had a sugar-sand beach and seagulls and a myriad of local shops with all sorts of souvenirs and pretty things to buy. Harley and Alice never noticed.

They'd managed to get checked in and they looked out the window at the beach. Then they looked at each other.

Clothes fell. Buttons popped. Intimate garments went everywhere. Alice threw back the covers and dived in just a few seconds ahead of her brand-new husband. In a tangle of arms and legs, they devoured each other in a surging crescendo of passion that lasted for what seemed hours.

"What are you waiting for?" Alice groaned. "Come back here!"

"I was only…trying to make it easier…" he began.

"Easier, the devil!" She arched up, grimacing, because it really did hurt. But only for a few seconds. She stiffened, but then the fever burned right back up again, and she dragged him down with a kiss that knocked every single worry right out of his mind.

"Oh, wow," she managed when the room stopped spinning around them. She was lying half under Harley, covered in sweat even in the cool room, shivering with delight. "Now that was a first time to write about!" she enthused.

He laughed. "I was trying not to hurt you," he pointed out.

She pushed him over and rolled onto him. "And I appreciate every single effort, but it wasn't necessary," she murmured as she kissed him. "I was starving for you!"

"I noticed."

She lifted up and gave him a wicked look.

"I was starving for you, too," he replied diplomatically, and chuckled. "You were incredible."

"So were you." She sighed and laid her cheek on his broad, hairy chest. "No wonder people don't wait for wedding nights anymore."

"Some of them do."

"It isn't night, yet," she reminded him.

He laughed softly. "I guess not."

She kissed his chest. "Should we go down to the restaurant to eat?"

"Mr. Parks gave us a one-week honeymoon with room service. I do not think we should insult the man by not using it," he replied.

"Oh, I do agree. I would hate to insult Mr. Parks. Besides," she murmured, shifting, "I just thought of something we can do to pass the time until supper!"

"You did?" He rolled her over, radiant. "Show me!"

She did.

THEY ARRIVED HOME bleary-eyed from lack of sleep and with only a few photos and souvenirs of where they'd been. In actuality, they'd hardly seen anything except the ceiling of their hotel room.

The ranch house was one level. It was old, but well-kept, and it had new steps and porch rails, and a porch swing. It also had a new coat of white paint.

"It's just beautiful," Alice enthused. "Harley, it looks like the house I lived in when I was a little girl, growing up in Floresville!"

"You grew up in Floresville?" he asked as he unlocked the door and opened it.

She looked up at him. "We don't know a lot about each other, do we? It will give us something to talk about when we calm down just a little."

He grinned and swept her up in his arms, to carry her into the house. "Don't hold your breath waiting for that to happen," he advised.

She smiled and kissed him.

He put her down in the living room. She sighed. "Oh, my," she said softly.

There were roses everywhere, vases full of them, in every color. There were colorful afghans and two sweaters (his and hers), a big-screen color television set, a DVD player, an Xbox 360 gaming system and several games, and a basket of fruit. On the dining-room table, there were containers of breads and a propped-up note pointing to the refrigerator. It was full of cooked food. There was even a cake for dessert.

"Good grief," Harley whistled. He picked up the note and read it. "Congratulations and best wishes from the Scotts, the Parkses, the Steeles, all the Harts, and the Pendletons." He gaped at her. "The Pendletons! Jason Pendleton is a multimillionaire! I thought he was going to deck me in San Antonio…" He hesitated to tell his new wife that he'd tried to date Jason's stepsister Gracie, who was now Mrs. Pendleton. He chuckled. "Well, I guess he forgave me. His mother has a craft shop and she knits. I'll bet she made the afghans for us."

Alice fingered the delicate stitches. "I'll be still

writing thank-you notes when our kids are in gram-mar school," she remarked. "Harley, you have so many friends. I never realized." She turned and smiled at him. "We're going to be so happy here."

He beamed. He opened his arms and Alice ran into them, to be held close and hugged.

"Are you hungry?" he asked.

She peered up at him and laughed. "We didn't get breakfast."

"And whose fault was that, Mrs. Fowler?" he teased.

"I said I was hungry, it just wasn't for food. Well, not then. I could eat," she added, peering past him at the cake on the table.

"So could I, and I noticed fried chicken in the fridge. It's my favorite."

"Mine, too," she agreed. "I don't cook much on the weekdays because I'm on call so often." She looked up at him worriedly.

"I can cook, Alice," he assured her, smiling. "And I will, when I need to."

"You're just the best husband," she sighed.

"Glad you think so." He chuckled. "Let's find some plates."

THEY WATCHED TELEVISION while they nibbled on all sorts of delicious things. It was a treat that they both liked the same sort of shows. But they didn't watch it for long. The trip back had been tiring, and in many ways, it had been a long week. They slept soundly.

The next day, Alice had to drive up to her office to check on what progress had been made into the murder investigation while Harley got back to work on the ranch. He had things to do, as well, not to mention getting his own present of purebred cattle fed and watered and settled before he went over to Mr. Parks's house to do his job.

Longfellow welcomed her at the door with a hug. "Did you have a nice trip?"

"Lovely," Alice assured her. "But it's good to get home. We had food and presents waiting for us like you wouldn't believe. Mr. Parks had Harley's house renovated and he actually gave him a small herd of purebred cattle for a wedding gift—not to mention the honeymoon trip. What a boss!"

Longfellow smiled. "Surprising, isn't it, how generous he is. Considering the line of work he used to be in, it's a miracle he survived to get married and have a family."

"Yes, I know what you mean," Alice replied. "Any word yet on that scrap of paper we sent to the FBI lab?"

She shook her head. "The holidays, you know, and we're not at the top of the line for quick results." She pursed her lips. "Didn't you once bribe people to get faster service?" she teased.

Alice laughed. "I did, but I don't think my new husband would appreciate it if I did that sort of thing now."

"Probably not."

"Anything on the woman who died at Senator Fowler's house?" Alice added.

Longfellow frowned. "Actually, the senator stopped by and left you a note. I think I put it in your middle desk drawer. He said you were going to be a terrific daughter-in-law… Oops, I'm not supposed to know that, am I?"

Alice's eyes widened. She hadn't considered that she was now the daughter-in-law of the senior senator from Texas. She sat down, hard. "Well, my goodness," she said breathlessly. "I hadn't thought about that."

"You'll have clout in high places, if you ever need it," the other woman said wickedly. "You can threaten people with him!"

Alice laughed. "You idiot."

"I'd threaten people with him," came the reply. She frowned. "Especially Jon Blackhawk," she added.

"What's Jon done to you?"

"He called me at home at midnight to ask if we had lab results back on that thermos that Sheriff Hayes gave you."

"Now, why would he want to know about that?"

Longfellow's eyes sparkled. "The investigator who was working with Marquez on the Kilraven case recalled seeing one like it."

"Where? When?"

"At the home of her ex-husband, actually," she said. "Remember that spiral design on the cup? It was rather odd, I thought at the time, like somebody had painted it with acrylics."

"Can we find out who her ex-husband is?" Alice asked excitedly.

"I did. He died a few weeks ago. The woman he was living with couldn't tell her anything about his friends or visitors, or about the thermos. The investigator told me that the woman was so strung out on coke that she hardly knew where she was."

"Pity," Alice replied sadly.

"Yes, and apparently the ex-husband had a drug problem of his own. Poor woman," she added softly. "She worked her way up to sergeant in the homicide division, and lost her promotion when she helped Marquez reopen the Kilraven cold case files."

Alice was only half listening now. She recalled the note the senator had left, pulled it out, opened it and read it. He'd talked to the police commissioner, he wrote, who had promised the reinstatement of the investigator on the Kilraven case. He'd also spoken to his colleague, the junior senator, and informed him that they were not going to try to hinder any murder investigations, regardless of how old they were. He'd talked to the coroner as well, and the autopsy on the senator's kitchen worker had been reclassified as a homicide. He hoped this would help. He reminded her that she and Harley should call and let them know when they were coming to supper. They had a wedding gift to present.

Alice whistled softly. "He's been busy." She told Longfellow the results of the senator's intercession. "What a nice man."

"Lucky you, to be related to him." The other woman chuckled. "See, I told you that... Wait a sec."

Her phone was ringing. She picked it up, raised her eyebrows at Alice and pulled a pen and paper toward her. "That's very nice of you! We didn't expect to hear back so soon. Yes, I'm ready. Yes." She was writing. She nodded. "I've got it. Yes. Yes, that will be fine. Thank you!" She hung up. "The FBI lab!" she exclaimed.

"They've deciphered the rest of the numbers on that slip of paper you found in the victim's hand in Jacobsville!"

"Really? Let me see!"

Alice picked up the slip of paper and read the numbers with a sinking feeling in her stomach. Now there was no doubt, none at all, who the victim had come to Jacobsville to see. The number was for Kilraven's cell phone.

CHAPTER ELEVEN

KILRAVEN WAITED FOR Alice in the squad room at the Jacobsville Police Department. Alice had driven down in the middle of the day. She didn't want him to have to wait for the news, but she didn't want to tell him over the phone, either.

He stood up when she walked in and closed the door behind her. "Well?" he asked.

"The number on that slip of paper in the dead man's hand," she said. "It was your cell phone number."

He let out a breath. His eyes were sad and bitter. "He knew something about the murder. He came to tell me. Somebody knew or suspected, and they killed him."

"Then they figured that Dolores, who worked for Senator Fowler, might have heard something from the man, and they killed her, too. This is a nasty business."

"Very," Kilraven replied. "But this case is going to break the older one," he added. "I'm sure of it. Thanks, Alice," he added quietly. "I owe you one."

"I'll remember that," she said, smiling. "Keep me in the loop, will you? Oh, there's another thing, I almost forgot. That thermos that Sheriff Hayes found, the one wiped clean of prints? Your investigator in San Antonio actually recognized it! It belonged to her ex-husband!"

"Oh, boy," he said heavily. "That's going to cause some pain locally."

"It is? Why?"

"Her ex-husband is the uncle of Winnie Sinclair."

"Does Winnie know?" Alice asked, stunned.

"No. And you can't tell her." His eyes had an odd, pained look. "I'll have to do it, somehow."

"Was he the sort of person who'd get mixed up in murder?"

"I don't know. But he's dead now. Whatever he knew died with him. Thanks again, Alice. I will keep you in the loop," he promised.

She nodded and he left her standing there. She felt his pain. Her own life was so blessed, she thought. Kilraven's was a study in anguish. Maybe he could solve the case at last, though. And maybe little Winnie Sinclair would have a happier future than she expected. Certainly, Kilraven seemed concerned about her feelings.

ALICE AND HARLEY went to supper with the senator and his wife. They were hesitant at first, with Harley, but as the evening wore on, they talked. Old wounds were reopened, but also lanced. By the time the younger Fowlers left, there was a détente.

"It went better than I expected it to," Harley said. "I suppose all three of us had unrealistic expectations."

She smiled. "They were proud of you when they heard what you'd done with your life. You could tell."

He smiled. "I grew up. I was such a cocky brat when I went to work for Cy Parks." He chuckled. "But I grew up fast. I learned a lot. I'm still learning." He glanced at her as he drove. "Nice presents they gave us, too. A little unexpected."

"Yes. A telescope." She glanced through the back window of the pickup at it, in its thick cardboard box, lying in the bed of the truck. "An eight-inch Schmidt-Cassegrain, at that," she mused.

He stood up on the brakes. "You know what it is?" he burst out.

"Oh, yes, I took a course in astronomy. I have volumes in my office on…" She stopped. The senator had been in her office. She laughed. "My goodness, he's observant!"

"My present isn't bad, either."

They'd given Harley a new saddle, a very ornate one that he could use while riding in parades. "Somebody must have told them what you were doing for a living while we were on our honeymoon," she guessed.

"My father is a digger." He laughed. "I'm sure he asked around."

"We have to spend time with them," she told him. "Family is important. Especially, when you don't have any left."

"You have uncles," he reminded her.

"Yes, but they all live far away and we were never close. I'd like very much to have children. And they'll need a granny and granddaddy, won't they?"

He reached across the seat and linked her hand into his. "Yes." He squeezed her fingers. "We're going to be happy, Alice."

She leaned her head back and stared at him with

utter delight. "We're going to be very happy, Harley," she replied. She closed her eyes with a sigh, and smiled. "Very happy."

* * * * *